The Red Monarch

Also by Bella Ellis

The Vanished Bride
The Diabolical Bones

BELLA ELLIS

The Red Monarch

HODDER

First published in Great Britain in 2021 by Hodder & Stoughton
An Hachette UK company

This paperback edition published in 2022

1

A CIP catalogue record for this title is available from the British Library

Paperback ISBN 978 1 529 36340 1
Trade Paperback ISBN 978 1 529 36338 8
eBook ISBN 978 1 529 36341 8

Typeset in Plantin Light by Hewer Text UK Ltd, Edinburgh
Printed and bound in Great Britain by Clays Ltd, Elcograf S.p.A.

Hodder & Stoughton policy is to use papers that are natural, renewable
and recyclable products and made from wood grown in sustainable
forests. The logging and manufacturing processes are expected to
conform to the environmental regulations of the country of origin.

Hodder & Stoughton Ltd
Carmelite House
50 Victoria Embankment
London EC4Y 0DZ

www.hodder.co.uk

For my niece Victoria

I knew not 'twas so dire a crime
To say the word, 'Adieu';
But this shall be the only time
My lips or heart shall sue.

That wild hill-side, the winter morn,
The gnarled and ancient tree,
If in your breast they waken scorn,
Shall wake the same in me.

I can forget black eyes and brows,
And lips of falsest charm,
If you forget the sacred vows
Those faithless lips could form.

If hard commands can tame your love,
Or strongest walls can hold,
I would not wish to grieve above
A thing so false and cold.

And there are bosoms bound to mine
With links both tried and strong:
And there are eyes whose lightning shine
Has warmed and blest me long:

Those eyes shall make my only day,
Shall set my spirit free,
And chase the foolish thoughts away
That mourn your memory.

'Last Words' by Emily Jane Brontë

Haworth, August 1852

It seemed as if all was in the doldrums. Though the weather was seasonably warm, the summer concealed itself behind a low barrier of cloud, making even the outdoors close and confining. To Charlotte it felt as if time stood still that August, trapping her in one identical day after the next, condemning her to a purgatory of isolation.

Ellen had written again, concerned by Charlotte's listless correspondence in recent months. It was in a state of near despair that Charlotte had been obliged to reply, explaining once again that she was silent because she had nothing to say. That she might indeed repeat over and over again that her life was a pale blank and often a very weary burden, and that sometimes the thought of the future appalled her. Indeed, no matter how she tried to muster her old vitality, it continued to elude her.

That day's pages of *Villette*, her most recent work, lay before her, only two and a half of them, and not one word even near satisfactory. Charlotte pushed them away from her unhappily, averting her eyes from the papers, unable even to look at them. There had been a time when to write was an easy impulse. But now, without her sisters and her brother at her side, it felt as if her joy had been buried, piece by piece, along with Branwell, Emily and Anne, part of her soul rotting alongside them. What had once been a fiery passion as effortless as the arrival of spring had become a hard laborious winter that brought forth nothing but misery. Charlotte could write no more today.

Instead, she drew her writing slope to her and opened the concealed compartment where she kept her greatest treasure. With the utmost care she gently took out a small notebook with dark red covers, measuring no more than four by six inches, and held it for a moment between her palms, as if in prayer. Within the covers were contained more than forty of Emily's poems, each one written in her minute printed hand, the seal of approval that showed a poem was complete. Charlotte held it to her breast. It was almost like having a small portion of her sister's spirit, pinned to the pages by the sheer force of her words.

For a few precious moments the poems returned Emily to Charlotte, seating her dear sister beside her at the table to talk and fight and wonder, restoring to her at least a portion of the sisterhood that Charlotte so deeply mourned.

The truth is that no one would ever truly know Emily. No one ever had, not even during her lifetime. Charlotte knew that her sister kept secrets even from her. From everyone, except her own heart and mind. And if in a hundred or two hundred years, people still talked of Emily Brontë, they would be obliged to piece her together from the poetry and fiction she had left behind. Even then they would find not one identity but at least a dozen, for Emily moved as fluidly as a river from one persona to the next, each one seemingly just as natural and as true as the last.

Emily had been a buccaneer and a wild moorland faerie. She had been a sour-faced misanthrope, a boisterous playmate, a gentle creature who cared for all that were not made human, and a human being unlike any other that Charlotte had ever known, or could ever know, even if she lived a thousand more years. Emily could be as beautiful as she was ugly, and as frightening as she was mild, but always, always through it all, her spirit shone like a beacon calling Charlotte home.

As she read, Charlotte hesitated over one poem in particular; one that brought back to her a time so strange and full of

2

dark adventure that – had she not witnessed it herself – she would have believed it to have been a half-mad fantasy.

Except that the dreadful events of that particular excursion had gone on to haunt them all for years to come, with consequences they could have never foreseen.

Yes, it had been real, the London detection. As real as the dull grey day that now stifled Charlotte's every breath. The terrors and the cruelties they had seen there, the murkiest corners of the human soul they had revealed, often lay in wait for her in the darkest hours of the night.

That time was her own secret to carry alone now, and she would carry it to the grave, burning every trace of evidence to protect her beloved sister's privacy. For if in a hundred or two hundred years, people still talked about Emily Brontë, then they would never truly know her.

Charlotte was certain that was exactly how Emily would want it to be.

The door exploded inward in one splintering thrust, ripping Lydia Roxby from her restless slumber in an instant. Clambering backwards on the bed until her back met the wall, she struggled to make sense of what was happening. It was as if her fragmented nightmares had spilled into reality. Suddenly their room was full of men, crowding around their bed, peering with menacing intent. Lydia thought she saw clubs and blades, though the lanterns held aloft blinded her against making out more detail.

'Harry!' she cried her husband's name as he was dragged from bed and thrust up against the wall of their chamber by the huge hand that encircled his throat. Lydia tried to scream, only to realise that filthy fingers were clamped so firmly over her mouth that she could taste soot and sewage on her captor's skin. Was this how she was to meet her end? But she could not, not now. She could not allow it, if not for her own sake and for Harry's, then for the life that grew within her. This was no time to die.

'I always thought you a fool, Roxby,' a deep rasping voice growled at Harry. 'But to steal from me and then to neglect to hide yourself is a grave error indeed.' The huge man tilted his head to one side as he observed the life draining out of his prey. Harry's eyes bulged in fear and desperation, his lips turning black in the lamplight. Some alien rage, unlike any emotion she had ever known before, engulfed Lydia.

Biting down viciously on the hand that stifled her, Lydia elbowed the man in his guts hard enough to wind him as she scrambled to save Harry. With more strength than she might ever had supposed she possessed, she shouldered her way into the arm that had Harry pinned, barging the assailant with enough force to surprise him into releasing Harry, even if he laughed as he let her husband go.

'Please! Leave us alone, you vile creature!' she shrieked, much to the amusement of her tormentor, but Lydia stood her ground between him and her husband.

'Oh, my dear,' he said, holding the lamp up so that finally Lydia saw his face. 'You are far too fine a specimen for this limp fool. Perhaps I'll take you tonight instead of him; for you are a beauty, with fight to match.'

The identity of their attacker stunned Lydia into a terrified silence.

For this was death himself, who had kicked his way into their room. This was Noose, lord of The Rookery, general of thieves and murderers, who had turned a thousand criminals into his own deadly army, and who controlled half of London – the darkest half – as his own. A man who would kill you for crossing him without a second thought. Icy dread filled Lydia as she felt a cold sweat break upon her skin.

What had Harry done?

'Please,' Harry whimpered, 'I swear, I have stolen nothing. I went to collect the jewel as you told me, but the seller did not appear. I waited the whole night and came to tell one of your men at dawn. That is the truth of it, Noose, I swear it is. Like you said, I would have run if I had stolen from you! I have been honest in all my dealings, I swear it. I beg you, do what you will to me, but let my wife go free. She knows nothing of my work for you, and she is with child!'

Lydia sat down on the bed, feeling the weight of her belly on her knees. In that moment, amid the chaos, confusion and fear, all she could think was how much satisfaction her mother would feel when she heard the manner of her wayward daughter's death.

'Take him!' Noose barked at his men. Lydia remained frozen as she watched her husband being dragged away as he cried out her name. Cradling her arms around her baby, she said a silent prayer, and looked up at the man who was about to slit her throat.

'You have a week,' Noose told her. 'Be sure not to waste it.'

'What? What do you mean?' Lydia asked him.

'I mean that if you want to see your husband again, you will find what he has stolen from me and bring it to me. You have until exactly midnight, seven days from now, to return what I need and save both his life and yours.'

'But . . .' Lydia struggled to order her thoughts. 'You said you had to kill any man that wronged you.'

'I did and I do,' Noose said, suddenly seating himself in the one chair they had in the room. 'But here's the thing, Mrs Roxby – I need that jewel back. I need it more than I need vengeance. And if there is one lesson I have learnt in this long life of mine, it is that a woman in love will fight to the death for the man who holds her affections. It's clear to me that you love that useless fool with all your heart. So, if you help me, I will help you. Return the jewel to me within the week and I will let you both go free, as long as you leave this city behind you for good. Fail and I will kill your husband, and you soon thereafter, no matter where you flee. For, I promise you, there is no corner of this earth that is safe from me. Are we in agreement?'

Lydia wanted to shout that no, they were not in agreement. For how could she, a weak, unworldly woman, who was heavy with child and had not a friend in this vast metropolis, search for and find something that she knew nothing about? Yet this proposal gave her precious time, and it was all she had. So, instead, she straightened her back and lifted her chin.

'We are in agreement, sir,' she said.

The room was suddenly empty, the broken door mewling on its hinges.

How Lydia wished she could run home. How she wished she could run into her mama's arms and lay her head in her lap, and beg to be forgiven and that Mama would be kind to her once again. But that path was closed to her now, and not only because her mother, the elder Lydia Robinson, would never forgive her for what she had done.

Noose was quite correct: Lydia did love Harry with all her heart, and she loved their unborn child a thousand times more. There had to be a way to save them both – there had to be, and she had to find it, or at least call on the help of someone who could.

One name came to mind at once.

For there was only one person in all this world she could call to her aid now. One person who, she was certain, would not let her fall prey to Noose's deadly threat. Going to her trunk, she pulled out her writing slope and, opening it on the floor, dipped her quill into the last of the ink and began to scratch out an urgent plea for help.

A letter, addressed to one Miss Anne Brontë, The Parsonage, Haworth.

TWO

Charlotte

'Of course, he then became intolerable. Throwing all about him into hubbub and confusion with his emotions,' Charlotte said, as she and her sisters took to the heights of the moor in search of some respite from the gloom that their brother Branwell had cast over their little home in recent days. 'It is as if no one else has ever felt an emotion, ever lived with a broken heart, ever had to plough on with life in the face of bitter disappointment.'

It was a fine July day. The sky, traced here and there with little wisps of wind-laced cloud, opened ever upwards towards heaven, and the cotton grass danced in amongst a fresh crop of tender green heather. Flossy ran on ahead, leaping over ridges and furrows with joyful abandon, her long ears streaming after her. Keeper kept close to his mistress's side, occasionally lolloping after Flossy, but always returning a few moments later to bump his head against Emily's hand. As for the three sisters, they climbed ever higher without any particular thought as to where they were going, yet somehow all agreed on their destination.

'I fear we have lost him for ever,' Emily agreed unhappily, pausing for a moment to kiss Keeper's head. 'He was not in full possession of his wits *before* Mrs Robinson's husband passed, but now . . . He cannot conceive that she still will not have him. Poor broken soul, he's a near lunatic howling at a moon of his own creation, with his whole future snuffed out in an instant. And to send her coachman to reject him on her behalf, it is intolerable.'

Emily gathered her skirts and hopped in one bound from the lower path on to a higher trail, which, judging by the expression on her face, pleased her enormously, as it did her dog, who was happy to follow at her heel.

'I believe you do Branwell a disservice,' Anne said presently, as Anne was wont to do. Charlotte exchanged glances with Emily. They had noticed that as their baby sister came into her own, she was altogether more opinionated, and much less obliging. Oddly, it only made Charlotte love her more.

'Is he not languishing in our parlour as we speak, filling the air with his putrid misery?' Charlotte asked Anne. She had not meant to sound quite so harsh, but the nerves that had kept her awake most of the night had sharpened her edges.

'Yes, indeed he is,' Anne conceded. 'But I have seen a change in our brother these last months, and not all for the worst. A deepening of thought and sensibility, as if he is awaking to the seriousness of life, and the marks we leave upon this world when we depart it. Just this morning he showed me something he had written, and though he did not specify, it seemed clear to me that it was about . . .'

Anne trailed off, not knowing if she would mention the very thing that none of them ever mentioned, not even to one another.

'The child.' Emily released the words for them to be borne away by the breeze. 'Yes, he showed it to me too.'

Charlotte did not wonder why Branwell hadn't asked her to read his work, for he knew that she would not be able to bear it.

'Yes,' Anne confirmed, bowing her head. 'His heart has travelled to many dark places of late and it has brought him low. I am certain that in each past transgression he has revisited, he has become a little more steadfast, a little more true. There *is* a promise of a future for our brother yet, though he might not believe it; as those who love him, it is our duty to help him find the reason he needs to live.'

Neither Charlotte nor Emily commented further, and the walk fell into silence – as silent as it could ever be on the constantly whispering moors. It was impossible for her to speak of their brother's illegitimate daughter, the weight of shame was just too great. Even thinking of it brought Charlotte to anguished tears. That a baby girl lay cold in her grave, without a father's name to shelter her, was intolerable. Why had her brother not been born a better man? She hoped that Anne was right, that Branwell could be saved yet, but it was harder to believe such a thing was possible this summer, when every day that passed etched away another layer of hope.

When she looked up, Charlotte was glad to see they had found their way to Alcomden Stones, for it was as beautiful a place as any that God had ever created. Here at the uppermost reaches of the moor, great ancient stones lay scattered, or piled one upon another as if carefully placed to make a natural temple in homage to the landscape. The stones were warm to the touch, and Charlotte wrapped her arms around one, laying her wind-chilled cheek against its rough surface as she looked out at the blue-hazed horizon, her heart full of love for the landscape. It was the perfect place to carry out their very important and serious business.

'Well?' Emily said, as she scrambled atop one of the rocks, smoothing her wild hair back from her flushed face, only to have the air tangle it free again one moment later. Keeper, who couldn't scramble up the stone as Flossy had, lay at its foot, his head resting on his crossed paws, his expression most disconsolate, for he hated to be parted from Emily, even by a few feet. 'Let it be done with, then. If it is to be done, t'were well it were done quickly.'

'It's a book review, Emily,' Anne laughed, 'not a Shakespearean murder.'

'That we know of,' Emily said, grimly. 'For many a murder of an author's hope has been committed by a critic.' Emily had been against the publication of their work from the outset and now that there was tangible proof that it had been read by outsiders, she was all the more unsettled. Indeed, as Charlotte took the long-awaited copy of *The Critic* from her basket, she found herself balking at opening it, the very thought of its judgement stealing the breath from her lungs.

'I cannot,' Charlotte quailed, thrusting the publication at Emily and then Anne and then Emily again.

For it had been her who had pushed her sisters into this venture; she who had convinced them that their words were sufficiently good to be examined by the world. If the review was cruel and damning, she would feel as if it were her who had dealt her dear sisters this blow, and though she could take criticism from a stranger, she could not bear the thought of hurting them so.

'Well, I shall not read it,' Emily said. 'Anne, you must do it.'

'Gladly,' Anne said, arranging her skirts about her on the flat surface of the stone she had sat upon. She looked so uncommonly pretty in that moment that Charlotte already regretted the tears that she felt certain were about to stain her dear Anne's complexion when she read of her abject failure at producing any work of literary merit.

Regretfully Charlotte handed over the papers and waited. As Anne opened the magazine, a letter slipped out, fluttering down, and then almost gusting away on the breeze. Darting forward, Anne was just able to catch it in time.

'Why this letter is for me!' she said, examining the address. 'From London! Who do I know in London?'

'Open it, and then you will find out,' Emily said dryly, crossing her arms impatiently.

'Oh yes, I picked it up with the magazine this morning and then forgot about it,' Charlotte said. 'Still, there is time enough for letters, Anne. Please let us know the worst, for I cannot bear it a moment longer.'

'I know this hand,' Anne said, tucking the magazine under her skirt and instead tearing open the envelope. 'For I schooled it long enough. This is the hand of Lydia Robinson, or Mrs Roxby as she is now called.'

'Runaway Lydia?' Emily said, happy to be distracted from the review, much to Charlotte's annoyance. 'Eloped and disinherited Lydia?'

'The very same,' Anne said, as she hastily tore open the envelope and began to read.

'Yes, but the review?' Charlotte reminded her sisters, as Emily joined Anne on her rock, perching her chin on her younger sister's shoulder so that she could read the contents simultaneously. 'Surely the review of our first ever published work takes precedence over the empty-headed prattling of a Robinson girl?'

It seemed that Emily and Anne were too immersed in the contents of the letter to hear her. Charlotte resigned herself to wait.

'Oh dear,' Anne said, looking up at Emily at length. 'Oh dear, poor child.'

'A devilish mystery to be solved indeed,' Emily said.

'Let me see,' Charlotte sighed and, taking the letter that Anne handed her, she scanned it, her eyes widening with every word.

'Well,' Charlotte said, once she had finished reading. 'Lydia is alone and at the mercy of ruffians in London. What are we to do about it?'

'What we have become accustomed to, and rather expert at, of course,' Anne told Charlotte. 'We shall save the day, shall we not?'

At that precise moment, a sharp gust of air whipped their copy of *The Critic* from where Anne had secured it, its pages flapping like an inelegant bird, away and up into the sky, where it was torn asunder and borne rapidly in several directions, one page plummeting directly into the path of Flossy, who pounced on it with great glee and made sure to thoroughly kill it before returning it in soggy shreds to Anne.

'Oh,' Anne said, inspecting the remains that Flossy presented to her. 'Oh well, I don't think this was the relevant page, and anyway there are more pressing matters at hand.'

For now, at least, they would not know what the world thought of their book of rhymes; and perhaps, Charlotte thought as she watched the remnants of the paper fly ever closer to the sun, that was for the best.

THREE

Anne

'We cannot just go to London,' Charlotte said, once they were at home and settled around the table, two exhausted dogs stretched out underneath it, Keeper snoring with rhythmic wheezes.

It was clear that Charlotte was rather out of sorts after Anne had let their unread copy of *The Critic* get swept away on the west wind and partially mauled by Flossy. Anne observed Charlotte, who sat at the table with her arms crossed under her bosom, and all her corners turned downward and glum, and prepared herself for some considerable persuasion. Fortunately she knew exactly how to coax her elder sisters, with the insight that only a youngest child could obtain.

'For once I am in accord with Charlotte,' Emily said, picking the fallen petals from a bowl of overblown pink roses that sat on the table, arranging them into the shape of a heart. 'It is one thing to traipse through the snow into the wilderness to certain peril. But it is another thing entirely to go to *London*. For one thing, it is full of people, and for another, it is not in Yorkshire.'

Charlotte nodded in agreement.

'You forget, Anne,' Charlotte said with arch superiority. 'Emily and I have experienced London. And we found it to be very disagreeable, did we not, Emily?'

Bella Ellis

'We did,' Emily nodded. 'Very disagreeable. People everywhere you looked, and no Yorkshire at all.'

'I hardly think passing through on your way to Brussels counts as experience,' Anne said, doing her best not to sound too scathing. 'I expect you hardly saw more than the inside of a coaching inn. And this is different. We wouldn't be going to see the city! We'd be going to bring aid to a young woman who is all alone. Estranged from her family, and in terrible danger. How can we possibly say No and live with ourselves?'

'I'm prepared to try,' Emily said.

'Come now,' Anne sighed, shaking her head. 'Emily, you have travelled before, much further than I! You are not the bumpkin you pretend to be!'

'One doesn't have to be a "bumpkin", as you put it, to know where the best place on earth is and to determine to stay there,' Emily said firmly. 'You do not understand, Anne, the constant demands upon one to make small talk and look interested. It's exhausting.'

'Well yes, perhaps if we were making a conventional social visit, but that is not our purpose. We will be traversing into the dark and undoubtedly dangerous underworld of the grimmest and most violent parts of the city.' Anne crafted her temptation with the greatest care.

'As appealing as that sounds, we do not have funds to travel to London,' Charlotte interrupted. 'We spent all of our aunt's money on having our book published, and we are not paid for detections. Where should we stay and how should we keep ourselves while we are there, never mind afford transportation? I agree that Lydia must be helped, but I am not sure we can be the ones to do it, Anne. At least not in person.'

'Of course we can!' Anne thumped the table, taking inspiration from Papa in the pulpit on a Sunday. 'Are we the sort of women who simply accept defeat as soon as any difficulty is presented to us? Is our aid not a Christian duty that cannot

16

be weighed in coin? Besides, we could stay with Lydia in her room above the theatre for no expense at all.'

'In a *theatre!*' Charlotte's eyes widened in horror.

'In a *theatre?*' said Emily, clearly warming to the idea.

'And as to the other expenses,' Anne went on, 'I have a few precious things that I might sell. My shell and turquoise lariat perhaps, or my carnelian beads. Though I do love them, they are but trinkets, and Lydia's need is more important than my mementoes.'

Anne bowed her head, looking up at Charlotte through her lashes just as she used to when she was very small, when she wanted Charlotte to take her on her knee and read to her.

'Anne,' Charlotte said rather more tenderly. 'You would part with your treasures for a Robinson?'

'Of course I would,' Anne said at once. 'Lydia is a foolish girl, and yes she was selfish and vain when I first met her, but she is still a human being that I have known and done my best to guide towards goodness.' Anne stood up abruptly. 'Charlotte, Emily; Lydia's father is dead and her mother has disowned her. I owe her a debt of care. If all I can do, by journeying to London, is to be at her side and offer her a little comfort and protection, then I shall feel that I have done my duty. And I shall go whether you come with me or not.'

Anne crossed to the window, gazing out at slab after slab of grey gravestones, the afternoon light gilding the church spire with a golden glow. Her home was so safe, so dear to her. The thought of catching a coach and then a train, and then finding her way through the streets of London to Lydia made her heart quell and tremble. And yet she couldn't turn away from Lydia, she simply couldn't. Her well of courage must be deeper still – she had to make it bottomless – for she would never turn back from defending the weak. Not on any account.

'I shall go,' Anne said, turning back from the window. 'And

I shall discover the truth at the heart of all this. I shall free Harry and save Lydia. For is that not what we do, sisters? Drag the darkest matters into the light for all to scrutinise? As we did at Chester Grange, and last Christmas at Top Withens. Yes, there will be danger . . .'

Emily's expression altered fractionally at the thought of Anne facing danger alone, and Anne knew that she had her.

'And intrigue,' she went on, catching Emily's eye with a smile. Now for Charlotte. 'And I dare say some quite scandalous situations that three spinsters such as ourselves should never be associated with. But that means there will also be adventures aplenty and fiendishly difficult riddles to be solved. Something to stimulate our stagnant minds and test them properly once again. What do three such as we have to fear in London, for it is nothing to us.'

'It is nothing to us,' Emily said. 'As the case must be solved by a certain date and time if Harry is to be saved, then I suppose we should be home again inside a week, one way or another. I will not like it there, no decent person could, but I will accompany you, Anne.'

'Thank you, dear Emily.' Anne went to her sister and kissed the top of her head, causing Emily to shudder like a wet dog.

'As for funds,' Emily said, 'I have a little set aside from the housekeeping. Enough to get us there and back, at least, so you may keep your trinkets.'

'You have been setting aside housekeeping?' Charlotte asked Emily. 'What for?'

'For occasions when we might have to travel to London to save Branwell's mistress's daughter,' Emily said, most provokingly, though Anne could not help but smile at Charlotte's furious expression. Now was the time to smooth her ruffled feathers and make her feel indispensable, for in truth, without Charlotte's clear mind and flawless reasoning, they would be much the weaker.

'Charlotte? Please will you accompany us?' Anne asked Charlotte coaxingly. 'If you let Emily and me go alone, I dread to think what we might do without your steadying wisdom to guide us.'

Charlotte preened a little, plumping up her breast like a little wren.

'I suppose I can't very well refuse,' Charlotte said. 'After all, the last time I left you to your own devices, I nearly ended up dead.'

'You make it sound as if that were our fault entirely,' Emily laughed. 'It was you, my dear sister, who walked right into the monster's trap. In any case, console yourself with this: London is the home of all the publishers, Charlotte, and you will easily and expediently find a copy of *The Critic* there to torture us with.'

'That is a fine point,' Charlotte said, significantly cheered. 'Anne, write to the girl. Tell her we will leave at dawn.'

'Do you leave me?' Branwell asked as he entered the room, crumpling on to the black sofa like so much unwashed linen. 'I should not be surprised. All whom I love leave me. I must be a detestable person. A loathsome object of pity and misery. The sooner I am dead, the better for all of you.'

Anne glanced at her sisters warily. It had been only a few weeks since Mrs Robinson had sent her coachman to tell Branwell there was no hope of them ever being married. But it had been enough time for her already diminished brother to be cut in half yet again by misery. How thin he had become since his hopes were finally dashed, and how wretched in every breath and action he took. To mention the name Robinson now might be the last straw that broke the camel's back. And yet to lie would be another betrayal, and Anne could not find it in herself to do that to him, even for his own good.

'We are going to London at dawn,' Anne told her brother. 'With a view to rescuing Mrs Lydia Roxby, that was Lydia

Robinson the younger.' Charlotte threw her hands up in despair at Anne's frankness, and Emily simply landed her forehead on the tabletop with a soft thud and a deep groan. Nevertheless, Anne went on, certain her path was the right one, especially when she saw Branwell raise his bloodshot eyes to meet hers with a glimmer of life that she had not seen in days. 'It seems her husband has fallen into the clutches of a bad lot, and Lydia must pay a ransom to assure his release and her safety. The trouble being that she does not know what the ransom is exactly, other than it is some kind of jewel that Harry is alleged to have stolen, though he claims to know nothing. So you see, she really is in rather a dreadful predicament.'

'But this is wonderful!' Branwell stood up, clapping his hands together in delight. 'It's as if this mission has been sent by God to aid me.'

'I'm not sure I follow, dear,' Charlotte said anxiously.

'I must prepare,' Branwell said, pushing his bone-white fingers through his red hair. 'I must gather my belongings and find my copy of Cruchley's *New Plan of London*. I have no coin.' He pointed at Anne. 'Do you have coin?'

'Branwell, we were rather thinking that you might not come with us this time,' Emily said, gently. 'You haven't been well, and we fear the excursion might be more than you can bear—'

'No,' Branwell shook his head firmly. 'No, don't you see, I *must* join you. I must! It is my one chance of redemption. In saving Lydia from this dreadful situation I will prove myself to her mother! My beloved will see that her fortune is nothing compared to the love I have for her and her children, and she will be moved to accept me, I know she will.'

'It's not entirely clear that Mrs Robinson loves her children even,' Emily said. 'Lydia was disowned and disinherited for marrying Harry, Branwell. And it is not her mama she has asked for help, but our Anne.'

'But . . .' Branwell wagged his finger at Emily, looking a little like his old self again, all devilish smile and sparkling eyes. 'When I bring her daughter back to her bosom and heal every rift single-handed, all that will change. How can it not?'

'Branwell,' Anne took a turn to reason with him, 'this is not an opportunity for you to try to rekindle your "attachment" with Mrs Robinson. Poor Lydia is in dire straits – her husband is under the threat of murder by scoundrels, as is she! The situation could not be more serious.'

'Exactly,' Branwell said, happily rubbing his hands together. 'Now what are we to tell Papa? Nothing close to the truth, I presume?'

Emily

The journey was long, uncomfortable and arduous, spanning an entire day, more or less. They had taken an early coach to Bradford's newly opened train station, and from there they had hour after hour – six in total – of rattling, noisy, machine-born transport on the train that cut its way through the countryside like a butcher's bloody knife.

Emily would have been in no mood for conversation even if the din of the locomotion hadn't made it necessary to raise one's voice in order to converse. Instead she left it to Branwell to go on and on about how he was to transform his expectations and that he had within his grasp the power to snatch victory from defeat *ad infinitum*.

Her brother seemed entirely gripped by this delusion, for Emily was certain it was just that. While she loved to see his eyes glittering with excitement and the rosy flush across his pallid face, she knew his renewed optimism could only be temporary, no matter what success they had in London. Mrs Robinson would never want her brother as a husband and that was that. The thought of watching Branwell fall yet again, and yes, the misery of it dragging their entire family down with him into his pit of despair, was almost too much to bear. Yet she loved the fool and could no more bear to confront him with the dreadful truth than any of them could. Let him be happy for a little while at least, though it was bound to cost them all in the long run.

Besides that, her conscience was troubling her dreadfully. They had left Papa at sunrise with tales of a short visit to Scarborough to take the air and meet Charlotte's old school-friend Ellen Nussey. The dear old gentleman had been so glad to see his four children, happy and united at the prospect of an outing, that he had given them his blessing and even a little money to make their visit more pleasurable.

Emily hated lying to her papa. He was a man who valued honesty above almost all things. But there was one virtue he considered greater still, and that was honour. Emily only hoped the vice of deceit was somehow cancelled out by the good they sought to do in helping Lydia. She knew her sisters held similar reservations. This must be the last lie they tell him, she was resolved. Should the need arise to travel once again, or engage in a detection nearer to home, she determined that she would tell her papa all, no matter what the consequences might be. For it hardly seemed right to expend so much effort in pursuing the truth if they did not live by the same standards themselves in every respect.

Though it was probably best not to tell Charlotte, she had decided, and that was one little piece of truth she would keep in reserve for now. That and the cool, comforting weight that rested against her hip, nestled in a drawstring bag that was concealed in the large pocket she had sewn into her skirt. Something she had taken at the last moment from her father's desk drawer, just as they had bade him farewell.

Keeper had been tugging at the hem of her skirt, sensing she was about to leave him behind, and Emily had been watching Papa embrace Charlotte and Anne, when she felt a shiver of portent spider its way down her spine, webbing her with a heavy sense of doom. In her heart, Emily suddenly knew somehow that death was very close to them, and edging ever nearer. Well, she would be ready to fight its greedy grasp until the last. For she was not ready to die. Nor was she ready to lose one more soul that she loved.

This city was a beast, a living creature that, though it was made of many individual organisms, existed as one great living, breathing animal with its own intent. That much was clear to Emily from the first moment its great, sprawling carcass came into view.

The train brought them slowly past the scaled tip of its devilish tail, which thickened and flexed into the bulk of its spiked, crested body, until it swallowed them whole in its great jaws and they arrived in the very heart of London, grinding to a shuddering halt with a cacophony of screams and shrieks.

Stiff with sweat and exhaustion, they followed the other alighting passengers into the Greek-style cathedral of the station ticket hall, Anne tipping her head back to admire the splendour of the gilded marble interior.

As tired and travel-grubbed as they were, Emily saw the awe and excitement in the faces of her brother and sisters. For herself, she mistrusted this Frankenstein's monster of a city, stitched together as it was from the remnants of a thousand years of corpses. Nothing good could come from anything that grew out of such decay.

'Well,' Branwell said, lifting his chin with an air of the adventurer as the four of them, seeming very small in comparison to the looming buildings that surrounded them, wandered under the majestic Doric arch that straddled the entrance to the station like the front of a temple from antiquity. 'We are arrived on our adventure.'

He didn't seem to be cowed by the stink and din of the metropolis; in fact he threw open his arms wide to greet it, as he might an old lover – or, Emily thought, a bottle of gin.

'We are arrived,' Charlotte repeated, looking around her in dismay at all the strangeness and unfamiliarity.

Coming from Haworth, they were no strangers to filth or the stench of industry and close living. Indeed, on any given day, a person had to watch where they trod on the steep incline that was Main Street for fear of treading in something unmentionable.

Even so, Emily had never encountered anything quite like the unpleasantness of London. The stink of the city was at once apparent: an acrid concoction of all that is unhealthy, every possible by-product of animal and human life that had been strewn about to rot and ferment, its repugnance concentrated a thousand-fold, as if trapped under a great invisible glass dome that kept the putrid air still and heavy.

'How far from here is the theatre located?' Charlotte asked rather wanly.

'I suppose we could take a cab,' Anne said, looking towards the row of hansom cabs that lined one side of the street, their horses fussing and fretting in the heat.

'No need for that expense,' Branwell said happily, as he loaded his rather large bag into Charlotte's arms, all but obscuring her face. 'I have my Cruchley's! I bought it from a stationer the last time I was in Keighley – I knew it would come in useful one day.' With some difficulty he unfolded the map its full width and, the tip of his nose just above the finely printed streets, located their position.

'Fear not, women,' he said as he traced out their route with his fingertip, muttering street names to himself. 'Your brother will navigate you to the desired location on foot! It is but a short walk, less than half an hour.'

'You do realise we are going to see Lydia, and not to find a public house, don't you Branwell?' Emily said.

With a guffaw of pleasure, Branwell slapped her lightly on the back, and after a moment's thought, bade them follow him and marched decisively off.

'Can this go well?' Charlotte murmured to her as they fell into step behind.

'I fully expect us to be robbed and thrown in the Thames by sundown,' Emily told her. Oh, how she longed for the familiar dangers and evils that lurked around her little home. Those at least she understood; those at least she knew she could defeat.

Anne

Despite Branwell's continued confidence in his memory, after two hours of walking and the passing of the same tall, thin, black-painted house, not once but three times, it was Anne who decided to enquire for directions from a passer-by.

A great many carriages had tracked back and forth through the dusty streets, and people from every corner of society had streamed past them, and on occasions almost through them, as they had walked and walked, growing hotter and wearier with every passing moment. Fine ladies and gentleman strode about with an air of entitlement that seemed entirely different from the bearing of the folks that Anne knew, and she felt suddenly very far from home.

As for the tradespeople and the poor, even they seemed to have a specific air about them that Anne found rather intimidating. The former seemed busier, louder and angrier than any Anne had ever encountered, and the latter more desperate and impoverished than the worst that she had ever seen. Here, amidst the filthy grandeur, it seemed all the more abhorrent.

Yet, as far as she could tell, all three strands of society seemed to exist alongside one another with complete indifference, as if each universe was invisible to the other for the greater part of the time, only interacting when their worlds were forced to collide by necessity.

'Excuse me,' Anne said, bowing to a pleasant-looking woman who was sweeping the street in front of her shop. 'Can you tell me the way to the Covent Garden Theatre on Drury Lane?'

As fortune would have it, they were only two streets away, and, it would seem, had been for some time, though none of the sisters mentioned it, for not one of them wanted their brother to fail on his very first mission in some time.

'There,' Branwell said with some satisfaction, 'I told you I knew the way.'

The nature of the streets seemed to change in but a few steps, Anne noticed as they approached the theatre. The neat and respectable shops were replaced by taprooms and gin palaces, the scent of ale perfuming the heavy air that was, from time to time, punctuated by a snatch of a song or a cheer from within such an establishment. The pace of life slowed and the shadows lengthened as it became clear they were entering a part of town that was meant for leisure and scandal, whatever form that might take.

Anne found herself dawdling behind her sisters, fascinated by the strange creatures that inhabited this new, alluring but sinister world. Where others might only look ahead, Anne took in every detail: the irregular skyline and rooftops that cut into the summer sky, and below, the basement steps and sheltered alleyways that suggested a hidden world, cowering just out of sight. As she neared Drury Lane, she began to notice something curious that repeated itself at ever-increasing intervals. A roughly painted or chiselled insignia that seemed to be two capital Rs, one mirroring the other, back to back, topped with a crown and contained within a five-pointed star, or pentagram, as the Wise Woman of the Wage of Crow Hill would have called it.

Whenever the sigil appeared, it was either so low to the ground it was hardly likely to be noticed, or secreted high above lintels and windowsills. Never where a person might naturally look. Each mark had to be sought out, and she felt sure carried a secret meaning to those who were in the know, but what the meaning might be was unclear. Anne had paused in front of one such example to look at it more closely when she realised she had lost sight of her party.

'Good afternoon, miss.' A young man, tall, with a lean, hungry face approached her with a cold smile. It was only as he did that Anne realised he had been watching her for some time, and that it had been his slender, flat-capped figure that had vaguely registered in her peripheral vision for a few moments before he approached her. 'You look lost to me, my duck. Would you like me to escort you somewhere?'

'I know where you'd like to escort her, Jack,' another voice called. As she turned towards the second voice, Anne was dismayed to see a group of young men surrounding her, reminding her of an illustration she had seen of a pack of hungry hyenas leering at their prey.

'No, thank you,' Anne said with as much confidence as she could muster. 'I am with my brother and sisters; they are just a little way ahead. Good day.'

'Don't leave us just yet.' The one called Jack stepped into her path, catching hold of a fistful of her skirt. 'I know that accent! You come from the north, don't you? Have you come down here to find your fortune, or a feller with one at least? A pretty face like yours could earn a penny or two round here, my dear. I'd be happy to show you how.'

The jackals cackled once again.

'Please remove yourself from my path at once,' Anne said, reminding herself that she was the woman who had stood up to Clifton Bradshaw and made him cower under her wrath.

'I will as soon as you give us a kiss,' said Jack, leaning towards her so that she could smell his rotten breath. 'Come now, my little rabbit, don't make a poor man miserable.'

31

'Stand aside at once or I shall—' Anne began, but was soon interrupted.

'Do as she tells you.' Anne heard Emily's voice a fraction before she turned to see her, and as she did so her jaw dropped open in exactly the manner her aunt Branwell used to scold her about. For her sister was levelling one of Papa's pistols at Jack's head.

'Good lord, what have we here?' Jack guffawed. 'A lady with a firearm? This is a new amusement.'

'I daresay you won't be so amused when you are missing half your head,' Emily replied with such cool certainty that Jack's leer receded quite considerably.

'The lady is a crack shot,' Branwell added, genially enough as he stepped forward into the fray, taking Anne's hand and putting her behind him. 'So accurate with that firearm that she seldom misses. As for me . . .' He clenched his two fists before him. 'I'm a boxing man, Irish born and as vicious as a terrier.'

Jack observed them for a moment, as if taking in their every detail, and then seemed to nod to himself.

'Come on, lads,' he said, his smile returning. 'We've had enough fun with these foreigners for now. There'll be time enough to play with them again at our leisure.'

Anne waited until they were out of sight, lost in the crowds, until she turned to her siblings and said, 'I could have dealt with them perfectly well myself.'

'Of course you could have,' Emily said, pocketing the pistol after returning the safety catch home. 'Only thanks to your sister, you didn't have to.'

'And to me,' Branwell said, puffing out his chest. 'In truth, I am rather disappointed. I felt sure I could best the lot of them.'

'Emily, you stole Papa's pistol!' Charlotte said, appalled.

'Not his favourite one,' Emily said. 'He hardly ever looks at this one, and besides, this is the very gun he showed me how to shoot with. It is not stolen but borrowed. I felt that – when entering unknown territory – it made sense to be well armed against all eventualities, and it does fit perfectly in my pockets, see?'

'Pockets in your skirts,' Charlotte said disapprovingly, 'whatever next?'

'Well, a great deal of inconvenience is solved,' Emily said. 'On my right I have the loaded pistol, and on my left a small flagon of powder and some shot. And look, Charlotte.' With great delight she pulled back a spring positioned beside the pistol's trigger, which shot forth a short but deadly bayonet spike. 'If I run out of shot or time to reload, I can stick any villain with this! Is it not marvellous?'

'I am aghast,' Charlotte said, frowning deeply. 'However, I suppose this is a dangerous area, as it is plain to see, so for now I shall allow it.'

Emily gave Anne a look that said quite clearly that Charlotte had no say at all, but at least she didn't say it out loud and delay their arrival yet another half an hour.

'As your brother,' Branwell said, 'I must insist that you hand the pistol to me.'

'No!' Emily and Charlotte said together.

'Emily is a much better shot than you, Branwell,' Anne said soothingly, taking his arm. 'Besides, with fists like yours, you need no further weapon.'

'That is true,' Branwell said, somewhat mollified.

Within, Anne was still shaking.

If some wanton boys, chancing their luck on a lone, lost young woman could scare her, then how would she have the strength to face whatever came next?

SIX

Charlotte

'Well, at least we are here,' Anne said as they beheld the theatre at last. Charlotte looked up at what was to be their home for the next few days and shuddered despite the heat of the early summer eve.

From without, the Covent Garden Theatre looked rather magnificent, built, as much as the grand architecture of the last century had been, in the manner of a perfectly proportioned Greek temple. Four great pillars upheld the grand portico, which in turn was carved with figures and wreaths of flowers, and Charlotte could tell that the plaster it was rendered in had once been white. Now it was ingrained with dirt, and at its base a kind of green damp reached up with long feathery fingers, as if the earth itself was attempting to drag the building into the underworld.

Later Charlotte would come to realise just how pertinent this observation was, but just then she felt a little thrill at the glamour of their destination, mingled with her distaste.

The main entrance to the theatre was closed and locked, a fact that Branwell had only ascertained after stepping over a collection of drunks who had made their beds on the regal steps, and one young woman who simply sat on the step with her head in her hands, weeping. For a moment Charlotte wondered if the girl might be Lydia herself, but when she was certain it was not, she steeled herself and turned away.

They were here to help Lydia. Charlotte could not trouble herself with the great sea of need that washed all around her, for she did not have it within her grasp to ease the suffering of all. Anne, it seemed, could not be so pragmatic, stooping down to press a few of their scarce pennies into the girl's hands, and giving her a fresh, folded handkerchief that glowed snow-white against the dreary grime. This was typical of her sister, who was ever searching and striving for the best way to bring equality and fairness to every living person, no matter their status. If Anne was certain of one thing, she often told Charlotte, it was that she wanted her life to have changed the world, if only a little, for the better. Charlotte feared for any soul who was so full of hope, but for Anne most of all, for how would she survive when she truly learnt that at least half of life must be filled with bitter disappointment?

The narrow alleys at the side of the theatre were dank and rats darted away as they approached, but at least there was a gentleman to ask for aid, if one could use that word about the whiskery, beerish man who manned the stage door.

'Good day to you, sir.' Branwell approached the person. 'We are here to visit one Miss Lydia Robinson . . . Roxby. Mrs Lydia Roxby, the wife of Harry Roxby, and daughter-in-law of your manager, I believe? Can you direct us to her apartment, for we are led to understand that it is within the theatre?'

'Yer what?' the fellow said, leaning on the lower portion of the stable-style door that barred their way inside, chewing something odious. Charlotte felt she were as like to be sent to a cattle market as to be invited in.

'We are calling on Mrs Lydia Roxby,' Branwell repeated himself. 'At her invitation. She gave us the address of the theatre, but if you would be so kind as to direct us to her lodgings, that would be much appreciated.'

The whiskered man continued chewing for some moments more as he regarded them, as if weighing up the benefit of complying against murdering them where they stood, before stepping back and swinging the door open.

'Roxby's boy has a room here,' he said, thumbing over his shoulder in the general direction of the murky interior. 'The girl hasn't left that I know of, not since her man abandoned her, anyways. I should think the mister will put her out on the street if his boy ain't back soon. Maybe you can remove her before she is booted out and do us all a favour. Never ceases her wailing – you can hear it even down here. Scare off the ghosts, she will.'

'Ghosts?' Emily said, but Charlotte hooked her arm and led her away before they were delayed any further by her fascination for the supernatural.

Their party advanced into a long, dark and narrow hallway that seemed to offer only one direction.

'Imagine living in a room in a theatre,' Charlotte whispered. 'Surely there is only one dwelling that could be any less desirable for a young woman of quality than this one. And where in such a building as this would one lodge anyway? Young Lydia must have quite lost her senses when she consented to elope with Mr Roxby.'

'The thing is,' Branwell said, 'never having known what it is to be in love, you can never imagine what trials a person would endure to be with the one who has captured their heart and soul.'

Charlotte bowed her head, determined to keep the fury that rose within her chest contained, for now was not the time to vent it. Indeed, there was never to be such a time. Even so, it hurt her deeply that Branwell was so immersed in his own sorrows that he had no sense that each of his sisters had suffered too, in their way. It was just that they were not as free to wallow in their feelings as he was.

She felt Emily's hand steal into hers and give her fingers a comforting squeeze.

'He pointed upwards,' she said. 'I suggest we find a staircase and ascend.'

'They call the highest parts of the theatre "the gods", don't they?' Charlotte said. 'Then why do I feel as if we are seeking out devils?'

'Actors are terrible fellows with scant morals, I admit,' a tall and willowy young man – dressed as a king's cavalier – said, emerging from a room to their right, his shirt spattered with what Charlotte hoped was stage blood. 'But though we may be heading to hell, I can assure you that we aren't all demons yet.' He smiled and Charlotte could not help but be charmed by his dark eyes, though his true features were obscured by a thick layer of white greasepaint, his lips painted red. 'You all look rather lost, and by the melodious tones of your voices, I suspect I know who you are looking for: another who speaks with that delightful accent – Mrs Roxby. Am I correct?'

He bowed deeply, flourishing his long, ringleted wig as if it were a hat.

'You are, sir,' Charlotte said.

'Will you allow me to assist you?'

It was hard to discern what kind of man lay behind the mask that transformed his face into a villain, but Charlotte supposed they had no choice.

'We should be most grateful, sir,' she said. 'We are the Br . . . Bells, from Yorkshire, come to see Mrs Lydia Roxby.'

'Good news, for the young lady is very much in need of friends,' he smiled, bowing once again. 'Allow me first to introduce myself! Louis Parensell, at your service.'

SEVEN

Anne

When, after several moments of knocking and calling, at last Lydia opened the door to her chamber, the sight of her drew a barely stifled gasp from all present. All four siblings were caught in shock at the wraith that had once been pretty, plump Lydia Robinson.

'Lydia, dear,' Charlotte said, perhaps seeing that Anne was momentarily too stunned to act. 'Do you remember me? I am Miss Charlotte Brontë, Anne's sister, and this is Emily, and Branwell,' she added rather apologetically, 'whom you will know, of course. As soon as she received your letter, Anne insisted that we come to your aid at once. May we come in?'

Lydia opened the door wider.

'Is it you? Have you really come?'

'Of course we came,' Charlotte said, as she entered the attic room first. Anne noted that the stifling hot room must sit in the very centre and the very highest point of the theatre, judging by the several back staircases they had been led up, each one becoming gradually less substantial and more terrifying, the very last being hardly more than a ladder. The only source of light in the fetid room was a small round window of four panes, which for some reason was not open. Battling to keep the dismay from her face, Anne scanned the room, which under different circumstances could have delighted her with childlike glee. Here was a room that had five walls instead of four, and on the fifth, slanted wall, there was a small fireplace, next to which stood a copper kettle, and, it seemed, a quantity of tea.

You must collect yourself, Anne told herself sternly. You must resume your old duty as nurse and confidante, and see your charge safe and well again.

'I believe that we could all do with some refreshment,' Anne said, gesturing to her sisters to guide Lydia to the unmade bed, the only substantial piece of furniture in the room. 'You must rest, Lydia dear.'

'I am Mrs Roxby now.' Lydia smiled at the sound of her married name as Charlotte and Emily helped her on to the bed, and her billowing gown settled over her. 'I do so like to hear *that* name, Anne. Will you say it often to me?'

For a moment, Anne could not see what her sisters were staring at, and a large portion of Lydia was hidden behind Emily, but as she moved around her sister, the truth came into view.

Lydia was altered utterly from the blossoming young girl that Anne had last seen. She was painfully thin, her pale skin sinking into the sockets around her eyes and stretched thin across her cheekbones. Her abundance of dark hair no longer shone like polished ebony but rather seemed as if it was coated with the same grit and grime as the rest of the city, and perhaps most shockingly of all, pressing down on her narrow frame was the swollen belly of an expectant mother, very close to confinement.

Lydia had not mentioned her condition in the letter, perhaps as a young and inexperienced wife with no mother to guide her, she had not known how.

'My dear girl,' Anne said warmly, seating herself on the edge of the bed and taking Lydia's limp hand in hers. 'How terribly you have suffered alone. But we are here now.'

'Oh, Anne, you came.' Lydia seemed to suddenly recognise Anne anew, as if the last few minutes had vanished from time.

In one lunging movement, she clasped her arms around Anne's neck, dragging her down into a desperate embrace. 'You alone in all this world have not abandoned me.'

'Of course I came,' Anne said. 'We have all come to your aid, Lydia dear – come to solve the mystery with our finely honed skills of detection. Would it ever have been in doubt?'

'I used not to think so,' Lydia said, releasing Anne and sinking back on to a single limp pillow. 'I used to think I had Papa and Mama, and sisters and brothers who would care for me always. And yet here I am – quite, quite alone.'

'You are alone no longer, Mrs Roxby,' Charlotte said, passing a chipped cup of weak tea to Anne to minister to the girl. 'We are here to protect you now.'

Branwell sat in a rickety chair that stood next to a narrow table, which seemed to serve as both a desk and a dressing table. Then he leapt up again, seemingly greatly vexed by the intimacy of the room and the situation. Hardly surprising, Anne supposed. After all, the last time Lydia saw him he was being sent away from Thorp Green in disgrace. He wanted to help Lydia – Anne could tell that. And to make all good, including himself. But he did not have the first clue as to where to start. And so he paced and sat again, repeating the cycle with Lydia's increasing agitation. Anne laid a calming hand on his shoulder.

'Be still, Branwell,' she whispered. 'Time for action will come.'

With great reservations, Charlotte had lowered herself on to the very edge of the bed, as had Emily and Anne, the three of them forming a guard around Lydia.

'And how long has Harry been gone now, my dear?' Anne asked Lydia, whom she had propped up with her single pillow and, when that would not suffice, added her own luggage to act as a bolster behind the thin padding. Lydia sipped her tea.

'He has been gone four days now, including this day,' Lydia told them. 'Which just leaves three days for me to return this prize they say Harry has stolen. I agreed in the moment because I was afraid and I thought that a solution would present itself. But I am so weak, Anne! I have done nothing to save Harry – nothing at all. Except to speak to Harry's papa, which was of no use at all, and to write to you. Which is just as well, for Henry Roxby had no pity for his son. He told me that if Harry was so foolish as to get himself into such a situation, then he must find his own way out of it. I was all at once overwhelmed with a feeling of panic, and found that I could do nothing at all, not even leave my room. All I could do was cry, and now I am too weak even for that.'

'That is not true at all, dear,' Anne said, patting Lydia's wrist. 'You did the best thing you could when you wrote to me. My sisters . . .' Branwell caught her eye, and raised his brows at her, 'and brother have become quite adept at providing for persons who find themselves in difficulties. Three days is a good amount of time, and I am certain that between us we shall set this situation right in no time.'

Anne withdrew her hand, doing her best to disguise her discomfort. It was impossible not to notice that the bed they were sitting on had not been made in several weeks, the sheets were crumpled, the impression of a man's body still indented into the thin mattress. The sheets smelled pungently of sweat and married intimacy that Anne found equally repulsive and enticing.

'Tell us again what you told Anne in the letter, Mrs Roxby,' Charlotte said. 'Just in case you omitted any detail that may aid us in our next course of action.'

'They came in the night and took him,' Lydia said. 'They took him, and told me I have seven days to return to them the jewel he took from them! But if Harry stole such a thing, he did not confide in me, and I cannot fathom where he would have hidden it, or why he would not simply tell them? This room is my sole kingdom, and I have searched every inch of it

I can, pulled the mattress off the bed, crawled along the floor looking for a loose board or crack in the wainscot where such a thing might be concealed, but there is nothing.' She glanced towards the small circular window. 'And I am too cowardly to go out there, without Harry at my side.'

'Not cowardly.' Emily spoke for the first time since they had entered the room. 'You are in no condition to be searching out stolen goods. It is a difficult task, but I am certain we will find a way to unravel it.'

'We shall!' Branwell said, leaping to his feet and then finding himself at a loss for words and sitting down again. 'Depend on it,' he muttered.

'There is yet a more immediate solution,' Charlotte said cautiously, glancing warily at Anne. 'I should be remiss if I didn't present it . . . Mrs Roxby, what you have undergone is intolerable, but your present circumstances are easily and quickly resolved if you will allow it. I am duty bound to suggest that we stay here tonight . . .' Charlotte looked around the room with more than a little dismay, 'and upon the dawn, take you home to Yorkshire. You will stay with us at first until we can broker a peace with your mama, and I am certain that before long you will be reunited with your family and your condition managed with discretion and kindness.'

'Charlotte!' Anne stood up to emphasise her disagreement. 'We came to help Lydia, not to remove her.'

'I agree that removing her would be for the best,' Emily said with a shrug. 'I am no expert in love, but it does seem to me that when a person is very young and very charmed by another person, that sense and reason become lost. Future lives are gambled in an instant, and on an impulse. Removing Lydia from this place would not remove her from her marriage, or its issue.' Emily nodded at Lydia's belly. 'But it would at least give her some space to recover her senses, away from the heady poison of love. And mother and child would be safe.'

'I will not be taken away from Harry,' Lydia said, sitting up, and then standing with some purpose until all of them were on their feet, obliging Branwell to remove himself from the chair he had been occupying, with his arms outreached to catch her should she topple in any direction. 'You think me a silly-headed little fool, Miss Brontë. A stupid girl, who allowed herself to be seduced by a scoundrel and a cad, but you are quite wrong.' Her eyes seemed to shine like twin blue moons as she spoke. 'I am sure of one thing in this world, and that is that I love my husband and that he loves me, Miss Brontë. We belong to one another, body and soul, and I could endure a thousand more nights in this city if he is by my side. If you cannot help me find the jewel and return my husband to safety, then you must go. I will die before I leave him. And besides, our tormentor has promised to kill me too if I do not obey him. He tells me he will find me wherever I run, and take his payment in blood if he must.'

'Well, that does rather undermine my notion,' Charlotte said, with grim humour.

Anne could see that there was nothing to be done to alter Lydia's mind. They were to take on the very worst souls that inhabited this very worst of cities, but Anne believed that – with faith and determination – they would not only survive the battle but bring these thieving scoundrels to their knees.

Emily

'Well then,' Emily said. There was only one thing to be done now, and that was to discover the whereabouts of this mysterious jewel and rescue Harry Roxby. There was simply no point mithering about the difficulty of it a moment longer. 'How did Harry become entangled with the ruffians who took him, and what kind of men are they? It is best we know our enemies as well as we can. So, tell us everything you know.'

'It's my fault.' Lydia's voice trembled. The righteous ire that had brought her to her feet a moment previously had drained away, and she was reclining once again. 'Harry was determined that we should be independent from any help, but Papa, in his fury, had made it impossible for Harry to find a role worthy of his talents in the Yorkshire playhouses. The theatre managers were too afraid of Papa's influence to employ him.'

'He was indeed a man who must rule all with an iron fist, little caring for the tender hearts he crushed beneath his domineering boots,' Branwell said, before Charlotte quieted him with a withering look.

'Harry put my welfare before his pride,' Lydia continued, resolutely ignoring Branwell's presence. 'After a few days staying with old friends of his, he brought me here to the theatre where his father is manager.' She gestured at the roof above her head. 'Harry and his father do not care for one another, any more than my mama cares for me now . . .'

45

'Your mother cares for you a great deal, Lydia—' Branwell began, but Lydia cut him short.

'Sir, she cares for me as much as she does for you,' she returned, addressing him for the first time with just a hint of that haughty spark Anne had spoken of more than once. Foolish Branwell seemed rather pleased at this response, and Emily thought that – as time was of the essence – it was best not to enlighten him further.

'And so?' Anne prompted Lydia.

'And so, we came to ask his father for help. Henry is not a man disposed to coddle his son. He believes that if a man is to make a life walking the boards, then he must carve out his own way with resilience and fortitude. Harry has proven himself more than capable. He endured a desperately unhappy childhood without love or comfort. It cost him a great deal to ask his father for aid, and a great deal more to accept what little help Mr Roxby would afford us, which was this room, and casual work around the theatre. Not even the smallest part in any performance! And Harry is such a fine actor, Anne. You will remember how he set the stage alight in Scarborough, no doubt?'

'It is a performance ever burned on my mind,' Anne said gently.

'And so, I suppose . . . no, I *know*, that he determined to make enough to buy our way out of this hovel, to allow us to be independent again by any means. He did not speak to me of his actions, but I observed them. I sensed he was straying into danger, and I did not intervene. That is how he fell in with the Sharps.'

'The Sharps?' Emily asked, cocking her head to one side like Keeper at the prospect of cheese.

'Yes, all of Covent Garden, the Strand, as far up as Euston and below as far as the Embankment, and as far again in either direction – these streets are an empire for them, a group of criminals captained by a man they call Noose.'

'Noose,' Charlotte repeated the name with a shudder. 'How peculiarly thrilling.'

'You would not find him so thrilling if you met him, Charlotte,' Lydia said with a touch of coldness. 'They say he has murdered at least a hundred men and women. His soldiers crawl out of The Rookery of St Giles every night to pick off what they can from the drunks and theatregoers, and retreat again into the slums before day breaks, because they know that no man who wishes to live will follow them there. They'd kill you as soon as look at you, every one of them. Even the children they use as pickpockets are so absent of humanity or any notion of decency that they might as well have been raised by wolves.'

'I should think wolves would make far better parents than many humans,' Emily observed, thinking of her Keeper, who had shown her more love, loyalty and trust than most human beings – excepting her sisters, of course, and he was not nearly so disagreeable as them.

'They use children and young women to entice money from gentlemen of low morals, and more often than not employ outright thuggery to beat what they want from their victims,' Lydia continued, her voice quivering with exhaustion. 'Noose is so named because he was twice sentenced to hang for murder, and twice escaped. The burn of the rope still scars his thick neck, as if he had been branded by the devil himself.'

'And which of these crimes did Harry engage in?' Emily asked, not entirely sure she wanted to rescue him any more. 'Theft or murder?'

'Nothing so *very* terrible,' Lydia said, shamefaced. 'I did not know precisely, so the morning after Harry was taken, I ventured downstairs and spoke to one or two of the theatre folk who are kind to me, and not too fearsome. I discovered that his role was to walk among the audience finding targets

47

for Noose's men to rob. He'd listen to ascertain what amount of cash was being carried by whom, and making note of any jewels and silks being worn, and such. For he looks like an agreeable gentleman, not someone to be wary of. Later, when the thieves struck their victims, they could be direct and discreet. For this subterfuge they paid Harry a portion of their profits.'

'Harry brought these men to your door?' Anne asked, failing to hide her horror as she heard, despite Lydia's protests to the contrary, how very poorly Harry Roxby was caring for his young wife.

'Not until the night they kicked the door in and took him. That night Noose told me his terms on this very bed, and I wrote to you that same night, for I could not think of another person as sensible as you, Anne. I had no idea that you had become practised at helping people in such a particular kind of need, but I am glad to know a detector.'

'And now you know three,' Emily said.

'Four,' Branwell reminded her.

'Three and a half,' Emily smiled, before turning to her sisters. 'For this jewel to inspire such violence and fear, it must be something very rare and difficult to obtain. Something that would cost our criminals very dear to lose, otherwise they could simply steal a replacement and punish Harry accordingly. It must be very singular, or hold some threat for Noose, should it fall into the wrong hands. So we know we aren't looking for a commonplace piece of jewellery.' She thought for a moment. 'We have but one objective: to determine the specificity of the jewel we are looking for and where it might be.'

'Is that not two objectives?' Charlotte questioned her, as she was prone to do whenever Emily took the lead.

'They are two components of the same objective,' Emily said, 'that come under the heading, "find the jewel". The second objective—'

'Or more accurately the third,' Charlotte muttered.

'The *second* objective is that we need to discover where Harry might be being held by this Mr Noose. For if we cannot find the ransom in time, then we will have to free him from his prison and find a safe refuge for Lydia and her husband. Even if it means sending them to the Continent – Brussels, perhaps, where we have acquaintances. No one would willingly chase them there.'

'Tell me, Emily, where shall we begin to search for this unknown object?' Charlotte asked, glaring at Branwell until he offered her the rickety chair and retreated into a corner, no doubt to brood on being declared but half a detector. 'How do we find something when we do not know what it looks like, where it has come from or where it is hidden?'

'It is a devilishly hard task, I grant you,' Emily said, picking up a pile of unread newspapers that were on the desk. 'But we shall find it with rational logic and diligence. Charlotte, Anne – read through these, searching for any reported thefts of note. Branwell, you and I shall begin in the very place where the Sharps ply their trade, of course. We shall begin here, in the theatre. And we shall begin now.'

Charlotte

Emily departed with all the flourish one would expect of a major leading a charge into battle, leaving Charlotte to ruminate privately that for all Emily claimed to hate society, she was never happier than when utterly alone, and did not have one moment's patience for the usual troubles that might furrow a lesser brow. Emily, nevertheless, did have a talent for the dramatic.

It rankled with Charlotte somewhat, because this was Anne's detection, the case had come to her little sister. It was Anne's expedition that she had instigated and led, and yet here was Emily, charging off into the night with Branwell in tow, as if she had uncovered this matter, leaving Anne alone in this dingy room to act as nursemaid to Lydia with Charlotte to read newspapers. Where was the adventure in that?

Silently she chided herself for allowing even a glimmer of resentment to trouble her brow. What she must admit is that each of them had their specific talents when it came to detecting, and each came into their own at the appropriate moment. Emily was the adventurer, and it was the adventurer who should be sallying forth in the crowds below. What mattered was that the mystery was solved, and that Lydia and Harry were saved. Not who solved it. Still, Anne looked troubled and constrained by their confinement with Lydia. It would not do, Charlotte decided. If they were to get to the bottom of this conundrum, the hunt must involve all of them.

'I fancy Emily believes she will have the answer by midnight,' Charlotte said to Anne as she sorted through a pile of linen, folding what seemed clean enough and setting aside the rest with a view to finding a place to launder it. 'As if somehow, just by being foolhardy and impulsive, she is a better detector than you or me.'

'Emily has her moments, and we must allow them to her,' Anne said evenly. 'You will have yours soon enough, Charlotte. No one could forget your bravery and cleverness when in grave danger last Christmas.'

'This much is true,' Charlotte agreed with a small smile. 'I was marvellously clever and courageous. And so were you, Anne. Of all of us, I believe you have the greatest ability to intuit revelations that are invaluable. You seem to be able to read the very soul of a person.'

Anne smiled, and Charlotte was pleased to see her a little fortified by their conversation. For all that Anne had become such a formidable woman, she would also always be baby Anne to Charlotte. The truth was that the darling, golden little child that Anne had been when they had lost their mother all those years ago had given Charlotte someone to love and dote on when she was too young really to understand exactly what she had lost. Someone who loved her unconditionally in return. She'd done her best to love Anne in the way she knew their mother would, and no matter how old they grew, or how far Anne's magnificence might take her from Charlotte, she would always love her so.

'Lydia, when did you eat last?' Anne crossed to the bed, where Lydia lay listlessly, her hand resting on her belly, her face turned to the window, where the setting sun brought a little colour to her alabaster skin.

'I'm not entirely sure, Anne,' Lydia said. 'I believe I had a little bread yesterday.'

'You need sustenance, and urgently,' Anne said, looking at Charlotte, who inclined her head in silent concern.

'And these papers are from two weeks since,' Charlotte said. 'We must seek news of more recent events.'

'Is there a kitchen in the theatre where I might find something for you?' Anne asked. 'We have some coin.'

'No,' Lydia shook her head. 'There are stalls and shops on Drury Lane, Anne. But you should not go alone – you must take Miss Brontë with you, and you must look at all times as if you know what you are about, and are very sure of your direction, and you must keep your hands on your belongings at all times.'

'Is it really so dangerous, Lydia?' Charlotte went to the circular window and peered out at the street below. Though it was almost eight, the sun was only just now beginning to sink below the horizon, casting a coppery glow along the street, making the fine white buildings glow so that they looked almost like the Greek palaces they mimicked. 'Surely not everyone hereabouts can be a cutpurse or thief?'

'No, not everyone,' Lydia assented, her voice barely more than a whisper. 'When Harry first brought me to London, I believed I had stepped into the most beautiful and exciting place on earth. The colours seemed so bright here, the noises louder somehow. And how fine the ladies are, how fashionable. I imagined that one day soon, Harry and I would live in a fine house on Bedford Square with a maid and a housekeeper and I should be a very cosmopolitan lady. But the world is not kind to you if you are poor. If you are poor the world sees you as a sinner and a target both, and it will do all it can to bring you lower still until eventually you may do nothing but let yourself die.'

'Come now, it is not quite so bad as all that yet,' Anne soothed the poor girl. 'You will feel much brighter when you have eaten. I will go and fetch some food for you directly.'

'You stay with Lydia,' she told Charlotte, as she gathered some coins from her purse and tucked them into her glove. 'I will go out – find something to make us a decent supper.'

'You cannot go alone, Anne,' Charlotte insisted. 'Lydia has done well enough here alone for the last few days. I shall come with you and we will take care of one another, and that is the end of it.'

The interior of the theatre was now in total darkness, the doors that ran along the attic all firmly shutting out the last of the daylight. Charlotte reached for Anne's hand and stretched her fingers to use the crumbling, damp wall as her guide. When at last they came to the narrow wooden staircase that bent and twisted to the floor below, she stopped.

'There is a faint light at the bottom,' Charlotte told Anne in a whisper, though whispering was not strictly required. 'I am afraid if we make our way down the stairs in the dark we are likely to break our necks.'

'Call out!' Anne urged her. 'Ask the light-bearer below to illuminate the stairs. After all, Emily and Branwell must have descended this way, and if they have, I am sure that we shall also, else never hear the end of it.'

That was true enough, and after all they could not stay trapped on this floor for ever. The descent must be conquered.

'Hello there!' Anne called out, down into the pit of ever-deepening dark. 'Is there someone there?'

'Who's that calling?' a female voice returned.

'We are the Miss Brontës come to visit Mrs Roxby. We are very much alive and hope to remain that way, so we should be grateful for the use of your lantern to help us on the steps?'

A moment later the flame of the candle began to illuminate the staircase, almost as if it were floating entirely alone, but then, just before it reached the top, it cast its orangey light on a young face.

'Here I am to light your way, Miss Brontës,' the young woman said. 'Kit Thornfield, at your service.'

The descent went quickly after that, and Charlotte was very glad when they were met at the foot of the stairs by a door that let them out in the upper floor of the theatre, and the hallway that encased the highest tier of boxed seats. The gaslight illuminated a narrow corridor that ran in a circle, given the illusion of being twice the width it was by the regular positioning of gilt-framed mirrors on the walls. Best of all, it was a firm and secure footing that could not be further removed from the perilous stairs to the attic, which had swayed and trembled underfoot, or the shabby room in which Lydia now lay, half starved.

As they walked into the light, Charlotte saw that Kit Thornfield was a person unlike any she had ever seen before.

About Anne's age, a tumble of flame-red hair curled down over her shoulders and back, quite untamed by pin or bow, and she wore – well, gentleman's garb. A collarless white shirt, untucked, over breeches. She could almost have been Branwell's lost twin, if it were not for the fact that her features were so finely made, her green eyes set wide and large, her nose straight and small, her mouth a pretty rosebud of pink, all framed by a heart-shaped face. If she had been standing there in a gown of any description, Charlotte would have thought her the most beautiful woman she had ever encountered. As it was, she simply didn't know what to make of the curious creature, except that she was at once intrigued and unsettled by her.

'Good evening, Miss Brontës,' she said with a soft Irish accent that Charlotte at once warmed to. 'Pleased to meet you. May I introduce myself formally? I am Kit Thornfield, also known by the stage name of Celine Varens. I perform opera at the theatre, but I also paint scenery and study art, hence my frightful garb, which fares so much better than silks and satins when it comes to paint and ink.'

'How marvellous,' Anne said, at once taking Miss Thornfield's hand and curtseying. 'I should love to wear my brother's clothes, but I fear that my papa and neighbours would all die of apoplexy on the spot. I'm Anne, by the way, and this is my sister Charlotte.'

'Good evening, Miss . . .' Charlotte began awkwardly, feeling robbed of the comfort of the rules of society when addressing a stranger.

'Kit, just call me Kit,' Kit said, holding out her hand. Charlotte took it first, and found her own warmly shaken. 'Of course, theatre people are used to such eccentricities; we are a family of strangeness here. I would usually change into a gown to leave the theatre, but even then, as long as I don't stray too far, the local people pay me no mind now.'

Charlotte so wanted to talk to Kit, to ask her about her art and her singing and what life was like in the theatre, but she found her lips suddenly sealed by shyness. It was often so, when she was introduced to someone she truly found interesting. All at once, the experience and self-possession she had worked so hard to garner flew out of the window, and she was just a small, plain spinster with nothing to say.

'Are you going out?' Kit asked them. Charlotte nodded. 'Then let me show you the way – the theatre can be like a maze to those who do not know it. I've been a resident performer here for two years, and I am still uncertain as to where some doors lead, and which passages go where. There is the theatre itself, worn like a beautiful gown over a bone-thin old lady, and then there are the innards of the place, which I swear are designed to thwart any who dare to venture into them. They are floors below, tunnels and dungeons almost! I'm sure those passages must be littered with the skeletons of those who have tried to navigate them!' Kit laughed at the thought, and then seemed to check herself. 'I apologise, I am being most unseemly. I meant to say that I'm so glad you are here to help Mrs Roxby. It's been such a perplexing business, and many of us are cautious of going to her, for fear of making matters worse. It does not help that Old Roxby seems to have a vendetta against her and his son. Have you come to take her home to Yorkshire?'

'We hope not,' Anne said. 'At least not before we have found her husband, liberated him from his captors and brought him safely home.'

Kit, Charlotte noticed, did not even blink at the notion of two women presenting a daring rescue as their purpose. Perhaps theatrical people weren't as terrible as Charlotte imagined. This one was rather splendid, that was certain.

'Can you tell us what you know of Harry?' Anne asked, taking the lead when Charlotte remained silent. 'With whom was he associating before he was taken? We are most anxious to find his captors and demand his release.'

'I fear I don't know enough to help,' Kit said, her creamy brow furrowing. 'My position as an unmarried lady in the theatre means I must be constantly on my guard on all fronts, largely from the great quantity of gentlemen who believe that, if they offer to keep me, I shall surrender to them all that I am at once. To keep the many at bay I am obliged to keep one influential aristocrat closer than I would like, but still at arm's length. The moment you give them what they want, they lose interest in you. It's a constant, tiresome game of chess and I cannot wait to be done with it.'

'How awful,' Anne exclaimed.

'To have all those gentlemen obsessed by you,' Charlotte added a little less robustly. 'Dreadful.'

'So, beyond the company, I stay away from other business that goes on in and around the theatre. But I will say there is plenty of it, if you dare to observe. If you have a few minutes, we can sit in an empty box and I can show you where you might look.'

'We are engaged in securing a meal for Lydia and ourselves, and searching for newspapers,' Anne said, glancing at

Charlotte, who had gone quite pink. 'Perhaps you could accompany us, and we could talk as we walk?'

'I'd be most glad to escort you,' Kit said. 'And I will be able to guide you away from the worst establishments.'

As they headed into the bustle of Drury Lane, Charlotte struggled to both look and not look at Kit Thornfield, also known as Celine Varens, for this frank and frankly scandalous young woman was entirely unlike any other person she had ever met before.

TEN

Emily

'Now then,' Branwell breathed, as they entered the auditorium. 'This is grand.'

'No better than the Royal Theatre, Duke Lane,' Emily replied loyally, talking of their Bradford counterpart, although this was not strictly true.

Branwell's mouth fell open as he pointed towards the stage, agog. 'Emily, Emily, there is a tiger upon the stage! A live tiger!'

There were indeed not one but three tigers on the stage, though two of them seemed to be not much more than cubs. Emily watched, beguiled by their beauty, yet horrified by the predicament of such majestic creatures. How cowed the poor whipped creatures looked, how miserable.

Neither brother nor sister had ever seen a tiger outside the pages of a book before. Both were mesmerised as they slowly approached the stage, gazing at the great muscular creature that should have dominated her trainer – a large moustached man in purple – in both beauty and power, but was somehow conquered by him.

The injustice of it! Tigers such as these should be stalking the jungles of India, not performing tricks for an infinitely lesser being.

'Are you not afraid they will turn on you one day and bite your head off?' Emily asked their trainer, who, according to the signage on his props, was titled 'The Great Brute Tamer of Pompeii'.

'They're too afraid of me to do that,' the man said, with a decidedly home-grown accent and altogether nauseating swagger. 'That's the key – get them when they are cubs and beat the fury out of them before they know different.'

'I hope they do eat you,' Emily told him sincerely, as the beautiful beasts were harangued back into a cramped cage. 'I hope they eat you slowly and with great relish.'

She was roundly insulted as the trainer departed with his animals, but she didn't mind nearly so much as she minded the thought of those poor animals in that inadequate cage. No creature as fierce and free as a tigress should ever be imprisoned so.

'There were tigers on stage,' Branwell said to her after a moment, his mind still stuck on the spectacle. 'Actual tigers, Emily!'

'I know,' Emily said, forcing her mind back to the present predicament. 'Let us concentrate on the matter in hand, Branwell,' she said. 'I shall release the tigers later.'

Turning her back to the stage, which was now occupied by six ballerinas and a pianist, she took in the sumptuous wonder of the theatre's interior. The opulent gilded circus rose upwards to a vaulted ceiling, which at first glance looked as if it had been painted as expertly as the Sistine Chapel to be a blue sky dotted with perfect white clouds. But this was no place of worship – at least not of heavenly things, Emily thought. This was a palace to take pleasure in earthly delights, to flirt with sin and temptation. And what a palace it was, made of gold leaf and all manner of beautiful adornment that cast a glamour over the observer, making them blind, at least for a little while, to the coarse reality that existed beneath the illusion. The scent of sweat and blood, the splintered floorboards sticky with substances that Emily didn't like to dwell on, faded into nothing when there was such dazzling artifice to distract from them.

'This is a place where a man could get himself into trouble,' Branwell said, entranced by glimpses of stockinged ankle as the dancers' gauze gowns flared open like petals in the sun as they pirouetted in unison.

'Everywhere is a place where you can get yourself in trouble,' Emily said, adding thoughtfully, 'perhaps you *should* get yourself into a *very* little trouble, preferably not the expensive kind. At least then it might give you some respite from your unhappiness.'

'I cannot,' Branwell said regretfully. 'As much as I wish I could distract myself with some dalliance, I am in *love*, Emily. No matter how you might wish it were not so, no matter how *I* might wish it were not so. I am in love and I am a slave to that love.'

It was true that they were all so busy condemning Branwell for his terrible decisions and array of resulting afflictions that they never did pay tribute to him for his constancy to Mrs Robinson, and yet constant he was.

'I shall never fall in love,' Emily said. 'To lose one's agency to any other, even willingly, is unthinkable to me.'

Branwell smiled at her fondly.

'You know, Emily, you will never be able to truly understand the human condition until you have lived at least a little of it yourself.'

'What nonsense,' Emily said. 'Now to the detection.'

'Where to begin, though?' Branwell gestured around him. 'There is so much to examine.'

'Let us begin with the theatre folk,' Emily said, peering past the elegant dancers and into the dark recesses of the wings where several people were engaged in all manner of mysterious and intriguing business. 'Harry must have made friends here, and if not friends, enemies who will know more of what he was about than poor, ignorant Lydia.' Her eyes searched out a small set of wooden steps to the left of the stage.

'Let us begin there and find our way behind the stage, and see what we shall come across, Branwell. And we must pay close attention and never forget that all we encounter is false-hood. We must search amongst the spectral for what is true and solid.'

'The talent of the players on the stage is true and solid,' a young gentleman said with a lazily amused smile as he came upon them from behind. 'For what is all this but a mirage, without an actor to bring it to life?'

Emily turned to him and knew his dark eyes at once from their brief encounter earlier that day when he had shown them the way to Lydia's room.

'But what is an actor but a mummer with no mask, without such a glorious setting to trick our eyes and minds into believing their pretensions?'

'We are the mages,' he returned, tilting his head slightly as he looked at her. 'Masters of reality, bringing forth imagination into being and making more of this world than it is, would you not agree?'

Under normal circumstances, Emily found it very difficult to know what to say when confronted with whimsical nonsense, but for some reason she encountered no such issue with this gentleman. Perhaps it was his attire, his true likeness hidden behind stage make-up, his eyes lined with kohl, that kept her at ease. It was hardly like talking to a real person at all, but more like conversing with a character from a book, or a resident of Gondal. And since Emily was excellent at doing both those things, she was not at all beset with her usual shyness. Instead she smiled broadly, to her brother's astonishment.

'I do believe I agree with you, sir,' she said. 'It is very surprising, as I almost never agree with anyone at all.'

'Allow me to introduce myself formally,' he said, 'though we have met once before.' He bowed deeply, removing his plumed hat and ringleted wig with one flourish, revealing a mass of dark, unruly hair.

'I am Louis Parensell, principal actor at the Covent Garden Theatre, Drury Lane. Pleased to make your acquaintance. Again.'

'I am Emily Brontë, and this is my brother, Branwell Brontë,' Emily replied.

Somehow, in this theatrical setting, the whole tiresome ritual of becoming acquainted seemed almost appropriate to Emily. It seemed there was a time and a place for curtseys and bows after all.

'Now, I know why I am in the theatre,' Mr Parensell said, 'as our curtain rises within the hour. But I find I must ask why you are here. Have you come to seek employment?'

'Lord, no!' Emily laughed. 'We have come with our two sisters from Haworth in Yorkshire to visit Mrs Roxby and offer her our aid.'

'Ah yes, but that still doesn't explain why you are here and not by her side?'

'My brother and I are hoping to discover the whereabouts of Mr Roxby, so that we may retrieve him from his captor, a Mr "Noose", and return him to his wife. If you would be so good as to tell us what you know about the matter, we'd be most grateful.'

Mr Parensell ran his fingers through his unruly hair, and attempted to pat it flat, until it was at least a little more groomed.

'I heard he was in trouble, I didn't realise it was that kind of trouble,' he said. 'Have you brought an army of men to retrieve Harry from the den of the Sharps?' he said quite seriously. 'For that is what you will need.'

'Well,' Emily looked at her brother, who had been mute all this time, his attention divided between their conversation, the dancers, and a gentleman with a monkey on his shoulder, who seemed to be setting up some equipment on the stage, which Emily had to admit was rather diverting. 'As it happens, my sisters and I have found that even though we are but weak and feeble women, we can do most things that must be done entirely ourselves without the slightest bit of aid from any gentleman.'

Mr Parensell regarded her with a half-smile that irritated Emily, though she could not precisely decide why. Perhaps because it was rather too charming to be irritating in the right way.

'Madam, I am surrounded by actresses, dancers, acrobats and opera girls. I do not doubt it for one second,' he said. 'However, I am duty bound to caution you. I don't know where the Sharps have closeted poor Hal, but I do know they are dangerous animals to a man. I am practised in the art of defence and attack, and I would not wander into that region without at least fifty trained men at my back.'

'I am also practised in the art of defence,' Branwell said rather loudly, perhaps hoping one of the dancers might hear him. 'My friends say I am like a terrier in a fight – small but deadly.'

'Even so,' Mr Parensell said, 'your cause is honourable but foolish. Any decent man would advise you to stay away from that particular brand of difficulty.'

'I see,' Emily said, giving Branwell a pitying look before turning back to Mr Parensell. 'Where and what is this "rookery" we have heard spoken of?'

'A slum,' Mr Parensell said, leaning back on the stage and looking up towards the dome, as he sought the right words to expand on his explanation. As he did so he exposed the length of his warm brown throat, in which Emily could faintly detect his blood pulsing. It was almost as diverting as the monkey.

'The streets where the poor are penned in and piled one upon another like cattle,' Mr Parensell went on. 'More than one such area is called a rookery, but The Rookery of St Giles, the one I speak of, is the very worst place in London. More so even than the treacherous streets that surround this very building, or even the Adelphi arches that run along the Strand.'

He directed a dark look at Emily once again.

'But I urge you to go home, to where you are safe.'

'Sir, if decent people never take a stand against the encroaching dark, then soon the entire world will live in constant terror. I thank you for your concern, but you cannot turn us from our purpose. Please, tell us more about this Rookery.'

Louis sighed and shrugged.

'Once the parish of St Giles was a fine place to live,' he went on. 'Filled with gentlemen's residences, wide avenues of fine houses populated with decent people of good society. But that was more than a hundred years ago now. Within the last century it has fallen into despair. The streets are crammed with derelict houses full of desolate souls seeking the cheapest roof they can afford.' He shook his head gravely.

'It is a pity indeed that good men and women must suffer so,' Emily said. 'But the portrait you paint so vividly, Mr Parensell, seems one of people to be pitied, not feared.'

Mr Parensell nodded.

'I would agree, Miss Brontë, and in truth those people should be pitied, not just for their lot in life but for the greater crimes that are done to them. I was like them once, and I'm afraid to say it cost me a good part of my soul to drag myself clear of the mire.' He cast down a look of dismay. Emily could not tell if it was real or an affectation, but in any case she found his sorrow moving, and the length of his dark lashes objectively beguiling. She resolved to write a poem about him, recast as a Gondal hero of course, at some later date. 'For those who live there are not only trapped in degradation, but also at the mercy of a king of criminals known as Noose and his army of reprobates. The lawful inhabitants must do his bidding, must pay his tariffs and taxes, and even shield him from the law if they want to be left alone. There is none that dares disobey him, not if they wish to see another dawn, for if Noose puts a price upon your head, you may be assured that you will pay for it with your life, and within the week.'

Emily thought of the tigress made meek, bowing her beautiful head to the hateful brute that beat her, and a flush of anger bloomed across her nose.

'Such a terrible man holds so many in his thrall and none have sought to vanquish him?' Emily demanded, astounded.

'No one cares for the poor, the ill, or the lost in this city, or throughout this nation,' Louis told her with a frown. 'Why, the general consensus is that if you are selfish and foolish enough to be poor, the best thing you can do for yourself and society is to die, and even then you are forcing the parish to pay for your grave. Those who have sufficient means seem to walk through this city as if in a dream, ignorant of its true directors, who orchestrate their pantomime lives. Once I longed for nothing more than to make England my home, but now . . . let us just say that my boyhood dreams have faded away to nothing under the burden of harsh reality.'

Suddenly Louis paused, looking around him as if he had become aware of the possibility of being overheard. Emily wondered what he meant by his boyhood dreams, where he might have grown up and if it were very far away, but there was no time for those questions now. Louis replaced his hat and wig in one decisive move. Lowering his voice, he took one step closer to them.

'I have a little time before tonight's performance,' he said *sotto voce*. 'I am not on stage until after the first interval. If you wish I can tell you more of what I know, but not here. Noose has men everywhere, and some might say he is the least of your worries.'

Before Emily could answer, there came a bellow from the back of the stalls.

'What's this! What's this! Still rehearsing? Clear the stage at once, you fools; our audience will be upon us within the hour! Claude, put away those props and set places for the first act. And I want curtain down by eleven, theatre clear by midnight. I have business to conduct later. Ladies!' One of the ballerinas reluctantly stayed at his command while the other dancers fled the stage. 'Do your best to look like you are enjoying yourselves tonight!' the yellow-whiskered and ruddy-faced fellow told her. 'No one comes to look at a troupe of miserable old crones prancing about. Smile, for God's sake, lift your skirts a little, and I'll need two or three of you to entertain my associates tonight, so sort out amongst yourselves who is to stay.'

The poor girl curtsied and fled. Emily deduced that she was in the company of Mr Henry Roxby, Harry's father. And what an unpleasant individual he was.

'Why are you standing there clacking, Parensell?' Roxby demanded of their companion as he waddled towards them with an air of menace that Emily would previously have thought unlikely in a man of his rotundity. 'Why are there fishes about the stage before curtain-up, Parsensell? Don't I always tell you, no fishes before curtain-up?' He eyed Emily with far too much familiarity. 'This one does not look a bit like your usual fare – far too skinny for you, I'd say.'

'I am not *for* anyone, sir,' Emily said quietly. Louis coloured deeply, the tip of his nose turning pink.

'I say – that will not do,' Branwell added in her defence.

'Sir, they are not fishes. They are Miss and Mr Brontë, come to see Mrs Roxby and your son Harry, if only they can find him.'

'Oh indeed.' Mr Roxby exhaled a great phlegm-rattling sigh. 'I am glad to see you, then,' he said. 'You will do me a great favour if you take that mewling idiot girl away with you, and I am no longer obliged to keep her here.'

'You are not at all concerned for the whereabouts of your son, Mr Roxby?' Emily asked him, her eyes narrowing just a little. 'Nor of what might befall him?'

'Boy's a fool,' Roxby told her, unapologetically. 'It's no surprise to me that he has been, or shall soon be, murdered by despicables.' He hooked his thumbs into his coat lapels, as if he were addressing a rapt audience. 'I knew, from the moment he was born, I tell you, that he'd amount to nothing. Sickly, dull child he was. When he told me he was to take to the stage, I told him, I said, you will fail at the first hint of trouble, a weak-minded dullard like you. You will amount to nothing, my boy. Not a thing.'

Emily thought of her own dear papa, and wished with all her might that she might be allowed to box Mr Roxby smartly on the nose. But Charlotte had told her more than once that such a thing was not generally considered acceptable in polite society, no matter how tempting it might be, and one had better always refrain. So, in honour of her sister she merely balled her fist, hiding it amongst the folds of her skirt, hoping the action alone would be enough to relieve some of her mounting ire.

'Mr Roxby the younger was doing rather well when Lydia met him in Scarborough, so perhaps you were wrong,' Emily said, her tone dangerously quiet and mild, her fingernails biting into her palms.

Mr Parensell caught her eye, shaking his head slightly. That and something else in his expression warned her to hide her true feelings towards Harry Roxby's father at all costs.

'In the north,' Mr Roxby went on, oblivious of her disapproval. 'Yes, he did make a living in the north for a time, before that girl caught his eye. Of course he did – a man with a bottle of wine becomes king in the land of the thirsty, does he not, no matter how bad the wine is?'

Emily pressed her lips together with all her might, but though she managed to silence herself for the sake of the detection, her eyes flashed like lightning over the moors. It was only because of Mr Parensell's steadying look that she was able to restrain herself further from rebuking the buffoon who had so casually abused her homeland. Even so, she knew she had to be free of his presence within the minute, else risk violence, Charlotte or no.

'Mr Parensell,' she said briskly, 'I would very much like to see the place we spoke of earlier, if you would be good enough to show me. Branwell,' she turned to her brother, 'we can reconvene at Lydia's room.'

'Emily,' Branwell said uncertainly. 'I don't suppose I should be allowing my unmarried sister to disappear on to the streets of London with a gentleman, an actor no less, whom she does not know from Adam.'

'Then it's a good job you don't have any say in the matter, isn't it?' Emily said.

ELEVEN

Charlotte

Every particle of their surroundings stifled Charlotte in every conceivable sense, including her ability to make intelligent conversation, it seemed. It was true that the day had been long and arduous, but no more for her than for Anne, and Anne was as full of vivacity as Charlotte had ever seen her, finding no shortage of things to say to the very original Kit Thornfield. Charlotte could find no such ease.

The heat of the day, though it was almost over, still lingered in the air, caged in by the tall buildings and narrow streets. Each breath they took was hazed with dirt and grime, and the stench of humanity bound so closely together with animals and industry. The lane, which once would have meandered through a meadow bordered by hedgerows, was now thronged with more people than Charlotte thought she had ever seen in one place. Even her visits to Leeds and Bradford, to Bruges and beyond, had never affronted her with such a great proximity of people.

Charlotte had hoped that her excursion with Anne and the exterior of the theatre would afford at least a little more of a sense of liberty than the dreadful apartment Lydia languished in, but it was hard to decide which location was more hateful.

Anne had taken to Kit at once and, before they had exchanged two words, was sharing confidences with her as if they had always been good friends. This, Charlotte summarised, as she tried to make sense of exactly why Miss Thornfield made her feel so uncomfortable, was the trouble with this particular detection.

Murderers and monsters she had no fear of, and she was almost certain that this Mr Noose Lydia had spoken of was probably not nearly as clever or as dastardly as he or anyone else thought, for none could be more dreadful than the horror they – or more precisely, she – had defeated last December when they had found the bones and hunted down the diabolical beast that had hidden them away at Top Withens.

But these London people, these *theatrical* people were another matter altogether. They might as well be consorting with fairies and elves, so strange and frightening were these folk, who seemed not to adhere to any single convention that made the world a navigable sea. Kit Thornfield was a case in point. She was perfectly pleasant, candid and forthright, made no pretences and put on no airs. Indeed, Charlotte sensed she was an honest and decent person, though her certainty about her intuition on such matters had been shaken to the core a few months since. But it was also because of Kit's strangeness that Charlotte felt acute uncertainty about how to be in her company. And she, who made it her motto that just because a person is odd to others, they should not be overlooked or ignored, was struggling against committing the same injustice. Anne seemed to have no such quandary, which only made Charlotte feel all the worse for her prejudice. Perhaps she had been told so many times to stay away from a certain kind of person that she forgot they too were made only of flesh and blood, with a soul and heart just the same as hers.

'There's a cookshop just across the street,' Kit said, as she shepherded them between the crowds of people and carts, her outstretched arm a constant buffer between them and the crowds that surrounded them. 'Been there since time immemorial. They say the highwayman Jack Shepherd dined there regularly before he was hanged. I must own that it is still a den of thieves and frequented mostly by convicts and ticket-of-leave men, but the food is honest and cheap. Better that than The Dog, which is a proper thieves' paradise, and The Cock and Magpie, which ladies such as yourselves should avoid at all costs.'

Kit stopped for a moment to emphasise her point. 'Misses Brontë, please have a care while you are on the lane. Only these last few months we've had two attempts at murder on this very street that we know of, and one of them successful. A man was shot dead in the copper foundry and my own friend and mentor, the lithographer Mr Blewitt, was almost shot to death in April by a young man hardly more than a child. Some might argue he deserved it, but I will defend him to the end, for he is willing to apprentice me in his trade, which, as you can imagine, is a rare opportunity indeed for both a lady and an opera girl. Besides, one could argue that crime would be much worse if it were not for the criminals. They keep themselves in order, so long as we do not interfere.'

'But what about the Metropolitan Police?' Charlotte asked. 'The new force, built to fight and solve crime? We took our inspiration from their founding!'

'I have never yet met one who is just for the people, or just interested in truth,' Kit said, with more bitterness than Charlotte expected. 'The constables follow the orders of their seniors, and their seniors serve another master, and whoever that man is, they all bow to him.'

'That sounds like a kind of infernal imprisonment to me,' Charlotte muttered, though from the expression on Kit's face, she thought the other woman had heard her.

'But why not simply sing for ever?' Anne asked her, fascinated. 'If you are so talented as to be employed at the theatre, you need not ever ply another trade if you do not wish to.'

'Ah, but I do wish to,' Kit told her. 'Celine Varens is another person who has nothing to do with me. She is a coquettish, vain and dubious person, whose garb I am obliged to wear from time to time in order to beguile, amuse and earn my keep. But she is a fine-feathered bird who has nothing in common with my plain, uncomplicated sparrow's heart. Truth be told I do not like her at all, and shall be glad to see the back of her. Besides, a theatrical career is not for ever, not for a lady. Soon Celine will be too old to please the audiences any more, and before then I would like to have completely shed her skin, and to make my living through my art, principally through the lithograph, because I wish to make prints that can be seen by ten thousand people instead of the few who might see a painting in a gallery or fine home, or even the scenery I paint at the theatre. Art should be for the masses, don't you agree, Miss Brontë? Why should only those who have money and fine houses enjoy the pleasure of being moved or educated by something beautiful or informative?'

'I do – I do agree,' Anne said enthusiastically. 'As do you, Charlotte?'

Charlotte wondered at what to say, and found she had nothing coherent to add after her last comment, so instead just made a vague affirmative noise, which seemed to amuse both of her companions, whom she was certain were thinking her silly and stuffy.

'How did you come to London from Ireland?' Anne asked her.

Kit smiled vaguely as she surveyed the scene around them. 'Ah, but it is a long tale. Suffice it to say I came here looking for a home and I found it, eventually, though it took rather longer than I imagined and cost me more than I would rather have given. Yet, it was to be found in the place I least expected it.'

'Here, in the theatre?' Anne said, glancing back at the imposing building.

'Well, somewhere close to it, anyway,' Kit said with an enigmatic smile.

'Miss Thornfield, I believe that you were going to share with us what you knew about Harry and his associates?' Charlotte said, changing the course of the conversation on a ha'penny. 'Forgive me, but the hour grows late, and we have just a little time to try and help him and Mrs Roxby.'

'No, forgive me, I am so very fond of talking of myself – it's a terrible affliction,' Kit laughed. 'Harry was involved in a number of less-than-legal ventures in order to free himself from his dependency,' Kit said, without taking offence at Charlotte's bluntness – unlike Anne, who shot her a horrified glance. 'I believe you know what kind of work he undertook for the Sharps, marking targets for their thievery. However, I did see him a few days before he vanished, deep in conversation with Noose, their faces so close to one another they looked as if they were trading secrets. I was afraid then that he was being pulled even deeper into their dealings.' She shook her head regretfully. 'Later that evening, when Harry was alone, I went to him and warned him against entangling himself further, for Lydia's sake, but he told me the deal was done and that he and Lydia would be gone away from London within days.'

'Were you close to Harry?' Charlotte asked, sounding more suspicious than she meant to.

'Not so very close, for he has hardly been here a few months and much of his time was engaged with "earning" a living and with his wife. But the company is composed of genial folk; we treat one another with familiarity as a matter of course, and turn a blind eye to some of the more unsavoury things we are often obliged to do to get by. Even so, I was afraid for him, to see him in cahoots with Noose. For I know all too well what befalls those who cross that man.'

Charlotte wanted to ask Kit how she knew, but upon seeing the shadow of pain that passed over the young woman's face, refrained.

'We have heard that once this Mr Noose demands something, it must be done or else,' Anne said, as Charlotte played over Kit's last words in her mind. Her first instinct was to trust Miss Thornfield, but she must be wary of trusting too soon in search of friendship, for the last time she had made such an error it had almost cost her her life. She longed to be as at ease with Kit as Anne was, but was afraid of it too, afraid of what unknown avenues such an acquaintance might lead her down.

'But there was something else, too,' Kit added, slowing to a standstill as they arrived outside the cookshop. Charlotte inhaled the scent of something richly savoury and realised how very hungry she was, her whole person suddenly quivering with exhaustion.

'I can't tell you the detail of it, for I do not know any more than I observed,' Kit went on. 'All I can say is that Harry was engaged in some business with his father that troubled him greatly. They came to blows the day that Noose came for Harry. And Harry, who is a gentle fellow, quite clearly restrained himself from freely attacking his father and came off the worse for it . . .' Kit paused for a moment. 'I cannot be sure what I tell you is true, and you must consider that what I say is my opinion only, but it seemed to me that Harry had discovered something that would put his father's reputation at risk, and Old Roxby was hell-bent on silencing him one way or another. Or it could be some kind of family feud . . .'

She turned to regard Charlotte and Anne seriously. 'What you must never forget is that everything here is beauty and death in the same breath. The moment you forget it, the dogs will hunt you down.'

'We are not afraid of dogs, Miss Thornfield, nor of danger,' Charlotte said with a spark of indignation. 'You might think to look at us that we are country bumpkins and poor, pathetic women who have never strayed from our father's parlour, but you would be wrong. We are detectors, Miss Thornfield. We have already vanquished one killer and solved one disappearance when no others could.'

As soon she spoke the words, Charlotte bit her lip hard enough to hurt. Her outburst had been prompted half by pride, and half by feeling dour and ordinary alongside Miss Thornfield, and yet further still by the fear that pricked the back of her neck when she thought of the nest of vipers they had found themselves in. Even so, Kit still did not find offence in her words, but rather looked very sorry to have upset her so.

'I beg your pardon, Miss Brontë,' she said. 'You are right, I did make assumptions about you, and I should have known better. Please, forgive me and let us begin again. And if you would address me as Kit, I would be most grateful.'

'Certainly, Kit,' Charlotte said, exchanging a rueful glance with Anne's arched eyebrow. 'And you may address us as Charlotte and Anne. But I beg you, please be discreet about what you have learned of us. We find it vital to keep our . . . accomplishments hidden.'

'You need not explain further,' Kit promised them, glancing inside the busy establishment where the queue was ever lengthening. 'We all have our secrets that we must keep close. Please, wait for me here and let me know your wishes. I shall procure whatever you require and bring it to you.'

'Are you quite sure?' Charlotte asked. 'I feel that we impose too much upon you.'

'Not at all. They are a rowdy crowd, and it is far too soon after your arrival to inflict them upon you. Perhaps if you are still here in a decade or two . . .'

'Thank you, Kit,' Anne said, removing a shilling from her glove. 'We need nourishment for five: milk, cheese and bread, perhaps – whatever you can manage – and if possible, a little change? Our budget is very strict.'

Charlotte watched as Kit disappeared into the mêlée, turning away as she heard the jeers and comments that followed the highly original young woman, most of which she was glad she didn't understand.

'Is Miss Thornfield not remarkable?' said Anne, her eyes wide. 'I do so enjoy meeting unusual people like Kit. She reminds me of Celia Prescott and Isabelle Lucas – women who have found a way to lead life as they choose, escaping the ties of expectation.'

'You might say the very same thing is true of us,' Charlotte said, pleasing Anne a great deal. 'Not many would look at us and guess of our adventures, or even that we are poets, and yet we have a book of poetry in the world . . .'

'Why, Charlotte, I do believe you are right,' Anne said. 'I do believe that we too might be considered remarkable, though I hardly feel it.'

It was only then that she noticed a boy of perhaps ten or so sitting on the street, leaning up against the wall of the cookhouse, his thin arms wrapped around his knees, with such a desolate and tragic expression on his face that it moved Charlotte at once.

'Have you no home, boy?' she asked him, perhaps a little too strictly, for when he looked up at her his eyes brimmed with unshed tears.

'I used to, miss,' he said, his voice light as a feather. 'But I was sent to London when I was nine by my ma to make my own way in the world because she could keep me no more. Sent here, to this house.' He inclined his head towards the cookhouse. 'And told to call them that live here Mother and Father, though I never saw them before the day I arrived. But they beat me, miss, and they starve me, and they hate me. I would run away, excepting I'm so tired that all I wish to do is fall into a deep sleep and never wake again.'

Kit emerged from the establishment carrying in her arms four newspaper-wrapped parcels, a pitcher of milk and what looked like a small pan of soup.

'Here,' Kit dropped the change into Anne's palm, who began to offer a halfpenny to the desolate child.

'Wait,' Charlotte said. She smiled at Kit, who stood as she unwrapped the bread that was still in her arms, and broke a portion off, before doing the same with the cheese; for when she looked at him she saw all the unknown children they had been too late to save last December – children whose disappearances went unnoticed because no one marked their presence in the first place.

'Take this,' she said to the child, kneeling so that her clear grey eyes were level with his red-rimmed brown ones. 'Eat this and take this coin. It's not much, I'm afraid, but it's enough to give you some strength. Don't give up your spirit, boy. Life has been unkind to you thus far, but your heart still beats and the Lord still watches over you. You will find a place where you will be happy and safe again, I swear it.'

'Do you really, miss?' the boy asked her, taking the food gratefully.

'I have to,' Charlotte told him. 'I have to believe that we are the masters of our own destiny, otherwise this world would be a very hopeless place to live.'

As the boy ate, she rose, and when Kit offered her an arm she took it gratefully, for indeed there were moments where the injustice of this society that man had built in his own image almost brought her to her knees.

'What a fascinating woman you are, Charlotte,' Kit remarked.

Charlotte felt the heat of the day even more keenly than before, and took that to be the reason her cheeks were blazing so fiercely.

Emily

'Thank you, sir,' Emily said, the moment they were clear of the theatre. 'I fear another moment in that odious man's presence, and I would have said something that would impede our detection and shame myself.'

'You are a detector?' Mr Parensell said, with a quizzical expression, as he shepherded her through the crowd. 'Meaning that you investigate a crime, like our London detectives?'

'A little like them, I suppose,' Emily said, secretly suspecting that their own efforts were bound to be far superior. 'But often there is no obvious crime, only an injustice or a wrong that we seek to rectify. So, a little like your London *detectives*, but from Yorkshire, so better. What an unnatural word "detective" is, now I come to think of it. It doesn't sound right at all.'

Mr Parensell laughed delightedly. 'I have met a great many people in my life, Miss Brontë, but never any such as you.'

'I should think not,' Emily said.

'In any event,' Mr Parensell went on, 'I'm not sure you should be thanking me for taking you from your brother, even at your own request.' He raised a rakish eyebrow. 'You seem like a respectable young lady, and generally respectable young ladies should not be seen with me because I have a terrible reputation as a seducer and a cad.'

Emily snorted a laugh which came out of her nose, harmonising delightfully with a pen of pigs just a few feet away.

'You are not worried by my dangerous notoriety?' he asked, looking a little put out.

'Sir, I am an aged spinster of twenty-eight and a Yorkshirewoman,' Emily told him, wiping tears of mirth from her eyes. 'I doubt that you would attempt to seduce me, but if you did you would find yourself stabled with the geldings a very short while later.'

Mr Parensell separated the space between them by one more step. He had left his foolish hat and wig in the theatre, and a sideways glance at him confirmed that he was a man of very fine looks. His complexion was dark, his hair a mass of black curls and his form tall and erect. There were worse things to occupy a person's time with than gazing upon him, even covertly.

'Besides, it is one of the many good fortunes of not being young or beautiful or rich, that there are very few people who know or care what I do; and as I am accountable only to myself, my papa and God, I largely do as I please.'

'Well, that's a relief,' Mr Parensell said, smiling at her. 'Now we are quite certain that we are not likely to develop an attachment for one another, we can get on with the business of being friends.'

'I do not require a friend,' Emily said, picking her skirts up out of the mire and walking purposefully, as if she had the first clue about where she was going. 'I do require you to tell me what you know about Harry Roxby and his associations, and if you know anything of the jewel he has taken and where he might have put it.'

Mr Parensell appeared to be quite confounded by her demands as he fell into step beside her.

'Make haste, sir,' she added.

'May I?' He offered to take her arm. Emily nodded, and Mr Parensell guided her out of the path of a flock of sheep that had suddenly rounded the corner, with the kind of gentlemanly courtesy that would have Charlotte falling in love with him within the hour.

'You have brought us to Covent Garden market,' Louis Parensell explained as they emerged from the narrow alleyway that Emily had marched down and into a wide, palatial square.

'As was my plan,' Emily lied as she surveyed the scene. Even though the day was dwindling away, the square was still a cacophony of life, festive in air, undercut with a sense of urgency to close as many transactions as possible before the evening dropped her velvet cloak over the proceedings. Darkness would usher in a new world of commerce that had nothing to do with these innocent endeavours.

'Here animals are bought and sold, slaughtered and cooked, skinned and tanned, all within the same few yards,' Mr Parensell told her. 'Any goods or foods or flowers you wish for, you will find it all here. The finest hour to visit the market, though, is long before dawn, when the flower sellers display their blooms in a breathtaking wall of colour and scent . . .'

'We've got all that in Halifax,' Emily said, 'and besides, I do so hate cut flowers. I'd much rather see a primrose growing sweetly in her home than ripped from the earth for our transient delight.'

'You are quite right,' Mr Parensell said, stopping as he thought on the matter. 'This philosophy will save me a great deal on the cost of bouquets and win me a few hearts to boot, I dare say—'

'Sir,' Emily interrupted him, 'I am glad that my opinion will make your philandering so much more economical, but I wonder if we might now turn to the facts of which you are in possession.'

'Very well,' Louis Parensell said, his hand dropping from Emily's elbow. 'I didn't know Roxby before he came back to the theatre with Lydia, but he seemed a decent fellow. Old Roxby made it clear he thought Harry was a fool to elope, to throw away his position in the provinces and a regular income. He seems to have cared little for him – indeed, when he spoke of him, which was hardly ever, he seemed rather to hate him. I remember thinking that perhaps I should be glad that I have never known a father after all, if fathers can be so cruel.'

'Not all fathers are cruel,' Emily said. 'Mine is kind and worthy indeed. I am very sad for you and Harry that you have never known paternal love.'

'Don't feel sorry for me,' Mr Parensell said. 'One cannot miss what one has never known. In any event, when Lydia came to ask Roxby for help after Harry was taken, he asked her what business it was of his, and said that he would help her if she helped him, by which he meant—'

'I can suppose what he meant,' Emily interrupted, wrinkling her nose in disgust. 'Go on.'

'Hal is as good an actor as any, saving myself of course,' Mr Parensell said. 'He should have been given a role on the stage, and a weekly wage. Some might have thought it nepotism, but none would have been surprised by a man handing his son a living. In fact, I was certain I was about to find myself in want of a role, but no. Roxby told Hal that he and his wife could have the room I showed you to earlier, but that he must make his own way without any help from his father. And that's what Hal did.'

'How?' Emily asked, buying a sprig of heather from a gypsy, though she knew it was not Yorkshire heather, and that the seller was no true travelling woman, but just in case she happened to be a witch, as no one ever wants to fall foul of a witch.

'I believe you know the most of it. He started with good intentions,' Mr Parensell said. 'Got a job, minding donkeys in the market, and he'd sing for a penny to passers-by. He'd walk from stall to stall asking for employment, stood up in the taprooms and clubhouses, reciting and singing, and he was doing well that way; that is until he came to the attention of Noose, and all was lost.'

They had stopped in front of a grand-looking building; if it hadn't been spewing forth men and women that were clearly the worse for wear, Emily would have thought it was a fine establishment, perhaps a coffee house or some kind of boutique. The door was flanked either side by huge plate-glass windows, and bright gaslight flamed above the door like a beacon. It glowed like an Aladdin's cave promising all who entered fistfuls of treasure.

'A gin palace,' Mr Parensell explained, seeing the curiosity on her face.

'It does not look seemly,' Emily said, peering in.

'Yes, but you are an elderly spinster and I would like a drink,' Mr Parensell said. 'Or are you afraid for your reputation after all, Miss Brontë?'

'Certainly not,' Emily said, 'but neither am I foolish enough to be goaded into a dare, sir. Particularly when it involves the addiction that is likely to murder my own brother if he cannot soon turn from it. You may enter and drink of the poisoned well if you wish, but not until after you have told me, in haste, what I need to know!'

Mr Parensell pressed his lips together for a moment as he assessed Emily, and though the results of this study were not clear, Emily felt certain now that he knew she was no fool to be trifled with.

'So, ours is to be a sober acquaintance,' he said. 'Very well, perhaps you will be a good influence on me, for a short while at least. What Noose offers is the opportunity of improved financial prospects very quickly. This is the lure that has ensnared many a desperate man. The work Noose will offer will often seem simple, over in one transaction, and the rewards more than worth the fleeting risk. But there will always be a catch, a hook hidden somewhere within the maggot, that holds the fools who trust him forever in his service. He will lie to his employees, make it his business to compromise them, tempt them into a debt that they did not know they owed, and will never be able to repay. I can only imagine that whatever the business is with this jewel, Noose was playing the game once again with Harry. There would have come a moment when Harry found himself in the frame for the theft with the law or a rival gang, and Noose would have protected him in exchange for his loyalty. Only it never came to that, did it? The jewel vanished and no one knows what became of it.'

'Do you believe that Harry does not know where this jewel is?'

'It seems improbable that he would lie about it to a man who will certainly kill him for withholding its location. It *must* be that Harry doesn't know where it is.'

'Do you know who might have procured the jewel, where from, and who it was to be sold on to?' Emily asked him.

'I would risk my certain death to tell you if I did know,' Mr Parensell said, repressing a smile, 'so charmed am I by your uniquely direct manner. However, I do not. I have my reasons to steer clear of Mr Noose and his ilk.'

'I see,' Emily said thoughtfully. 'Then it would seem that the best I can do is go straight to the source for information. Where might I find this Mr Noose?'

'You don't find him,' Mr Parensell told her, his tone suddenly deadly serious. 'Have I not succeeded in making this abundantly clear to you, Miss Brontë? Noose is never found, he only appears when he wishes it, and when he does you are likely to wish that you had never seen him at all. And once his business is done, he is gone. Vanished into the labyrinth where he is king. Make no mistake, there have been eyes on you since you arrived at the theatre.'

'But—'

'Braggard!' Quite suddenly a heavyset gentleman shoved Mr Parensell hard, causing him to stumble a few steps before regaining his balance. Once he did, he returned to his assailant and slapped him smartly across the face.

'How dare you, sir,' Mr Parensell roared, for a moment looking genuinely dangerous, his hand flying to the hilt of the sword that he wore around his waist. Emily took a step back against the wall of the gin palace, searching to her left and right for the fastest escape route.

'How dare I? How dare you!' The other man was clearly very inebriated. Emily was all too familiar with the sway of his body, the exaggerated gestures, the bleary, unfocused and bloodshot eyes. 'You who have stolen away my only love and made her your strumpet!'

Emily was reasonably sure she would be able to retrace her steps and find her way back to the theatre, and yet it felt disloyal, somehow, to abandon Mr Parensell, when he had done exactly as she had asked him and been as helpful as he could have been. Seeing a broken brick at her feet, she picked it up, concealing it in her skirts in case she might be called upon to deploy it.

'I know not of whom you speak, sir,' Mr Parensell told the drunk, gesturing at Emily. 'Can you not see I am escorting a lady, and if you persist in this accusation I will be forced to take action.'

'Sarah Smith! Her name is Sarah Smith!' The man spat forth the name in accusation. 'I love her, and will never love another. And yet she will not accept my proposal because she pines for you! An ... an ... *actor!*' He jabbed his finger in Mr Parensell's face. 'You must release her to me! Or I shall murder you here, where we stand! By God I shall!'

87

'My dear fellow, you can hardly stand at all,' Louis said, grinning at the crowd that had begun to gather round, and rather starting to enjoy himself, Emily thought.

'Let me be clear – do you accuse me of stealing your young lady's heart merely by walking the stage?' Mr Parensell asked. 'Sir, it is my trade, and I will not be held accountable for the considerable number of young ladies who fall helplessly in love with me when they see me perform. If handsomeness and charm are a crime, then I should have spent my life in prison.'

The crowd laughed and cheered, and Mr Parensell bowed, winking at two giggling maids and blowing a kiss to another. Emily was beginning to think that perhaps the brick she held might be better directed at his very large head.

'I'll kill you!' the drunk said, and suddenly he produced a vicious-looking blade with a wicked-looking point. A gasp ran through the crowd, and Emily could not be sure if it was one of fear or delight. Even so, the threat of it didn't seem to dim Mr Parensell's confident manner.

'What the deuce!' he cried, parrying the thrust of the knife with his sword, steel singing against steel. Again and again the drunk lunged at him, as each time Mr Parensell sidestepped or ducked out of his way with the flourish of a matador, delighting his audience with amusing comments or little bows that only inflamed his attacker all the more.

Emily knew that such a sight was utterly despicable, and certainly not the sort of thing that even an old maid such as herself should be exposed to, and yet she could not help being thoroughly delighted by the entire spectacle.

'I'll cut your throat, you wagtail cad!' the drunk cried, lunging once again. 'I'll cut you up and feed to you to my dogs, I will!'

At that moment the man lost his footing, staggering back into Emily, and shoving her so hard against the wall that she dropped the brick on her foot, crying out in pain.

'Well, now, sir, I find I am obliged to fight you in earnest,' Mr Parensell said, narrowing his eyes into an expression of intent. In one deft movement he somehow tripped the man, who fell crashing on to the cobbles, to find himself with the tip of Mr Parensell's rapier at his throat.

'I will kill you for the harm you inflicted on my friend,' Mr Parensell said with quiet menace. Emily, seeing the steel in his expression, believed his threat completely, as did the poor fellow he had at his mercy.

'Please don't, sir, I'm sorry, sir, I didn't mean to hurt the lady, sir, I just want my Sarah back – that's all, sir. I love her so much, you see.'

'Sir, I do not know of any Sarah Smith,' Mr Parensell told him. 'But even if I did, she would not be mine to return to you. A woman is not an object to be handed from man to man like a chattel. A woman is a soul, as fine and as complicated as yours and mine – a great deal more so, in your case. If you wish to win your Sarah's heart then you must treat her as such. Do not make demands of her, you fool – woo her. Don't expect her to care for you, rather behave in such a way that makes it impossible for her not to. In short, be a man deserving of her love, not a drunken, brawling buffoon.' The small crowd applauded, the women cheering particularly loudly, Emily noticed.

'Now slit 'is throat,' came an enthusiastic call from the crowd. Louis pretended to consider it.

'Please don't murder me, sir,' the drunk begged, his thick voice filling with tears.

With a swish Louis removed the end of the rapier from the man's neck and re-sheathed it in one fluid movement, just as a musketeer might, causing several of the ladies audibly to sigh and swoon.

'Begone then,' he said, 'before I change my mind. And to you, ladies and gents, come and see me perform tonight as daring Jack Shepherd at the theatre on Drury Lane, second half after the tigers!'

However, once the promise of a murder was over, the crowd had dissipated as quickly as it had assembled, and they were alone again.

With a shrug Mr Parensell turned back to Emily. 'Are you hurt?' he asked her kindly.

'Not a bit,' she replied.

'Then I had better escort you back to the theatre and make sure I am made right for tonight's performance. Old Roxby will not stand for lateness.'

'Would you have killed him?' Emily asked, curious about the chill look in his eyes she had caught, just like that of her dear, lost hawk Nero before he went in for the kill: precise and merciless.

'I would have had trouble with a stage sword,' Louis told her. 'The blade retracts into the handle, you see.' He showed her how the blade shot up into the hilt when any pressure was applied.

'But his knife was real! You were not afraid?'

'My blade was a prop, but prior to this life I have survived many other existences, and most of them required me to be able to fight in order to survive,' Mr Parensell said, intriguingly. 'Besides, a man as drunk as him was never going to be a danger. I just thought I'd make a little sport of it, that's all.'

'I would love to be able to use a fine blade with such skill and prowess,' Emily said wistfully.

'Well, I would be happy to teach you a little rudimentary swordplay, if you truly mean it,' Mr Parensell said. 'There is a flat portion of the roof of the theatre behind the portico where I like to practise on occasion. If you are not afraid of a very little peril in reaching it, then I would be honoured to instruct you.'

'And I should be honoured to learn,' Emily said, smiling openly. 'I must admit that I quite like you, Mr Parensell.'

'I feel that such a declaration from you is a compliment indeed,' he returned with a smile. 'I quite like you too, Miss Brontë, so may I beg that while you are here in London you will call me Louis, and allow me to be your guide and aid in your detecting? For I am certain you don't need a protector.'

'My sister would consider it most irregular for me to call you by your Christian name, Mr Parensell,' Emily said, already imagining Charlotte's expression with pleasure.

'But we are irregular people, are we not, Emily?' he returned with a sweet smile.

'Indeed we are, Louis,' Emily said. 'Indeed we are.'

THIRTEEN

Anne

It was a great relief to see Lydia so much improved after their meal, as were they all. Now she had eaten and drunk there was some colour in her cheeks, and her eyes had regained some of their lustre. Best of all, she smiled as she took in the small group that had come to her aid. Even the sight of Branwell did not dim her pleasure.

'I feared you were a fever dream,' she told Anne, reaching for her. 'That I had imagined you in my desperation for aid, and that if I woke I would find myself quite alone as before. I dreamt of the girl I used to be, Anne, when you first tried to school me and show me how to be a decent person. I think of how silly and selfish I was, of how I thought nothing of others' troubles, so long as I was content and occupied. It was as if I did not know how to love until I did love. And then, as soon as I truly cared for another, for my Harry, all the pain and troubles of the world became mine, to feel and to rail against. A thousand times more now that my little one grows within. Suddenly I know I must do what I can to improve this earthly life for all. I know I must do my best, no matter how small an effort it might be. And yet I had all but given up hope of finding any such strength until you, whom I teased and cursed and made miserable, came to my aid, loving me still, though I scarcely deserved it. I would have been more prepared to die than wake if it hadn't been for you, dear Anne, and this little one moving within.'

Unexpectedly Lydia placed her former governess's hand on her abdomen. Anne took a sharp breath of astonishment as she felt the undulation of the unborn babe beneath her palm.

'See how he appreciated his cheese?' Lydia said fondly, imitating a childlike voice. 'Thank you for taking care of Mama, Miss Anne.'

'How extraordinary,' Anne said, leaving her palm there for a moment more, as she felt the rump of the infant pass under her palm. 'Charlotte, place your hand here – you might feel a little fist or elbow greet you!'

'I will refrain,' Charlotte said with a small, anxious smile, as if she had been invited to touch something longed-for but forbidden. 'Lydia, you must stay in bed and gather your strength, for we may need to travel at short notice.'

'With Harry.' Lydia held Charlotte's gaze firm. 'I will not leave without my husband.'

'With Harry,' Charlotte nodded, glancing up at Anne once Lydia, pleased by the assurance, had settled back into her makeshift pillows.

Seated variously on the bed, trunks, and the one chair that Charlotte had made her own, they gathered around Lydia's bed to discuss what little they had learnt since arriving at the theatre earlier that day. The clock was ticking on Harry's life, and Lydia and her baby's lives hung in the balance along with it.

Charlotte told Emily and Branwell what they had gleaned from Kit Thornfield, and Emily told them about Mr Parensell, though Anne was certain from Emily's ever-so-slightly-pleased-with-herself air that she had not told them everything, which was just as well as Charlotte had already been made anxious by Emily venturing into the streets with an unknown male as it was. Branwell told them after Emily had departed that Mr Roxby the elder had passed no further comment on the situation his son was in, and had excused himself when a

young boy arrived to tell him he had urgent correspondence
that must be answered by return.

After that, Branwell had ventured beyond the auditorium
and found the fascinating green room situated above the
stage, where he had met many delightful young ladies – some
singers, some dancers, and one lady who had a marvellous
propensity for twisting her frame into any shape. Branwell
told them about all this enthusiastically, but hadn't an awful
lot to say that might be of help, except that the ladies all said
Hal Roxby was one of those men who truly loved his wife, and
that every girl knew that you weren't to find yourself alone
with old Mr Roxby, if you knew what was good for you.

'Hal is a good husband,' Branwell summarised, speaking to
Lydia. 'A man who loves steadfastly and sincerely, no matter
what external forces may dash him from rock to rock – a man
worth saving, Mrs Roxby.'

'I believe so, sir,' said Lydia, her demeanour still cool when
it came to Branwell. After all, he was the cad who had stolen
her mother's affection and good name.

'And yet we are no further on with our detection,' Anne
said, rising impatiently. 'Everything we learned today, Lydia
had already told us. We do not know where Harry is kept, or
where this stolen jewel might be hidden, if it is not already
sold on.'

'We have gained allies,' Charlotte said steadfastly, seeking
to calm her. 'I believe that – though she is not a person we
might ordinarily associate with – Kit Thornfield will be a
friend to us, once she has seen that we can be trusted. It seems
that this Mr Parensell has useful inside knowledge of the
Sharps' operations, and Emily says he has offered us his help.
He *is* a decent fellow, is he not, Emily? Not a drinker or a
reprobate?'

'I believe he is both those things,' Emily said. 'I believe that,
as with Miss Thornfield, he is obliged to be rather . . . flexible.

But he is honest about it, and I am minded to trust him. After all, we brought Branwell with us.'

'I say,' Branwell said, glancing at Lydia. 'You do me an injury, Emily Jane. Do not make sport of my very real afflictions, which all come from my being a steadfast and true heart that should never waver, not for one moment, from its devotion, despite the harm that is done to it by indifference.' Branwell paused with a sorrowful look. 'And furthermore, who—'

'Besides,' Emily interrupted him for his own good, before he ruined his chance of making amends with Mrs Roxby for good. 'Anne is right, we *are* no further along. No one knows where this missing jewel might be, only that Harry is most likely being held in this place they call The Rookery, which all describe as a living hell on earth.'

'We must go there then,' Anne said. 'We cannot go forth with our detections until we know more, and we cannot know more unless we talk to this Noose himself. We must ask him for more information about this jewel and what – if any – compensation he will accept if we are able to provide it.'

'We should broker a deal with the very devil?' Charlotte asked Anne. 'How can such a thing be the right path, Anne? We should not make peace with evil, we should vanquish it with all our might, just as we did in December, though it nearly cost us our own lives.'

'I would agree with you,' Anne said, 'if that was what I am proposing, but it is not. We appear to make peace with the devil, we lure him into feeling powerful and in control, and then we bring him down into a fall from which he will never recover.'

Anne heard the vehemence in her own voice, and was not surprised to see the expression of alarm on Charlotte's face, for she sounded more than a little crazed by her certainty.

'Caution, Anne,' Charlotte said. 'For, in these past months, I have begun to see within you the strength and resolve to do exactly that which you say is impossible. But you must not ever think us invincible; for the moment that you do, you will bring us all down with you. We are but mortal women, Anne, and though we might wish every miracle were within our reach, it is not. We can only do what we *can* do – which is a great deal more than many think, but not all.'

The words stung, and Anne rose from the bed, crossing to the small window. After but a few hours, it seemed to her that Noose and the Sharps could only be one small thread in this great web, seething with trapped souls who would do harm to each other over and over just to survive. Anne thought that when all humanity was in such a tangle, unravelling just one dark knot could release the whole. She was tired and over-whelmed, but still had hope. Her core of steel would not bend, and neither would her determination. Half an idea began to form in her mind.

'Kit said that The Rookery was the first place most travel-lers arrive at when they come into London. It sits at the convergence of three roads, one from the north, one from the south, and the route into London from Ireland. It is the neces-sary haven for desperate people looking for work and a roof.'

'Yes,' Charlotte nodded. 'And so?'

'Then we shall be those people when we infiltrate the slum,' Anne said. 'For in many ways we *are* those people: travellers looking for a shred of hope when all is lost, just as Papa was when he first arrived on these shores from Ireland. Tomorrow we shall gather what we have brought with us, perhaps a few things from the theatre to aid us as props, and continue our detection unseen in the heart of The Rookery.'

'And how will this help us?' Charlotte asked. 'Are we to live in the slum while the clock ticks down to Harry's de . . .' Charlotte remembered Lydia just in time, '. . . deadline?'

'It gives us a reason to be there,' Anne said. 'A reason that won't draw attention from the criminals that run the place. A reason to ask questions and see what we can discover, and perhaps even find our way to Noose. And, yes, The Rookery may be a kind of hell, but it is still a hell populated by ordinary people like you and me – people who want to do good and be decent, despite their circumstances; people who will help us, given the chance. And whom we may be able to help a little in return.'

Charlotte smiled and softly said, 'My warrior sister. Ready to lead us into battle.'

'Anne is a good general,' Emily said. 'And I am happy to be her major. This is a classic tactic of war – the element of surprise and misdirection. Louis told me the Sharps have ears and eyes everywhere hereabouts, so we should rise with the dawn and make our approach before he comes to know more of us and our intentions. I believe that Mr Parensell will accompany us if we request it.'

'Except that he is known to Noose and his gang, and his presence will alert them to the charade,' Anne said, studying Emily's face, for it was so unlike her to request help from anyone, let alone someone she had just met. 'Surely he is more likely to be a hindrance than a help.'

'That might be true if it weren't for the fact that he is a master of disguise,' Emily said, with quiet pleasure. 'And we ourselves are adept at going all but unseen, are we not?'

'Well, I for one am not afraid to face death,' Branwell said, with suitably dramatic intonation. 'It holds no fear for me when I am kept from the one person who made my life tolerable. Until I am at her side, death is my constant friend.'

'Excellent,' Emily said. 'So, it is agreed. I shall go and find Mr Parensell and alert him to our plans.'

'Not alone,' Anne cautioned. 'The crowds are leaving the theatre, and we are certain that Noose's men will be amongst them. We must keep ourselves hidden and take care not to be seen or fall into danger. I will accompany you.'

'Or perhaps Branwell should,' Emily said. 'As the protector of the group.'

'I believe you can evade Branwell's attentions far too easily,' Anne said, warming to her role of general. 'I shall come with you, my dear. We will need this candle for the staircase.'

Anne lifted the only candlestick from the table.

'Will you be well, Charlotte? In the dark?'

'I daresay the dark will aid us to our rest,' Charlotte said, sitting beside Lydia on the bed. 'Covering all the conditions that might keep an imaginative mind awake. But I shall not sleep until you are safely returned, so be quick about it.'

They could not find Mr Parensell at first. Not in the wings of the theatre, in amongst the bustle of the performers and stage-hands putting to bed that night's performance in readiness for tomorrow, or anywhere backstage. Each time they asked, they would be pointed in a direction that led them deeper into the bowels of the theatre, and below it. First they carried the faltering candle down into the musician's pit, and then down another level into a great dark chamber filled with old scenery and props.

Anne paused to lift the candle around them, the movement of the flickering light seeming to bring the two-dimensional scenes to life.

'Louis?' Emily called impatiently.

'There is yet another staircase leading down here,' Anne told her, peering down more half-rotten stairs. 'What could anyone be doing down here?'

'How are we to know what actors do or why?' Emily said, taking the candle from Anne, and beginning the descent. Once at the bottom of the steps they appeared to be in a long tunnel, one that ran in both directions from where they stood, with a series of small arched compartments that stood to one side of the central route.

'How extraordinary,' Emily said, slowly turning to light the mysterious place as much as possible. 'It feels as though we've wandered into the catacombs of Paris, or the lost burial chambers of the Knights Templar.'

'Down there,' Anne whispered to Emily, noticing another light a few yards away, faintly glowing round a gentle bend. As they approached, Mr Parensell stepped into the tunnel before them.

'There you are,' Emily said, seeming to think nothing of the odd moment. 'We've been searching for you, Louis, we have a plan to . . . oh hello.'

Anne and Emily were both taken aback when Kit emerged from the dark, just a little beyond Louis, her hair dishevelled, wiping her eyes with the heel of her hand, as if she had been crying. As the two parties met, Anne glanced into the impenetrable black of the chamber out of which Louis had stepped.

'Please excuse us,' Anne said uncertainly, glancing at Emily, who was unperturbed by the scene.

'Emily, my dear, how I've missed you.' Louis beamed at her sister before noticing Anne. 'What's this? A second Miss Brontë? My cup runneth over!'

'Louis, this is my sister Anne,' Emily said. 'Anne, earlier today, Mr Parensell and I were engaged in a sword fight with a ruffian, which seemed to render social niceties somewhat irrelevant,' Emily said by way of explanation.

'I see,' Anne said, feeling that from the moment the four of them had entered the theatre, so far from home and Papa, everything they knew as real and predictable had begun to ebb ever so slowly away. It was almost as if here they could be players too, acting the parts of the women they could have been, had fate dealt them another deck of cards. Rather as though they had brought down their imaginary world of Gondal to this earth, and were at last able truly to walk amongst their own stories of intrigue, dashing gentlemen and fascinating ladies. It was not an unpleasant thought.

'And Emily, this is Kit Thornfield, whom Charlotte and I met earlier, and who helped us secure our meal this evening.'

'Pleased to meet you.' Emily shook Kit's hand. 'Are you well? You seem to be upset.'

'Oh, it is nothing,' Kit said. 'Theatre life is always full of drama, but Louis is like my brother, always there to comfort me or tease me rotten – one or the other. Sometimes we are obliged to go quite far to find a quiet place to talk in private.' Kit smiled at Louis, who gently tugged one of her ringlets in return.

'Hold hard, Kit,' he said. 'Your trials will soon be over.'

Anne glanced into the chamber once more; the impenetrable pool of darkness made her shudder.

'What is this place?' Emily asked him.

'Old tunnels left over from the last theatre. Few know they are here, otherwise they'd be fully occupied by vagrants and miscreants. I believe they were built for royalty or other such great folk to come and go discreetly.'

'What a great deal of effort and expense when a hooded cape and mask would do the job,' Emily said thoughtfully. 'You London people really have no idea of economical living.'

'Well then, Mr Parensell.' Anne thought it best to go on before Emily asked yet more questions about the tunnel. 'We have a plan to infiltrate the lair of the Sharps at dawn. And, if you are willing, we require your assistance and utmost discretion, sir.'

'I fear for the sanity of this plan but, as an afternoon's acquaintance with your sister has shown me that you will not be deterred, you may consider me your loyal soldier, Miss Brontë.' Louis bowed. 'Oh, and Emily, this is for you. Practise how to wear it, and when you have time, balance the weight of it in your palm – becoming used to its weight will enable you most effectively to thrust and parry.'

To Anne's immense surprise, he presented Emily with a weapon: a short, curved sword, enclosed within a leather scabbard that was embossed at either end with finely engraved silver casings. Delighted, Emily took it, pulling it half free from its home to reveal a fine blade that gleamed in the candlelight.

'Goodness, Louis,' Kit said. 'I never thought I'd see the day.'

'What a very beautiful thing,' Emily said as she turned it over to examine it more closely. 'Far too beautiful for a theatre prop.'

'Oh, that is no mock sword,' Louis warned her. 'The blade is true and wickedly sharp. It is a scimitar and, according to my mother who gave it to me on the day that she died, it once belonged to my grandfather, who made his living on the high seas. I have carried it around the world with me, my only true possession.'

'Louis, you can't lend me such a treasure,' Emily said, unsuccessfully attempting to return the weapon to him, for she clearly wanted it so very much. 'I am bound to lose it or break it.'

'I do not think you will,' Louis said. 'And besides, I thought – as it is rather discreet – you might be able to wear it about your waist on a sash or something similar, and it would hardly be seen in the folds of your skirts. The perfect weapon for a fighting lady.'

Anne was quite aghast at Louis' casual reference to Emily's person, but she did her best to hide it, for neither Emily nor Mr Parensell seemed to notice the indiscretion at all, so fascinated were they by the sword and all the stories that it told, more like childhood playmates than lady and gentleman. Kit looked on with a fond smile, though whether it was truly one of a sisterly nature, Anne couldn't determine.

She could see why a typical young lady might be impressed by Mr Parensell. Emily had never been tempted by such surface attributes before, however, so Anne could only imagine that she saw something else in this extravagantly appointed young man – some reason for trusting him with their very lives. All she could do was put her own trust in Emily's judgement. After all, it had never erred before.

'We should go back,' Anne said. 'The others are waiting for us.'

But just as she turned to head towards the staircase, a particularly large rat reared up on its hind legs before her. Before Anne could react, she felt something fly past her ear, and the rat lay dead, with Louis' knife buried deep in its belly.

'Some of them are the size of dogs,' Louis said, stepping forward to remove the knife, and cleaning the blade on a handkerchief. 'Don't worry, I wouldn't have struck you. I'm skilled with the blade, and I am not a violent man, except out of necessity.'

'I always say the same thing about myself,' Emily said.

It certainly seemed that for the first time that Anne could remember, her sister's head had been well and truly turned by a gentleman, or something close to one, anyway.

FOURTEEN

Charlotte

The Rookery was both worse and better than Charlotte had anticipated; both more serene and yet more terrifying than she could have imagined.

The day was but a promise still when, shrouded in shawls wrapped around their faces, with cloth bags and bundles under their arms, the party of five emerged from the theatre, playing the parts of weary travellers with quite some conviction.

A bright, glittering mist lay over the filth and much of the street, hiding its brutal ugliness with a low, shimmering cloud that gave Drury Lane an unearthly feel. Morning dew bejewelled every surface, encrusting once grand columns and palisades with brittle, fragile beauty. For a moment Charlotte could imagine this once elegant road as it had been a hundred and fifty years before, when great ladies in fine coaches paid calls with feathers in their ornately dressed hair.

She had not slept well; barely at all, in fact. Most of the night had been spent lying down across the width of the bed with Emily's, Anne's and Lydia's feet at her back, and Branwell snoring in the chair. Hours passed by with her eyes fixed on the window, tracking the progress of the moon as it rolled sedately across the sky. There had been muddled dreams, half memories, half hopes. One moment a familiar touch had glided across her cheek, as light as a feather, and, for a second, she was very far away indeed, feeling the warmth of another's hand. But, for the most part, all she had done was feel the ache in her back and worry that this detection was beyond them, despite Anne's youthful confidence.

That their detections mattered to them was in no doubt. That they had genuinely helped people – saved lives, even – could not be denied. And yet, this was so very far from the life Charlotte had dreamt of for them all – the peaceful, respectable, literary life, where they might make their living from the gentle art of placing words, and take their leisure in the society of her literary heroes, as equals.

What must not be done, Charlotte had reminded herself throughout the night, and once again now, was to lose sight of that dream, which seemed almost within reach; even more so, now that their book of rhymes was out in the world. That it was attainable she did not doubt. That it would require great fortitude and determination to attain, she was certain. And she could allow nothing at all to sway her from her purpose for her precious little family, not even them themselves.

'This way,' their ostensible leader, the young Mr Parensell, told them rather gruffly, apparently assuming the mantle of the character he had given himself the moment they left the building, and intending to carry it on, regardless of where and with whom they were. In addition to his assumed accent, which was so peculiar that Charlotte doubted anyone could precisely identify it as either foreign or English, he had outfitted himself in an old army greatcoat, a battered top hat, a rifle slung over his shoulder, with, swaying at his belt, a sword, not dissimilar to the one he had given Emily.

'I shall not allow it!' Charlotte had said just before bed, when Emily had delightedly succeeded in devising a way to attach the cursed object about her waist with Lydia's silk scarf. 'Emily, we are not savages, bent on attacking our foes in battle.

We fight with our intellect, and our love of God. Not . . .' she waved at the sword, 'such objectionable foolishness.'

'I am not going to use it,' Emily said, twisting this way and that to see if she could glimpse the scabbard from every angle. 'I have no idea how to, for one thing, but I shall wear it, Charlotte. I must become accustomed to it – Louis said so.'

'I do believe on this particular occasion that it would be impossible to underprepare in any way,' Branwell had said. 'And besides, if a sword or a pistol is required, I can wield either passably well.'

The Rookery did not precisely begin or end anywhere; instead its dark tendrils began to weave and choke amongst the healthy, wholesome lanes and streets in subtle degrees until they were mired in its jungle.

Roads and alleyways became narrower and darker, and the houses and buildings that had once been fine and grand grew steadily more decrepit, like half-rotted corpses, the outline of their disintegrating structures visible like ribs amid patches of decaying flesh. Gradually the windows that had been looking benignly down on them became gritted with black, their frames swollen from years of neglect. Above all, there was the slick, dark rot that clung to every molecule, as if it were a living presence itself, and not merely a remnant of constant, universal death.

When Charlotte dared to lift her eyes for a moment from the steady progress of her feet, she'd meet the beady gaze of a rat or two, roaming quite freely, with no fear of human inter-vention. Or a dead one, eyes glazed, its grasping, clawed hands echoing the last throes of its agony. Sewage ran down the gutter, and the stink that rose from every corner followed them, an always moving baleful presence.

It was not so very different from Haworth.

Except in that beloved little village, the people had a means to an end, a way to make an honest life even if it was a hard one. And – always rising above the poverty and hardship – was the backdrop of the surrounding moors, the beauty of God's creation showing them a promise of a better world. Here in The Rookery, it was easy to believe that these streets were the beginning and end of time.

'Slice of bread and butter, friends?' A young woman stood before them, holding out half a loaf and a small amount of butter on paper.

'Thank you, for we are weary travellers,' Mr Parensell said.

'We're looking for a place to rest our heads,' he continued. 'Can you tell us of a decent boarding house or room for rent?'

'They are all much the same,' the girl said bleakly, pocketing her coins in her apron. 'You'll find many houses will give you a length of floor to rest on, or string out a rope for your sleep hung over, like a bit of washing. They all pay to one master in the end, so take your pick.'

'Perhaps best talk to that gentleman, then,' Charlotte said. 'Can you tell us where he is?'

'I cannot,' the girl said, retreating into her doorway, pushing open the door at their back. Without another word she darted inside and shut the door.

'Perhaps a little too blunt, Charlotte,' Anne murmured. 'We are, after all, playing a part.'

'I am only trying to get to the point,' Charlotte said, pulling the shawl away from her face as the heat of the morning began to build. 'We could wander this maze for a year and not find the information we require.'

There was a scuttle of footsteps running away, a clatter of shutters drawing swiftly closed. Above them, a bedraggled-looking caged songbird was taken in off the sill. A hush fell over the streets; the morning held its breath in anticipation.

'I'd be grateful if you'd accompany me, Miss Brontës, Mr Brontë, Parensell.' A short, thick-set gentleman, wearing a battered bowler that sat low over one eye, appeared behind their party as if he had vaporised into being. At his back lurked some keen-looking lads; one of them, Charlotte was certain, was the young man who had called himself Jack, one of the thugs who had accosted Anne soon after their arrival. So, they were Noose's men too. How far did his tendrils extend?

'You . . . you know our names?' Charlotte said, finding the air suddenly very chill, as she noticed four inch-long scars that seemed to have been purposely placed in an orderly row just behind his ear. If the man could do that to himself, what could he do to them?

'Indeed,' the fellow said. 'The Brontës from Haworth; your father is the parson there. I have known of you since shortly after your arrival, and have followed you since you began your journey this morning. You wish to meet my master, and so I am come to escort you to him.' He grinned, revealing a mouth almost empty of teeth, except for one or two that stood like gravestones. 'I suppose I had better introduce myself. I am Mr Skeet, and these are my boys. My master is very curious to meet you. Very curious indeed.'

The rasping laugh that followed gave Charlotte no comfort. How foolish they had been, how naïve to think they could track this predator as if *he* were the prey. He knew everything about them, where their home was, who their papa was. That the rogue had revealed it to them, intending it as a threat, was in no doubt, and Charlotte was afraid. For here, in the heart of this labyrinth of unhappiness, all that they held dear was at terrible risk from a man described by all who knew him as the very embodiment of evil.

FIFTEEN

Emily

Until the appearance of the menace that had been sent to fetch them, Emily had almost been enjoying their progress into The Rookery. The surroundings were certainly dire, and the threat real enough. Yet so was the thrill at being totally detached from her own life. Here she could be – and was – anyone in the world, as if nothing that had passed before in her life meant a thing. There was the constant pleasure of the swing of the scimitar at her hip, giving her the sensation of being a true adventurer, and the weight of the pistol in her pocket, which gave her a feeling of power that was quite intoxicating.

Her love for her homeland hadn't been severed; if anything it was magnified by this strange untethering of her spirit, and Emily knew that her soul would never willingly part with the moors she loved so much. And yet here, amongst dangerous strangers, she felt as if she roamed the streets of her true home, her own imagination. Here she could freely seek out intrigue and dangers and truly be herself. Here she was pirate, thief, empress; an altogether different woman. The prospect of giving flesh and form to a thousand hidden dreams both terrified and thrilled her.

And then Noose's henchman arrived and made the danger all too real. Hearing the name of their papa on his lips made her blood run to ice, and she remembered that she was only

Emily Brontë, and that what they did here could bring harm and hurt to those she loved the best.

Warily Louis removed his false beard and eyebrows, stuffing them in his pocket as they followed the bowler-hatted man deeper into Noose's lair, unable to refuse on any account.

'I am a little acquainted with the gentleman we go to visit,' he said by way of explanation, catching Emily's enquiring glance. 'He is not a man who responds well to any hint of artifice.'

After a moment or two they came to a house that would once have been an elegant London residence, but now rather staggered into its neighbour, as if it had recently been dealt a deadly blow.

Anne nudged Emily, nodding upwards at a rather strange symbol that had been chalked over the door.

'I've seen it before,' Anne told her. 'First when that scoundrel accosted me, and now here.'

'Perhaps it is an insurer's mark?'

'I think not,' Anne said shortly as she turned her face from Jack's leer.

'The first floor,' Skeet told them, nodding up the staircase. 'You will find him in the room to the right of the landing. You may leave all your weapons with us.'

Louis relinquished his shotgun to Jack, and Emily, glancing at him for assent, untied the blade from her waist, placing it at the man's feet.

'Want me to search you, Annie, my girl?' Jack asked Anne, who ignored him steadfastly.

'All of them.' Mr Skeet stopped Emily as she was about to pass. 'The pistol too.'

Emily rather regretted levelling it at Jack's head now, for had she not, she might have been able to keep it concealed upon her person.

One after the other, with Branwell leading the way, the party ascended the creaking stairs, past empty picture frames and splintered banisters, until they reached the closed door they had been directed to. There they hesitated, uncertain. At last Emily reached forward and knocked on the door. There was no answer for several seconds, and so, unable to wait a moment more to learn of their fate, she opened it and went in.

The gentleman, if he could be described as such, was seated at a very fine Regency desk that had been carefully positioned in a rectangle of sunlight, his huge frame bent over a tiny book that he held in his massive hands as tenderly as one might a flower. He was entirely bald, and looked as if his nose had been broken on multiple occasions, for it could not seem to settle on a direction of travel. He was of a muscular build, and seemed to occupy the dainty desk chair he was seated in at his peril. He paid them no mind at all.

Apart from this furnishing, the apartment was entirely empty, although Emily could see that it had been richly appointed once. Green silk wallpaper hung off the damp walls in shredded loops and skeins. At her toe, Emily noticed half a plaster rose that had once formed part of the ornate ceiling plasterwork above, where a shattered chandelier still swung with heavy, precarious menace.

'Excuse me,' Emily said. 'We are arrived.'

'One moment,' Noose replied, his voice heavy and gruff. 'I shall get to the end of this page and find out what sort of fellow this Wickham is before our meeting commences.'

'Apologies, but no,' Emily said. 'We cannot wait, sir, for you to finish your page. It was you, sir, who set the clock ticking when you took Mr Roxby from his wife and set a deadline on his life. Every second counts. Miss Austen will wait for you, I am certain.'

Had there been a slamming-down of the book, a leaping-to of booted feet and a flinging of the little book across the room, it would have been a deal less terrifying than the quiet closing of that volume, the meticulous setting down of it, precisely aligned with the corner of the desk. Noose looked up at her, his angular visage thrown into sharp relief by the silvering of sunlight, and met her gaze with eyes that were so pale blue they might almost have no colour at all.

There was a mild curiosity in his expression, one that most resembled the look on a small boy's face as he examines the spider in his palm, just before he removes its legs one by one.

'What have you to do with Roxby, Miss Brontë?' he asked, rising from his seat and walking towards their party, displaying his powerful height and breadth to maximum advantage. He was well dressed, yet his clothes sat ill on him, fighting with his savage nature.

Emily lifted her chin to show she was not cowed, although to tell the truth she was very near to it. That he had the physical strength to crush her neck with his bare hands was not in doubt. 'We have been appointed by the Robinson family of Yorkshire to negotiate the safe return of their son-in-law, Harry Roxby,' she said, noting the thick twist of a livid scar that roped around his neck, rising just above the silk cravat he wore, lending him an air of the charnel house – a corpse dressed for his own funeral.

'There is no negotiation to be had, Miss Brontë,' he said. 'I set out the terms to Mrs Roxby when I visited her . . .' he checked the pocket watch that was secured to his waistcoat with a chain, 'five days since. And she accepted them. Once my terms are set, they are set, and cannot be altered.' He tilted his head as he looked past Emily to where Louis stood, his hands clasped behind his back. 'That reminds me, sir – our business is yet to be concluded, is it not, Mr Parensell?'

'It will be shortly,' Louis said, his eyes as downcast as his voice was low. Emily glanced at him sharply. Louis had alluded to having reasons to avoid Noose, yet had readily agreed to accompany them today? He must have known he would be questioned on whatever their business was. That made him either foolhardy or underhand. Emily preferred the first explanation.

'Sir, we are only trying to help our friend, and find a resolution that will suit us both.'

'There is only one solution,' he said. 'Harry Roxby stole what has already been promised, and I must have it returned within the next two days, or he shall find himself taking a swim in the Thames with manacles around his ankles. Do you take my meaning, Miss Brontë?'

'Your meaning is not exactly subtle, sir,' Emily replied. 'But see sense. If Harry had stolen your jewel, what reason would he have for not revealing its whereabouts when his life is threatened?'

Noose considered the question.

'It is just such a conclusion he is gambling on me reaching. But I am a sensible man, Miss Brontë, and my good sense tells me that Harry Roxby will return the jewel to me, tell me where it is, or die.'

'His wife is with child.' Emily took a step forward, but Noose did not move a muscle.

'I am aware of that, and I will be sorry to kill her,' he said. 'But she wouldn't have been the first, and needs must.'

He smiled at the thought of murder. It took every ounce of Emily's self-control not to show the horror she felt in her expression.

'Sir,' Anne stepped forward, the two pin-spots on her cheeks alerting Emily to the passion simmering in her sister's breast. 'We can find your jewel, but you must tell us more – where did it come from, what kind of jewel is it, where might it have been sold on? You cannot expect anyone, least of all Lydia, to find something we know nothing about!'

'I cannot tell you more,' Mr Noose said with an impatient gesture.

'But that is impossible!' Anne stamped her foot, unable to contain her frustration. Noose crossed his arms across his broad chest and gave a look that spoke of patience that was almost at an end. Emily gave her sister a warning look, and Charlotte took Anne's hand, drawing her back a step.

'I was told to procure the item in question for my . . . a buyer who was determined to have it. I brokered a deal with Harry – he would fetch the thing from an agreed hiding place, so that he'd never know the identity of the one who had taken it, and he'd bring it to me. I in turn would deliver it to its new owner and all would be compensated. I know nothing more about it than that. Look, all I need is the location of where it is hidden, I'll take care of the matter from there. But if you cannot give me that at the hour stipulated, then I will have vengeance, for it will be my body rotting in the gutter not long thereafter, and I don't aim to die alone for another's mistake.'

Noose stopped abruptly, checking himself too late.

'Who threatens *you*?' Emily questioned.

Noose took a short breath, looking down for a moment, before returning his gaze to them, icily steady. But there had been the moment of that slip, when he had shown something altogether more human. Emily was sure of it – there had been the briefest flash of fear. What on God's earth could make *this* man afraid?

'I have some admiration for your party,' he said. 'That you have come here shows courage that not many of the men I know possess. So, I will tell you one thing, but be advised – if you fail to locate the jewel, or any of what I tell you is spoken of by another's mouth, I will slit your necks myself and then travel as far as I have to, and do the same to your father and anyone else you might love. Are you in any doubt of that fact?'

Emily held Noose's gaze for as long as she dared, and in the icy depths of his eyes saw nothing that would dissuade her from believing him.

'We are not,' Emily said, reaching for Anne's hand in the fold of her skirts, feeling all the braver when she was linked with her sister so.

'Then I will tell you that there is one above me – one I must answer to. He calls himself the Red Monarch, for his true name must never be spoken. I rule my part of this city, but it is him and his followers who hold all of London in his grip, from the very lowest beast to the highest personage you can imagine.' He brought his fist level with Emily's eyes to illustrate his point. 'There are none who are free of his reach. If I fail him, he'll take my head and I'll deserve it. So, you see, the jewel *will* be returned to me, or death will come for me too. Do not think I will flinch from taking any with me that I can. I am a bad man, Miss Brontë – the worst of them – but the Red Monarch is the devil himself.'

'We've dealt with devils before, sir,' Emily said. 'They do not frighten us.'

'Then you have never met true evil yet, Miss Brontë,' Noose told her. 'For if you had, you'd know that to be frightened is the only sensible thing to be.'

CHAPTER

SIXTEEN

Anne

Mr Skeet and his thugs accompanied them out of The Rookery, lest – as Mr Noose put it – they got gutted like fish before they could finish their work for him. But seeing how Jack had leered at Anne, Noose had instructed him to stay behind, and told them all that not a finger was to be laid on the Brontës until he ordered it.

Despite his threats, Anne had not felt afraid in his presence, or anywhere else in The Rookery, a peculiarity that she was still trying to fathom. The situation was so very bad. Harry's life hung in the balance, the sand in the hourglass was running down at a perilous rate, and there were forces at play that cared not one jot if three Yorkshirewomen and their brother fell victim to their schemes. Anne understood perfectly clearly how perilous the situation was, and yet somehow she could not feel it within her breast. Instead she felt invincible.

It was as if she were watching events unfold from a very great distance, as if each minute that passed was nothing more than one of the plays shown every night in the theatre, and she was sitting on the very back row, or high up in the gods, with an eagle's-eye view of everything. It was because she had faith, Anne realised, that she was able to maintain clarity and calm: faith in her own abilities and those of her sisters, and a certainty that, though the solution may not yet be to hand, they would uncover it, and, through God's grace, would do so in time.

London might be enmeshed in a network of crime, but not even this Red Monarch or his mysterious 'followers', whom Noose had spoken about, had faced a Brontë sister before.

They had returned to the theatre and were making their way to Lydia's room, when a flurry of red hair and fury met them head on. Charlotte collided with Kit as the younger woman stormed away from something that had clearly upset her.

'Oh, oh, I do beg your pardon, Charlotte,' she said, once she had righted herself. 'I was in a fury and not looking where I was going, I'm so sorry.'

'Are you well, Kit?' Louis asked her, stepping forward.

'I am,' she said, with a brittle smile. 'Did you have any luck in The Rookery?'

'Not much,' Charlotte said, bowing her head. 'In fact, rather the opposite. We have nothing.'

'We have something; we know there is another agency at work, and perhaps that has some bearing on the next step,' Anne said. 'A direction will become clear, if we are calm and allow it. Kit, Mr Parensell, would you join us for a moment in Lydia's room? I know you feel that you have shared with us all the intelligence you have, but perhaps you might be able to contribute some local insight if we collect our thoughts?'

'I have a few minutes I can spare,' Kit nodded, looking at Louis, who nodded as if acceding to a request. Once again, Anne wondered about the nature of their friendship, about the nature of Mr Parensell. Yet, it hardly seemed to matter to Emily, so she supposed it should not matter to her either, at least that's what Emily would say. Anne determined to watch him, even so.

Some fifteen minutes later, Lydia's room was crowded with company.

'So, another half-day passes, and still we are nowhere,' Anne said. 'Except that we have to search an entire city for a jewel that we know nothing about – not its colour or its size or cut. We don't have a single marker from which to begin, and have only succeeded in attracting the attention of one man of violence. If we are not careful, this other character is likely to be on our heels too at any moment.'

'What do you know of this Red Monarch?' Emily asked, looking from Louis to Kit.

'Nothing,' Kit said. 'That isn't a name I've ever heard.'

'I've heard rumours,' Louis added. 'Whispers; but I always have thought of it as a half-supernatural legend, like Spring-Heeled Jack or another ghoul with which parents attempt to tame their unruly children at bedtime. I've never seen evidence that the Red Monarch is a man of flesh and blood.'

'Mr Noose was afraid of him,' Anne said. 'I cannot imagine that he would fear anything that was not a real threat.'

'I should like to go home,' Charlotte said, removing her bonnet, for a moment looking very tired and gaunt. 'I should like to go home to Tabby and seedcake, and my own dear bed, and to never having heard of Mr Noose or this Red Monarch of whom he spoke. I do so miss the common decency of a good, honest, Yorkshire mystery.'

Lydia, who had risen from the bed while they had been out, washed and dressed, was now seated in the chair, having listened intently to everything they related to her.

'You should go home, Charlotte,' she said gently, reaching for her hand, and looking around at the party. 'You should all go home. You came here at my request, and have already risked more than I should have allowed to try and help me. But there is nothing you can do – I see that now. Mama was right. Everything that has unfolded has done so because of my own actions. She told me there would be a price to pay for eloping, and I told her I was willing to pay it, but I didn't realise the price would be my darling Harry himself. But there you have it – there is no solution, and I must face the prospect of my own death too. I wouldn't mind it so very much if it were not for my child.' She laid her hand over her stomach. 'I mind so very much for this little one, who has never even drawn breath.'

'We are *not* going home,' Charlotte said at once, straightening her shoulders. 'Forgive me, Lydia, I am tired and a little bewildered, but you are not alone. You have your friends and we will not leave you, not until we have brought Harry home and all is well. Will we?' Charlotte looked at Emily and Anne in turn.

'Not at all,' Anne said.

'Would never,' Emily added.

'We simply need to think through everything we know from the beginning, sift through every grain of information we have, for somewhere in there we will find, if not the solution, the beginning of the solution,' Charlotte added.

'There is an unknown jewel that has been stolen . . .' Anne got up from the bed and began pacing up and down the length of the room.

'It could have been taken from anywhere and anyone,' Emily said, joining Anne in her looped walk. 'But it isn't just where it came from that matters, it is also what would be done with it once it is acquired. If we can identify those who would acquire a stolen jewel, and from whom it was taken, we might find something useful.'

'The newspapers we acquired revealed nothing of note,' Anne added, 'no report of a jewellery theft. So perhaps the person from whom the item was stolen doesn't want it revealed, or perhaps they don't even know it has been taken? Or perhaps it was stolen to begin with.'

'Which is of no help to us,' Emily added.

'Say that Harry did have the jewel,' Charlotte said, following Emily and Anne as they worked through the problem.

'That he did collect it from the secret meeting place as directed, and then, instead of passing it to Noose, decided to sell it on himself and make a fortune for himself and Lydia . . .'

'He would not have done that,' Lydia insisted. 'My dear Harry is a man not given to deep thought, that is true, but he is a good man, and a man of some principle, if misguided. He would have performed his part in the transaction, and that would have been all. I cannot conceive of him doing anything foolish enough to take him from me and our child, and put us at risk also. Perhaps he never did see it, just as he has told Noose.'

'Perhaps, Lydia,' Anne placated the young woman. 'However, for the purposes of detection, we must consider every scenario, however unlikely it might seem. So, if Harry had – having seen the jewel and perhaps realising its value – decided to take the risk and cut out Noose and his mysterious master, he would have been able to find plenty of nefarious candidates within the environs of this theatre, either to conceal or to sell on the jewel.'

'I'm afraid I'd have to disagree,' Mr Parensell said from his position at the door. 'Noose may have his own master, but he is the lord of every dark deed done in this quarter, from every pocket picked to throat cut. None who enjoy living would dare defy him, including, in my view, Harry.'

'Greed is a powerful lure, though, Louis.' Emily stopped before Mr Parensell, their eyes meeting as they exchanged a rather too familiar smile, Anne thought. 'Are you certain there is not one who'd risk fleeting danger to make a fortune and escape the city?'

'Well, there have been such men in the past,' Louis conceded, with a slight bow of his head. 'They usually turn up cut into quarters, scattered about the place so that all may learn of their folly.'

'That *would* be a powerful deterrent,' Emily mused, taking up the walk again.

'Then, if he could not sell it quickly, he would have hidden it,' Charlotte said. 'Told Noose it wasn't in the hiding place. That it had been taken before he even got to it, and concealed it until it was safe to turn it to profit.'

'But it is not hidden here,' Lydia exclaimed. 'I searched every crack, and floorboard, unstuffed the mattress even . . . It is nowhere.'

'We must check the room again,' Anne said. 'And we must check the whole of the theatre. Harry might not have liked residing here at his father's mercy, but he must know this building like his own hand, and are there not dozens of passages, nooks and crannies to conceal something in?'

'It will take much longer than the two days we have to search this theatre,' Emily said, exasperated. 'The task is too great. The place is a labyrinth, as Anne and I saw for ourselves when we came upon the tunnels.'

'There is one other possibility that *might* help,' Kit said, suddenly.

'Go on, Kit,' Anne prompted her.

'Well, Mr Roxby keeps a safe in his office. Spent a fortune on it a year ago. The most modern model, with an impenetrable Bramah lock.'

'No lock can keep me out,' Louis said cheerfully. 'Not even that one, though I have yet to attempt it.'

'Are you a thief, sir?' Anne asked Mr Parensell.

'Indeed, there have been times when breaking a lock is all that kept me from starvation,' Louis told her. 'But I have only ever stolen out of necessity, and not for many years now.'

He held Anne's gaze with a sweet smile until she looked away.

'The point is,' Kit went on, 'in the past only a strongbox was ever used for takings and such, but then suddenly a safe seemed to become of the highest importance and urgency. From time to time, I have caught glimpses of Roxby opening it, and it always seems to be stuffed with documents and papers, nothing obviously valuable. The last time I saw him add an item to its contents, it was so full that he had to force the new addition in. But to my point – I think perhaps . . . I think perhaps Harry knew how to open it.'

'Why would Roxby trust his hated son with that secret?' Charlotte asked.

'I don't believe Mr Roxby knew, but rather that Harry might have found a way into the vault himself?'

'Elucidate,' Emily said, stopping her pacing to focus on Kit, hands looped behind her back.

'I hadn't thought of it before, because it seemed of little importance, but the day before Harry was taken, I came upon him in his father's office, kneeling on the floor next to the safe. That night's performance was in full swing, and Mr Roxby was front of house to see the new acrobatic act perform. Harry would not have expected to be seen.'

'You saw him with his hand in the safe?' Emily asked.

'No, just on his knees before it, almost as if he had dropped something and was searching for it. But when I spoke to him, he started and leapt away from the safe as if he had been caught at something.'

'But why would Harry be stealing from his father, if he had just stolen a valuable jewel?' Charlotte asked. 'It makes little sense.'

'Unless . . .' Anne thought for a moment. 'Unless he wasn't stealing from the safe . . . but hiding something in it?'

SEVENTEEN

Emily

There had been no question that it would be anyone but Emily who took charge of the task of searching the office, though the plan could not be executed until much later, when both Louis and Kit – in her Celine Varens guise – had left the stage. Louis had returned just after midnight, with Kit, who still wore her pink silk gown, her hair dressed and crowned with a wreath of pink blooms. It had been Emily's decision to take Louis with her that had been a bone of contention.

'A moment,' Charlotte said, when Emily announced her plan to visit the office as soon as the theatre slept. 'Anne? Branwell?'

The four of them congregated in the hallway, standing together in the small pool of light afforded them by the lantern Branwell held aloft.

'Emily,' Charlotte said in a tone that had immediately made her sister roll her eyes. 'Our secret life is not conventional. I own that this matter of detecting has caused us to make decisions and take actions that a respectable and educated spinster ordinarily would not. However, I must . . .' Emily's sigh was a warning, yet Charlotte persisted. 'I *must* caution you against destroying that which cannot be recovered. What we do here is important, no doubt, but it is not your life, Emily Jane.'

'Who else's life can it be but mine?' Emily retorted.

'Charlotte doesn't mean that, and you know it.' Anne joined her sister in the intervention, infuriating Emily all the more. 'Your true life is not playing at make-believe in a London theatre with a man you have known but five minutes, Emily. Your true life is at our home, and in your heart – to write, and to be free to do as you please as a respectable spinster authoress. This strange adventure that only a few will ever know of, this can't be the sum of our existence. Don't throw your good character away for the sake of a pair of dark eyes.'

'I see.' Emily crossed her arms under her bosom and set her chin in such a way that both her sisters took heed that a storm was brewing. 'So, you tell me I may break into a theatre manager's office and attempt to gain access to his safe in the dead of night, without fear of impropriety, but to take a person with me who knows the theatre better than any of us and is an expert at picking locks would likely cause my ruin?'

'You seem very familiar with him, that is all,' Anne said, her discomfort at the conversation plain to see, even in the dim light. 'And as charming and as . . . beautiful as he is,' she added hurriedly, 'he concerns me, Emily. His intimacy with Kit seems more than just brotherly, and I fear that he is not a decent man. And I don't mean that he has stolen, or seduced, or even worse. I mean that I am not sure he is worthy of your trust. I just wish you to take care.'

'Ha,' Emily barked a laugh. 'A dishonest former thief and a seducer? You could have just described our brother! And you trust him with your life!'

'Emily,' Branwell said, injured. 'I have near destroyed myself, and worse still our father and my beloved sisters for my own heart's desire, and I never stole anything despite the accusations, I thought you knew that.' His expression was one of deep pain. 'The point is, I know very well what traps can lie unseen in the forming of an attachment, and you seem to be

128

throwing all caution to the wind with this gentleman. It's not like you, sister, to be so easily turned.'

Emily walked abruptly away from them for a few steps, before advancing once again on her siblings at some considerable speed.

The storm broke.

'Can it be true that none of you knows me at all?' she questioned them in a barely restrained hiss. 'Do you think me a fool? Do you think I would ever allow my heart to burn for *any* man, let alone one I knew I could not have?' Emily looked pointedly at Charlotte. 'Or one who lay rotting in the grave?' This time she turned her gaze to Anne. 'Or, my dear brother, to confuse the desires of the flesh with the true loyalty of the heart? No, and again I say no. I shall never love – I determined it long ago as we waited quietly for our mother to die. And again, when we buried our sisters, and again and again and again, when I watched my brother and sisters near wilt away with misery because of it. Emily Brontë will never love, she will never pine, she will never fall. She will belong to herself entirely until the day she dies.'

'Emily,' Charlotte said, soothingly, 'we only meant to caution you.'

'There is no need to caution me for the mistakes that *you* have made, Charlotte,' Emily told her furiously. 'It is true that somehow in this city of death I have found that rarest and strangest of flowers, a *friend*; a useful and brave friend who I refuse to judge on the circumstances of his past. And I will not surrender this friendship for you or anyone.'

Emily blew out the lantern and the hallway fell into shadow.

'Now, may I go about my work?'

'I have caused a rift between you and your family,' Louis spoke *sotto voce* as they made their way through the inner workings of the theatre.

'You have not,' Emily replied in the same tone. 'Whatever gave you such an idea?'

'Your rather heated conversation was easily audible through the thin partition,' he replied. 'I am used to mamas and papas despising me, of course, though normally I've done something to deserve it.'

'They are afraid that you will seduce me,' Emily huffed. 'Me!'

'And you are not?' Louis said, glancing back over his shoulder for a moment, his dark eyes alive with something Emily could not fathom.

'Of course not,' Emily said. 'We had the measure of one another very quickly, and you know that I am not a woman who will care for decorative words, false promises, or pretty looks. Perhaps if you knew how rare it was for me to feel comfortable with a stranger, then you would appreciate my simple friendship for what it is. You are likely attracted to frivolous beauty, so I should make a poor prize for seduction.'

'I think you judge me to be a *little* more shallow than I am,' Louis said, his tone wry as they edged along. 'For example, we have never discussed what qualities I look for in a lady. Suffice to say that an agile mind and a kind of originality are just as important to me as how a person looks.'

'Of course you are not shallow,' Emily said. 'You were broken at some point by some dreadful cruelty, I suspect. And though you seem full of ego and confidence, you are low in heart and esteem from some past error or circumstance that has changed the course of your path. You are fragile, even, and very alone despite all your friends. Yet even so, within your heart, you are a man who wishes to be good.'

Louis stopped and turned around to face her, so that Emily almost walked into him. He said nothing, but simply searched her face for several moments. Emily caught her breath at this sudden proximity, as she turned her face up to meet the strange, magnetic pull of his penetrating gaze.

'What?' Her voice was no more than a whisper.

'How did you do that?' Louis asked her. 'Are you a witch?'

His gaze was so intense, and full of something she could not interpret, that she took a step back, coughed and swallowed.

'No, just a writer. Should we go on, Louis?'

'Yes.' Louis seemed to come back to himself, his eyes blinking rapidly. 'Yes, we should go on. Have you heard the story of the ghosts of the theatre yet, Emily?'

Emily was relieved for the odd moment to have passed, and to be given a topic she could rely on to be solid and real.

'I have not – do tell me,' she said, her voice trembling, her heart beating as if she had run across the moor with Keeper. It was all very curious, as if her body knew something it had yet to alert her mind to.

'We have dozens that come and go, but two are resident much of the time,' Louis told her, something of his old laughing tone returning to him, offering her his hand as she climbed a jointed beam. 'The Grey Gentleman, and another who is to be much dreaded, for they say if you see him, it means you are to die young.'

'Oh, an omen ghost,' Emily said happily. 'We have dozens of those in Haworth. My friend Robert Heaton's family has a grey-bearded old man who only shows himself when one of them passes. And there's another, a flaming barrel rolling down a hill that suddenly vanishes, which we see so often we've entirely forgotten what it is supposed to portend, though I don't think it can be anything very bad. Tell me of your ghosts, Louis.'

'Well, the Grey Gentleman wears a cloak and tricorn hat – you might see him in the upper circle if you are unfortunate. I often wonder if it's my friend Jack Shepherd come to see if I am doing him justice in my performance of his life. But those who have met him talk of being paralysed with a terrible fear that doesn't pass until he has vanished.'

'Have you seen him?' Emily breathed, and only realised when her fingers tightened around Louis' that she had not released his hand. The sensation it gave her was something akin to stomach ache after eating too much of Tabby's boiled mutton.

'I think perhaps I have glimpsed him sometimes,' Louis said. 'A movement in the corner of your eye, and yet when you look directly, there is nothing there. If it is Jack, he has let me alone and I'm grateful.'

'And the other? The omen ghost?'

'I pray every day not to meet him,' Louis told her, quite seriously.

'Who is it?' Emily breathed.

'The ghost of Joseph Grimaldi.'

'The clown?' Emily asked, enthralled.

'The very same. He spent many years on the boards here, his wife and baby died while he worked here, his brother went to sea at eight and was never seen again, his son drank himself to death and he died poor, drunk and crippled from years of clowning and bringing joy to others. They say the ghost is full of fury and pain, and if you hear the jingle-jangle of the bells on his hat, you should run, for if you look upon his dreadful face, all got up in his clowning make-up and costume, then it means you are to die, and soon.'

'And has anyone ever seen him and dropped dead?' Emily enquired, making Louis smile.

'Not that I know of,' he said.

'Then he doesn't sound nearly as bad as Robert's gytrash,' Emily said.

'Who is this Robert Heaton?' Louis asked her.

'No one of consequence,' Emily said. 'Though he does have an excessively good library.'

'Well, in any event, I am glad you are so sanguine about the matter,' Louis said, lowering his voice as they came to a wider, brighter passageway. 'I have been terrified by clowns since I was a child, and should I ever meet him, I am likely to drop dead on the spot.'

'Well, that would not be a very good epitaph,' Emily whispered. 'Died from fright of clowns.'

'I shall endeavour to die in a more befitting manner for your sake,' Louis said, dryly. 'Now, no more talk until we are inside the apartment. There may still be people about, both living and dead, and we don't want to attract their attention.'

The door to the room was paned with etched glass, made yellow with years of smoke; it was locked, but Louis did not have a moment's trouble in picking the lock. Emily watched him, impressed by his speed and skill with the long, needle-like implements he had produced from his pocket, and wondered if she might trouble him to show her his techniques once all was done. To be able to conquer a lock would certainly be a useful addition for detecting. Grudgingly, Emily acknowledged that Charlotte had been more or less correct when she had reminded her their main aim was to be able to live securely from their talents. And it was true that what Emily loved to do more than anything was to walk and write and dwell in her imagination, building up civilisations only to watch them fall apart. And yet, it was Charlotte who had chosen to make their writing available to the public, not Emily. If the world were another place, then perhaps detecting would be her profession, and perhaps in that world she would be fully occupied and satisfied.

Once inside the small room, where the acrid scent of cigar smoke still lingered, Louis sat the glim, as he called the candle stub, on the floor by the safe.

'The famous Bramah lock,' he said, frowning.

'Is it a problem?' Emily asked him.

'It is unbreakable, according to the makers,' Louis said. 'But we shall see about that. I have yet to meet a lock or a woman's heart I could not devise a way to open.'

'This may be the hour,' Emily said dryly, sifting through the papers strewn over old Roxby's desk in case there might be anything of interest there.

'Kit said that Harry seemed to be looking for something on the floor,' Emily remembered, wrinkling her nose at a rug that had clearly not been beaten in at least a year, its original pattern and colour lost under layers of grime and stains. 'If he was unable to return before Noose's men took him, then perhaps it is still here, lying unseen. I'll search the floor.'

'Good idea,' Louis said, one long implement between his teeth, another in the lock. 'She is yielding to me – I can feel that she wants to give way.'

'Where did you learn your lock-picking skills, Louis?' Emily asked him as casually as she could, unable to dismiss Anne's caution as completely as she would like to.

'Along the way. Because I had to, and besides, as you know, an actor must possess an array of skills,' he said with a shrug. 'Be able to rise to any challenge.'

'Singing, perhaps, and a little dance,' Emily conceded. 'But you fought like a trained swordsman the first day we met, and you pick locks like Jack Shepherd himself. Come, now, entertain me while we work – distract my poor heart from girlish fear.'

'I do not believe your heart has ever been afraid,' Louis smiled as he pressed his ear against the safe, closing one eye as he made another adjustment. 'Very well, I was born in Spanish Town, Jamaica, to a mother I adored and a father who never owned me. My childhood was all happiness, though, with her by my side. We had very little, but all we had was our own, and she taught me to read and love nature and poetry.

My mama was the whole world to me.' His fond smile melted into sadness. 'She died when I was just eleven and I was left alone in the world.'

'Truly?' Emily paused to look at him. 'My mama died when I was a child too, and it hurt me deeply. At least I had Papa and my sisters and brother to cling on to for as long as God allowed it. It must have been very hard and strange for you – to be bereft at such an age.'

'There are a hundred who have had it worse than me, and all only a stone's throw from this very spot,' he said, brushing aside the kindness as if he were too afraid of feeling it. 'There were few options open to me, so I took a job on a ship running sugar to England, thinking I would find my future here. It was a hard life aboard that ship; I nearly died a hundred times a day. To avoid such a fate, I had to learn to fight, to steal, and to act the man I was so very far from being. I discovered that a joke or a recital could often soothe the savage breast long enough to stop it from killing you. Somehow, I survived the trip, and when I arrived in Liverpool I resolved to stay on these shores and never set sail on a boat again. The years from there to here I will not relate, as they are not suitable for a lady's ear.'

'And have you kept that vow never to set foot on a boat again?' Emily asked him.

'I have thus far, though lately I have begun to yearn for something . . .' He hesitated for a moment, and Emily heard another clunk from within the safe. 'Something more. A freer . . . cleaner life.'

'There!' Emily gasped as she caught a glint of something catching the light of the candle in the far corner, under a bureau laden with sheaves of paper. Diving forward, she stretched out her arm and reached under as far as she could until her fingertips touched something cold and hard. She inched the object towards her palm, and brought it out.

'I think perhaps I have found a jewel at last,' she said, sitting back on her heels, clasping the item in her palm, her dark hair pulled loose and her cheeks flushed with pleasure.

'You really are the most beautiful woman, Emily,' Louis said, as if he were really just seeing her for the first time.

'What in all hell is going on in here?' the voice of Mr Roxby suddenly thundered.

Emily had never been so glad to be caught in all her life.

EIGHTEEN

Charlotte

'Of course, it's so obvious!' Charlotte said, standing up quite suddenly, making the rest of the party start at her outburst.

'Is it?' Branwell asked, looking around him and rubbing at his bleary eyes, waking up Kit, who had refused the offer of a chair or a seat upon the bed. She had remained seated on the floor, leaning up against the wall and dozing off mid-conversation, which rather touched Charlotte. It was pleasing that Kit felt so at home in their company, that even at this late hour they talked and brought forth ideas and theories between them. And there was something about Kit that reminded her of her radically independent friend, Mary Taylor, a vibrancy and rebellion that she couldn't quite find the courage to aspire to herself, but that she admired so much in others. And there were so many questions she longed to ask Kit, questions that only a woman of experience could answer. Not that she was sure she had the courage to put all her questions into words and speak them aloud.

'What is? Shall I fight it?' Branwell said blearily.

'No, Branwell, if it was something that required fighting, it would be too late by now in any event,' Charlotte told her brother, handing him a glass of water to help bring him to his senses. 'The answer is out there – *listen* and we shall hear it, I am certain!'

Charlotte crossed to the circular window and pushed it open as far as it would go, letting the warm air of the outdoors replace the stagnant air within.

The sounds of the city at night were abundant: shouts and songs, laughter and chatter came from directly below, and beyond that music played somewhere; further beyond that dogs barked, and a fight broke out. Though it was more than an hour past midnight, the world below vibrated with life as vivid, if not more so, than in any daylight hour.

'I'm not sure I'm following you, Charlotte,' Anne said. Charlotte gave pause for a moment to look at her sister's frowning visage. It was impossible not to notice how very personally Anne took this detection; after all, they were here at her insistence, and if they could not help Lydia – if the detection was unsuccessful, or if any of them came to harm because of this escapade – it would be Anne who would suffer as a consequence. What was required was to liberate Anne from this room and let her brilliant mind follow its intuition to find a path forward.

'Noose refused to tell us more about this Red Monarch character because he said that gossip spreads like a fire around these streets,' Charlotte explained. 'That means that somewhere down there, at this very moment, people will be talking – about what happened to Harry Roxby, about Noose, perhaps even about the whereabouts of the jewel or the identity of this Red Monarch of whom Noose is so afraid. It seems to me that if we can find who this fiend is, then we will at least be able to uncover precisely what we are searching for, and what the plans are for it.'

'Yes,' Anne said, crossing to the window and taking Charlotte's hands. 'Yes, Charlotte you are quite right. We need to go out, now, into the night, and listen for the voices of the hidden city – the city that is only seen after dark.'

'Exactly,' Charlotte said, pleased to see her sister's eyes light up at the notion. 'We have approached this from the wrong direction. All we have done is talk, but it's listening we need to do now.'

'Charlotte,' Lydia said as she raised herself with some difficulty into a sitting position, 'I cannot recommend that you venture out at this hour.' She gestured with some concern towards the window. 'Those are not your people, Miss Brontë – people who frequent the streets and clubhouses at this hour are people of low morals and often dangerous intent.'

'Precisely,' Charlotte said, reaching for her cloak. 'And we need to hear what they are saying, for it is the people of low morals and dangerous intent who are the keepers of the secrets we are trying to uncover. Fear not, my dear Lydia, for I have vanquished evil single-handedly before.'

'Not quite single-handedly,' Anne muttered, adding, 'You need not fear for us, Lydia. We were brought up amongst working people. There is not much that we haven't seen or heard in our lives. And we will have Branwell at our side.'

'And I shall accompany you too,' Kit offered, 'if you will have me? I know this area and many of its occupants quite well.'

'If it is not too much trouble, Kit? You must be tired.'

'Not at all,' Kit said. 'It is very much more engaging to take a night stroll with my new friends rather than avoid my "admirers" at the stage door.'

'Should we not wait for Emily?' Anne asked. 'At the very least she is our armoury.'

'We cannot spend another minute waiting for her,' Charlotte said firmly, fastening her cloak. 'We must be out; we must be doing *something*. Besides, Lydia will be here when she returns. *If* she returns, that is, and is not at this very moment bound for a prison ship about to set sail for Australia . . .'

NINETEEN

Anne

The warm and heady night into which the party emerged seemed to transform the streets and buildings into places from another realm: one where dark fairy tales were born, and all the lost creatures of folklore might emerge from the shadows.

The summer sky was bright with stars, and it seemed to Anne as if some of them had fallen to earth to blaze as brightly as in the heavens, lending an ethereal witch's glamour to every dirty alleyway and vice-filled corner. It was easy to see why those who had so little in the daylight enjoyed the night hours so much more, for at least here – on the nightside of nature – everything was beautiful for a little while.

Flaming torches were posted outside the notorious club-houses, where drinking and singing went on late into the night. The gin palaces were lit up with gaslight, and fires burnt in braziers at regular intervals, where salesmen peddled warmed ale and cold pies. There was an air of gaiety to the evening which was quite cheering, and Anne soon found that any misgivings she might have had about advancing out into the unknown slipped away as she became just a background player in the lively scene, and a very inconsequential one at that.

They dawdled, strolling slowly, catching snatches of conversations as they wandered through Covent Garden, which was just as busy at night as it was in the day. Charlotte tried her best not to look directly at the ladies who had to resort to selling themselves to survive, as if somehow she might be tainted by observing them directly. Not Anne, though – she would not let herself turn away from any of the realities they encountered, for she felt sure that they must all be seen, all understood, if a person was truly to be able to know this world.

Kit drew them into a shadowy doorway as they came across a particularly rowdy, very drunk gentleman, being rather roughly handled by some ladies of ill-repute, who seemed to be having a gay old time of it.

Kit looked at Branwell as she nodded her head towards the boisterous group. 'See how, when the girls amuse their marks with kisses and tickles, the children are sent to dart in and out, as spry as swifts, lifting and thieving everything they can lay their little hands on, and spirit it away in moments?'

'Oh yes.' Anne watched, fascinated, catching glimpses here and there of the pickpockets at their work, as fast as a king-fisher spearing its prey, then gone again in a moment.

'And once they've picked the carcass clean,' Kit whispered to them, 'the women will vanish into the crowd, and the poor fellow won't know what became of his new friends until . . .'

Sure enough, the whirling party sped away, leaving the gentleman at first bereft, then confused, and then – upon the checking of his pockets – filled with fury and shame. Anne watched as he turned to shout after the girls and then thought better of it, not wanting the crowds around him to see what a fool he'd been.

'Ingenious!' Charlotte said, adding hastily, 'and quite, quite wrong, of course.'

'I have often wondered about the nature of sin,' Kit said, taking Charlotte's elbow to guide her through the crowd as they returned to the crowds of the square, Anne and Branwell following on behind. 'It must be better to steal from a foolish, lustful man than to sell yourself to him, must it not? Where does God forgive sin, do you think? Would he forgive you for every betrayal, or just the kind that cannot be avoided?'

'God forgives every sinner if they ask for it,' Anne told her. 'I am quite sure of it.'

'So I could do as I wished until the day I died, and – as long as I repented in time – still be saved?' Kit asked her. 'That rather seems like cheating.'

'No, not cheating,' Anne said. 'Though it is better to live as well as you can and please Him every day, of course. For in doing so, your life will be a content and fulfilled one, not filled with the misery and guilt of sin.'

Kit seemed to think on this for a moment more until something else caught her eye.

'Look, there are our ladies again,' she said. 'It is certain they will be run by Noose – he controls all such business around the Garden. Shall we get a little closer and see what we can hear?'

'Yes,' Charlotte agreed. 'Let's draw a little closer.'

They stopped a short way from the girls, who were talking to a couple of rough-looking types who lingered in shadows, clearly keen not to be fully observed. Anne almost cried out loud when she caught a glimpse of the very same Mr Skeet who had escorted them out of The Rookery, the hated Jack, and two more of his party.

'Noose's men,' she whispered. Branwell had brought them a mug of ale each, and guided them to an upturned barrel to use as a makeshift table.

'Keep your eyes on me,' Charlotte told them, 'but your ears tuned to their conversation.'

They each nodded in tacit agreement.

'I ain't saying I don't agree with him,' one of the women all but shouted, sounding greatly vexed. Anne studied her furtively, noticing that beneath the great quantity of rouge and the ringleted wig she was wearing, the woman was painfully thin and gaunt. 'I'm just saying, it ain't right. It ain't, you know it ain't, as sure as I do. He knows it too, though he don't care about it. It's all business to him.'

'Because it's not about what's right, though, is it, my love?' Mr Skeet said, pulling the woman tight against him. 'You and me aren't ones to talk about what's right. It's about what keeps the wolf from the door and food in our bellies, and our necks free of the rope. Besides, the boss has got more to worry about than himself if this jewel ain't delivered on time. Him upstairs is in on it, see?' Mr Skeet pointed upwards. 'And if he doesn't get what he wants, there will be hell to pay for all of us.'

'Blimey, the Monarch ain't God!' the woman said with a raucous giggle, finding herself very funny. Skeet lightly cuffed her round the head, gesturing for her not to mention the word.

'Might as well be, for all the power he's got,' he replied, tapping his nose twice with his forefinger to signify what he knew must be kept a secret. 'You mark my words – his power extends everywhere. High as it can go, near as makes no difference.'

'You don't know who he is,' the woman scoffed, shoving him in the chest playfully. 'You suppose you are as high up and as feared as Noose, that you are one of them lot, but you ain't, Leonard.'

'Oh, I know all right,' Mr Skeet said, looking decidedly put out. 'And you should treat me better than you do, love, if you know what's good for you.'

'Who, then?' she asked him, cajolingly fluttering her lashes.

'Do you think I'm fool enough to say his name to you? I like my life too much, my dear,' Skeet replied, skirting around the edges of kissing her.

'Because you don't know!' The woman made to laugh again, but it was brutally cut off by one short, sharp backhander across the mouth from Skeet that knocked her sprawling to the ground. Anne gasped, turning her face into Branwell's shoulder.

'Come,' Charlotte said, taking her arm and hurrying her away. 'We've seen and heard enough for tonight.'

'No,' Anne pulled herself free. 'We must go back! We must find that woman and rescue her. We must send her to our friend Mrs Prescott in Bradford – she gives decent employment to fallen women. We can't leave her to be beaten and abused by that monster.'

'She won't thank you for it,' Kit told her. 'The truth is that the workhouse and parish aid is so often worse than the life they have now, where at least they are free from constant punishment and scorn. And even if you did save her, there's likely thousands more just like her in this city alone. You can't save everyone, Anne – that task is impossible.'

'I do not believe that,' Anne said. 'I shall never believe in minding only for myself and looking away. This world will never be a place of equity if we count only our own blessings and never seek to share them.'

'But today you must,' Charlotte said, continuing to guide Anne away. 'For if you don't, you will be harmed, and it is my duty to keep you safe.'

'I do not require guarding,' Anne snapped, deeply upset by what she had witnessed. 'What an unhappy, unsuccessful venture.'

'Not at all – we have discovered something very important,' Charlotte said gently.

'What?' Anne replied, downcast. 'I heard nothing so significant.'

'We know that Mr Skeet knows the true name of the Red Monarch. It was fear that caused him to strike the poor woman down – I saw it in his eyes. He knows the name of the man that even Noose is afraid of, and he wishes to God that he didn't. And if he knows it, then we too can find it out.'

Emily

Louis sprang to his feet, his heel against the safe door, which Emily saw creak open just a crack as Mr Roxby entered. He picked up an old cloak that was tossed over the back of the chair and threw it over her head.

It was such an absurd attempt at subterfuge that for a moment Emily was infuriated by the indignity, and then minded to laugh out loud at the silliness of it all. Reminding herself what her papa would say if he were to hear of this episode tempered both impulses, and Emily remained still and quiet, choosing to let Louis throw the dice and see where it would land.

'Sir, you catch me compromised,' Louis said. 'With a lady, whose name I must protect at all costs.' Though she could see nothing, Emily imagined Louis gesturing at her covered personage, and the urge to laugh almost overcame her once more.

'She's no lady, then.' Roxby roared at his own joke, and under the cloak Emily clutched at the object she held in her hand, digging her nails into her palm to keep herself silent. 'For heaven's sake, man, you have your own apartments to retreat to, not two minutes' walk from here! Or if you could not contain your amorous passions a moment longer, are there not a hundred places in this theatre more comfortable and befitting to tip a lady than on the floor of my office?'

'Momentum overtook us, sir,' Louis said, strangely subdued. 'A quite uncommon passion, like none I have ever known before, in fact.'

'You are a bloody fool, and as likely to be murdered by a husband or father as you are to remember your lines. And as for that article . . .' Emily sensed she was being pointed at, '. . . get the strumpet out of my theatre now. This is a respectable place, and I will not have it tainted by your tomcat behaviour. Take her away.'

There was an awkward silence, during which neither Emily nor Louis moved one muscle.

'Could you give us a moment of privacy, sir?' Louis said, his tone tight.

'I shall dock you rent from this week's wages, Parensell!' Roxby raged. 'You chase me from my own apartment!'

'I shall gladly pay the fine,' Louis said, and Emily heard a great deal of huffing and many colourful terms as Roxby exited, slamming the door behind him.

At last Louis pulled the cloak from Emily, who regarded him, her dark hair come entirely undone and tangling around her neck.

Looking at her, Louis let out a long breath, and shook himself into action.

'We'd better be quick,' he said, holding out the offending cloak for her to wrap herself in. 'He is bound to try and discover your identity, to see if you are someone's wife or daughter who he can blackmail.'

'But you opened the safe?' Emily asked as she wrapped herself in the cloak and drew the hood up to hide all but her mouth.

'I did, but there's no time to look now. We must get you away from Roxby's clutches and back to the safety of Lydia's room, otherwise your sisters' fears will have been proved correct.'

'Do not fear for me. I shall leave the theatre by the main entrance and return to Lydia's room through the stage door. Roxby is very much mistaken if he thinks he is a match for me.'

'Be careful.' Louis' hand hovered towards her as if he might touch her, and then fell once again to his side. Emily was glad of it, for she did not like the confusion that his touch inspired in her person. Such a discomfort was to be avoided at all costs.

Emily left the office, closing the door behind her, and after a moment headed for the auditorium with a view to finding her way to the main entrance.

'I beg your pardon, madam, are you lost?'

As Louis had feared, Roxby was indeed waiting to pounce on her like a fat spider, every one of his legs aching to ensnare her in his sticky web.

'*Nein werter Herr, vielen Dank, aber ich kenne den Weg sehr gut*,' Emily replied in German, which at that moment seemed like the perfect defence against his drooling lasciviousness.

'Eh?' Roxby said. Wrong-footed, just as Emily hoped he would be.

'*Ich sagte bereits, dass ich den Weg sehr gut kenne. Solltet Ihr mich erneut belästigen, werde ich Euch den Kopf vom Körper trennen, mit einer sehr scharfen Klinge, verborgen in meinem Mieder*,' Emily told him firmly. Most of her German had been learnt from Gothic novels, and she was sure he wouldn't understand her threat to cut off his head; nevertheless her accent was good enough to persuade him she was foreign-born, and her tone sharp enough to make the hated man back away. Just a fraction, but it was enough for her to find a gap to hurry past him, and through the empty theatre. Aware that time was of the essence, Emily knew she should press on into the night, but she couldn't quite stop herself from pausing, just for a moment, in the hope of meeting one of the theatre ghosts, but the dead were quiet that night. Disappointed, she found an unlocked door and made her way out of the theatre, then hurried around to the stage door, where Louis was waiting for her with a lantern.

'You would make an excellent highwayman,' he told her, as she removed the cloak and laid it over a young man who slept huddled against the wall, an empty bottle at his side.

'I would,' she agreed.

'Just before Roxby entered, you had found something. Was it the jewel, do you think?' In her haste Emily had quite forgotten that she was still clutching the item. Unfurling her fingers, she held her palm out to catch the lamplight. It was a single earring that lay in her palm – a rather beautiful one, a large drop pearl topped with a faceted diamond, that if it was genuine would be worth more than a penny or two.

'I don't think this is *the* jewel,' Emily said regretfully. 'I suppose it could be a clue.' She turned the trinket over in her fingers. 'But I am certain it is not the reason for all this violence.' Putting it in her pocket, she turned back to Louis as he held the stage door open for her. 'Did you find anything in the safe?'

'Not a jewel,' Louis said. 'But receipts – dozens and dozens of them – and each one I put my hand on seemed to be stamped with this insignia.'

He held out one, which had been folded and sealed with wax.

Emily took the bundle to examine later, in better light, tucking it into her bodice for the moment.

'I'm sorry it's not your jewel,' Louis said.

'As am I,' Emily said. 'But it is something, Louis. Something that may be important. Thank you for all you have done to help us.'

Emily offered him her hand and he shook it once, and gave her the lantern to light her way back to Lydia's room.

'You could stay a while longer – I could give you your first lesson with the blade?' Louis offered.

'I should like that very much indeed,' Emily said. 'But if I am not back soon, my sister will have a fit of the vapours, and I can't bring myself to torment her further, for she is a dear old thing.'

Emily did not look back once as she ascended the stairs, but somehow she knew that Louis remained at the foot of them, watching after her, until she was out of sight.

TWENTY-ONE

Charlotte

They had been returning to the theatre, when there seemed to be a sudden upswell in the crowds that had previously been drifting along the streets in a steady flow.

With hardly any warning, an influx of people coming from somewhere transformed the busy street into a press of bodies, each struggling to attain a different direction. For a few minutes, Charlotte found herself caught in the current, twisted and turned this way and that. The heat, noise and stink of bodies threatened to overcome her senses, and she feared herself lost until she saw a slender hand, garnished with a pink silk cuff, reach for her in the mêlée, the fingers outstretched towards her. Grasping it in hers, she held on to it for all she was worth, until at last she and Kit were side by side. But when the crowd receded, Anne and Branwell were nowhere to be seen.

'Where can they be?' Charlotte said, standing on her toes to try and get a glimpse of her brother's bright hair.

'I fear they were taken quite far from our path,' Kit replied, glancing around. 'But they will be together and quite well, I'm sure. The best thing to do is to return to the theatre and hope that we meet them along the way.'

'Very well,' Charlotte said anxiously, in the hope that Anne was with Branwell, knowing that her brother let loose amongst such temptations would quickly succumb. As for Anne, she worried for her too, but a little less so, knowing that Anne was sensible and intelligent.

'I admit,' Kit said, smiling at Charlotte, 'I am glad we have a few minutes alone.'

'Oh?' Charlotte found herself instantly folding herself away, fearful of scrutiny.

'Of course, I meet so many fascinating people at the theatre. Dear friends, like Louis, more family to me than any I have ever had, but hardly have I ever – I daresay never – come across a person like you.'

'Like me?' Charlotte touched her hand to her hair nervously.

Kit made the comment with such warmth and ease that Charlotte wished with all her might that she might return it in the same manner. But here was Kit, pink, golden and glowing, and here was she, small, pale, stiff with shyness, and aware that the last time she had put her trust in a generous new friend, it had turned out to be a dreadful mistake.

'Yes, and your sisters too, of course,' Kit said unhappily after a moment. 'So brave, so determined to do what is right and good, and to make your own way in the world. And to stroll through the night with an opera girl, and treat me as an equal. I wish I were more like you, Charlotte.'

'Like me?' Charlotte exclaimed. 'When you are so beautiful?'

'My beauty has not made me happy,' Kit confessed. 'Once I thought of it as a kind of currency. Now I see it has led me into a trap, when I thought I was chasing freedom.' Kit dipped her head as her voice trembled with emotion.

'Kit, can I help you?' Charlotte asked her. 'You may think you are trapped, but I promise you there is a way out. You are halfway to finding it already. You can remake yourself entirely, I've seen it done.'

'You are too kind to me, Charlotte,' Kit said.

'Not at all; every living soul deserves kindness,' Charlotte said.

'Then you should be kind to yourself, and recognise your own brilliance,' Kit said, turning to smile at Charlotte.

Charlotte blushed again.

'I rather think I recognise it too well, Kit,' she replied ruefully. 'I sometimes think I see myself as something far greater than I can possibly be. My ambition burns me like flame. It shames me.'

'You must not be ashamed of ambition,' Kit said. 'Though it may cost you something of the comfort a quiet, small life might afford you. But such a life is not for you, Charlotte. I can see that by the fire in your eyes.'

Kit linked her arm through Charlotte's and squeezed her close to her side, as their walk slowed to a companionable stroll. Charlotte Brontë, strolling alone in small-hours London with an opera girl and artist, Charlotte thought to herself with a good deal of pleasure. Perhaps she *was* rather fascinating, after all.

'How anyone like you can feel so uncertain is beyond me.'

'Charlotte, you have brought your family here not just to nurse Mrs Roxby, but to *rescue* her, putting yourselves in great peril in the process. You are astoundingly courageous.'

'Well, it was not me alone,' Charlotte felt compelled to say. 'From time to time my sisters and I seem to fall into step together, working as one mind, and when that happens it rather feels as if we are powering a Faraday dynamo that could light the entire world with its brilliance.' Charlotte dipped her chin. 'I must sound quite insane.'

'Not at all,' Kit said. 'You are a solver of mysteries!'

'Oh, I don't mean that,' Charlotte said. 'That all happened rather by accident, though we do show a propensity for it, it is true. Yet it is not what we really do. What we really do is *write*.'

Making the declaration aloud gave Charlotte a thrill. She rarely admitted to anyone outside her family her true desire, her real purpose on this earth.

'Oh, yes,' Kit said with gratifying enthusiasm. 'Yes, of course, you are a writer. I can see it in the way you regard the world around you, and how you unravel the threads of lives and make sense of them. It's in your remarkable eyes, for they are the apertures of the soul, are they not? I look into them and see fathomless inspiration.'

Charlotte blushed, unaccustomed to such warm praise. 'Well, we are recently published poets,' she admitted. 'And I plan to complete a novel too. But it won't be just a novel of manners, a polite drawing room romance. It will speak the truth – the truth about the pain of existence, the search for freedom, the longing for that one soul that connects with your own. Do you see my meaning, Kit?'

'I do,' Kit said, stopping to gaze at her. 'I hope you write your novel, Charlotte. And when you do, don't forget people like me, I beg you – lauded one hour, and despised the next. Oh, how I long to leave this tawdry life behind.'

'Ah Kit,' a tall top-hatted figure emerged from the dark quite suddenly. 'I thought you had escaped me tonight, but I see the streets have conspired to bring you to me.'

'John.' Kit forced a smile as the gentleman took her hand, brushing it with his well-groomed whiskers as he kissed it. Straightening, he noticed Charlotte for the first time.

'Have you taken a maid?' he asked.

'No indeed, sir,' Kit said sharply. 'This is my friend, Miss Charlotte Brontë.'

Charlotte curtsied, though she could not bring herself to speak to such an impertinent man; though he was certainly drunk – she recognised the stench all too well.

'Charlotte, this is my . . .' Kit looked up at the gentleman's face, ruddy, plumped and, Charlotte surmised, a good deal past sixty, with uncertainty. 'Mr Smith.'

'Well,' Charlotte said, taking a step back. 'If you will just point me in the right direction, Kit, I will bid you goodnight.'

'Don't be in such a hurry to leave us, Miss Brontë,' Mr Smith said. 'We shall escort you back to your lodgings, of course.'

'There is no need, sir,' Charlotte said stiffly, as she observed how he put his hand on Kit's waist, bringing her tottering close to his side.

'Of course there is. It is but a few minutes, I'm sure.'

Kit gave Charlotte a glance that told her to accept the offer, so she bowed her head, and fell into step beside them.

Kit, she noticed, was silent and tense, her gaze fixed straight ahead and her jaw clenched, as if awaiting her execution.

'So you come from the north, the workshop of this great nation,' the gentleman said, seemingly intent on making polite conversation.

'I do, sir,' Charlotte replied.

'Then tell me, how fares our great city in comparison to those grey regions you hail from? Are they as blighted with the poor and insufferable as London is?'

'There is poverty sir,' Charlotte said. 'The poor struggle a great deal in Yorkshire as they do anywhere.'

'It is a futile struggle,' he replied. 'There are too many of them, breeding like rats, infesting every corner. I am of the opinion that the only way to make our city a great and good place again is to rid it of them once and for all.'

'Drive them out, sir?' Charlotte asked him, appalled.

'Stamp them out,' he replied. 'What good are they to our nation, but a drain on it? Cull them, like we would any animal that had multiplied too much.'

'John, you are being deliberately provocative,' Kit said quietly.

'Not at all,' Mr Smith replied. 'I say only what I believe. Our nation should be built on strong, solid English shoulders. If we were to sweep away the vermin into the sea, now would that not leave a bright future for us all, Miss Brontë?' He gave her another appraising look. 'Or for the best of us, at least.'

They had arrived at the theatre, which seemed to surprise Mr Smith rather.

'You are staying in this building? You seem ill-suited to such a life,' Mr Smith commented. 'It is rarely for the ordinary.'

Charlotte shook off the insult, quelling her rising indignation.

'Kit, will you come in with me?' Charlotte took Kit's hand and tugged at it a little. 'For I must speak with you on that matter we discussed.'

'Kit owes her time to me tonight, Miss Brontë,' Mr Smith said, removing Kit's hand. 'That gown she is wearing is the receipt that shows it.'

Kit turned towards Mr Smith, pressing her hands to his chest.

'Sir, it is so very late, and I am so tired. Please may we meet again tomorrow? I promise I shall be far better company then.'

'This is not our arrangement, madam,' Mr Smith said.

'I beg you sir, we can meet tomorrow . . .' Kit began again, with a gentle smile.

'You will comply with our arrangement,' Mr Smith said, grabbing her wrists.

'Sir,' Charlotte stepped in between them, 'whatever your "arrangement" with Miss Thornfield, she is still a human soul and not your property. Tonight, she will stay with me.'

Grabbing Kit's arm, she pulled her inside the stage door and slammed it shut, leaning her weight against it. There was a thunderous hammering at the door.

'You will pay for this!' he shouted through the door. 'You will pay for this, do you hear me?'

After a moment or two of silence, Charlotte peered out of the small square window panel into the night.

'He has gone. Kit, I'm so sorry,' Charlotte said. 'I did not mean to make things worse, I just . . . I could not bear to think of you having to go with him, when you looked so unhappy at his side.'

Kit looked perfectly white in the lamplight, her face drawn and pinched.

'He hurt you?' Charlotte asked her tentatively.

'He would have if I had gone with him tonight, in any case,' Kit said. 'But now at least I have a few hours more to be free of him. He is angry now, but I know how to sweeten him.' She smiled. 'Fear not Charlotte, all will be well.'

Kit held Charlotte's hand tightly as they made their way to Lydia's room.

'You can come home with us,' Charlotte said suddenly. 'To Yorkshire, and then you will be free of that man.'

'You are so very kind,' Kit said in a quiet, mournful tone. 'But there are some things that only death can free you from.'

TWENTY-TWO

Anne

All at once, Charlotte and Kit were lost to them, and Anne found herself alone with her brother. Keen to steer Branwell away from the drinking establishments that seemed never to close, Anne had linked her arm through his and guided them onto the Strand. Even this broad, long street was just as busy at night, lined with gaslights, as it was in the day. It felt a little to Anne like stepping into future years, far from now, when the world would look quite different from anything they knew or understood. The infinite possibilities of the future excited her imagination endlessly. But Branwell was growing restless.

'I am certain we have learned all we can,' Anne said, 'and we have lost Charlotte and Kit. It hardly seems right to leave our small sister alone and unprotected.'

'I don't think we need fear for Charlotte – she is a fierce little creature!' Branwell paraphrased Shakespeare.

'Yes, but being fierce in the face of a brute like Noose or one of his henchmen will only exacerbate her troubles,' Anne worried. 'Come now, Branwell, let's return to the theatre and make sure she is safe.'

Branwell was just about to concede when Anne stopped in her tracks. There, almost invisible in the lintel of the window, a hastily chalked version of the same sigil she had seen on their first day in London, the back-to-back letter Rs.

'There is something about these marks,' Anne said thoughtfully, showing it to Branwell, who peered at the odd little drawing.

'For the firehouse, I expect,' Branwell said.

'No,' Anne said, as she scanned the doorways, lintels and gutters in either direction for another one. 'Insurance marks are made of sturdy plaques and screwed into the wall, not chalked on in moments . . . Here!' She beckoned her brother to her side. 'Another. Let's follow them.'

'Follow them where?' Branwell asked her, his shoulders slumping. 'I am weary, Anne. It's exhausting staying sober amid such gaiety. Can we not return? For I am unable to see another such mark, and you know temptation is my nemesis.'

'Here's another one!' Anne called, quite a few yards away from him now, before noticing that other folk in the square had begun to pay attention to her. Dipping her head, she walked swiftly to her brother's side, hooking her arm through his.

'You may retire if you wish, but I feel certain these marks mean *something*. The first time I saw one, I met Jack. And there he was again today, and so was this design. It seems obvious to me that if we follow them, we are bound to find out something more about Noose, the meaning of the mark, or something about Harry and the jewel. So go back, if you must, but should anything befall me, it will be you who has to live with our sisters.'

'Very well, lead the way,' Branwell said, with a sigh.

'I will, and let's be discreet about it,' Anne told him, glancing around. 'I sense eyes on us. We must appear as if we are just taking an aimless stroll.'

'We *are* just taking an aimless stroll,' Branwell said.

Before long, Anne had searched out another and yet another drawing down towards the river.

'The Adelphi building.' Branwell's eyes lit up as the majestic, palatial building reared about them. 'I read that it is inspired by a Croatian palace. What an icon of design and architecture. On a moonlit night such as this, it shines like a temple on Grecian shores.'

Anne was pleased to see her brother's face alight with interest.

The Adelphi building was indeed marvellous, rising from the street like a great towering homage to the classical age. A series of vertical columns made elegant supports to the palisades and perfectly placed windows of Georgian design, some of which still glittered with candlelight. Anne imagined the elegant rooms beyond, the gilded furnishings and crystal candelabra, conjuring a scene from every Austen novel she had ever read of self-possessed ladies taking a turn about the room with proud gentlemen. Everything above the built-up embankment looked in perfect proportion and alignment, a hymn to the beautiful virtues of order and serenity. In contrast the dark, cavernous mouths of the arches over which the Adelphi was built yawned open like mouths gaping with hunger.

'What makes it all the more remarkable,' Branwell said, leading her closer to the building that loomed above them, 'is the underground network of storage and streets that the Adelphi is built over, providing easy transportation of cargo and storage for goods, with access to the river. Is it not remarkable? Come, let us take a closer look at the engineering of it.'

Branwell walked on with vigour, but Anne pulled back a little at the dense gloom he was so eager to pierce. It was not that she had any fear of the dark, more that she could feel that great wave of human suffering that was contained within its cloak, rolling out towards her with brutal clarity. And then she saw it, carved with precision and care into the keystone of the arch, doubtless by a mason – the sigil once again. They must go in.

*   *   *

Little flickers of light could be glimpsed here and there. Quiet murmurs could be heard; a baby's thin cry was drowned out by angry shouts and drunken laughter, and underneath it all an outpouring of soundless sorrow somehow made itself heard.

'Branwell, I am fearful,' Anne said, surprising herself at speaking the thought aloud.

'People come and go from here at all hours of the night,' Branwell assured her, utterly oblivious to the pain she was sensing. 'Come now, Anne – Emily is committing theft with an actor, Charlotte is carousing in Covent Garden with an opera girl. Do you wish to be the most sedate and sensible of your sisters?'

'I suppose not – not when you put it like that,' Anne said reluctantly, pointing to the mark. 'And if there is a clue to Harry's plight here, we must seek it out.'

She looped her arm more tightly through Branwell's as they advanced, even though Anne could not shake the idea that she was walking into a hellish underworld, bordered by the lapping waters of the River Styx.

As her eyes adjusted to the light, Anne made out a family – a woman and her four children, a baby at her breast, huddled into one of the arches, doing their best to sleep on the hard ground. Fires were lit here and there, and the odd candle and lantern afforded small points of illumination that revealed another such family and then another, each at the very end of hope. As Anne passed the silent pinched faces of so many, clinging on to life for the sake of life itself, she felt a grip take hold of her heart so fiercely that she thought it might stop beating then and there.

Where was God in this place?

Anne's grip on Branwell's arm loosened. As he walked on towards the river, she found herself coming to a halt, stopped dead by the crush of unhappiness that swirled around her in the smoke-filled shadows. Then she heard a cry in the dark – not a baby this time, but still the cry of a child, of longing and pain. How could she turn her back on such agony?

Anne glanced towards her brother's back, his stride purposeful and direct, and she knew that she should follow him. But she also knew that she could not ignore the cry – not if she were to continue to consider herself a Christian woman.

'Hello?' Anne called out into the dark, taking a few steps towards the sobs. 'Hello, who is there?'

More than one voice answered her, each calling out in their own kind of misery.

'Spare a penny for my baby, miss?'

'Come over here, my love, and let me show you who's 'ere.'

'How much do you charge? Or how's about you give it me for free?'

The impulse to turn around and run was very strong, but Anne continued to advance towards the weeping. These were only human beings like herself, she told herself – people brought low by circumstance and bad luck, raging against the lot they had been given with anger and violence – and she for one could not blame them. They were not monsters, but God's children. And if she took one step after another, steadily and with determination, then they would not harm her. At least, that's what she told herself as she sought out the source of the tortured wailing.

After what seemed an age, but was probably no more than a minute or so, she came very close to where the noise was, though she could not make out a human form at first. Then she saw a pile of rags lying in a corner, rags that shivered and trembled with every wracking sob.

'Good evening,' Anne said, stooping down so that the hems of her skirts became mired in whatever damp concoction coated the floor. 'Who is there? Who is crying? May I help you?'

The crying ceased and there was a movement in the rags, as they shifted and uncurled, and from within them rose a small, oval-shaped, pale face that seemed to shine in the darkness.

'You shouldn't be out here, miss.' A girl's voice, better spoken than Anne had expected, trembled. 'Not a nice lady like you. They'll rob you, given half a chance, or all the king's men will take you away to sea, they will, and you'll never be heard of again.'

'Well, I shan't let anyone's men take me anywhere,' Anne said, with more bravado than she felt, assuming the girl must be half delirious with pain. Raising her voice, she added, 'Besides, my brother is near, and is carrying a pistol. Any who seek to harm me will find themselves harmed instead.'

'Even so, you should not be here, miss,' the small voice said. 'I shouldn't want any ill to come to you.'

'What's your name, child?'

'Clementine, miss. They call me Clementine now, though I had another name once, before I died and became a ghost.'

'You aren't dead, Clementine,' Anne said softly as she approached a little closer, making out a pale, shoeless foot, and small skeletal hand clutching at her rags. 'You feel very bad, but you are alive.'

'I can't be, miss, I've seen my own grave. So I know I must be dead, and only thirteen when I died, miss, though that's better than some, I suppose.'

'Is that why you are weeping so, Clementine?' Anne asked her. 'Are you hungry? Do you wish to find your mama and papa?'

'No, miss,' Clementine replied. 'I mean – yes, I am always hungry, though I don't think a ghost ought to be. And as for a mama and papa, they buried me long ago.'

'I see.' Anne did her best to keep the horror and sadness from her voice, for fear her pity would injure the disturbed mind of the child further. 'So tell me, Clementine, why do you cry?'

'Because I'm hurt, miss. And awful tired, and I didn't even get a penny for my troubles. He told me he'd pay, but he didn't. A ghost ought not to hurt, should they, miss? But I do. I hurt so badly.'

Anne was still for a moment as she interpreted the girl's explanation, and then as she unravelled the meaning, her heart almost burst with anger and pain. And yet the fury that raged in her breast remained hidden in the dark, her voice as gentle and as warm as a summer breeze.

'Clementine?' Anne asked.

'Call me Clem, miss – everyone does,' Clem said.

'Clem, I would like you to come with me, please.'

'Where, miss?' The girl's voice trembled.

'Well, to a safe place to sleep and rest,' Anne told her. 'A place where I will see if I can ease your pain a little, and feed you and find a happier situation for you. Would that be amenable, Clem?'

'What of your brother with the gun, miss?' Clem said, the terror in her voice palpable. 'Only I am ever so hurt, miss, and I don't think I could please another, even for coin.'

'None shall touch you,' Anne said, and this time it was her voice that trembled – with rage. 'You shall be safe from harm with me, Clem. Let me help you, please, I beg you.'

'If Noose finds out . . .'

'Noose?' Anne asked, alert at once.

'It's him that made me dead and holds my soul for safe-keeping, miss,' Clem said. 'It was another at first, then another, and now that I am almost done, he's the one that will have the last of me.'

'Can you walk?' Anne reached out her hand, encircling a thin wrist, feeling the birdlike bones flex under her touch.

'I'm not sure, miss,' Clem said.

At length Anne found the girl's waist and, encircling one arm around it, hooked the other under her knees and picked her up gently, horrified by how easily she was able to lift the child.

Closing her eyes for a moment, Anne sent up a silent prayer.

'Branwell Brontë?' she called out. 'Are you nearby with your pistol at hand?'

There was a beat of silence, and then a torch flared not far ahead.

'I am here, and I am armed,' Branwell said, catching on to her pretence at once. The shadows and whispers retreated into angry silence. Anne walked steadily towards him, keeping her eyes on her brother until at last she was safely by his side.

'Let me take her,' Branwell said gently, with an expression of sorrow and sweetness on his face as he saw Anne's cargo.

'No,' Anne refused. 'Thank you, dear brother, but I shall manage. This is Clem, and she has had quite enough of the touch of men in her young life.'

'And in my young death, too,' Clem muttered, winding her slender arms around Anne's neck. She looked up into her face in a half-abstracted awe, as if she were being borne along by a vengeful angel.

TWENTY-THREE

Charlotte

There were but two hours left before dawn when Charlotte opened the door to Lydia's room, first with a rush of relief and then a great deal of shock and concern. Kit had been silent since they had returned, sitting next to Lydia on the bed, lost deep in inward thought. Charlotte worried she had done wrong to drag Kit away from 'Mr Smith', though Kit refused to admit it. She was sure she had made things even more difficult for Kit by her inept attempt to rescue the young woman. And to make matters worse, as every minute passed without the arrival of her siblings, her anxiety for their safety grew.

Anne and Branwell were the first two to return. Charlotte was so horrified by what she saw in Anne's arms that she had to muster all her resolve not to cry out, as it looked for all the world as if her sister had brought back a corpse with her.

'Good Lord, Anne,' Charlotte exclaimed, unconsciously barring her sister's entrance. 'What on earth have you done?'

'The girl, Charlotte,' Anne said, engaging her in a solemn look. 'We found her under the Adelphi arches. I fear she is but days away from death, and all for want of a good meal and some decent care. How could I leave a child to face that alone?'

'You could not,' Charlotte acknowledged, turning to where Lydia was sitting up in the bed, she and Kit alert. 'But you cannot bring the girl in here. She is probably infested with all manner of afflictions, and Lydia has only enough strength for her and her child. There is another room along the hall. I have never heard a sound from there. We'll take her there if we can.'

Charlotte went in to fetch the candle with Lydia's blessing.

'Can I help?' Kit asked her, the colour returning to her cheeks for the first time since Charlotte had sent her suitor away.

'Of course,' Charlotte said. 'If you can find another light, and perhaps some sheets, that would be most welcome.'

As Kit hurried down the dark hallways in search of those items, Charlotte breathed a sigh of relief. Emily returned to find her outside the next-door chamber, holding the candle high as Anne cradled the sleeping child, Branwell hovering a few steps back, in case the girl should wake and take fright at the sight of him.

'What did you discover?' Charlotte asked her.

'Nothing, precisely, but what we did find I will tell you about shortly. It seems your findings should take precedence. Who is this poor soul?' Emily peered at the girl with concern. Her sister's hair was dishevelled, Charlotte noticed, and her face flushed with some exertion. At least her dress, though worn through and fraying at the hems, appeared to be in good order, and not as if it had recently been troubled. Of course it hadn't been; Emily had been right when she had demanded that Charlotte should know her character better. There had never in all her life been a gentleman to trouble Emily's equanimity with promises of love. Charlotte should and could feel confident that the vapid actor Louis Parensell was most certainly not the man to change that.

What Emily and Anne might guess at, but never openly mentioned, was that Charlotte did her best to care for her sisters, as their mother might have done had she lived. However, the trouble with her sisters was that they were independent beings who far too often had ideas of their own. How

Emily had become so untidy was a matter she chose not to dwell on for now. Better to focus on this poor strange being that Anne cradled in her arms, and hope there was at least some little good they could do on this strange night.

'Poor thing,' Branwell said, covering his mouth with a trembling hand to hide his distress. 'She's ever so fearful of me. The things she must have suffered.'

'We will protect her now,' Emily said gently, rubbing her brother's arm. 'You did well to bring her here, both of you.'

'Come then, let us tend to her,' Anne said, shifting her weight a little.

Thankfully the door to the empty room was not locked, and though it was not furnished with a bed, as Lydia's room was, there was a dusty old chaise pushed against a wall. Anne laid the girl down there, and Charlotte pulled an empty crate closer to the girl to sit on, so that she was able to see her more clearly. Kit returned with another candle she had found, and arranged a clean cotton sheet over the chaise, remaining kneeling on the floor as she observed the girl, with not a care that her pretty pink gown became stained with dust and dirt.

'It breaks your heart,' Kit said softly.

Indeed, Charlotte had to bite her lip hard to repress the horror of what she saw as she examined her patient thoroughly. The child was bone-thin, her arms and legs covered in bruises and sores. There was blood on her spindle legs, though Charlotte could not quite discern where it came from, and her mind could not muster the detachment to speculate. If only her dear friend Celia Prescott – the doctor's wife and her husband's equal in medical matters – were nearby to offer her clear-minded, expert aid. But she was not, and all this girl had between her and death were the Brontës and Kit Thornfield.

'Branwell,' Charlotte said, steeling herself. 'Ask Lydia for some hot water, and soap if she has any, a comb, scissors and . . . go out and find what clothes you can for a girl of this size.' A thought suddenly occurred to Charlotte. 'One moment – find boys' clothes; I saw they sell second-hand and repaired boots and garments in the market. Though the sun has yet to rise, the vendors will more than likely be there – seek them out.' Charlotte delved into her sleeve and produced a few coins. 'I brought a little extra I had saved for emergencies. Bring also thin broth and some bread and milk – enough for us all. Oh, and something that will do as dressings for her wounds. Do you have it?'

'I have it,' Branwell said, tapping his heels together and saluting.

'I'll go with him,' Kit offered at once, climbing to her feet. 'I know the best places.'

'But Kit,' Charlotte said with concern, 'what if Mr Smith should still be waiting for you?'

'I doubt he will be,' Kit said. 'He is a determined man but not a patient one. He will find me tomorrow, at his leisure.'

Emily and Anne exchanged glances but didn't say a word, sensing a delicate subject.

Though Branwell looked exhausted, he left the room with the vigour of a man of purpose, and Charlotte could only hope that this would result in a permanent change in her brother.

'Here.' Lydia appeared in the doorway, offering a white cotton nightgown she had retrieved from her trunk. 'When you have removed the garments she is wearing, burn them on the fire.'

'Anne,' Charlotte murmured, once Lydia had left, 'we must cleanse and change her. I believe that – as she trusts you – you should lead her nursing, and I will assist you. Emily guard the door – make sure that no one enters without our permission.'

For once Emily, who had never taken very well to the notion of sickness or infirmity, even in herself, was happy to take a step back, and did as she was told.

'Clem, we are going to take these clothes off you now,' Anne told the half delirious girl gently. 'And we have something soft and clean for you to wear. Is that agreeable? There are only ladies present, and all but I shall avert their eyes as the business is done.'

Clem did not respond at all, and Charlotte prayed it was just that the child slept, now that she was comfortable and safe, rather than that she was slipping into that unknown realm of the fever dream that so few returned from. Removing the garment she was wearing took Charlotte and Anne much longer than anticipated, particularly as they were obliged to pull away some of the material that seemed to have fused with injured skin in several places. Many painstaking minutes ticked by, during which Lydia delivered a pail of warm water, and the sisters were able at last to free the fragile person from the garments that had all but entombed her, gently washing her as best they could. Charlotte held her head as Anne cut away the lice-ridden and matted hair, revealing beneath the mud-brown clumps a fair, soft down of blonde. It was all that Charlotte could do not to weep at the sight. No wonder she thought the girl dead, as Anne had told them, for she looked as if she had been in the grave at least a month, so wasted and fragile was she. What kind of a world was this, where so many were left to suffer and die, while all those who had enough for themselves walked over their bones?

With the utmost tenderness, Charlotte lifted Clem's frail form as Anne drew the soft, white nightgown over her head and arms.

'She sleeps, I think,' Anne said, her hand resting below the girl's chest, feeling the rise and fall of her abdomen. 'I pray she has enough strength until Branwell returns with some nourishment.'

'How old do you think she is?' Charlotte asked.

'Perhaps fifteen?' Anne wondered. 'She has been lost since the age of thirteen.' She and Charlotte exchanged unhappy glances.

'Perhaps if we are able to feed her and bring her to some level of health, we might be able to send her, more safely guised as a boy, to Mrs Prescott,' Charlotte told Anne. 'With her patronage, the girl might have a chance of a life at least. I shall pen a letter explaining the situation.'

'Thank you, Charlotte.' Anne caught Charlotte's hand and kissed her on the cheek. 'Thank you for not sending me away and calling me a fool to bring her to you.'

'If only there were more like you, Anne,' Charlotte said regretfully, 'then this earth might be a gentler place to live.'

'There are more, though – there are Emily and you; and Branwell, Kit and Lydia didn't hesitate to help, despite their own troubles,' Anne said, turning to Emily and gesturing for her to come away from the door. 'I also came across something that might be pertinent to the detection. Above the arches I found this sign once again. In fact, it was a trail of such images that led Branwell and me to the Adelphi and thus to Clem. Most were drawn or scratched, but this was carved with purpose.'

Anne drew an approximation of the mark in the dirt on the windowsill with her fingertip. The two capital letter Rs, back to back, encased in a pentagram that was topped with crenellations.

'They must be the initials of a name or an organisation,' Charlotte said as she peered at the drawing. Emily frowned deeply as she took in the image, pulling out a slim bundle of papers from her bodice.

'Who put those there?' Charlotte asked her, rather concerned.

'I can't recall his name,' Emily said. 'One of my secret lovers. I have taken at least a dozen since we arrived, you know.'

Smoothing out one of the receipts, she examined it closely.

'This appears to be a bill of sale for a rather expensive Regency desk,' Emily muttered.

'What has *that* to do with *this*?' Charlotte asked her sister, pointing from Anne's sketch to the letter.

'Dozens of receipts just like this one were all we found in Roxby's impenetrable safe,' Emily said. 'Such security for nothing of value . . . except . . .' Charlotte watched as her sister refolded the paper, reuniting the broken wax seal that had once closed it. Embedded in the wax was exactly the same motif as the one Anne had drawn in the dust.

'Roxby is connected to this seal, as are Noose and his Sharps,' Anne said in wonder. 'Perhaps he isn't really called Henry, perhaps he's a Richard or a Robert Roxby? Perhaps *he* is this Red Monarch!'

'I don't think so,' Emily said. 'Roxby doesn't strike me as someone fearsome enough to make Noose cower – though men are ever deceivers. Perhaps he is much cleverer than he looks. Nevertheless, he is involved somehow, and Harry did not know. Or perhaps he did, and perhaps that's why they fought? That, or perhaps Noose was keeping more concealed than we accounted for.'

'Yet more questions and no answers,' Charlotte said desperately.

'Yes, but now at least we know where to look and . . .' Emily trailed off. 'Of course, it is so obvious once you see it.'

'Once you see what, Emily?' Charlotte asked.

'These aren't two letters, it's a stylised butterfly, and these aren't castle ramparts, it is a crown. I don't why it is enclosed within the pentagram, but I am certain this is the crest of the Red Monarch. It seems that – of all the fearsome creatures he could have named himself after – he has taken on the identity of a butterfly native to the Americas, I cannot fathom why.'

'And, judging by the quantity and placements of that mark, we are in the heart of his kingdom,' Anne said. 'So the Red

Monarch is no fairy tale told to frighten children. It seems a little odd, does it not Emily, that a man like Louis would not know of the Monarch's existence?'

'What do you mean by "a man like Louis"?' Emily snapped back.

'I mean a gentleman of the world,' Anne glanced at Charlotte, who raised her eyebrows.

'Well, not really,' Emily went on. 'It's clear that he presides over some kind of secret society . . .'

'Not that secret,' Anne said. 'We have discovered the marks; others with decent observation could too. And Louis seems to know about everything that goes on in the theatre. It seems a little strange to me that he claimed to know nothing about the Red Monarch.'

Emily frowned deeply, but the fact that she did not answer for a moment indicated that she was considering what it meant if Louis had indeed been holding something back.

'It does seem likely that he would know about the Monarch,' she concluded at length, speaking slowly, as if every word weighed as heavy as a rock. 'I will bring it up at our next meeting.'

'Then be careful, Emily,' Charlotte said.

'I have nothing to fear from Louis.' Emily dismissed the comment.

'How can you be so certain?' Anne asked.

'In the same way I know which direction is north,' Emily said. 'I just feel it in my bones.'

'When I first talked to Clem under the arches,' Anne remarked, 'she said she was afraid that if I did not leave at once, I might be snatched away as she had been.'

'You might well have been,' Charlotte said. 'What our brother was thinking, leaving you alone, I have no idea.'

'It wasn't Branwell's fault,' Anne said at once. 'He was so thrilled by the architecture that he was quite transported.

Anyway, once I had happened upon Clem, she told me that her master now, the man who owned her, was named Noose.'

'Noose.' Emily repeated the name in a low growl, her hand clenching around the hilt of her sword.

'Then she may know more of his business, and who he deals with,' Charlotte said thoughtfully. 'Perhaps when she awakens, we might be able to glean some information from her.'

'She is a little strange to talk to,' Anne warned them. 'She seems to think she is already dead and a ghost.'

'The horrors that child must have seen,' Charlotte said, glancing back sorrowfully at the sleeping girl. 'We also uncovered a granule of information, Emily. We happened upon Mr Skeet in Covent Garden, bragging that he knows the identity of this all-powerful Red Monarch.'

'Do you think he spoke true?' Emily asked her.

'I know he was greatly afraid that he had said too much,' Charlotte said. 'And I suppose that such power and influence could be coupled with a kingdom of criminals if the individual behind the name was indeed a person of high rank and social standing.'

'It would explain why Noose was afraid of the Monarch. A powerful man could bring him and the whole of The Rookery down in an instant.'

'To think that it might be one of those who govern us, who also seeks to oppress and exploit us!' Anne said furiously. 'We must go to Mr Skeet and ask him for a name.'

'We can hardly ask Skeet to reveal the identity to us,' Charlotte said, thinking of the way he had dealt with the last woman to question him.

'No, but if he knows, and if he is minded to talk about his knowing when he has taken a drink or two, then there will be someone else whom he has told – someone who might reveal the Monarch's identity. For if we can expose him, we can save

Harry with or without the jewel. Noose won't need to keep him any more, the whole house of cards will come tumbling down, and we will have done some real good.'

'These papers make little sense to me,' Emily said, still sifting through the receipts. 'There's a piece of silverware here, a rare book there, a crate of wine and so on, each one costing far more than the listed item should, which might be because we are in these foreign southern parts, I suppose, but also might be because they are deceitful. But for what reason?'

'I cannot fathom,' Charlotte said, fraught with frustration. 'Damn Noose, and damn the Red Monarch!'

'Don't let him get me!' Clem suddenly screeched from the chaise, scrambling herself into a tight ball until her back was pressed against the wall. 'I beg you, please don't give me over to him – he will be so angry that I've spoken even though I am dead, he will throw me in the sea, he will.'

'Who will, Clem?' Anne rushed to her side. 'There is no one here but us – there is no need to be afraid. You can say what you like, and no one will hear.'

'But you spoke his name, you summoned him,' Clem whispered urgently, her dark eyes darting here and there. 'You spoke the name of the king and he'll send all his men to snatch me away again, and take me to the tall house, like he did before when I was alive.'

Anne sat down next to Clem, and wrapped her arm around her thin shoulders.

'Do you mean Noose?'

'Not him; he's but a demon, not the devil himself,' Clem said.

'All the king's men?' Anne repeated the phrase that Clem had spoken in the murk of the arches. 'Clem, was it the Red Monarch's men who took you away, and changed your name and told you that you were dead?'

'It was,' Clem said, clutching at Anne's wrist tightly. 'I don't remember much about being alive now. It's like a dream that comes in bits and pieces and is always in a muddle. But there was a mama and a papa.' Her face softened as she spoke. 'A warm fire, and enough food. I think there was a baby brother and two sisters. I can hardly remember it, but I think that when I was alive my name was Mary. Yes – Mary. That's the name I saw on my grave.'

There was knock at the door, and Charlotte let in Branwell, who came with nourishment, a parcel of clothes, and a pair of sturdy, patched boots, which looked only a little too big. He saw the girl staring at him from the corner, her eyes huge and terrified.

'I escorted Kit back to her lodgings and I shall retreat,' he said. 'She does not wish me near.'

'But where will you go?' Charlotte asked.

'The sun rises and the day is fine, I'll take a walk and return soon.'

The atmosphere within the chamber had become so fraught with horror and grief that it heartened Charlotte to remember that there was a world outside, a world where the sun rose and flowers still bloomed.

'Clem ... *Mary*,' Anne spoke both names gently. 'Tell me – what happened to you?'

'I was a little girl when I was alive,' the girl they would now call Mary said. 'One day I was taken right out of my garden. I was reading in the arbour and then ... then I don't remember.'

'Was it Noose who took you?' Anne asked.

'No, I didn't meet him until a long time after I was dead. Another man took me. He was kind and well dressed and told me I was to go with him and he'd take me to my papa. But he didn't. I was taken from there to another place – a room in a tall house, where I stayed I don't know how long, because there was no window and it was all painted in black, even the mirrors. And then at last they took me from there to see the

Monarch and told me that if I was not obedient then my family would suffer because of me.'

'Where did the king see you?' Anne asked her. 'Do you remember the address?'

'In a grand palace,' Mary said. 'The finest place I ever saw, all the gold and silver in the world.'

'And what did the king look like?'

Mary closed her eyes and shook her head, her face screwing into a tight knot.

'Red,' she said. 'Red with eyes that shone yellow like a goat's and great big wings that stretched out across the whole of the room, turning it all scarlet.'

'Horrifying,' Emily breathed.

'And then what became of you, Mary?' Anne asked her.

'I was married,' Mary said. 'I was put in a pretty frock and married to a gentleman with a silver beard. The king was there at the wedding. He looked down at me and my husband, and he told him he had given him a well-bred girl from a decent family, that's what he called me. Pure and untouched, he said. Much better than any street urchin you find in the gutter. He said his generosity was never to be forgotten, for so rare and precious was his gift of this fine jewel.'

'He called you a jewel,' Anne breathed, turning to look at her sisters. 'You were a stolen jewel?'

'The finest,' Mary said with a hint of childlike pride. 'The prettiest he ever stole away, he told me so.'

'The jewel isn't a gem or something made of gold,' Charlotte said, gazing from Anne to Emily. 'The jewel we have been searching for, the jewel Harry refused to give up to Noose, is a stolen child.'

Anne

'Of course Harry would not surrender a child,' Lydia said, after Anne and Emily went to her room to apprise her of developments. 'My dear, brave husband, risking everything to protect another. That is the Harry I love, the man I know.'

'He is indeed a worthy man,' Emily said. 'Not many would risk their necks for another.'

Lydia stifled a sob at the thought.

'Don't worry,' Anne reassured her. 'Now we have unlocked the heart of the mystery, all that remains is to find the child, find Harry, and rescue them both.'

'You make it sound like nothing more than a ride in the park on a summer's morning,' Lydia said.

'Not quite,' Emily told her. 'But though it may not seem it yet, this is an important turn in our fortunes. An upward turn.'

'We have much to do,' Anne said. 'And must return to Mary for now. But in the meantime you should rest and then make your things ready so that as soon as we have Harry, we can leave at once. Pack only what we can carry with ease, and Lydia, make sure you eat and drink. You will need your strength – for you, Harry and your child.'

Lydia nodded dumbly, as Anne embraced her, before putting her thumb and forefinger under Lydia's chin to raise it a little.

'There is hope, dear girl,' she said. 'Have courage.'

★   ★   ★

'I wasn't married long – Silver Beard soon tired of his bride.' Clem was still talking to Charlotte when they returned, in a low monotone. It was as if, though her body was weak, her soul was determined that she should tell all about her pitiful life, before it was too late. 'Afterwards I tried to run away, to find my way home to Mama and Papa. But the Sharps caught me and took me back to the tall house. And the Monarch had me dressed up all nice, and he took me to see my grave. It was my grave, for it had my name on it, my birthday and my baby sister's, who died when she was one.' Mary's voice grew a little stronger as she ate her broth, and as more and more fragments of memory seemed to return to her. 'So, it was my grave. The Monarch told me that I was dead, and that my soul belonged to him now, for as long as he wanted it, to put all thoughts of the living behind me, for they had forgotten me.'

Mary leaned back into the chaise, finishing the last of her soup, and looked around her. It seemed to Anne that she looked a good deal better for the food and the rest, though most of her arms and legs were bandaged, and she had yet to notice that her hair had been cut away. She made a strange sight, but had more than enough of the spark of life to stay in this world a little longer.

'I don't know how many years ago that was, but I should think it was at least a hundred,' Mary said. 'I should think I have been a ghost for a very long time. It seems like forever.'

'Do you know where the tall house is, Mary?' Anne asked her.

'Near to the arches, right enough,' Mary said. 'Sometimes I'd find myself outside, wondering if they'd let me in again. It were so nice and dark in there, like it should be sleeping in your coffin.'

'Rest now, Mary,' Anne said gently, determined not to use the name Clem's captors had given her. 'You rest and we shall keep you safe.'

'I was a jewel,' Mary muttered as she drifted back off to sleep.

'A jewel,' Anne repeated. 'Our purpose is clear, sisters, we have two lives to save and a lost daughter to return to her family. All as the clock ticks on.'

TWENTY-FIVE

Emily

Emily had done her best to sleep, but it was near impossible. Her whole body itched for action and her whole heart ached for home.

There had been unexpected benefits to their trip to London. The detection was the most difficult and challenging they had faced, beset by danger at the outset, and almost impossible to make sense of. Yet she liked the freedom to become whoever she chose for just a little while. All the mutterings and opinions that she pretended not to hear at home meant nothing here.

Amongst the theatricals she was no longer 'the strange Brontë' or the 'wild sister' or 'that mannish girl'. Here, despite her loathing for society and urban decay, she felt as if she could at last walk in the shoes of her Gondal queens and duchesses, and cast herself in any role she chose, unchained from expectation.

Yet, despite the unforeseen pleasures she had found here, Emily knew she could not survive much longer without the heather under her feet or the lapwings in the sky over her head. She would not be able to endure much more of this filthy air, or another night without dear Keeper creeping up the stairs, to spend the night at the foot of her bed. She missed her dear papa, and Tabby's scolding, and the powerful charge of energy that always flowed from the rolling hills and valleys into her veins, making them glow.

This life was a diverting one, but Charlotte had been frustratingly right when she told her that it was not *her* life, and could never be, not forever. She would pine away here, wither and die like cut bluebells in a jar, before long.

Before they were able to return home, though, there was work to be done, and dark and dangerous work at that. And for her part she would need the help of Louis Parensell, a prospect that thrilled and frightened her in equal measure.

That Louis inspired something within her that she was unaccustomed to feeling could not be in doubt. Precisely what it was or what it meant was not entirely clear to Emily, and she was certain that to attempt to find out would be an act of wanton foolishness that would result in the kind of disaster she had seen her sisters and brother endure. It was best to ignore the skin-tingling and heart-racing effects of his proximity altogether, for she was sure it would wear off once he was at a safe distance. And yet, the thought of him near to her, the glance of his eyes on her skin, and the delicious curve of his smile, was provoking, bringing forth images she dared not dwell on for more than one or two racing heartbeats.

Louis was not to be found in the theatre, however. The auditorium was as empty and as quiet as Emily had seen it since she arrived, its silence echoing with the traces of memories that lingered in the air.

Taking her chance to explore more, she crept up the wooden steps that led onto the stage, and walked to its centre. Looking back at the theatre her eyes rose upward, searching out the boxes and circles for any sign of life, or – in the case of the grey man that Louis told her haunted the theatre – signs of death. But all was still, and the great uproarious, bejewelled lady slept for a little while, dreaming of what glories she would reveal when next she woke. Shuddering at the thought, she peered into the shadowy wings. There was a hint of movement in the dark, just beyond the fringe of where the spirit light faded away to nothing. Supposing it was either someone employed by the theatre or one of the ghosts, Emily advanced towards it, well disposed towards either. She was to be disappointed, though.

'Hello there?' she called out. 'Who is there?'

She heard a scuffle, the light footsteps of someone departing at speed, and then the gait of a heavier person lumbering towards her.

'What's this?' A wheezy, mucus-fuelled tone replied, making her heart sink. 'Oh, now, Miss Brontë. How may I be of service, my dear?'

Emily had taken against Mr Roxby the elder the moment she had met him, but she did her very best to repress this now, for she was certain he was a man who was more likely to bend to a little soft talk and womanly ways than a punch on the nose. However, soft talk and womanly ways had never been Emily's forte.

'I was hoping to find Mr Parensell?' Emily said with a smile as sweet as she could muster, which she conjured by imagining she was visiting a litter of puppies. 'If you could direct me to him, sir, I'd be most grateful.'

'Parensell, eh?' Roxby said, beckoning for her to follow him deeper into the theatre, towards where he kept his office. Instinctively, Emily resisted the implicit command, knowing that once she was isolated and alone with this beast, he might assume he had the upper hand and attempt some impropriety. However, with her sword at her waist and her pistol in her pocket, she also thought she'd rather like to see him try, so follow him she did.

'Now, Miss Brontë,' Roxby said, closing the door of his office behind her. 'You are in this great city without your papa, and though I have no daughters myself, I feel that it is my Christian duty to act as your papa certainly would, and warn you against Mr Parensell. Only last night I caught him in here taking advantage of a young lady, without a thought for her character! And you wouldn't want your reputation sullied by such base and vile activities, would you, Miss Brontë?'

He put the question in such a way that it sounded as though he rather hoped she might say yes.

'I thank you for your kind consideration,' Emily said, wondering how she might draw him round to discussing more pertinent matters. 'But you have no need to be concerned for me. I am a confirmed spinster and determined to remain one as long as I live.'

'Oh, I see,' Roxby said. 'Well, the male of the species has much to regret in that case, Miss Brontë. But watch Parensell – he's a nice enough man if you are his friend, but I've seen him charm the diamonds from elderly ladies' necks, and much more besides. He's a rogue, make no mistake.'

The first spark of anger ignited in Emily's breast at this slight against her ally.

'I can only judge him from what I know of him myself, not from hearsay,' she countered. 'And I find him very honest about who he is. Indeed, he has shown himself worthy of my trust.'

'I daresay,' Roxby chuckled. 'I daresay he has. But that's a female heart for you, is it not? Ruled by impulsive passions instead of intellect.'

'And what about you, sir?' Emily said tartly. 'Do you see yourself as an honourable man? When your own son has been under threat of death these past days? When your daughter-in-law and unborn grandchild are left alone without care or support, and you do nothing to aid them? Despite knowing exactly what crimes take place around and within your theatre, and being acquainted with his murderer-in-waiting, and presumably having some influence with him? Is that honourable, sir?'

The question was delivered with as polite a tone and smile as Emily could manage, though now her thoughts had wandered from a litter of puppies to the image of that tigress breaking free from her cage to take exquisite revenge on all who had wronged her.

'I have done my part,' Roxby said, bristling at once. 'I have done more than my part in that respect, Miss Brontë. Now I am responsible for more mouths than his. On every action I take rest the livelihoods of a hundred souls – more! Should I endanger all of them for the sake of one who will not benefit from my guidance one bit?'

Roxby made a rather good point on the face of things, but Emily found herself unable to reconcile herself with it.

'You presume to style yourself as having fatherly concern for me – a person you hardly know – but you are content to see your own flesh and blood murdered?' Emily asked him. Roxby grew redder with each word she uttered, his yellowed beard quivering with indignation. 'Can there ever be a justification for such neglect of your duties?'

'You know nothing of what I contend with to keep this building open, my people employed. You have no idea what I will do, what I have done for the folk who need me, and respect me. The things I am obliged to let go on unseen below our very feet.' He pointed furiously at the floor. 'And I do it all for my folk, each one of them worth ten of that fool boy who put us all in danger when he—'

Roxby came to a shuddering halt, checking himself abruptly.

'Tell me what you know of the Red Monarch,' Emily demanded.

'How dare you speak his name here!' Roxby said, surging up from his seat, his face gone quite purple. 'What business have you talking of him?'

'It's for his sake that Harry has been taken,' Emily said.

'Harry must break under threat and deliver the "jewel" meant for the Monarch, or die. But you know that, don't you, sir? And you know the said jewel is an innocent child taken from her home. You are part of this evil operation, aren't you, Roxby? Perhaps you may even *be* him?'

Roxby stared at Emily for a long moment, during which she thought he might actually explode with rage, but then – most unexpectedly – he laughed. He guffawed, hiccuped and laughed again, until he could hardly catch his breath and the tears ran down his face. Emily feared he might have gone quite mad.

'Me, the Monarch? Oh my dear, I thought better of you than that. You think a fat old actor like me could be a creature like him?' His face suddenly darkened, as he levelled his deadly serious gaze at her. 'He is not like human men, my dear. There is no heart in him, no soul. He is an automaton that exists for one purpose alone: to crush the world beneath the heel of his boot.'

He turned his face away from her.

'I have already said too much, I beg you leave here now, and my theatre as soon as you are able. For if you are meddling with the Monarch, you won't have many chances to leave with your life.'

Emily did not see the benefit in questioning him further then, for he had already revealed much more than he realised. Besides, he seemed to have all but gone, sunken into himself and lost in despair. Perhaps there was more to Henry Roxby than met the eye, after all?

'Please will you let me have the address of Mr Parensell's lodgings?'

'I will,' Roxby said, taking a pen, and scratching out a few words on a piece of paper. 'Though I will take no responsibility for the consequences.'

Emily meant to leave without another word. She tried most sincerely to.

'I know that any father worth a jot would move heaven and earth to save his child, no matter the risk to himself,' she said, taking the paper from Roxby's hand. 'I can plainly see how much you despise yourself, Mr Roxby, and I can say that you are right to, for if you will not stand up to the Red Monarch, who can only be a man of flesh and blood after all, you are worth nothing more than that.'

As she left, Henry Roxby buried his head in his hands and wept.

It was fair to say that Louis was more than a little surprised to see Emily Brontë at the front door of his lodgings at just a little after 9 a.m.

After the bitter encounter with Mr Roxby, Emily had been glad to be out and in the morning sunlight, though she had taken care to avoid the attention of the Sharp spies by waiting in the deep shadows, her hair covered with a shawl as she watched for them to glance away from her position. Then she had darted a few feet more, and a few more still, ducking down behind carts, or joining with a group of market workers for a few steps, before repeating this method again and again until she was sure she had escaped the sentinels' notice and was no longer being followed.

Evading their watchers gave her a particular kind of delight, but there was something else behind that pleasure too: the prospect of seeing Louis again. Of course he was a philanderer, a thief, and perhaps even a killer, but for some reason, even knowing all of that, Emily felt at home with him. It was quite a conundrum.

'How did you discover where I lived?' Louis asked as he came to the door, his skin and hair still wet from the washbowl, his white shirt undone at the throat. Somewhere in the building Emily could hear a deep baritone voice practising scales, and elsewhere a pianist, who seemed lost in a piece she did not recognise, but which gave the meeting the air of a torrid romantic opera.

'Well, I am a detector,' Emily said primly, rather concerned by how very fetching he was. With a great deal of effort, she prised her head away from the moors where she had momentarily pictured them together, and back into the present moment.

'Now, I realise it is very early for an actor, but even so, you must get dressed at once and come down again directly. We have a dangerous mission to complete, and it must be done promptly.'

Louis crossed his arms, half smiling, with his head tilted back to reveal a little more of his naked throat.

'And how do you know I will accept your dangerous mission, Miss Brontë?' he asked her. 'You seem very certain of my willingness to risk life and limb for your endeavours.'

'I am certain, Mr Parensell,' Emily said. 'For one thing, you already offered me your assistance and I trust you are not a man to go back on his word, despite your reputation. And for the second thing, this adventure is the most interesting thing that has happened to you in many years. And lastly because you want to be a good man. And wanting to be so is half the battle.'

Emily couldn't read the expression on his face as he regarded her for a moment more. There was something of a need in it, she thought. A need for adventure, she told herself, together with some kind of sadness that she could not make sense of at all. In any event, Louis was willing, just as she had predicted.

'I need but a few minutes to choose the appropriate clothes for this adventure,' Louis told her, closing the door. Emily was content to wait for him.

★　　★　　★

As good as his word, Louis returned dressed, rather finely Emily thought, in a green overcoat with a ruby waistcoat beneath, and matching top hat. His dandy attire rather put her worn and dowdy dress to shame.

Emily was not the sort of person to worry about being fashionable. For much of her life she had happily worn and remade clothing that had belonged to her mother and Aunt Branwell, with very little concern for what others thought of her apparel, and today was no different.

'Dressing to appear inconspicuous, I see,' she said with a wry smile.

'Dressing to give me courage,' Louis replied, offering her his arm.

'Why, are you in want of it?' Emily was surprised.

'I am when it comes to a certain matter that I'd like to ask your opinion on,' he said.

'Oh, of course – as soon as we have finished our task, we can discuss your salvation,' Emily said, secretly pleased that he would consider her thoughts on any matter of value.

'My salvation?' Louis looked at her as if she might have guessed his purpose.

'Is that not what you wish to discuss with me?' she replied, intrigued by his discomfort. 'I can't imagine on what other matter I'd be qualified to advise you, but no matter. First to business.'

As they walked, Emily briefed him on the finer details of their mission.

'Emily – no.' Louis stopped walking and turned to face Emily, taking her hands in his. 'I cannot allow this folly . . .' Seeing the anger flash in Emily's eyes, he clarified at once: 'Not because I consider myself superior to you, or in any way able to command you on account of my sex. I shouldn't think there is a man alive who could.' His voice softened. 'But because you are my friend, and I enjoy this bleak world very much more with you in it. I will accompany you into The Rookery, and even face down Noose for you, if I must. But it is because I regard you so highly that I cannot allow you to try and unmask the Monarch, if such a man exists. For not only will you fail, but you will be killed for attempting it. And I . . . I should regret that outcome.'

'Louis . . .' Emily hesitated. 'How can it be that a man such as you – a man who knows everything there is to know about this city – does not know that the Monarch is as real as you and me? That he has tentacles everywhere about us, including in the theatre and the house you are taking me to? I know that, and I have been here but a matter of days.' Emily took a step closer to him, searching his eyes. 'It seems improbable that you do not.'

Louis gazed down at her for a moment or two.

'You're right, I did lie, and it was a foolish and weak deceit.'

Emily shook her head in disappointment. 'I was so certain you were straight with me,' she told him. 'I truly thought that you were the north!'

'I do not know exactly what you mean by that,' he said. 'But I do know that when I withheld what little I know about the Monarch, it was for your own safety. I hardly knew you then. I suppose I thought you would give up, go home. Be safe. It only took a few more hours in your company to real-ise that you and your sisters would never do anything so sensible.'

'What else have you lied to me about?' Emily asked him.

'Nothing,' Louis said, reaching for her hand. Emily allowed him to take it. 'Nothing, I swear to you Emily. I just found that I needed you to be out of harm's way.'

'Do you know who he is?' Emily asked.

'I do not,' Louis told her sincerely.

'Then you are kind, Louis, but whoever the Red Monarch is, he is just a mortal,' Emily replied, pulling her hands free of his as she walked on. 'And only one at that. How can any one person hold so many in his thrall? He cannot be impervious to justice, or to scrutiny. No man can be – for the day that happens, we are all lost, don't you see?'

'I do see, Emily,' Louis said. 'I do see and I agree, but does it have to be you who puts yourself in harm's way?'

'If those who one would have thought fear nothing in this world, such as Mr Noose, or you, Louis Parensell, can't face him, then I suppose it must be up to me and my sisters to unmask the Red Monarch. For there is no man alive that frightens us, sir.'

'I do not doubt it, Emily,' Louis said softly, taking a step closer to her. 'Just as I do not doubt that you have more courage than a city of men. It's just . . .' Louis lowered his eyes for a moment. 'It's just that I would very much like you to stay alive, Emily. Could you not send one of your other sisters? The short, angry one perhaps?'

'I cannot,' Emily said, smiling despite herself. 'It is impossible to send Charlotte, for once she has been met, no one can ever forget her, no matter how hard they try. And besides, she seeks a public life one day, and acceptance into the finest drawing rooms of society. I can't risk her becoming infamous before she has had a moment to make herself known for her considerable talents. Please never repeat to her that I said such a thing – I should hate for her to think I admire her excessively, though I do.'

'You always tease me about my rakish life,' Louis said, 'and in doing so you have made me see that there is more than one way for a man to live – that having begun on a certain path you need not stay on it, not if it hurts or degrades you, or could result in your harm. I suppose I mean to say that you can turn back, Emily – you *can* choose another path.'

Emily thought for a moment, looking down the Strand. There was a peculiar beauty to the dusty day, bristling with folk and carts, life plunging on like water over rapids, without a thought to the jagged rocks that lay beneath the surface. Emily could not live in such pleasant ignorance, however – she knew what dangers were hidden just from view, and she could hardly pretend otherwise. Another path would be a pleasant stroll in comparison, particularly with such a charming companion as Louis, but at its end she would still find a kind of ruin.

'You know of the tall, dark house, though, don't you?' Emily asked Louis. 'The tall, black, thin house, where the windows are painted black?'

'I do,' Louis admitted hesitantly. 'It is nearby, may I ask why?'

'Then direct me to it, Louis, and I shall go on alone to make my enquiries.'

'What sort of enquiries?' Louis asked her. 'You don't plan to knock on the door and ask for the Monarch, do you?'

'I often find the direct approach saves time,' Emily said with a deliberate shrug of bravado. 'Now, where is it, this house?'

Louis sighed deeply.

'You must know,' he said at last, 'that I cannot let you go there alone.' He looked down for a moment, shaking his head before meeting her eyes once more. 'It appears I am willing to die for you after all, Miss Brontë.'

'You will not die, Mr Parensell,' Emily said, breaking into a warm smile. 'Certainly not on my account. I should never allow it.'

'Very well,' Louis said. 'Then you must prepare yourself. The tall house is not exactly a den of iniquity, but it is very close to one. It's a place where the normal restrictions of society are somewhat relaxed, where gentlemen and ladies visit to make discreet assignations, or partake in particular pleasures without fear of discovery or judgement. And a place where certain business deals can be made invisible to any who might object. It's a house that promises to keep all your secrets within its walls.'

'Well,' Emily said, as they began to walk with purpose once more, 'I'm afraid that promise is about to be broken.'

TWENTY-SIX

Charlotte

Emily had already departed with her orders to find the black painted house that Mary had described to them, and to see if it was possible to discover any more of the Red Monarch's dealings there, or the terrible racket that stole children from their homes to be sold into the worst kind of evil.

Charlotte, Branwell and Anne remained, tasked with attempting to find the girl that Harry had hidden, fathoming a way to locate where Harry had been imprisoned, in order to rescue him from captivity before Noose did away with him.

Charlotte feared – given the complexity of the situation they found themselves in – that it would be impossible to solve this detection without paying a heavy price. If that happened – if Harry was lost, or the poor child he was trying to save, and if they couldn't protect Lydia either, what then? Would their deaths be on the head of Charlotte and her sisters? Had their arrival in London to help Lydia made an awful predicament better or worse? Charlotte knew that anything less than a perfect outcome would plague her until the last of her days, and as such she could not allow the adventure to end any other way but happily – not if it was in her power to influence events.

After a few hours of sleep and a little more nourishment, Mary seemed a good deal improved, with enough strength to be able to walk, with the support of her beloved Anne, into

Lydia's room, where Emily and Branwell had moved in the chaise, beating as much dust off it as they could in the hallway.

Now Mary sat upon it, looking round the room as if it were the most wonderful place she had ever seen, better even than those golden rooms where she had been interviewed by the Red Monarch, for within this apartment she was safe and cared for. That she was pitiful to observe was evident. Her body was bruised, her head shaved close, and she was so thin it seemed almost impossible that she could live. However, her eyes were clear, her voice strong and growing stronger and gradually, under Anne's sweet influence, she came round to the notion that she was not a ghost at all, but a girl of about fifteen years of age. And a girl who still had a family some- where. A family with whom she would be reunited as soon as it was safe. Heartbreakingly, as the possibility dawned on her, she seemed to struggle to be able to accept anything so hopeful.

'I shouldn't think I should go home, miss,' Mary had said when Anne first mentioned the possibility. 'My poor mama and papa will have got used to me being gone, it doesn't seem right to upset them. And I am sure they have forgotten me by now. I shouldn't like to know that they have. It would be better never to know that, miss.'

'Mary,' Anne had said, 'my sisters and I have all grieved the deaths of people we love most dearly, our mama and our two precious sisters, Elizabeth and Maria. I promise you that if by some chance I could open the door tomorrow and see any one of them standing there in the flesh, nothing would matter more than just being able to embrace them again and rejoice.'

Mary had been musing on this ever since, and Charlotte thought it likely she would wish most dearly to go home once she truly understood that she was free from enslavement and that fear was not her only companion now.

The most pressing issues for now, though, were finding Harry and securing the safety of the other child he had hidden away from Noose and the Red Monarch, and – at least in the instance of Harry – time was running out very fast.

'Lydia, you know Harry better than all of us. Where might he have hidden the child? Did he have any friends in London that were not associated with the theatre?'

Lydia shook her head, searching for any thought that might be useful, returning her gaze to Charlotte, disheartened.

'I'm afraid I knew hardly anything of Harry's life before Gretna Green,' Lydia admitted. 'Mama told me what a fool I had been to place my fortunes in the hands of a virtual stranger, but I never considered it a matter of import. I believed that our love would always be enough, and it is. Only now do I wish I had some more knowledge of his life before I set eyes on him in Scarborough.'

'I suppose it is possible that he sent her out of London,' Anne said at the mention of her favourite place in the world. 'Just as we were minded to do with Mary, until we heard of her family. Perhaps he might have dispatched the child to friends from his old company in Scarborough?'

Charlotte considered the possibility for a moment before dismissing it.

'I do not believe there was time to make such an arrangement,' Charlotte said. 'Not between Harry realising the jewel he was to receive was a human being, and Noose's men snatching him the following day. It would take finances, time and risk to dispatch the child on a train. Moreover, how could he be sure that she would arrive safely? It's unlikely that Harry would have been able to execute any such plan in the short time he had to conceal the child. I believe she must be in the city – somewhere nearby, more than likely.'

'Why, there *is* someone Harry knew from his schooldays – someone quite respectable now, who lives with his young wife near Fleet Street, on Bouverie Street, if I recall correctly,' Lydia said, sitting up at the thought. 'I had quite forgotten – we visited with them when we first came to London, before Harry realised he'd have to petition his father for help. A Mr and Mrs Murray – he is making his way in the world as a solicitor, and Mrs Murray was very kind to me when many would have treated me as a pariah.'

'Fleet Street,' Charlotte said, crossing to the window. 'And where is that, Lydia? Is it far?'

'I'm afraid to say that I hardly know,' Lydia confessed. 'Everywhere I have been has been on Harry's arm, and I paid no mind to street names or directions of travel, but I'm certain Kit will know.'

'I know the way, miss,' Mary said. 'T"isn't very far, and I should be happy to take you, if you don't mind me being a bit slow.'

'No, Mary,' Anne told her gently. 'You are in no state to go anywhere, and besides, you must stay out of sight for now. We don't want anyone to know that you are in our care until we can deliver you safely home to your parents.'

'Thank you, Mary, but Anne is right.' Charlotte smiled at the girl as she crossed to the window, looking out at the life that went on below as if nothing of any great import had happened, and as if it would go on tomorrow and day after day after that, because nothing in creation – not even a terrible crime – could stop the rise and fall of the sun. 'The city is large, but not so much larger than Brussels, where I wandered often by myself and came to no harm. Besides, it is a fine day, and I am in need of some air and exercise. If you will but give me the address, Lydia, I will call on the Murrays, and pray they have the child under their protection.'

'And we shall try and locate Harry once more,' Anne said, looking at Branwell. 'We know he is in The Rookery; it is just a matter of finding out where. Someone must be willing to talk.'

'There was the . . . night woman,' Charlotte said. 'We heard her talking to Mr Skeet. I believe she thought that what had happened to Harry was a shame, and wrong. I suppose she might be persuaded to discreetly divulge what she knows, if we can find her again.'

'There will be eyes on you at all times, though, miss,' Mary said anxiously. 'If Noose knows you are looking for him or his, he'd have a swarm of spies on you, ready to cut you down if you got too close. On my life, miss. I know I have been out of my mind, but it comes back to me now, piece by piece. And I am certain that way is too dangerous.'

'Every way is too dangerous,' Anne said in frustration. 'It seems to me if we are to defeat this evil, that we must accept that danger is our lot.'

'No,' Charlotte said. 'Not if it can be avoided, Anne. Imagine how Papa would feel if any one of us was struck down here, hundreds of miles from where we are supposed to be? There must be a safer way – a way conceived by minds that are far more imaginative and inventive than those of Noose or Skeet or that banal devil the Red Monarch himself. We are clever enough to out-plot them all, if we try.'

'Mary,' Charlotte said, kneeling down at the feet of the girl. 'You must know the streets and houses in The Rookery well if Noose managed you?'

'Oh yes, miss, I lived there for some time – before I lost my bloom, that is. For a happy time, I worked as a maid for a couple who had a taproom. He was a hard, vicious man, but she treated me kindly enough, and it kept me from having to . . .' Mary's pleasure at the memory dimmed for a moment. 'That was a good summer, miss – decent work and a kindness here and there. I could have stayed like that for ever, and not have minded. But Noose said I had forgotten I belonged to him, and I was no use to him scrubbing floors, and he took me away from there. There is a back room at the inn, and he'd sometimes meet fellows there. I remember the missus saying that he moves around The Rookery all the time from house to house so that none is ever able to betray him while he sleeps.'

'What else do you know of his arrangements, then?' Anne asked her. 'Would you know of places he keeps prisoners, or enemies?'

'Not I,' Mary said. 'But my mistress might – she might have heard things. She told me more than once that folk talked as if she weren't there half the time. And I think she would be willing to tell, for she was very angry when Noose took me back to work on the street. She begged her husband to step in, but he refused and gave her a beating for asking. And that was that.'

'Then, Mary, you must tell us all you remember of this lady, and we shall do our best to find them, and attempt a discreet conversation,' Anne said, glancing up at Branwell. 'Do you remember, Branwell, when we disguised ourselves to pay a visit to Chester Grange?'

'I am hardly likely to forget it,' Branwell said with a smile. 'It was a most diverting caper.'

'I believe the time has come for us to strike such a ruse again. Perhaps Kit might help us with our costumes.'

'Then let us make haste and get to business,' Branwell said, rubbing his hands.

'Take care, my dears,' Charlotte said, suddenly rushing to her brother and sister to embrace them. 'I know what we do is right and necessary, but I could not live another day if I were to lose you.'

'That shall never come to pass,' Anne told her. 'We shall always be at your side, irritating your every thought always, I swear it.'

A shadow passed over the window, and Charlotte shuddered, as if someone had just walked over her grave, as Tabby would have put it – an unwelcome message delivered from an uncertain future. But the die was cast, the plan was set in action, and now they must bear up and stand strong to face whatever happened next.

TWENTY-SEVEN

Anne

Once they had established that old Roxby was not anywhere about in the theatre, Kit agreed to help Anne and Branwell get ready.

Together they had settled on the story of a brother and sister looking for cheap but temporary lodgings before beginning shop work on Regent Street; the kind of folk who might wander into The Rookery full of hope and be lucky to depart with a farthing to their names.

Anne accompanied Kit to one of the many compartments below the stage as she rummaged through a rail of dresses, at last settling upon a becoming pale green flower-print cotton day dress that suited Anne very much, bringing out the hazel in her eyes and showing off her creamy complexion.

'Are you quite well, Kit?' Anne asked as Kit held the dress up against her. 'You are awfully quiet and pale. I don't mean to pry, but I couldn't help but notice last night that Charlotte was worried about you.'

Kit dipped her head.

'My gentleman,' she said. 'The one I am obliged to endure to keep myself safe. He found me last night, when I was with Charlotte instead of him, as he wished. He showed Charlotte what kind of man he is, that's all. I didn't go with him, and I know I shall pay the price for my disobedience today.'

'What . . . what kind of price?' Anne asked hesitantly, not sure that she wanted to know but unable to turn away from the bleakest truth.

'He will hurt me for his pleasure,' Kit said matter-of-factly. 'But not where any injury can be seen on stage, and that is a mercy.' Kit saw the expression on Anne's face and hurried to her, taking her hands.

'Now don't fret my dear,' she said, kindly. 'I am used to this. It is the price I pay for freedom. A kind of freedom, at least.'

'Was the life you ran from so very bad?' Anne asked her.

'It was,' Kit said, closing the subject with a nod.

Then, sitting Anne before a mirror, she dressed her hair, and found a delicate straw bonnet to keep the sun from her face, completing the ensemble with white cotton gloves that buttoned at the wrist. The result was a neat, presentable young woman with high hopes for her future. Anne found her new appearance so convincing that she almost felt sorry for the poor girl, who was sure to have her dreams of a prosperous London life dashed at the hands of Noose and his Sharps.

'They will see us like rabbits wandering into their traps,' Anne muttered to Branwell as she tied the satin ribbon beneath her chin. 'Little knowing that we are rabbits with teeth and claws.'

'Don't all rabbits have teeth and claws?' Branwell questioned.

As for Branwell, the main part of his disguise was the removal of his eyeglasses and the darkening of his coppery hair with a deal of boot polish. Anne did have to admit that without the bright hair that was always aflame above his snowy brow, her brother did look quite a different man. His face had absorbed some colour from the sun, and he even held himself more erect and with more confidence. It was as if the simple alteration eased him in his own mind for a little while, providing a welcome break from the torture of his own existence.

'You are ready,' Kit said, pleased with her handiwork.

'Thank you, Kit.' Anne took her hand. 'You have helped us without hesitation from the moment we met. Perhaps when all this is settled, you will allow us to help you find a true kind of freedom.'

Kit returned Anne's warm smile.

'Return safely; if you are recognised, just be demure and come back to the theatre at once, do you promise?'

'Kit, a coach is waiting for you,' one of the dancers called to her. Kit's expression fell in an instant.

'We will,' Anne said, 'but I am certain we will not be recognised now.'

Kit nodded, but Anne could see the fear in her eyes, and for the first time she wondered if perhaps they should believe what everyone they had met had made clear in both word and deed: do not take on the Monarch and his men – not if you value your life.

A moment later and they were turned outside into the noise and bustle of Drury Lane. The day was still so young that it wasn't possible yet to feel the promise of the heat that shimmered over the steeples and spires of the city, as the streets were still swathed in the long shadows the great buildings cast, dark bars across the causeway.

Anne discovered that it was hard not to feel quite gay and in something of a holiday mood. The day was so fine, her dress was so pleasing, it made her wish that she and Branwell were simply visitors to the city, free to explore its pleasures and delights, rather than detectors who must cut their way through to its seedy underbelly and pick away at its scars. Indeed, Anne was forced to remind herself with every footstep of the gravity of their situation, and how vital it was that she should not fail in her mission today.

'Your new appearance suits you,' she said to Branwell, hoping that some conversation might alleviate the fear she felt growing within her as they drew close to the streets that heralded the entrance to The Rookery. 'Your step is lighter, somehow.'

'It is tempting,' Branwell said, his mind not entirely present. 'I will admit it.'

'What is, brother dear?' Anne asked him, perplexed. 'What is tempting?'

'To make another life for myself,' Branwell told her. 'To take another name and become another man – one who has not weighed himself down with so many mistakes and so much unhappiness as a certain Patrick Branwell Brontë.'

'Branwell!' For a moment Anne could only utter his name in shock. 'Your life is not so very terrible, is it? You have a family that loves you, and you could have your health, if you would only allow it to flourish.'

'I am glad of my family that loves me, despite all the unhappiness I have brought down upon their heads. And grateful that my sisters allow me to escort them on their detections from time to time,' Branwell said. 'But look at me, Anne, the only son of a man who made himself out of obscurity into someone educated, good and respected. What have I, who had every advantage that Papa did not, achieved with my life, other than wallowing in an ever-deepening pool of misery? So yes, the temptation to begin anew is very strong indeed.'

Anne was silent for a moment; it was hard to refute her brother's argument when he put it in those terms. His life had been a series of mistakes and missteps, there was no denying it. If only she could make him see that all he had to do was to decide to change his fortunes himself, and that then it would be so.

'I know that Mrs Robinson's refusal to see you has hit you hard, brother . . .' she began as they passed the last respectable house before the slums of The Rookery waited for them, like rotting teeth in a gaping maw.

'It has done more than that, Anne,' Branwell said unhappily. 'It's crushed every atom of hope out of my body. For as much as you all mock me and despair of me, you must understand that I *love* her. I love her and I always shall, no matter how she crushed my heart beneath her heel. It may transpire that she is not worthy of my love, but even if that is so, I shall still love her, for in that one thing I am consistent and steadfast. In never failing to love her I am successful, at least, even if it will be the death of me.'

'Then I cannot persuade you that now is the time to withdraw your love?' Anne asked him. 'To begin again with fresh impetus to make yourself a man worthy of your father's pride, and to place your heart more carefully in the arms of another who will love you in return?'

'It is impossible,' Branwell said.

'Today it seems impossible, Branwell,' Anne told him. 'I know a little of being separated forever from seeing the one person that you hoped for, however foolishly. And I also know that the impossible days do pass eventually, and that, unlikely as it seems, you can hope again for a little happiness in this life, if God is minded to grant it.'

Branwell smiled fondly at his sister, taking her hand and bringing it to his lips.

'You are the best of us, Anne,' he said, 'the truest reflection of our father. Charlotte, Emily and I try to remake ourselves in your mould, for there is none finer, but we will never be your equal.'

Anne could not contain her laugh.

'That our sisters would ever consider changing themselves, for one moment, is a thought that would make an excellent comedy at the theatre,' she cried cheerfully, touching her fingertips to Branwell's face for a moment. 'But you, my dear brother, you will have me at your side on this impossible day, and every impossible tomorrow that follows, until one day you wake to a new dawn and realise that your heart is mended.'

'And if it never mends?' Branwell asked her, as the grubby houses gathered round them in a tight, querying press.

'Then every day I shall feel your pain with you,' Anne promised him. 'I shall share the burden of it until the Lord comes to lift it from your arms.'

Anne looked up to catch a face at a window just as it darted out of sight. A group of ragged children had begun to follow at their heels, growing bigger with every narrow alley or decrepit doorway passed.

'And now to put aside our troubles and find The Three Pennies,' Anne said to her brother. 'For our work has begun.'

TWENTY-EIGHT

Emily

The tall house was just as Mary had described it.

Set back from the street, pressed between two large, grand, pale buildings, it skulked, wrapped in discretion and secrecy. Painted entirely black, including the windowpanes, it almost succeeded in the illusion of not being there at all. Indeed, since her arrival at the theatre, Emily had walked past it on more than one occasion without giving it a second glance. Lurking unseen in its own shadow, it reminded Emily of a ghoul, waiting to pounce on unwary souls that might stray within its grasp.

'This must go in a story,' Emily said, her eyes travelling upwards to the very top of the building, her expression one of admiration.

'Stand behind – I shall knock,' Louis said. 'There is a secret code.'

He rapped once and then twice in quick succession, and then once again. Emily raised a single eyebrow, but refrained from remarking that as secret codes go, it was hardly the most devious and impenetrable one she had ever encountered.

At length a slot opened in the doorway and a single eye took in first Louis and then Emily.

'Who?' a voice sounded.

'The lady is with me,' Louis said with a smirk. 'We require a . . . little . . . privacy.'

Emily heard bolts being drawn back behind the door, and it opened a crack. She made a move to venture in, but Louis stopped her.

'We wait for one minute before entering,' he said. 'To allow our host to withdraw, so their identity is also hidden.'

Emily wondered how one found out about all these rules in the first place, but kept her questions to herself for the sake of expediency.

Louis glanced at her anxiously. 'I would really rather you let me go in alone, Miss Brontë. Let me glean what information I can, while you wait outside. I have no wish for your fine mind to be tainted or brought down by anything unsavoury you might witness inside.'

'I shouldn't think there is anything more traumatising than watching Farmer Thwaite's prize bull procreating with a long-suffering heifer,' Emily said. 'And as I have witnessed such a thing, I should think I will manage to survive, somehow.'

'There are practices that you will not know of,' Louis cautioned her.

'Unlikely,' Emily assured him. 'Now, may we go in, as time is rather pressing and I don't have the will to reassure you further, except to say that I am very widely read.'

Louis relented at last and ushered her into the house before him.

The interior was no brighter or more festive than the outside.

Every surface Emily could see was swathed in shades of black paint, velvet or silks, as were all items of furniture and the carpets. Even the paintings on the walls had every face painted out with washes of grubby oils. For Emily it was not too much of a leap to imagine that they had entered the devil's London residence, especially when she thought of what young Mary must have gone through here. At first the idea of this place had seemed rather exciting, but it wasn't just secret lovers consummating their forbidden passions within this place. It was an executioner's block for victims too.

Catching her breath at the awful thought, Emily wondered if perhaps this was where the Monarch hid himself away – his very own lair?

A long, languorous moan came from what one might expect would be the parlour. Intrigued, Emily went to peer around the slightly open door, but Louis called her back to his side. He picked up a key from a black lacquered plate that stood on a table in the hallway.

'For our room,' he said, rather furtively, quite unable to look Emily in the eye. 'It is on the second floor.'

'Then let us make our way slowly upwards,' Emily said. 'Listen at every door for any snatches of conversation that might provide fruitful.'

However, there were no coherent or useful words to be gleaned from their eavesdropping, only here and there the kind of cry or shriek that made Emily wonder if Farmer Thwaite's prize bull was a tender lover after all. Within a few minutes, they arrived at 'their' room, as Louis had referred to it, and Emily felt an unexpected flutter of nerves in her chest. What nonsense, she cautioned herself sternly, pushing the sensation firmly away. This had nothing to do with him and her, and everything to do with detection.

Louis unlocked the door and opened it, for want of knowing what else to do. As he did, Emily went to the foot of the staircase that rose up to the next floor, looking upwards. There were two men stationed on the landing above theirs, well dressed in good-quality attire, unlike Noose and his men. On their shirt cuffs, just visible below the sleeves of their coats, she saw a flash of red against the white. Emily was all but certain that they were embroidered with the Monarch's crest. His men were here, and therefore could it be that the very fiend himself lay but a few feet away? Emily gazed up the staircase, wondering if the villain could really be within her reach at this very moment. Could their luck have turned at last?

'Emily.' Louis murmured her name, beckoning for her to join him in the room. Emily obeyed and found herself somewhat taken aback to be confronted by a large bed and nothing else within the apartment. Where did a person sit, she wondered?

'I cannot see what we can possibly gain from being in here,' Louis said restlessly, pacing over to the painted-out window, back towards Emily and immediately off towards the window, which he appeared to gaze out of, even if there was nothing to see. It was quite peculiar behaviour, Emily thought.

'Not very much,' Emily agreed. 'It is what is going on above our heads that requires further investigation. Whatever it is, if it requires two guards to stand sentinel, it must be a very secret business indeed.' She told him about the motifs she'd seen embroidered on their cuffs. 'Louis, I am quite sure the Red Monarch is in residence at this very moment!'

'He won't be here,' Louis dismissed her, with disappointing speed.

'How can you know that?' Emily asked him, narrowing her eyes.

'Because whoever he is, he will send others to do his grim work for him, I'm certain. All the whispers I hear about him, and all that you have heard yourself, tell us he is a man of great importance and wealth. He will hide in the full glare of society, supposing himself untouchable, while others sin at his command.'

'Yet we know he visits here,' Emily persisted. 'It was here that he interviewed poor Mary before dispatching her to . . .' Emily cut off the sentence, her expression of disgust finishing it for her.

'Yes,' Louis conceded.

'And those men are his – I am certain I spied his mark on their attire, Louis. They are protecting him even now, as we stand here conversing.'

'What do you propose?' Louis asked her. 'That we storm up there and engage them in a fight? For I left my sword at my apartment today.'

'I have mine, but on this occasion I mean something more subtle,' Emily said thoughtfully. 'You should create a diversion.'

'A diversion?' Louis asked her.

'Yes, a distraction,' Emily replied.

'I know what a diversion is, Emily,' he told her. 'I am just uncertain what you plan to do with one.'

'You create a fuss, call for help, do anything to get the two sentries to come to your aid, and while everyone is gathered around you, I shall flit upstairs and see what I can find out.'

Louis turned back to the window, as if he were gazing at the most fascinating and beautiful view, such was his concentration.

'I should think that any man who loved you would live a very short life,' he said, more to himself than Emily.

'Well, none does, thank goodness,' she said, batting the comment aside. 'And anyway, do you have a better plan?'

'It just so happens that I do,' Louis said. 'I suggest we take the servants' stairs.'

'Will we not meet servants?' Emily asked.

'There are none – too much risk of gossip. All who come here must do for themselves while they visit. Even the proprietor is never seen.'

'That plan is better than mine,' she admitted at last. 'Though substantially less exciting.'

'Leave your boots here,' Louis told her, nodding at her feet. 'The servants' stairs aren't carpeted, and you could hear those great, clumping things a mile off.'

'Very well,' Emily said, unoffended. 'However, my stockings are darned more than once at the toe and the heel, and quite unsightly. I am a parson's daughter and a Yorkshire lass, you see.'

'I shall not look at your feet,' Louis said, turning his gaze away from Emily as she unlaced her boots and left them at the end of the bed.

'I am ready,' Emily told him. Louis looked up then at her, and down at her boots, placed neatly side by side. A strange expression of deep discomfort passed over his face, before melting away into a smile.

Trying to understand Louis' expressions was a little like learning to read in German, Emily thought. His face was much harder to comprehend than any she had ever studied before. Yet, Emily discovered, with a peculiar kind of pain that was something like indigestion, she would like nothing better than to do so.

'Come on then, Miss Brontë,' Louis said. 'Let's go and get ourselves horribly murdered.'

It was quiet and bright on the servants' staircase, for there the walls were unpainted, and the windows still let in light.

Gathering up her skirts, Emily led the way up the stairs, taking great care with each step not to alert anyone to their presence. Once they had reached the next landing, she turned back to look at Louis, who nodded.

Ever so slowly, Emily opened the door that led to the forbidden landing – a crack that was just wide enough to afford her a view of the two gentlemen who stood there. One leant against the banisters, picking at his nails with a wicked-looking pocket knife. The other reposed against a wall, staring up listlessly at the ceiling.

'You must go down and execute your distraction,' Emily whispered to Louis. 'I can't hear or see anything from here. I need a moment to put my ear to the door.'

'I can't leave you up here alone and unprotected,' Louis whispered in return.

'I protect myself.' Emily pointed over his shoulder. 'Go down and act the drunk or something. I don't care what you do, but get those men away from this door so that I might learn something.'

'Very well.' Louis left without another word.

Emily was waiting in silence when she heard a sudden burst of drunken singing on the stairs below, and then the sound of Louis stumbling up the steps.

Opening the door a fraction, she saw first one man go down, then the other peering over the banister after him. Then there was a shout, some colourful language, and what sounded rather like two men tumbling down the steps. At last the other sentry went to his colleague's aid, and Emily darted out from her hiding place.

Only one door on the landing was closed – the one at the farthest end, the greatest distance from her escape route. Undeterred, Emily pressed her ear against the door and listened, and was rewarded instantly.

'Will it be done or not?' A gentleman, for it was a gentleman's intonation and arrogance, spoke. 'For if it is not, I will have your head served to me on a silver platter.'

'It will be done, sir, I swear it.' Emily recognised Noose's rough-toned voice, cowed by fear. 'Harry Roxby's a fool, but his friends care for him – or for his wife, at least. They don't doubt my word, sir, when I say I will dispatch him at midnight tonight if the jewel is not returned – and his missus soon after. I believe they will rectify the situation.'

'Three northern old maids,' the gentleman said. 'You truly believe that? I must say it seems like quite the gamble to put your own life in their hands, my man. Besides, they can hardly find what they don't know to look for. If you disappoint me . . .'

Emily heard a chair toppling, and envisaged the unknown person leaping to his feet in anger. Desperate to understand more, she crouched down, putting her eye to the keyhole. Thankfully, the key had been removed, affording her a glimpse of the interior.

This room was empty of a bed. Noose was seated in a chair opposite the keyhole, and the other man stood to the right, just out of Emily's eyeline.

'They know the jewel is a person, sir,' Noose said, sitting with his head bowed. 'They picked up one of the Clementines the other night and took her back with them. The girl was fit to die, but if they got to her before she gave up the ghost, she will have told them her sorry tale. And if they know that, they will find your missing prize.'

'One of my jewels has been taken in alive?' The gentleman, now certainly identified as the Red Monarch, roared at Noose, coming at him so ferociously that the great, hulking criminal flinched and cowered.

Still Emily could not see a face – only half a well-dressed torso looming over his underling.

'Yes, sir, they've kept her in the theatre.'

'Well, tell Roxby to dispatch her, then!' the Monarch roared. 'That little whore met me, knew me, saw my face. She could identify me if she breathes a moment longer! If I am unmasked, then it will not be I who suffers, sir. No, I will simply retire to the Continent and carry on from there until it is safe to return. It will be you who swings, sir – you and every one of those you run, and every house in that fetid kingdom of yours will be burned to the ground, whether it be occupied or not.'

'I have always kept you safe, sir,' Noose said stiffly, his voice bristling with hatred.

'So then have Roxby do away with her, and quickly.'

'Old Roxby is no killer, sir,' Noose said. 'He'll do what he's told, even stand by while we take his son, but I reckon he'd faint at the sight of blood.'

'Who, then?' the Monarch bellowed in Noose's face. Emily caught just a glimpse of a bearded chin.

'Parensell will do it,' Noose told the Monarch. 'I got him keeping an eye on the goings-on over there, and he's no stranger to drawing his blade when required.'

Emily stepped back in one sudden movement, an audible gasp escaping her mouth before she was able to clamp her hand over her mouth.

There was no time to think now. Shouts from below told her that Louis had been bundled into 'their' room, and the door slammed shut. The guards were returning.

Emily raced to the servants' staircase just as they returned to their post. She heard the door slam behind her as she ran down the steps to the landing below. Pressing herself against the wall, she froze as someone opened a door above her.

'Anything?' a voice asked from within.

'Nothing,' came the reply.

Emily sat down on the bottom step and buried her head in her hands, hot tears of hurt and anger staining her hands with shame.

Could it be true?

Yes, it was true. It came from Noose's own mouth, and he had no idea that she was standing on the other side of the door, no reason to lie.

Louis was a spy. Whether he had been from the moment Emily had met him didn't matter. He had been sent to unravel their plans and reveal their every move to the enemy, regardless of what harm it might bring them. Nothing they had done to evade the eyes of the Sharps mattered, not when Louis was reporting on them at every turn.

The realisation hurt more than Emily could fathom; it bored a wound into her breast and filled it with ice-cold misery and desolate rage.

Her friend, her conspirator and fellow adventurer. She blanked the unthinkable thought from her mind at once, and focused on the only fact that mattered.

Louis Parensell had betrayed her. He had betrayed them all. And if he could do that, what else could he do?

In her stockinged feet, her face set in stony contempt, Emily crept down the servants' staircase to the ground floor, and left the tall house without once looking back.

She would have vengeance.

TWENTY-NINE

Charlotte

The benefit of being small and of a less than impressive appearance was that Charlotte had been able to leave the theatre right under the noses of the spies that Noose kept posted on Drury Lane, and not one of them, not even that terror called Jack, gave her a second glance.

Departing alone, though undisguised and with no companion to offer protection, Charlotte was nevertheless the epitome of inconspicuousness. In her simple brown dress and matching bonnet, she hardly looked like an intrepid detector about to do battle, and it served her purpose well. Still, it vexed Charlotte a little more than she would like to admit. For all that she wished for her talents as an author and intelligent mind to be acknowledged, there was a sting to her intrinsic invisibility, no matter the benefits it afforded her.

The walk to Fleet Street had been a pleasantly uneventful one, taking less than a quarter of an hour, though thoughts circled continuously in her mind. Thoughts of Harry, that lost child, and of unhappy, trapped Kit repeated themselves over and over until they became a tangle of impossible problems. Charlotte feared that resolving all would be beyond her and her sisters. And yet, they could not fail; the consequences would be devasting. Somehow, they would prevail. They had to.

It took only a few moments more to find the entrance to the narrow passage that was Bouverie Street, where the lady and gentleman that Lydia spoke of lived. She could only hope that Emily, Anne and Branwell were faring as well with their employments. Charlotte came to a stop as she looked up at a board above a many-paned bay window and caught her breath.

'Bradbury and Evans, Printer and Publisher,' the sign read.

Bradbury and Evans, the most recent publisher of one Mr Charles Dickens.

For a long moment, Charlotte stared at the sign, her heart caught in a kind of wonder. For here was one address that she had only previously seen in her imagination, picturing herself sending a copy of her own manuscript to this building; and now here it was, made real in bricks and mortar.

Should she go in, she wondered, and inform them of her forthcoming submission?

If she had been Branwell in his glory days, she would have done so directly, and told them with the utmost assurance that she was in possession of a rare talent for the writing of novels, and they should at once offer to publish her works, sight unseen, if they didn't want to make a terrible mistake in passing up her brilliance. But Charlotte had never been like Branwell. Not even in her most determined and confident moments would she have found the courage to present herself so, and anyway, who would believe her? She did not look like a brilliant literary talent ready to be unleashed upon the world.

The home of the Murrays lay just another two doors down, in apartments on the second floor of a building. Charlotte allowed herself to linger for a moment more, wondering what it might be like to enter that building as one of its published authors. How glorious it would feel, and how satisfactory. And to be taken on by the very publisher that published Mr Charles Dickens, the toast of London and far beyond, would be an almost unimaginable pleasure.

The craving for such recognition pulled at a thread of longing that remained tightly knotted in Charlotte's heart, no matter how hard she tried to sever it.

Charlotte yearned for her name to be known, just as Mr Dickens's was. It was her guilty desire, more passionate than the one she had nursed for Monsieur Héger – and something she would never admit. Just to be published would be the most wonderful achievement for any person, but for Charlotte it was not enough.

Insignificant though she might look to passers-by, Charlotte Brontë knew that she would never be content until she had burned her name across the world, and perhaps not even then.

But where to begin, and how? All she could do was write – write as if she had the devil at her back, and never stop until she had breathed her last. But not today – today there were more pressing matters to be dealt with; lives were at stake, and dependent on Charlotte's actions.

Swallowing the bitter taste of her ambition for now, Charlotte made her way to the Murrays' apartment.

'Why yes,' Mrs Murray told her, as soon as she had been welcomed into their small but neatly appointed parlour. 'The Roxbys stayed with us for a short while. Mr Murray was rather concerned about the circumstances of their union – an elopement rarely ends well, he said. We are working hard to improve our circumstances, you see, but we let them rest here for a little while, so long as it would not undo all our hard work. I'm sorry if there has been yet more scandal, but I'm afraid my husband and I will be unable to help, Miss Brontë. We have our own reputations to think of.'

Despite her pre-emptive refusal of help, Mrs Murray was well mannered enough to send a maidservant to fetch some tea.

'That's Edith,' she told Charlotte. 'She's a dear, but I long for the day we can accommodate a proper cook. My dear

Ernest hopes to secure a junior partnership soon, so that we may rent an entire house and not just part of one. Now, is that not something to be proud of?'

'It certainly is,' Charlotte said politely, trying her best to discern if Mrs Murray might be keeping anything from her – like a hidden child, for example.

'So, what trouble are the runaways in now?' Mrs Murray asked, her expression all wide-eyed innocence.

'It's a delicate matter,' Charlotte said carefully. 'Mrs Roxby is confined due to the nature of her condition, and is weak with worry, as Mr Roxby has been missing these past six days.'

'Oh dear, has he abandoned her?' Mrs Murray said serenely, as the girl brought in a tray. 'Mr Murray will be very concerned to hear that. He said no good would come of their union. Lemon or milk?'

It seemed unlikely to Charlotte that the child was hidden within these rooms. Mrs Murray's tranquil expression showed no sign that anyone had called upon them in the dead of night, bundling a lost and frightened child into their friends' arms to protect against murderous thugs. The young lady was delightful to look at, with dark hair swept back from her porcelain skin and languid blue eyes that exactly matched the chiffon scarf in her hair; there was not the slightest suggestion that she was someone trying to keep a dangerous secret. However, as the lady poured her a much-longed-for cup of tea, Charlotte thought she ought to be direct, just on the off chance that Mrs Murray was an excellent liar after all.

'Mrs Murray, I am bound to ask as a matter of urgency,' Charlotte said, taking the tea gratefully. 'Mr Roxby didn't ask you to take care of a child on his behalf? It would have been a very grave matter, and he would have cautioned you and your husband not to reveal it to a soul on pain of death. If it were so, you could tell me, however, as my sisters and I are doing all we can to help Lydia at this terrible time.'

Mrs Murray blinked at her, apparently none the wiser.

'He most certainly did not,' she said, amused, as if the mere suggestion were a rather droll joke. 'Besides, we have only a few rooms in this apartment. We have nowhere to hide a child, or anyone else, for that matter.'

'Well, I shall trouble you no more,' Charlotte replied with a polite smile. The truth was she hadn't felt so at ease since they arrived in London as she did now, seated in a respectable parlour, drinking a decent cup of tea from a fine cup and saucer. It was only now that she realised how exhausted she was from lack of sleep, and how hunger gnawed at her bones. However, the clock on the mantel reminded her that she must return to the theatre, no matter how strong the temptation was to sit in the sunlit parlour and converse with the vacuous Mrs Murray about nothing at all. She could only hope that her sisters had fared better with their discoveries than she had.

It was as she emerged from the Murrays' home that Charlotte beheld a sight she could hardly believe at first, and it was not until she had blinked several times in rapid succession that she allowed herself to believe it was in fact a true vision and not a hallucination.

For, before her very eyes, she saw Mr Charles Dickens himself, exiting the publishers with a lady and a gentleman, looking very jovial and pleased with himself.

It was too much, and Charlotte entirely forgot herself.

'Mr Dickens!' she called out as she all but ran down the Murrays' steps and crossed the street towards him at a canter. 'Mr Dickens!'

Mr Dickens made a comically beleaguered face at his companions, before turning towards Charlotte with a look of admirable forbearance.

'Madam,' he greeted her with half a bow. 'Forgive me, I meet so many people, are we acquainted?'

'N-no, sir,' Charlotte admitted, suddenly conscious of her accent, and her worn attire. 'That is to say, not in person, sir, but I have read so many of your novels that I feel as if your voice is almost as familiar to me as my own.'

'Well, good lady, may I commend you on your excellent taste. Good day, madam.' Mr Dickens turned to go, but quite without knowing where such boldness came from, Charlotte found herself detaining him further by placing her hand rather insistently on his sleeve. The lady smiled with great amusement at Charlotte's forthrightness, and the other gentleman looked rather worried at her impertinence.

'Forgive me,' Charlotte faltered, but she could not let this moment pass by without speaking up, for what if it was this very moment that changed the course of their lives? 'My sisters and I have recently had our first volume of poetry published, by a small press, and it has been reviewed in *The Critic*, though I have yet to read the review because the wind snatched it away from me . . .' Charlotte was momentarily halted by the expression on Mr Dickens's face, but pressed on. 'And I am soon to have a novel ready to send out to publishers for their inspection. I wonder if you might have any wisdom you might share with me, sir? I should be so grateful to be guided by your advice.'

'My advice would be not to trouble yourself further with such aspirations, madam,' Mr Dickens told her. 'The world is already overrun with too many novelists. Why, it seems to me a thousand new serial volumes come out every week. A simple assessment of your person reveals to me that you do not have the stomach for it. A lady novelist, in particular, must be of independent means, provided for by either a husband or a fortune, and entirely robust in both appearance and spirit. I advise you to abandon your plan and marry. And if you cannot marry, teach. Both occupations would be far better for your health than wielding a pen.'

'Nonsense, Charles,' the woman at his side said. 'Why would you seek to discourage the young lady so?'

'Because I am tasked to speak the truth, Mrs Crowe,' Dickens said. 'Now, George Smith, are we to take tea following our meeting, as we discussed, or must we continue to linger in the street?'

'Tea at once, Mr Dickens,' the younger man said, smiling at Charlotte rather sorrowfully, which eased her indignation and shame a little and warmed her heart considerably, for it was a very kind smile.

'I shall not come with you,' Mrs Crowe said. 'I have had enough of gentlemen for today. I shall walk with our young friend here a while, and bestow upon her a better wisdom than you, Charles.'

Her comment was exactly what Charlotte should have longed to say if she had but the breath and courage. And yet it was delivered with such a pleasing, laughing countenance that it hardly seemed like an admonishment at all. The three parted ways with amiable joviality and Charlotte found herself alone with the lady.

'As Mr Dickens failed to introduce me, I shall have to do it myself,' she said. 'My name is Mrs Catherine Crowe, and I have been making my living from my pen alone for several years now.'

Catherine Crowe was a lady of middle age, comely, with dark hair and with an intelligent light in her eyes that added an air of fascination to everything she said and did.

'I know your work, of course,' Charlotte said, blushing. 'Why, you are better known even than Mr Dickens!'

'Indeed, and how it rankles him,' Mrs Crowe smiled. 'But when I began, I had nothing but my name, and my little son to feed. No husband to support me, no fortune to provide for me, and let me assure you that a little fear goes a long way to inspiring creativity.'

'Truly,' Charlotte agreed.

'Now, my dear,' she said, taking Charlotte's arm. 'Tell me your name.'

'Charlotte Brontë, and I am so very pleased to meet you, Mrs Crowe. I enjoyed your *Susan Hopley* very much, though I'm afraid I only recently read it. The thought of a young maid turning detector to solve a crime was a most novel one, and came to my attention soon after . . . well, soon after I had myself wondered what it would be like to investigate a mystery.'

'It was a novel idea, and a very good one,' Mrs Crowe agreed with admirable self-assurance. 'Though some of the critics insisted that any woman, never mind a low-born one, would never be able to do such a thing, and now all the critics speak of Poe's *Murders in the Rue Morgue* as the first of such fiction, though my novel was published months before his. Still, I'm sure history will record the facts accurately.'

'Your name will endure, I am certain.' Charlotte found herself suddenly bereft of all words and overcome with admiration.

'And you have a fancy to write too?' Mrs Crowe inclined her head as she spoke.

'More than a fancy,' Charlotte said quietly. 'A need so fierce it scorches my heart.'

'Then here is my advice to you, Miss Charlotte Brontë,' Mrs Crowe said. 'Never be told what you can and cannot do, even by my friend Mr Dickens. Never avoid writing on any subject for fear of propriety, and always, always make sure you get paid a fair and proper amount for everything you do. Your destiny is within your own hands and that of no other – do you hear me?'

'I do, thank you.' Charlotte managed a small smile. 'You have given me the courage to continue.'

'You don't need any courage from me, my dear,' Mrs Crowe said. 'I can see in your eyes that you have more than enough yourself. Here is my address in Edinburgh.' She handed Charlotte her calling card. 'I'm lodged for a few more days in London, at the Chapter Coffee House on Paternoster Row, should you have time to call on me before I leave. Please consider me your friend from this moment on.'

'I hardly know what to say,' Charlotte said, fighting back the threat of tears, partly at the kindness, and partly at the mention of an establishment she had visited in happier times, when she and Emily had been en route to Brussels.

'There is nothing to say, my dear,' Mrs Crowe said kindly. 'Now I must let you get about your day. I, for one, look forward to some peaceful hours ahead during which I might write uninterrupted by cockatoo-ing gentlemen. Good day, my dear.'

'Good day,' Charlotte smiled, 'and, Mrs Crowe?'

'Yes, my dear?' Mrs Crowe raised a dark eyebrow.

'I can assure you that women make excellent detectors. For we are discreet, mild in appearance, and so often readily discounted that we are hardly ever suspected, despite our strength and determination to resolve any wrongdoing.'

'It seems to me, my dear,' Mrs Crowe said, appraising Charlotte once more, 'that for anyone to discount you would be a grave error indeed.'

Anne

Branwell led the way into The Three Pennies taproom, guiding Anne to a rough-hewn corner table that was more of a turned-up crate, and two unstable three-legged stools in the corner, before he went to the long table where a tapped barrel of ale was situated, to enquire after refreshment.

'Bread and cheese with two mugs of ale will be brought by the good lady directly,' he told Anne as he sat down.

'Is that Moll, who Mary told us about?' Anne asked, and Branwell nodded in reply.

'I believe it is her we should attempt to question about Harry, as from what Mary told us, her husband does not seem an amiable man.'

'I agree,' Anne said, looking around her at the room. At barely midday it was now almost empty, save for a thin young girl who was sweeping old straw matting out into the street, and an older fellow who seemed to have fallen asleep with his nose in his ale. Anne would have feared he was dead, were it not for the rattling snore he emitted every half-minute or so. The place was well kept and clean if not neat, and evidently the persons running it had worked hard to make it a profitable establishment – quite an achievement in The Rookery, where any source of profit was hard to come by.

'New to round 'ere, are you?' the woman asked as she set down a plate of buttered bread and a small hunk of cheese on

233

the table. Anne thought she might be aged around thirty – her fair hair was free from streaks of grey, and her figure lithe and strong. Her face, though, was careworn: eyes circled in dark rings, cheeks hollowed out, and skin that particular shade of grey that seemed to come with city life and poverty.

'Yes, quite new,' Anne said with a smile. 'We've travelled far, and we were told we'd find cheap lodgings hereabouts until we are settled.'

'Cheap, certainly.' The woman looked over Anne, and then at Branwell, and seemed to come to a decision. Glancing over her shoulder, she bent closer to them and added in a lower tone, 'At least on the face of it, but mind you watch out for those who will rob you while you sleep. You look like decent folk; you'd do better to try anywhere but in The Rookery.'

'Oh goodness, thank you,' Anne said. 'It seems that my brother and I were given the wrong intelligence. You have saved us a great deal of trouble. Mrs—?'

'Moll,' the woman said, wiping her hands on her apron before shaking Anne's hand, and then Branwell's. 'Make no mistake, The Rookery is full of good, hard-working people, who labour every waking hour just to eat. And me and my Jack, we do better than most. It's not the good ones I'm warning you away from, but the men who control us all like their puppets, leaching every spare ha'penny we have out of us at every turn. If you can afford to stay out of The Rookery, you should, else you might never escape it.'

'Would these men be part of a gang called the Sharps?' Anne asked Moll. 'And their leader a man named Noose?'

'God in heaven,' Moll hissed, her eyes widening. 'How do you know that name?'

'You are a good and kind woman, Moll,' Anne said, glancing at Branwell. 'You deserve our honesty. Will you not sit with us for a moment?'

Frowning deeply, Moll went into the other room for a moment, and Anne heard her calling her husband's name with no reply. Returning, she drew a third stool up to the table.

'Be quick about it,' she said, her whole frame strung out with visible tension.

'We have a friend in common – a young girl you knew as Clementine . . .'

'Little Clem?' Moll's eyes at once filled with tears. 'She lives?'

'Yes, though she is very weak. Clem – Mary is her true name – told us you gave her a home, work and shelter for a few months, and that you might be able to help us in a related matter. In short, Moll, we are trying to end the tyranny that Noose has over you all, and that of his paymaster also.'

'I felt sure she'd be dead by now, the poor girl.' Moll held her apron to her mouth, doing her best to stem the flood of emotion that had come upon her. 'I found her sleeping in the street one night, as we were locking up. She were in a terrible state; had been so wrongly used. I persuaded Jack we needed to help, and she'd be cheap, and we took her in. All was well until Noose heard she was here. It ain't right what he did to her, forcing her to . . . I tried to stop it but . . . my husband said we didn't need any trouble.' Moll dropped her head. 'She was only a child.'

'She still is,' Anne said, covering Moll's hand. 'Moll, my brother and I are doing our best to help Clem, and another child just like her who is about to be sold into the same kind of servitude. We need your help.'

'If Jack knew I'd even spoken to you, he'd throttle me,' Moll said, shaking her head. 'Much as he loves me, and I love him, he'd kill me stone dead, and I can't say that I'd blame him.'

Anne bristled in her chair, to hear Moll speaking so casually about the risk to her life from her husband.

'There is never any reason for a man to lay a finger on his wife, Moll,' she said. 'Violence is never an expression of love.'

'Perhaps it ain't where you come from,' Moll told her. 'But he's been good to me, more than many men are to their women. He's a good man underneath it all. Or he used to be, anyway, and that's the man I love, even if I never see him these days.' She thought for a moment, gnawing at her lip. 'If I help you, I risk my life.'

'We don't need you to do anything,' Anne said. 'We just need a little intelligence, some information.'

Moll glanced around again, drawing her shawl around her shoulders, as if the warm day had just grown chill.

'You swear you will care for my Clem?'

'I swear it,' Anne told her.

'I will answer your question if I can,' Moll said, gesturing for Anne to be quick.

'We have a friend being held by Noose somewhere. He's being held because he hid the child that Noose plans to sell into servitude on behalf of the Red Monarch. If we don't return the child, he will be killed.'

Moll shuddered, and it was plain that it took every fibre of her will to remain seated on the stool and not flee at the mention of the Monarch.

'It is imperative we get to him before midnight tonight,' Anne went on, 'before Noose and his men cut his throat and put him in the Thames. If we can free him and locate the hidden girl, then we may be able to bring everything we have found to Bow Street, to the London detectives, and give them reason enough to defy the Monarch and clear The Rookery of his gang once and for all, and free all the decent people here, or else make their corruption evident to the world.'

'It can't be done.' Moll shook her head. 'Others have tried more than once, and any attempt ended in violence.'

'Moll, Clem told us that Noose would have meetings here from time to time, in your back room? If you are able to tell us where he might keep a prisoner, then everything else will be done by us. No one will ever know that you spoke to us. Is there a building or cellar you know of?'

'You're just a slip of a girl,' Moll said, looking first at Anne and then at Branwell. 'And he's not much more than a boy. This endeavour will kill you.'

'I am not afraid to die,' Anne said. 'Yet I hope very much not to – I would like to live a long and productive life – but if I must die in protecting a child from such unspeakable evil, then I will gladly go into battle ready to meet my Maker, as would my brother.' She glanced at Branwell. 'And besides, we are not alone. We have many allies.'

'There is a house,' Moll began, but before she could continue a huge shadow loomed over the table. Moll sprang up from her seat.

'Hello, my love,' she said, smiling broadly. 'I've just been directing these good people here to a place to stay for tonight. I said Esther's place was as good as any. What do you reckon?'

Moll's bright smile didn't waver an inch, and yet the fear shone out of her eyes and her body trembled.

'What's going on here?' her husband said, looking Branwell and Anne over. 'What you up to, Moll?'

'Nothing – I swear, Jack,' Moll said.

'Sir,' Branwell stood up and offered Jack his hand. 'My sister and I have arrived from the north, having recently secured positions nearby. We don't have much until we've been paid, and your wife was helping us find lodgings.'

It seemed Jack was more minded to accept Branwell's explanation than he had been his own wife's, even though they told the same tale.

'Well, you told them, ain't you?' He grabbed hold of Moll's arm and gave her a shove towards the back room. 'You ain't going to make us any money sitting around flapping your tongue, are you?'

'No, Jack.' Moll did her best to make herself as small as she could, scurrying for the other room. 'Sorry, love.'

'You're finished,' Jack said, picking up their untouched plate.

'I'm sorry, sir,' Anne half rose from the stool, holding his eye and taking the plate in her hand. 'But we have not, as you can clearly see.'

There was a moment of tension as Moll's husband debated whether to wrench the plate from her hand. Anne watched the calculated contempt in his pale eyes, saw the stiffening of his fingers around the pewter. Branwell stood up suddenly, and though he was no match for the other man in height or frame, he squared up to him with the bravery of David facing Goliath.

'Apologies,' Jack said, dropping the pewter platter on to the crate, so that half the bread slid on to the floor. 'My regulars will be in soon enough when their shift is over. I reckon you will want to be out of here by then.'

Anne waited for him to depart after Moll, certain that he'd be raining his anger down on his wife any moment.

'We can't just leave her here with him.' She turned to Branwell. 'We have to intervene – what happens to her now will be because of us.'

'We can't do any more, Anne,' Branwell said. 'It will be worse for Moll if we do.'

Enraged, Anne pushed herself up from her stool and flew out into the narrow street, her fists clenched in her skirts, her eyes tight shut, until she could eventually control her anger.

'Anne . . .' Branwell touched her arm as he came to her side. 'I've seen men like him a dozen times. There is no reason to his fury, nor rhyme to his violence. To attempt to intervene now would certainly cause Moll harm, and moreover distract us from our principal purpose, which is to find out where Harry is kept.'

Anne began walking on, unaware of where they were going, just certain that she could not be still for another minute.

'When Harry is saved,' Anne told her brother, 'and the children are safe, I will go to her because . . .'

Anne turned towards Branwell. 'I embarked on this detection so certain that we could change things for the better, Branwell, but how can we when there is so much that is wrong, and we have only one lifetime? There is too much – too much pain, too much cruelty. How can . . . how can it ever be healed?'

'I don't suppose it ever can,' Branwell said. 'Not entirely. But that you are willing to try is a kind of victory in itself. And your courage makes me a much braver man.'

Anne rested her forehead on his shoulder for a moment, drawing strength from his kindness. How good it felt to have her brother back for these few short days, even if she could not hope to keep him once the bottle got hold of him again.

'But what now, Branwell?' Anne looked around her. 'What hope do we have of finding Harry in time now?'

'Missus! Mister!' A child called out to them from the shadows of a narrow gap that ran between two buildings, not wide enough to be called an alley. Anne advanced a little further to see two wide eyes looming out of the gloom. It was Moll's servant girl.

'Missus says to tell you to look in the Dyott house,' the girl whispered, her eyes darting about right and left. 'No one goes in there, not for nothing. It's falling down and certainly full of ghosts, but Missus says that's all she can do for you, and not to bother her again.'

'Thank you.' Anne went to take the girl's hands, but she darted away like fry in dark waters, and was gone in an instant.

'We have something to go on,' she said, turning to Branwell. 'Hardly anything at all, but a little better than nothing. We must get back to the theatre and see what the others have learned.'

'But not the way we came in,' Branwell said, offering Anne his arm. 'We need to wander for a while, let it look to any casual passers-by that we are, indeed, seeking lodgings, until we can find a quiet way out that will not draw notice.'

'A sensible direction,' Anne said. 'And I pray that when we return this evening, we may be able to save Harry Roxby's life.'

'And I pray that we keep our own,' Branwell muttered.

Anne didn't reply to her brother, but his words struck home. For the first time since they had arrived in this huge, soul-devouring city, she felt the cold drench of fear in her veins.

Anne believed with all her heart that there was another, better place waiting for her when the time came. But she was not ready to die. She would never be ready to die until she had at least done enough to leave this world better than she had found it. And if this place was the measure of anything, she would need to live a thousand years to do so.

For now, all that Anne could do was pray to live through tonight, so that she might fight again tomorrow.

CHAPTER
THIRTY-ONE

Emily

The auditorium was quiet, at least, for a little while longer. Even during the few days that it had become her makeshift home, Emily had come to know its patterns, the hours when it would be busy and bustling with preparation and rehearsals, the times when the audience would trickle in, full of laughter and chatter, and when the roar of the crowds would raise the roof as they were swept up by the magnificent talent of arch betrayer – and now her sworn enemy – Louis Parensell.

The awful thing was that Emily had liked him so very much, in a way that she seldom liked anyone – even her sisters half the time, though she loved them fiercely. And she had trusted him, just as Keeper trusted her, without question or hesitation, because it had felt right. It had felt natural. For when they had met on that first day, it had felt as if somehow they had known each other long before they had ever met. Even now, knowing the truth, she could not bring herself to be afraid of him. She could not imagine him doing her harm; it seemed impossible.

Tears came into her eyes, and Emily banished them firmly, telling herself it was only because she missed her dog – the weight of his head in her lap and the print of his paw on her skirts – and no other reason.

All she needed was a minute or two to herself, sitting in the soft dark of this empty box until she found the courage to return to her sisters and reveal to them what she had discovered. Oh, how it galled her that Charlotte had been right to caution her. And how certain she was that her older sister would revel in reminding her of the moment she told them that it had been Louis who had been betraying all their secrets, and had been ordered to murder Mary.

'There you are!' Louis appeared on the stage, carrying her boots in one hand, as he peered up at where she was sitting. 'Why didn't you come and fetch me? I was sure you had been captured and minced into pies!'

'Were you indeed?' Emily said, reminding herself that this was a man who had been dispatched to murder a child and spy on her. And yet it was not fear that filled her breast, but pain. She wanted simply to get up and walk away, and let him slowly realise by himself that she had discovered his duplicity. However, she had only one pair of boots and she needed them.

'Wait there,' she told him, 'and I shall come down.'

Emily determined to use the few minutes that passed between her leaving the box and arriving at the stage to compose herself and gather her thoughts. The question was: should she reveal to Louis that she knew about his betrayal, or use her discovery to her advantage somehow?

Emily was not at all sure that she could dissemble so effectively. It was not in her nature to lie, to hide her true feelings, to wear more than one face. And yet she could not approach this unhappiness in the same way she would any other; she could neither meet it head on, like a charging goat, nor hide from it by burying her head in the sand. One way or another, it must be faced. But if she found a way to use Louis' betrayal to their advantage, then she need not tell Charlotte and Anne either, at least not until all was done and she could claim she had had the information since the outset, and worked a secret plan to aid their detection. How that would irritate her sister.

But how to engineer the right outcome?

In any event, after this whole affair was done, she would pack away her heart for good. For yes, though she would never admit it to another living soul, she ... she cared for Louis. From this moment on, she would nail up her heart in a wooden box, bury it deep and never risk such a painful blow again.

'Miss Brontë.' Louis was in the stalls, pacing as he waited for her. He greeted her with a relieved smile.

'Mr Parensell.' Emily made herself smile as she reached out for her boots, which he handed to her. Taking a seat on the wooden steps that led to the stage, she slid her sore, holed-stockinged feet into them and began to lace them.

'I was alone at the tall house for a further half an hour waiting for you before I began to wonder if you were captured or dead,' Louis laughed. 'That you managed such a feat without being detained is a truly impressive thing. But why didn't you come back to me? And your boots,' he added hastily.

'I did not like that place. I am a woman of good character and I feared if I stayed longer it would taint me with its lies,' Emily said. She had thought her voice light and teasing, but Louis' dark eyes narrowed a little at her tone; he frowned, detecting in her the very thing she was doing her best to hide.

'I thought you'd come for your boots,' he said gently. 'It is a very eccentric person who walks through the streets without them.'

Her boots secured, Emily stood up and took a few steps in them, like a child with a new pair of shoes, extending her toes before her to admire them.

'At home, when I'm alone on the moors, I like to strip off my boots and stockings and feel the warm rocks or the soft peat under my feet,' Emily said. 'I suppose I am eccentric. I suppose I am not a sophisticated person at all, Mr Parensell. I suppose I am just a simple country yokel, open to all kinds of exploitation that might amuse a more cosmopolitan man.'

'Emily, what did you hear inside that room?' Louis asked, his eyes clouding with shadows that made Emily reach for the sword in the folds of her skirt. For the first time, fear snaked its way through her veins, and yet she could not yield to it, she could not turn away from her anger.

'That Noose knew we had taken Mary, that he knew everything we had done thus far, which he relayed to the Monarch, who ordered that Mary should be killed at once before she became a threat to him.'

Louis dropped his gaze to the floor for a long moment, the muscles in his jaw tightening. When he looked again at Emily, his eyes were full of regret. Well, he was a fine actor, Emily reminded herself.

'Who did he say should carry out this deed?' he asked her softly.

'One of Noose's henchmen,' Emily replied coolly. 'A cold-hearted killer for hire, quite happy to shed blood for a fee, it seems. He hides his monstrous heart behind an exceptionally amiable front. I believe you might know him, Louis. After all, he greets you in the mirror every morning.'

The game was up.

'I see,' Louis said carefully. 'Please, Emily, let me explain . . .'

'There is nothing to explain, Louis,' Emily said. 'Except that I suppose I am obliged to take you prisoner, now, to prevent you from running to your master.'

'You do not need to take me prisoner,' Louis said. 'I am not serving Noose, or the Monarch, or any but *you*.'

'You expect me to believe that Noose and his master lied for the benefit of a woman they did not know was listening at their locked door?' Emily asked him. 'No wonder you were so keen to prevent me from going there. You must have known they were meeting at the very hour.'

'I did know,' Louis told her. 'And that was the reason I tried to stop you; but not because I feared for myself, but because I was afraid for you.'

'So, you concede that Noose did not lie,' Emily said, turning her face away from his, so that his sorrowful expression would not hinder her.

'No, he did not lie.' Louis ran his fingers though his hair, the dark curls falling over his eyes. 'I owe Noose a deal of money. After our first visit to The Rookery, he sent men to tell me the debt would be paid off if I kept my eye on you and your sisters. Needing a deferment, I agreed. But it was all an act, Emily. I have killed, in defence of my life – and it suits me to have Noose believe I am a violent man. But I would kill myself before I'd harm an innocent child. Can you not see that for yourself?'

Emily bit her lip. Despite the summer day burning outside, the theatre was dark and chill. Without its blazing gaslights it was a dead space, a mausoleum of artifice and forgotten dreams, populated only by shadows.

'You are an actor,' Emily said, meeting his eyes at last. 'I am not like you, Louis, I don't fall in love with every passing face, or gather friends as easily as one can the wild heather on the moor. For all I know, everything you say and do is a lie. Lies are your stock-in-trade, after all.'

'Emily, I am your true friend,' Louis said, taking a step towards her. 'I said "Yes" to Noose because I am a pragmatic man, and I wanted to live another week. But I knew even then, even before I really knew you, that I would never betray you to him. I have been planning to leave London now for a long time, saving my earnings to lay a foundation for a new life. I think I may have found a way to leave for good. I decided that once your matter was settled, it would be time to enact my plan. With the money I should have paid to Noose, I have purchased tickets on the next ship to New York, leaving tomorrow at dawn. There's a new and exciting life out there for anyone who wants it, opportunities to start again, to be the man I want to be – a good man. The man who only you believe could become a reality. Emily, if you only knew—'

'You told Noose we had Mary,' Emily cut him off. 'A good man would never have done that.'

'No,' Louis shook his head, 'that was not me. Noose has his eyes everywhere. It was not me, Emily. I have not given any information of any use to them. I am a fool; I am an impulsive man who rushes in at the first glimpse of—'

'A glimpse of what?' Emily asked him.

'A glimpse of what it means to know a soul that seems as if it could be half of your own . . . Emily, I . . .'

But before Louis could finish his sentence, his mouth fell open, and his eyes widened in terror as he gazed up at the stage.

'What?' Emily began to turn to follow his gaze, but Louis grabbed her by the shoulders to prevent her. Suddenly every shadow darkened, and the chill in the air grew bitter.

'Don't look,' Louis said, dragging his eyes from whatever was behind her and fixing them on her face. 'You mustn't look.'

'At what?' Emily asked, trying to shake his hands off her. But Louis would not release her, and when she saw the fear in his face, she understood why.

'The clown is here,' he whispered, his voice trembling. 'Grimaldi is on the stage and he points at me, Emily.'

At her back, Emily heard the dulled jingle of belled feet. A shadow lengthened until it fell over them both, engulfing them in black.

'All upon whom he looks die young,' Louis reminded her. 'Don't look at him, look just at me. Look only at me.'

Emily wrenched herself out of Louis' grip and spun around.

Just for a moment, for the briefest of seconds, she thought she caught a glimpse of something that should not be there: a blur of light in the velvet dark; a smear of jewelled colours; the flourish of a disembodied hand; an approximation of a face made gruesome by slashes of red and black around the eyes and mouth.

It was gone before she could truly be sure if it had been there in the first place.

The air in the theatre was as frozen as on a winter's day; so cold that she could make out her own breath. And the theatre was silent, every sound that usually whispered and creaked all around had quieted. It had become perfectly still, as silent as the grave.

'There was nothing there,' Emily said, despite the chill in her heart. 'You did not see a ghost, Louis. It is all part of your illusion, designed to try and divert attention from your true character. You will not die young.'

'Does your saying it make it so?' Louis asked her, falling down on to one of the benches, his face ashen. Forgetting their animosity for a second, Emily went to sit next to him. Taking his hand, she felt his pulse racing under her fingers, and saw his countenance drained of all colour, the terror that still inhabited his eyes. Louis was a good actor, but this was more than acting. He really believed he had seen the ghost of Grimaldi, and his fear touched her heart with an icy finger.

'I don't want to die, Emily,' he said.' I don't want to die before I have done enough good to balance the bad.'

'You won't,' Emily assured him. 'I have said it, and now it is so. You will live a long life, Louis. I feel it in my bones, and our housekeeper Tabby says I am half-fairy, so it must be true.'

'Then let me help you.' Louis turned back to her. 'Trust me again, as your true friend who would never harm you, I beg you, Emily.'

Emily withdrew her hand from his.

'I cannot trust you, Louis,' she said. 'My sisters will already think me the fool. As much as I wish I could believe you, Louis, I cannot be a fool twice.'

'If you are to go back into The Rookery again,' Louis argued, 'or chasing after what the Monarch wants, then you will need a man who can fight, Emily – who can really fight.'

'Perhaps, but that man can no longer be you.' Emily got up to leave.

'Emily, wait.' Louis stood too, catching her fingers in his. 'What if I told you that I . . . that I have a deep regard for you, Emily Brontë? A fondness that has grown within me so rapidly. I had never known that a man could feel such tenderness towards a woman who has hardly given him any reason to hope she might feel the same.'

'I would say that you were trying to charm me as if I were any ordinary girl who would have her head turned by such prettiness,' Emily said, tugging her fingers free.

'Then what would you say if I told you that the two tickets I have bought to sail for America on the morning tide are for me and . . . one for you, Emily, if you'll have it? I know I am half mad to even think it; but yes, I bought one for you, in the hope that you might come with me.'

'Come with you to America?' Emily could not fathom what Louis meant. 'You are more than half mad, Louis. I liked you, yes, but I barely know you. There was something, for a moment. A might-have-been moment that almost happened. But now? Now, you are nothing to me and never will be again.'

Louis said nothing, turning his face from her.

'I always feared that I was a nothing man,' he said. 'And now I have my confirmation.'

Emily stood there for one moment longer, and then she fled.

THIRTY-TWO

Charlotte

'Are you quite well, Emily?' Charlotte asked her sister, who had been silent since she had returned a few minutes earlier, the last of their party to do so.

Emily was most definitely out of sorts. Her sister's complexion was livid, and her eyes hot and glassy. Her mouth, pressed firmly shut, seemed to forbid tears to fall through sheer force of will. Emily had not spoken a word since she entered, crossing directly to the window and looking out of it steadfastly, her clenched fist pressed to her cheek, as if admonishing herself.

'I am,' Emily said flatly, without turning her gaze to the room.

It was not unlike Emily to be so sullen and still, and yet Charlotte fancied this was not one of her usual moods, which worried her. It had always seemed to her that Emily was the strongest of them, the rock that could withstand millennia of cold winds without alteration. Charlotte could not bear to imagine what might have brought her sister so low.

'Well,' she said, sensing the more general air of despondency in the room. 'Our efforts have been successful to a certain degree, and we have garnered some vital intelligence. We know that the child that Harry has hidden is not at the Murrays', which, though frustrating, at least eliminates that possibility. And thanks to Anne and Branwell, we also know where Harry is almost certainly hidden. Emily, what did you discover?'

Emily sighed heavily, shifting her weight from one foot to the other.

'The Monarch uses the tall house for meetings, and, as luck would have it, he was there when I arrived.'

'Emily, how terrifying!' Anne exclaimed.

'I cannot bear to think what could have happened if he had discovered you,' Charlotte added. Was this why her sister was so silent and wary? *Did* something happen?

'He never knew I was there,' Emily said; all the flare and drama with which she usually flavoured her recounting was entirely absent. 'I was able to listen at his chamber door. I heard him talking to Noose, scolding the great beast as if he were a bad dog.' She nodded at Mary. 'They know we have Mary with us, and they want to come after her before she says too much. We need to take her to a place of safety as soon as we can think of one.'

'Will they come back?' Mary asked, her voice trembling as she reached out for Anne, who went at once to her side, taking her in her arms. 'Will they make me a ghost again? I don't want to be dead again, miss.'

'They will not, never fear,' Emily told Mary, making her tone as gentle as she could. 'But we must find a place to hide you where the Sharps will not look. For tonight we must attempt to liberate Mr Roxby, and we can't safely leave you or Lydia here without us to defend you.'

'Were you able to get any idea of the Monarch's identity?' Charlotte asked Emily.

'I'm afraid not,' Emily said. 'I peered in through the keyhole as I listened. I could tell that he was well-to-do, educated and of high social standing. He had very fine shoes, a well-tailored suit, and I caught a glimpse of a grey beard, which ages him above forty, I suppose. I believe he must wear a jewelled ring on his right hand, for after he struck Noose around the face, he left a bloody cut on his cheek.'

'Emily, you must have been in terrible danger!' Anne said, embracing her sister, who remained stiff in her arms.

'No more than you and Branwell, or Charlotte,' Emily said. 'All of us faced the risk of discovery today.'

'And what else did you find out, Emily?' Charlotte went to her, taking her chin between her thumb and forefinger and turning her face towards her so she could look into her eyes. 'What don't you want to tell us?'

Emily dropped her head for a moment, and Charlotte felt her tremble.

'Nothing,' she said, looking up at Charlotte, with a silent plea that begged not to be made to say more. Charlotte held Emily's gaze for a while longer, and saw in her eyes pain and confusion. She knew that look – she had seen it herself in her own reflection more than once, felt it threatening to burst open her heart as it beat beneath her ribs. Whatever Emily was hiding, and Charlotte knew she was hiding something, she trusted that it would not alter the course of their plans or put them in danger. Emily would talk when she was minded to, which Charlotte knew perfectly well might be never. But that was Emily – one could not hope to completely understand her, and yet she would always be loved just as she was, indeed because of it.

'Well, then.' Charlotte turned back to the small, dejected party. 'Now is the time to plan our next manoeuvres. We know where Harry is, this Dyott house in the centre of The Rookery. We cannot make an assault on this building until after dark, and even then . . .' Charlotte looked at Branwell, Anne and Emily in turn. Each of them was only half listening to her as they chased their own thoughts through another landscape entirely. It really would not do.

'We are a sorry party indeed,' Charlotte went on, clapping her hands twice as she would to garner the attention of wayward pupils. 'Three women and a gentleman who have never undertaken such a rescue before. We are almost certain to be captured and killed. And then Papa will receive the news that his children were not spending a pleasant few days by the sea as he believed. He will discover that we have been murdered in the depths of hell, for a secret purpose he never guessed at, and that every one of his children is a deceiver. And that is if our bodies are found and identified at all. It's just as likely we will be thrown in the river, and that he will live the rest of his days heartbroken and alone, never knowing what fate befell his children. And our book of poetry will be the last the world will ever know of our writing, if indeed it is known at all.'

Charlotte finished with a dramatic flourish that she felt sure was likely to rile at least one of them into action, but none of her siblings raised their heads in the fiery defiance she was expecting, not even Anne.

'Well, shall we go home then?' Charlotte asked them, 'and leave Lydia, Mary and Harry to their fates? Not to mention the poor unnamed child.'

'I'm sorry,' Anne said, burying her head in her hands. 'I am so very weary, and there is so very much wrong with this world, Charlotte – so many living in dreadful conditions, their lives hanging by a thread every single day. It wears me to the bone. Even if we liberate Harry and find the lost girl, even if we are able to take Mary home to her family, all the crimes that have been committed against them will still have been committed. And will be committed against others just like them tomorrow, and the day after and for all time. We four are not a great enough army to alter anything.'

'Do you truly believe that, Anne?' Charlotte asked her sister. 'You, our firebrand, our crusader? Are you so easily defeated by mere magnitude?'

'In this moment I am,' Anne said unhappily. 'In this minute, I want to go home to our house, our little parlour, our dear papa and Tabby's cooking, and never think of London again. What we face here is nothing like it was at Chester Grange or Top Withens; what we face here isn't one individual who is capable of evil, it is . . . every cog and wheel of society. What can we do against such a machine?'

'Everything,' Charlotte said firmly. 'I believe that with courage and determination we can do everything we put our minds to. Of course I am afraid too.' She looked around the room as she spoke. 'I am very afraid. I am afraid of walking into Noose's lair with my brother and sisters already defeated and too weak to face him.' Charlotte put her hand on her brother's shoulder. 'Branwell, can I count on you at least?'

'I will be at your side until the last,' Branwell said. 'I admit, I came here hoping to win the favour of Lydia's mother, but in truth I have begun to see that that was but a dream of mine, a dream that I must wake up from if I am to survive. Even so, I won't turn away from your side, Charlotte. My heart is broken, and my spirit all but crushed to dust, but I am ready for the fight tonight.' Branwell smiled up at her. 'You and I marshalling our troops, just as we used to as children; planning our campaigns and vanquishing our enemies. I always thought we'd be rather good at waging a war.'

Charlotte bent to kiss the top of her brother's head.

'But Branwell and I are not enough,' she said. 'Emily, will you be with us? And will Mr Parensell?'

'I will be with you and ready for whatever may come,' Emily said, pondering for a moment. 'I cannot speak for Mr Parensell.'

Emily's cheeks flushed scarlet as she spoke, but Charlotte pretended not to notice.

'I hope so,' Charlotte said. 'I have been against him, I know. But I do not relish the thought of such an enterprise without him. Branwell, will you fetch him now while there is still a little time before the curtain rises? We need his help to plan the rescue. Of course we cannot go into The Rookery before dark, so I would say we should set off after tonight's performance – which will give us an hour to retrieve Harry before Noose's threat is due to be executed.'

'At once,' Branwell said.

'Wait,' Emily put her hand on his arm, hesitating for a moment. 'I do not believe he is in the theatre.'

'Well, I shall look for him, just to be certain,' Branwell replied, frowning briefly at Emily. She merely turned her face away.

'Mary?' Charlotte went to the little girl, kneeling before her as she lay in Anne's arms on the battered old chaise. 'Tell me, my dear, what has Anne changed for you?'

'She's brought me back from the dead, miss,' Mary said, her solemn eyes huge. 'Miss Anne has changed my whole life, and now I only long to live it, so I can be good like her.'

Charlotte glanced at Anne before turning to Lydia.

'Lydia, what would you have done if Anne had not brought us to your aid these past few days since?'

'I rather think I would have died in this room, alone, and my child with me, or been forced on to the street if Noose didn't kill me first,' Lydia said. 'And that Harry would die alone, and never know our baby. And the child he has hidden? Well, God only knows what would have happened to her.'

Charlotte took Anne's hand and lifted it to her cheek.

'So, my darling Anne, do you really believe that nothing you do changes anything?' Charlotte asked. 'Anne, you change the world with your every thought and deed. By choosing the right path again and again. By putting your nib to paper and expressing your mind. You change the world because you are determined to, and it only takes one broken cog to bring the greatest machine to a halt. We are close to cracking that mechanism tonight, though there is much to do still. I beg you, my dear sweet girl, don't lose heart. For it is your heart that keeps us all strong.'

Charlotte cupped Anne's face in her hands, Anne covered them with her own.

'I will never give up,' Anne told her in a whisper. 'I will not quit this world until I see it remade in God's image, one smashed cog at a time.'

'Excellent,' Charlotte said. 'Then I believe we are ready.'

There came a muffled knock at the door.

'Branwell and Mr Parensell already?' Charlotte murmured warily.

'Wait,' Emily said, removing the pistol from her pocket. 'We know that Mary is a target for the Sharps. We must be prepared for an assault.' Positioning herself on the other side of the door, Emily held her gun upright, readied for a possible attack.

Anne crossed to Mary, shielding the girl as the knock came again, more insistently this time.

Glancing at Emily once more, Charlotte opened the door just a little.

'Miss Charlotte Brontë?' A pleasant-looking gentleman was peering at her through the crack. That he knew her name concerned Charlotte. Only her enemies knew she was here.

'Who are you?' she asked him, drawing herself as tall as she would go, which was to just below his shirt collar.

'Forgive me, my name is Ernest Murray.' He produced a calling card from his breast pocket. 'You called on my wife earlier today, asking after Harry Roxby?'

'Ernest?' Lydia leant forward to get a better look at the caller, as Charlotte opened the door a little wider. 'Yes, it is Ernest Murray. Let him in, Charlotte.'

'Mr Murray,' Charlotte said. 'Please, come in – our present abode is humble, but we are facing rather trying circumstances.'

Ernest took a sweep of the room's occupants as he entered, his eyes lingering for one moment on Mary. To any who had not seen her pitiful state only yesterday, her dreadful condition would seem quite shocking enough today.

'I will speak plainly,' Mr Murray said. 'My wife told you that we did not know of any child connected to Harry, but she was incorrect.'

'Indeed!' Charlotte said, dismayed at her failure to read Mrs Murray. 'I was so sure she spoke true!'

'And you were right, Miss Brontë,' Mr Murray said. 'My dear wife simply doesn't know how to keep anything to herself, which is why when Harry came to me with a child he said needed urgently hiding from a grave harm, I did not tell my wife.'

'So, you do have the child?' Anne asked.

'I don't,' Mr Murray said. 'I trusted Harry, believed him when he told me that the child was in danger and must be hidden until he was able to resolve the matter. I was able to take him to a place where I knew she would be safe.'

Just then Branwell and Mr Parensell returned, with Kit at their side. Charlotte noticed how Louis' eyes were fixed on her sister, and how he nodded to her as if thanking her the moment she deigned to look at him. Meanwhile Charlotte sent Kit a questioning look, attempting to ascertain if all was well with her, and Kit nodded and smiled. Charlotte would have to wait to reassure herself further.

'Where then?' Charlotte asked him urgently.

'She resides at St Patrick's Catholic Church, in the care of one of the sisters who attends there, just a few streets from here at Soho Square. I have done some work there, establishing the deeds of the church, and they trust me. There are a few tunnels under the church, a remnant from before the church was built, when the land was owned by a mistress of Casanova, would you believe? She had tunnels built from her house to . . .' Mr Murray seemed to realise that his pleasure in the history of the hiding place was not nearly as important as its location and switched course abruptly. 'Harry and I took her there the same night he called on us – the poor child was too afraid to speak, though appeared otherwise unharmed. Harry told me that once he had discovered a way to get out, he would remove her to safety, and as I hadn't heard from him any more, I believed the matter closed. That was until you came to call on us, Miss Brontë.'

'The matter is most definitely not closed, Mr Murray,' Charlotte said, 'but you have advanced our case a great deal, and we are grateful.' Charlotte looked thoughtfully at Lydia and Mary. 'I wonder if I might ask another favour of you? Might you take Lydia and Mary home with you until we can be certain of their safety? You are not known to our enemies, and if Lydia wears Emily's cloak, with Mary disguised as a boy, I am sure they will be quite safe. Perhaps you could tell Mrs Murray that she is Lydia's nephew, Clement? Clem for short?' Charlotte looked at Mary for her approval and received it in a broad grin.

'My wife will not approve,' Mr Murray said. 'But of course I will help, how could I not?'

'Here, Lydia should take my bonnet,' Kit said, removing the broad-brimmed straw hat. 'Paired with the cloak, she is likely to be mistaken for me, and it will shield her face from view.'

'Thank you, Kit, and Mr Murray,' Charlotte said. 'For we must rescue Harry from a gang of thieves and find a way to unmask the evil creature who is stealing little girls away from their homes to be so ill-used. To know that Lydia and Mary are protected by a gentleman such as yourself means a great deal. I must warn you, though, there is some danger in help-ing us.'

'The risk in sheltering two ladies for a night cannot be that great,' he smiled, 'but you cannot mean to do this alone, Miss Brontë.' He looked around at the ragged and unlikely group of rescuers. 'From what little information Harry gave me, I know these men are dangerous.'

'You need not fear, Mr Murray,' said Charlotte, lifting her chin, 'for we are never alone when we have one another.'

THIRTY-THREE

Anne

'We have but a few hours until we can go to Harry,' Anne said, a little bereft after Mrs Murray had left with Lydia, her face hidden by the hooded cloak, and little Mary, who had been quite delighted with her boy's clothes and outsize cap, which she pulled down low over her eyes. 'I don't think I've ever looked so fine,' she had told Anne happily.

The three sisters and Kit had watched at the window as Mr Murray hailed a hansom cab, and bundled his precious cargo in, noting that the sentries posted around the theatre didn't pay them any mind. Anne sent a part of her heart along with little Mary, hoping that it would not be too long before she was able to see her again and take her home to her family at last.

'We should use the time wisely,' Anne continued. 'Soho Square is but a few streets from here. I propose we steal our way out of the theatre now, avoiding the attention of Noose's men somehow, and go to see the girl at the church. It's possible that since a few days have elapsed, she might be able to tell us something that will lead us to the Monarch, or at least enable us to contact her family, who must be worried to despair.'

'Kit and I must depart, however,' Louis said. 'If we are not below at the regular time, old Roxby will notice that we are gone.'

259

'However, I can go out to distract the Sharps that are keep-ing watch on the theatre.' Kit looked at a clock on the building across the road. 'If I go out there at a quarter past the hour, perhaps you can leave at the same time. It should help you get clear of their notice.'

'Thank you, Kit,' Anne said. 'And, Mr Parensell, will you accompany us tonight?'

'Indeed, I will meet you at the far corner of the garden tonight – at eleven, if that is agreeable, Miss Brontë.' He looked at Emily, who did not return his glance, though her complexion showed she was certainly aware of it.

'It is very agreeable,' Charlotte said, warmly, and Anne smiled her assent too.

They had ventured downstairs just as Mr Parensell had directed them to, and sure enough there was Kit in animated conversation with their enemies, allowing them a safe passage beyond their watch, and towards Soho Square.

St Patrick's Church was a fine Georgian building, designed with admirable economy to fit into the necessarily small space it occupied in an area crowded with older buildings. Its under-stated elegance appealed to the artist in Anne, though Catholicism held no fascination for her as it did for Charlotte from time to time. Anne felt it was a kind of worship that kept the ordinary soul at too great a distance from the God she loved, and filled that void with costume, symbolism and ritual. To her, that seemed to make a living, breathing belief become a magical, fantastical thing.

Yet St Patrick's modest, rather worn but imposing pres-ence, peering proudly over the square, offered her a good deal of comfort. Anne believed with all her heart that God was with her in step and breath, but there was more than a little relief in seeing the physical expression of sanctuary that the church offered, simply by standing there, its doors flung open.

The interior would have been very fine indeed, pillared and gilded with a majestic dome above the altar, and stained-glass windows of breathtaking quality. Time had taken its toll now, and in the gloom Anne could make out wide cracks in the plaster that shot heavenward from the foundations, and here and there stood an empty bucket, positioned strategically in readiness for rain.

Of course, she preferred her own church at home, with its clear glass windows and crooked spire. Even so, she was moved by the spectacle: scent and smoke of incense that hung in the air, the statues of Christ and the Virgin, and votive candles glittering in the cool shadows.

The four, not quite knowing what to do or how to behave in this unfamiliar terrain, advanced down the aisle to where a lone nun was leading a group of street children in the rosary.

Looking back at her brother and sisters, Anne, who seemed by mutual consent to have been chosen to speak to the sister, waited politely for her to finish her salutations.

The nun remained where she was for a full minute further, before crossing herself, kissing her crucifix, and sending the children to another sister who, she told the children, had a meal waiting for them.

Rising, she turned towards their party with an open smile. She was a lady of indeterminate age, but with an expression of such pleasant serenity that Anne envied her for a moment.

'Welcome to St Patrick's Church. I am Sister Justine Marie,' she said pleasantly. 'There is no more mass for another hour, but you may reflect and pray here; or, if you are here to take confession, I can fetch Father Thomas for you?'

'Thank you, we are not,' Anne said. 'We are here to pay a visit.'

'We don't generally receive callers!' Sister Justine Marie said with a smile. 'Except for those who have come to call upon the Lord. Tell me whom you hope to visit.'

'A friend of ours – a Mr Ernest Murray – brought a charge for your safe-keeping a few days since,' Anne ventured. 'A child, a girl of about ten, we believe. It must seem troubling that we don't know more about her, but we are the children of a parson, seeking to return the child to her family as soon as we can.'

Sister Justine Marie smiled broadly. 'Yes, but I'm afraid if it's little Eliza you have come to see, you've just missed her.'

'Eliza?' Charlotte asked. 'She told you her name then?'

'No, she was in a state of complete silence for all of her visit, but she ate on the second day, and would sleep as long as I stayed at her side. No, it was her father who told me her name. A very kindly gentleman, he came a few minutes before you, and so pleased to have his lost girl in his arms.'

'Her father?' Anne turned to Charlotte with a relieved smile. 'You were able to trace her father? That's wonderful. Did he give you an address where we might visit her?'

'Oh no, we didn't trace him,' Sister Justine Marie said. 'He found us somehow. In the joy of the reunion, I didn't think to ask how, except I thought that Mr Murray must have found him.' She smiled warmly as she recalled the event. 'He told us her name was Eliza and that he'd take her right home to her mother.'

'But how . . .' Anne bit her lip, a cold wash of dread drenching her all at once. 'How would her father know where to find her when Murray and Harry were the only ones who knew her location, and Mr Murray had only just thought to tell us?'

'He was so sweet to her,' Sister Justine Marie went on. 'Called her his precious little jewel.'

Anne closed her eyes in horror.

'Noose, or one of his men,' she said flatly. 'Somehow he found out where she was and came to claim her before we could. He's taken her; he'll take her right to the Monarch and deliver her into his very jaws.'

'Dear God – Louis,' Emily whispered, every speck of colour draining from her face in an instant. 'I will murder him.'

'What do you mean, Emily?' Charlotte asked. 'Emily?'

Emily turned on her heel and began marching out of the church, followed at pace by Charlotte. Anne remained, determined to gather all the information she could as she turned back to Sister Justine Marie.

'If you please, Sister, is there anything else you can tell us about the person claiming to be the girl's father? Anything at all that will enable us to follow her path somehow?'

'He was a working man, I thought, from his dress and manner,' Sister Justine Marie said. 'And he was gentle with the girl, who went to him without protest.'

'Was she pleased to see him?' Anne asked. 'Did she call him Father?'

'Not pleased, exactly . . .' Sister Justine Marie looked troubled. 'She was quiet and still, and clung on to me when I tried to pass her into his arms. But she eventually relented when I told her she need not stay in the church any more. I thought it was because of all she had been through – that the shock of it had rendered her mute and insensible.' Sister Justine Marie looked up at Anne. 'Oh dear, have I made a dreadful mistake?'

'No, Sister, the fault does not lie with you,' Anne said kindly. 'You are a good woman, who trusts in others to be like you. But is there anything else, anything at all? Did he say anything further to her, for example?'

The sister thought for a moment. 'I overheard him talk to her as they left, but I must have misheard because it was all so strange.'

'What do you think he said?'

'Well, he was talking to her like a mother to an infant, cooing and singsong. I thought I heard him say he would take her to see the shining crescent moon and then she'd be home for good with her family of . . .' Sister Justine Marie stopped abruptly. 'I thought it was rather strange when he said it, but you know how families have their little ways and sayings, things that sound odd to those outside their circles? And he was very glad to see her, so I didn't give it another thought until now . . .'

'What did he say, Sister?' Anne pressed her.

'He said he was taking her home to her family of little lost ghosts.'

THIRTY-FOUR

Emily

Emily paid no mind to where she was going as she flew out and away from the church, as fast as the whipping winds that tore the briar roses from the hedgerows at home, leaving their scattered petals to be squashed underfoot.

'Emily!' Charlotte called after her just as she marched across the pretty little garden that occupied the centre of Soho Square. 'Emily, please do desist. The hour grows late and we must not lose sight of Anne or Branwell!'

With a great force of will, Emily made herself stop in the middle of the oasis of green that offered at least some respite from the constant march of building after building, each one seemingly intent on hedging her in so that she would be trapped forever in this interminable maze of iniquity.

'What has vexed you so?' Charlotte asked, a little out of breath, when she caught up at last. 'I saw the shadow that fell over you after your return from the tall house, but had hoped it was a matter you had already dealt with, until now. Emily, I am your sister, tell me.'

Emily dug her heels into the soft grass to steady herself, and pulled up as much courage as she could muster to face Charlotte with the sickening truth.

'I did discover something else at the tall house,' she said, every word spoken costing her a heavy toll. 'I discovered that

Noose had employed Louis to spy on us, and he has been doing so almost from the first day.'

'Dear Lord!' Charlotte gasped. 'You knew this before he came to listen to our discoveries and plans this afternoon? Before we asked him to accompany us tonight?' Emily nodded. 'Why then, Noose knows everything, and we have nothing left at all to surprise him with. If we go to retrieve Harry, they will be ready and waiting for us. Emily, did he turn your head so far that you have lost all reason?'

The words mounted up at speed within Emily's breast – words that strove to explain how very sincere Louis had sounded when he swore to her that he would never betray her. The expression of hope and sorrow she had seen in his eyes when he begged her to trust him. And yet she knew that if she brought forth all those words to her sister, Charlotte would be incredulous at her foolishness. She knew it, because that is exactly how she would react if their situations were reversed; how she had reacted when Charlotte had tried to explain her feelings for Constantin Héger to her.

And so all Emily said was, 'It would seem so. But the next time I see him, I will kill him.'

'Who are you to kill?' Anne asked as she and Branwell hurried to their side from the church. Emily steeled herself for more remonstration, but Charlotte spoke first.

'Emily cleverly worked out that it is Mr Parensell who has betrayed us, and who must have told Noose the whereabouts of the girl,' Charlotte said. 'Only he could have relayed the information so swiftly, and it was he who delayed our departure to wait for Kit's "distraction" to enable him to send his intelligence.'

'Of course!' Anne said. 'That wretched man, he has made fools of us all. I suspected him at first, but let my concerns go. What very poor detectors we *all* were to take such a man at face value.'

Emily knew that everything Anne said was to ease her own sense of responsibility, but the kinder her sisters were to her over her failings, the more they drove home her mistake to its hilt and straight into her heart.

'It matters not,' she said, determined not to let her feelings sway her from their purpose. 'We run perilously short of time. Yes, thanks to Parensell, it is likely that Noose and his men will be expecting us, but we can still have the advantage of surprise if we arrive earlier than they expect us, as soon as it is dark, which should fall just before ten. That leaves us four hours to find the girl and save her from the Monarch. Anne, what did the sister tell you?'

Anne relayed the information at once, her sisters and brother huddled close to her in a tight-knit group. 'And he called the poor child his jewel. She must have been so afraid, and thought herself so friendless when the sister told her she must go.'

'Show her a "shining crescent moon" . . .' Branwell said, looking up. Though the sun had only just began to sink in the sky, a half-moon was visible in the faultless blue dome, rising just above the rooftops as if appearing through a curtain. 'There is no crescent moon tonight.'

'A crescent is not just the moon, though, is it?' Charlotte said eagerly. 'It must have another meaning here. Emily, what can you recall about the history and symbolism of crescents?'

'I am not to be asked,' Emily cautioned her sister, suddenly feeling that nothing she had once considered sane or logical could be a surety any more. 'We should not trust my guesses. What if we waste precious moments on a false presumption? What if we lose the child, lose Harry, because we have missed something in plain sight in our eagerness to proceed?'

The four fell silent as they considered this possibility.

'We know it is not the moon,' Anne said, gesturing at the sky. 'What other crescents could it be? A French pastry?'

'The white of a fingernail?' Branwell suggested.

'The symbol that represents silver in alchemy,' Emily added.

'And often found representing the Virgin Mary in Catholicism,' Charlotte said.

'In ancient times the crescent moon was a manifestation of the hunter goddess, Diana or Artemis,' Emily remembered, finding a salve from her hurt in the knowledge all her reading had protected her with.

'Emily,' Charlotte said, looking into her eyes. 'Your trust in your own judgement is shaken, but you must restore it at once. You alone of all of us have the greatest instinct for those invisible connections that bind a detection together. I trust you to know the best path to take.'

It was more than tempting to hide from the restorative cure that Charlotte was offering her, in no small part because it could just as likely prove deadly – and not just to her pride. But Emily refused to let Louis Parensell have her mind as well as her pride. She considered all that she knew.

'It's a street, of course it is,' Emily said as soon as the realisation came to her. 'They have crescent roads in Bradford, and we saw a crescent street from the train as we arrived into Euston Station, did we not? He could have been speaking of a crescent street, but which one . . .? Branwell – your map.'

'Yes, Emily, yes! Let us rationalise,' Charlotte went on, as Branwell brought out his map from his jacket, unfolding it. 'We know the Monarch is a man of social standing and wealth, therefore we could presume that if, indeed, he was referring to a crescent road that belonged to him, it could be named for him. And it would seem prudent, if not strictly methodical, to look for such a crescent in the vicinity of The Rookery. For that would allow the Monarch to carry out his awful dealings with Noose with ease and discretion.'

★   ★   ★

'All in all, the proposition of a street does seem to be the most logical path to pursue,' Emily said, feeling certain as soon as she had spoken that she was right.

'Very well,' Branwell said, hastily running his finger over the map that he spread out on the grass. 'There are only two such candidates that I can see surrounding The Rookery: Burton Crescent and Mornington Crescent. I can't see any other such streets, though the map is small and I may have missed one. Here, Anne – you check.'

'I believe he is right,' Anne said, after running her thumb over the map, scanning every square inch.

'But which one shall we go to?' Charlotte asked. 'We only have time to visit one.'

'Mornington Crescent,' Emily said at once, her eyes widening as she made the connection. 'The current Earl of Mornington, of course.'

'Of course?' Anne asked.

'Yes, I read about him in the gossips,' Emily said. 'They call him Wicked William. He is a cad, a philanderer, a gambler . . . a man of late middle age and fine tastes. In short, an excellent candidate for the Red Monarch.'

'It must be him,' Anne said. 'We are close – I can feel it!'

'Mornington Crescent is quite a walk from here,' Branwell said. 'I'd estimate half an hour from Tottenham Court Road.'

'Then we must invest in a cab,' Charlotte said as they turned to head northwards. 'Branwell, will you fetch one, please? At least from there we can go directly into The Rookery quite quickly.'

'Thank you,' Emily said quietly to Charlotte, as Anne went ahead with her brother to secure a horse-drawn cab. 'Thank you for not revealing to the others what a cursed fool I have been. For I cannot bear the thought of what the cost of my poor judgement might be.'

'There will be none,' Charlotte said, 'for we will correct it. And as for your judgement, Emily, you are but made of blood and flesh, and the best of us lose clarity when our hearts are the captains of our destiny.'

'I will never allow my heart a moment of freedom again,' Emily promised herself aloud. 'I will allow it only to be free in my mind and imagination, or at home roaming the hillsides, and there alone.'

'I hope that is not true, Emily,' Charlotte said, 'for I do believe that one heart joined to another in mutual love must be the greatest delight that any human can attain on this earth.'

'Not for me,' Emily said. 'Besides, I have been thinking of the crescent moon as the ancient symbol for the hunter goddesses.'

'Yes?' Charlotte asked her, as a growler cab pulled over to the kerb.

'The crescent belongs to *us*, Charlotte – to women who will hunt and fight and never be defeated. Let us go and reclaim our legacy and cut down any who try to prevent us.'

THIRTY-FIVE

Anne

Though the day was still warm, the shadows had lengthened and the afternoon light had taken on the distinctive golden hue of a fine summer's evening. It would have been almost pleasant, despite their situation, if they had not just endured a terrifying ten minutes of being jolted and tossed around in the elderly growler cab, which had never been designed for the speed that Emily insisted on from its driver with her constant hectoring. Though terrible danger was likely facing them imminently, Anne was nevertheless thoroughly glad to be out of the awful conveyance, her feet on stable ground again, privately swearing that she would walk everywhere from now on whilst they were still in this awful city.

As Branwell paid the driver to wait, in the event that they needed to make a swift departure, Anne wasn't sure if she hoped it would be required or not, so frayed were her nerves.

'There must be more than thirty houses here,' Emily said, standing at the apex of the crescent, looking first left, then right. The crescent was constructed of two quarter-circles of neat, terraced town houses, the lower parts painted white, the upper parts constructed of small dark bricks and embellished with wrought-iron balconies. Opposite, a semi-circle of a garden was all the greenery in sight.

As pretty as the houses were, Anne was sure that residences such as these wouldn't be the main residence for a man like the Red Monarch, whether he was the Earl of Mornington or not. No, if his lair was here, then this would be one of his many places of business, just as the Tall House was: a discreet abode in a quiet lane, where all manner of horrors could be executed without any fear of discovery – a network of oppression and evil.

'We should split into two parties,' Anne said. 'I shall go with you, Emily, and Charlotte with Branwell. Then one of each pair should have a weapon, if it is required.'

'But what are we to do – knock on every door and ask them if the resident kidnapper is at home?' Branwell asked.

Anne thought for a moment.

'Emily said that the men who worked for the Monarch at the Tall House had his mark embroidered on their cuffs, the same symbol that can be found in any corner where his evil is present. So, if he does have a lair here,' Anne said, 'it is likely that his symbol will be present somewhere, even if not in plain sight. We each take one side of the street, study every house closely and meet again in the middle to report what we have found – agreed?'

'Agreed,' said Charlotte and Branwell. Weighing up her sword and her gun, Emily handed the pistol to Branwell, and they parted.

'Why did you choose the sword?' Anne asked Emily.

'Because I need the practice,' she said. 'Besides, Branwell is such a terrible shot, think how much worse a swordsman he will be.'

Emily's anger was almost palpable, so Anne didn't question her any further. She only wondered why her sister needed to perfect her sword-wielding skills, and who she planned to fight. She could imagine, but thought it very much better not to ask.

Anne and Emily walked in silence, struggling between the urge to hurry and the need to take in every detail of each identical house, searching for that one mark that might single it out.

How strange it must be to live in such a place, Anne thought as they made their progress towards the end of the row. To live in a house exactly the same as your neighbour's, carrying out a life that must be all but identical too. It gave her a worrying sense of being imprisoned by respectability and aspiration, all portioned into a carefully designed grid. If all that a person could want is a neat life, in a neat house, in a neat city street, then what room could there be for imagination? For freedom and exploration and, most of all, what room could there be for change? Was it the will of humanity to resign itself to such sedentary limits? The very thought of such voluntary imprisonment, interred by contentment and blind to all the ills of the world, made Anne yearn to run, and not stop until she was at home and free once again.

And then she saw it. One of the half-moons of glass above a doorway had been altered slightly so that at its centre the panes formed a small but distinct butterfly. It was a detail that would hardly have been noticed, had one not been looking for it, but to Anne it stood out like a gate to hell.

'Emily,' Anne stopped her sister and nodded at the butterfly. 'Come, let us fetch the others.'

'No, there is no time to wait,' Emily said. 'I have my sword – let us go in now, Anne. For what if . . . what if something terrible happens while we fetch our brother and sister, and we are too late to stop the child being harmed? We go in and trust that they will find us soon enough.'

Anne looked into her sister's eyes and saw the fire that burned there. She had the good sense to know when Emily Brontë was not to be deterred, and when Emily was in such a mood, the best that could be hoped for was to temper her a little.

'There is no need for your sword just yet,' Anne said, pushing the weapon back into the folds of Emily's skirt. 'We shall knock on the door and try to gain entrance through the usual means. After all, there is the possibility that the resident of this house just enjoys butterflies.'

'Very well,' Emily said, with alarming compliance. 'Then you take the lead, little sister.'

Anne rang at the doorbell and they waited. Eventually a rather elderly butler opened it, but before Anne could open her mouth, Emily charged past him and up the stairs, her sabre rattling in her hand.

'What the devil . . .?' the old gentleman cried.

'I do beg your pardon,' Anne said to him, following her sister at a pace. 'I'm afraid my sister is really rather unconventional.'

Anne hitched up her skirts and raced up the stairs two at a time after her sister, who pushed open first one door and then another and then another, searching for the child. When she found none, she took another flight of stairs, repeating the exercise until she stopped on the threshold of the last room on this second floor and held the sword aloft.

'Let that child go this instant,' she said, with such furious menace that for a moment Anne felt terrified by her sister.

Arriving at Emily's shoulder, Anne saw a fair-haired girl of about ten dressed in white lace, sitting on the knee of an old man, his plump arms around her rigid body.

'Let her go, Mornington!' Emily demanded. Shocked, he complied at once. The girl, despite her terror, ran straight into Anne's arms.

'Don't be afraid,' Anne told the child. 'We have you now, and we will keep you safe.'

'Are you the earl?' Emily asked the abhorrent man. 'Otherwise known as the Red Monarch?'

'I . . . I don't know what you are talking about,' the man said, rising from his seat. 'I am a guest of the earl and that young lady is my niece.'

'You despicable coward,' Emily raised her blade, the man cowering under her wrath. It really was quite a sight to behold.

'Good Lord, what on earth is going on here?' A male voice spoke to them from the top of the stairs. 'How have these hoydens forced their way into my property and disturbed my guests, Berkley?'

'I'm terribly sorry, sir,' the old butler called from the bottom of the stairs. 'They overwhelmed me.'

'You are the earl,' Emily said, whirling round to face the new arrival. The man from whom she had taken the girl closed his bedroom door and turned the key firmly in the lock. 'You are the Red Monarch.'

'Oh, dear me, not me, young lady,' the gentleman replied, apparently amused – whether at the notion, or at the sight of a strange young woman brandishing a sword, it was hard to say. 'That is to say, I am the earl, but not the Monarch, although I am acquainted with him, of course.'

'What kind of man are you that would allow this to happen to a child under your roof?' Anne asked him, holding the girl tight to her side.

'I am the kind of man who knows not to question those more powerful than him,' the earl said. 'A man in debt, who cannot afford to anger his superiors; a man who does not blaspheme against his gods.'

'You are an earl!' Emily said.

'And the Red Monarch is king! He is a god!' the earl returned. 'There was a time he almost *was* our king, until that little bitch threw him aside. And if she can't keep him from doing as he wishes, then you, my strange little creatures, will be ground into the dirt by the heel of his boots if you insist on interfering in this matter any further.' He shook his head. 'Good God, what am I doing even conversing with the likes of you? Get out of my house now, or I shall have you removed to prison, and don't for one moment think that I can't or won't.'

'Tell us who he is,' Emily insisted, levelling the point of her sword at his throat.

'Tell me who you are,' he replied.

'We are the ones who will bring you down if you do not speak the Monarch's true name.'

'I would rather you took my head,' the earl said, eyeing her sword without much trepidation. 'If that ancient instrument could manage it.'

'Then stand aside and let us leave,' Anne told him.

'You had your chance to leave. Now I rather think that I will let the constable I have summoned detain you,' he said with a pleasant smile.

'The law would surely not stand by and see such evil done!' Anne said.

'Did you not listen to me, little girl?' the earl said. 'The Monarch is king, he *is* the law. Justice is done and undone on his say-so, and you two savages are nothing to a man like him. I'll give you one last chance: leave the girl and be gone before you are arrested.'

'Never,' Anne said, standing shoulder to shoulder with Emily.

'Step aside!' Branwell shouted from below, Papa's pistol levelled at the earl's head.

'There are more of you,' the earl said, turning to look down at Branwell and Charlotte at the bottom of the stairs. 'You are like a plague of rats. I rather think I won't, if you don't mind.'

'Run!' Emily shouted, as she shouldered into the earl at full pelt, knocking them both down the stairs in a tumble of knees and elbows, the blade clattering down ahead of their descent to the first landing.

Scooping the little girl up on to her hip, Anne ran as fast as she was able after them, as Branwell dragged his sister up from the floor, leaving the earl still sprawled, groaning and holding his head.

'You'll pay for this, you witch!' he howled. 'You've murdered me.'

'You'll live, unfortunately,' Emily said. 'Still, I'm sure the devil will be calling you home soon enough.'

And then they flew down the last flight of stairs, out of the terror of the house and into the serene evening, where all was peaceful and calm, not a trace remaining of what had just occurred within.

Bundling the child into the cab, Anne and Emily guarding her either side, Charlotte and Branwell sat opposite, the cab rattling along at the greatest speed its noble steed could muster, all but shaking their teeth loose in their heads. And as they flew along, with scarcely a moment to understand what had just happened, Anne realised that – no matter how respectable a row of identical houses might look – behind every façade there would always lurk the potential for horrors untold.

CHAPTER

THIRTY-SIX

Charlotte

Branwell asked the cabbie to let them out at the far side of Covent Garden. Branwell was first to exit, handing down first Anne, then Emily, and then he reached out for the girl, who cringed away from him, turning to fling her arms around Charlotte's neck, her small frame trembling against Charlotte.

Charlotte gestured for Branwell to stand back and then, with great difficulty, eased herself out of the carriage with the girl in her arms. Feeling exposed even here, Charlotte drew the child into the shadow of a narrow alleyway that ran down towards the river. The child trembled violently, her eyes huge with terror, her frame all but frozen, rigid with shock.

Kneeling in the alleyway so her eyes were level with the girl's, Charlotte searched her gaze for any sign that she could hear her.

'You are safe, now,' she said gently. 'No harm will come to you. I am Charlotte, these are my sisters Anne and Emily, who rescued you so magnificently. And that gentleman is my brother Branwell – he is very kind and good. Do you have a brother?'

The girl shook her head very slightly.

'Can you tell me your name?'

The child just stared back at her, unshed tears standing in her eyes.

'Do not fear,' Charlotte said, glancing at Anne. 'You are safe, we are fairies, come from the moors of the north to find you and return you home. You saw my sister with her sword, and my brother with his gun, and Anne who is armed with a mighty courage. And I, for though I am the smallest, I am the oldest, the queen of the fairies.'

'Like Titania?' the girl whispered, suddenly focusing on Charlotte's face.

'A little like her, but much, much kinder,' Charlotte assured her.

As she smiled at the girl, it was rather like watching her soul, her spirit, find its way back into her physical frame, returning each piece of it slowly to life.

'When you are ready, you can tell us your name, and your mama and papa's names, if you have them, and we shall take you home as soon as we can, but in the meantime you will have us to take care of and watch over you – do you understand?'

The girl nodded, taking Charlotte's hand, her grip so tight that Charlotte felt almost certain that she was not about to let it go.

'We have her – she is safe,' Charlotte said to the others, who had formed a barrier around them. 'And now we need to make our plans according to her needs.'

'We cannot take her to a constable,' Anne said. 'Not if the earl was speaking the truth when he said that the Monarch had control of the police.'

'And we cannot take her back to the theatre,' Emily said. 'Noose's men are stalking us there.'

'I think the only safe place to take her is to the Murrays',' Charlotte said. 'I am sure that Mrs Murray will be most confused by all the comings and goings, but Mr Murray is a man to be trusted. He will help us find Mary's family, and the child's. But if I travel there now, that leaves only you three to find Harry and free him from the Sharps. Will you manage it?'

'It will be difficult without your huge strength and stature amongst us, but I dare say we will manage,' Emily said, with such a faint echo of her old self that Charlotte could not be angry with her.

'Then go now,' Charlotte said. 'Go carefully, and don't delay. Hurry back to Fleet Street as quickly as you can, and then, my dear brother and sisters, home as soon as we are able.'

'The hour cannot come soon enough for me,' Emily said. 'I shall never set foot in this city ever again.'

Charlotte bid a farewell to her family, as if this might be the last time she saw them, and indeed that was a possibility, each of them knew. They held one another in turn, tightly if briefly, imparting a silent oath of love with every embrace, eyes meeting in affirmation of their loyalty to one another, and their determination to succeed.

Surveying the area until she had her bearings, Charlotte felt she could find her way to Fleet Street with relative ease, and so, with the child's hand still in hers, she set off, pausing to look back only once to see Branwell, Emily and Anne disappearing into the distance, and after one moment more, out of sight.

Please return them to me, she whispered in prayer. For I don't know how I should live without them.

THIRTY-SEVEN

Emily

The heat of the day had just begun to decline, the promise of the evening a cool, slippery silken shawl that draped itself over the shoulders of the city, when Emily, Anne and Branwell found their way back into The Rookery.

There was no time to fashion a disguise or to think of any pretext for the visit into the slum in a bid to evade Noose's sentries. Instead, Emily let her hair down so it curled darkly over her shoulders, Anne wrapped her shawl around her head, and Branwell, his hair still a shade darker from the boot polish, pulled his hat down low over his brows, throwing the bridge of his distinctive nose into shadow, and the three of them wove themselves silently into the steady stream of the silent weary returning to The Rookery after long hours of back-breaking work elsewhere in the city.

The Dyott house stood across the narrow road. The three of them regarded it from the shadows afforded them by the sinking sun. Mary had told them it had once been lived in by an evil old man who had made his living by sending the Irish back across the sea, deporting any who fell foul of the law; but it had been empty for the last thirty years at least, and it was all but fallen down.

'Before Murray took her, Mary told us that she heard stories about that place. That years ago, the last owner dug rooms underneath the house to make more rent, and the upper floors collapsed, killing a whole family. Now there is a certainty that it is haunted with vengeful ghosts, and that to step inside is an invitation to be cursed,' Anne recalled.

Emily thought of Louis' face when he told her he had seen the ghost of Grimaldi. That ghosts walked the earth was of no doubt, but could it be possible that the shadows of the dead could somehow exercise their will against the flesh of the living, harm or even kill them? As she stood there watching the old house, its caved-in windows regarding her with the same blank stare of the sockets of a skull, she felt it had to be true – that if a soul lived with enough misery, enough hate or enough love, they could force their spirit to spend an eternity screaming at the world of the living, never knowing if they were heard. The shadows must be full of the insanity of the dead, Emily thought – beings driven mad by eternity without resolution. It was surely safest to ask for nothing from anyone beyond your family in your mortal life, and then, when death came, you would be quite free from hurt and pain.

'If they are keeping Harry there, it will be in the subterranean rooms,' Anne said, interrupting her thoughts. 'Mary said she thought that the man who had those dug out was so keen on making more money that they went down not one floor, but two, and that is where Noose keeps his prisoners.'

'There doesn't seem to be a sentry on the door,' Branwell said, 'though of course they might be waiting in the rubble of the upper floor. Perhaps we should circle the building and discover the best way in.' Emily thought for a moment.

'Two of us must go in and one wait to see how we fare,' she said. 'I propose Branwell and I make the breach. Anne, you stay here and keep watch. If we do not return within twenty minutes, then go and find Charlotte.'

'You want me to wait while you risk your lives, Emily?' Anne challenged. 'Give me your sword, and you wait here.'

Emily shook her head.

'Anne, I don't say this because of who has a weapon. I don't say it because I wish to go into that house; for once in my life, I do not. I say it because Branwell and I have reasons to go in – reasons that you do not – and that makes us more effective.'

'We do?' Branwell asked his sister with a weak smile. 'Is there gin within?'

'Branwell wants to show Mrs Robinson that he is a man of strength and integrity, and besides, Harry knows him; he will see his face and know we are there to help him,' Emily said.

'Harry knows me also,' Anne said. 'We both met him in Scarborough. And you and I both know, Emily, that Mrs Robinson cares not a jot what kind of man Branwell is – she has forgotten him entirely.'

'Then Emily is right to choose me,' Branwell said. 'I have nothing to lose. Even my life is worthless now.'

'Branwell, your life is worth a thousand times the favour of one woman. No single human has the power to destroy another just by withdrawing their affection, not if you refuse to allow it.' Emily frowned at Anne. 'You are brave, and I have seen your right hook, Anne. But Branwell is at least a little practised with the pistol, and you are not at all. It may come down to that. And I know how to point a blade, at least, and am comfortable with the prospect if it is required. Your heart is much kinder than mine – even a moment's hesitation in the heat of battle could cost you your life.'

'Very well,' Anne said at length. 'And you?'

'I have to show Louis that you cannot betray a Brontë and live.'

'You cannot mean to try and kill him, Emily?' Anne said. 'My sister is not a murderer.'

'I am certain that every man and woman could be, if driven mad enough by another,' Emily said. 'But no, I do not mean to kill him. I merely need to . . . mean to show him that I am stronger without his friendship, and more dangerous.'

'Don't take risks,' Anne charged them both. 'Do your best not to be seen. Find Harry, release him, and leave. If you do not return by the end of the quarter-hour, I shall run down to Moll's and ask for her help; not that I expect there to be any forthcoming.'

'Why am I entirely sober in this moment of all moments?' Branwell demanded. 'For this terrible plan is certain to fail.'

'And yet, my dear brother,' Emily said, grasping the hilt of the scimitar in her hand. 'It is the only one we have.'

They chose to enter at the side, through a window where the sill had crumbled away, leaving an open wound gaping with shadows. What lay beyond was silent and still. Dreading every step, they made their first approach into what had once been the drawing room of a grand old house. Now the floorboards were half rotted away, and those that were left shifted loose and creaking on the boards that supported them. Staying close to the mould-covered walls, Emily led the way, edging around the old skirting, away from the doorway that had once led through to the main entrance hall and towards the next room at the back of the house.

As soon as they entered the second room, they lost all traces of daylight. Emily waited in silence until her eyes adjusted to the dark, and she could make out a dim rectangle of a covered window on the other side of the room and a splinter of light that denoted a door to her far right. It was impossible to know the quality of the flooring here, and so with equal parts trepidation and impatience, she began to feel her way along the edges of the room. Sometimes her foot would find a board to tread on, sometimes it would step into thin air and she would be obliged to silently right herself once again. It felt like an hour before they crept out of the room and into a debris-strewn hallway, where broken bits of furniture languished like the skeletons of an elephant's cemetery that Emily had read about once as a child.

The once-grand stairway ascended to the soft, blue sky, and all was perfectly silent. If Harry was here, he was being kept very quiet – either that or he was already dead.

Quiet as cats, they headed towards the back of the house, testing each step of their toes against the crunch of the detritus before they proceeded. After what seemed like an age they found a set of steps leading into a cellar. After three steps down there was nothing to be seen but the dark, and nothing to light their way. And yet they could not turn back.

Reaching for the wall, which was slick with damp, Emily began to feel her way down the stone steps, using her feet and fingers in place of her eyes, reassured by Branwell at her back, carefully following in her footsteps. Then there were barely any discernible markers to guide them, just a pool of nothingness, with the single feature of the dimmest of lights to alert them as to which direction to take.

They heard a cry, short and swiftly stopped, that came from somewhere below. Emily saw the briefest flicker of light, which for one moment illuminated another set of steps leading downwards, and then it was gone. Willing her pounding heart to slow she made towards it, not knowing if there would be sturdy wood to greet the soles of her feet, or only more of nothing. Their luck was in. Here the floor seemed solid, or at least repaired. At last a small rectangle of greyish light became discernible, and Emily was able to make out another short flight of steps that seemed to be made from clay. She could hear movement beneath her, and crouched down on her knees to try and gain some idea of what lay below. All she could see was a figure slumped against a wall, the light of a lantern turned down very low. It was Harry and judging by the sound of his breathing, he seemed to be sleeping.

Readying the sword, Emily edged down the stairs, ushering Branwell to go to Harry, who had been tied with thick rope to an iron pipe, while she fetched the lantern and carried it over to the prisoner, hoping that if he could see them clearly when he woke, he would rapidly understand that he was being rescued. For a brief moment she took in his swollen, broken face, so badly disfigured on one side that – even if he survived the next hour – she was certain he would never look the same as he once had. Bruises new and old extended below the neckline of his shirt, and by the look of his mangled hands, which lay palm up in his lap, his fingers had been broken.

Forcing every desperate emotion that threatened to over-whelm her down deep into the pit of her stomach, Emily steeled herself and looked at Branwell, who nodded. Placing her hand over Harry's mouth, Branwell shook him awake.

Harry's one good eye flew open in fear, the other was swollen shut.

Emily tried to quiet him, but all he did was shake his head frantically, panicking and struggling.

'Be quiet,' Emily hissed urgently. 'It's the Brontës – we are here to take you to Lydia.'

Suddenly the cellar filled with light, and Emily spun around to see three men emerge from the darkness where they must have been hiding all along. Two of them she knew: Noose and Louis. They had been lying in wait for them.

'I think it's a bit late for that, don't you, Miss Brontë,' Noose said, stepping forward. 'We had an agreement – the girl you took from Mornington Crescent in return for his life, but you have stolen the child. And now so many more people will have to die, starting with you and your brother.'

'Cut his ropes,' Emily told Branwell calmly, handing him her sword.

Standing up, she brushed the dust from her skirt, and sought out Louis' gaze for a moment. It surprised her that she felt not an atom of fear. It was as if they had stepped beyond fear, and that everything that came next was preordained one way or another, though she could not yet tell in whose favour.

'I knew you were a vile, violent man,' Emily told Noose, 'but I believed you when you told me you did not know what the jewel was. That you did not know it was a child you were stealing and selling. There is evil, and then there is you. You think yourself a noble kind of criminal, don't you, Mr Noose? But you are no better than the men who violate these children. You are not human at all.'

'I do what I must,' Noose told her. 'I take no pleasure in it. When you come from a living hell, as I did, Miss Brontë, you don't let it trouble your conscience. For no good man or woman came to rescue me when I was a boy, beaten and used. I had to claw my way up out of the dark, and I will not go back there, at least not while I breathe.'

'That may not be for very much longer,' Emily said.

Noose laughed again and shook his head.

'You are a rare bird, Miss Brontë,' Noose said, with warped appreciation. 'But now here we are, and I must kill you. The Monarch has a great hankering to feast his eyes on your corpses. He says if I bring enough dead Brontës, he will let me live.'

'Then tell me who he is,' Emily said. 'If we are about to die, give me his name so I might die with my curiosity satisfied, at least.'

'I cannot,' Noose said. 'I will not, for I am certain that – if it is within your power – you would come to this life from hell to make more of a nuisance of yourself.'

Emily turned back to Branwell, who had cut the last rope.

He nodded at Emily, handing her back the sword by the hilt, and taking the one-shot pistol from his pocket.

'I'm ready,' she said.

Everything that happened after that came at speed.

She heard the explosion of the pistol firing behind her; saw the swift flash of a knife slicing across a throat; glimpsed a gush of red that came forth in a violent, pulsing spout; and in an instant another muted struggle against the wall; the hammer-like action of several stabs to the gut. For a moment she did not understand what had happened, or even if she had witnessed her own death, and then she realised the truth of it.

Louis had killed two of Noose's men in under a half a minute, though Branwell's shot had missed Noose and lodged in Louis' right shoulder.

There was a brief, stunned pause, and then the eye of the storm passed, and they were swept up in the whirlwind of violence once again.

'Get Harry out!' Louis shouted to Emily, as he shouldered himself into Noose, knocking them both to the floor. The oil lamp toppled over, its flame leaping on to the floor and flickering up towards the beams that supported the ceiling.

'You have to take Harry, *now*,' Emily called urgently to her brother, as Louis and Noose fought, 'I can't carry his weight, but you can.'

'I won't leave you,' Branwell said. 'Emily, come now!'

'Just go!' Emily almost screamed at him, as she watched Noose and Louis tussle in the dirt, the room now a thousand times brighter as the fire took hold. Grabbing her blade, she waited for the moment when she would be able to swing cleanly at Noose without risking Louis. Then Noose's fist somehow came free and pounded down into Louis' head again and again as he found his knife with the other hand. The bigger man reared up, Emily saw a flash of steel bearing down on Louis, and then Noose collapsed on to him.

There was utter stillness, even in the midst of the flames.

A dark pool began to puddle outwards from the prone figures, creeping steadily towards the hems of her skirts.

Kneeling at Louis' side, she had to muster all the strength she possessed to push Noose's corpse away from Louis.

Gasping, she saw the hilt of a dagger buried in Louis' chest, a dark flower of blood blossoming over his shirt; a deep, bottomless wound at its centre.

'We must get you help,' Emily said. 'I shall fetch you help now.'

'There's no time,' Louis told her. 'Just go.'

'There is time,' Emily nodded. 'You will not die down here in the dark and dirt alone. I won't let you, for I said you would not.'

'It seems that I will,' Louis said, and pulled her bloodstained hand to his face, unfolding her clenched fingers and bringing her palm against his cheek. 'It seems that I will, Emily. There will be more men on the way before long; every second you stay beside me, you risk your life. You must go.'

'I will not leave you here to die,' Emily said, determined to refuse fate at every turn. 'We can find a surgeon – can you walk?'

'Emily, I cannot feel my legs,' Louis told her. 'There is no pain now, just the cold.' Somehow, he smiled. 'And with such a pretty fire burning, too.'

'I will not leave you,' Emily insisted. 'I cannot.'

'It doesn't matter now. You must go,' Louis said softly, 'or else I will have died for nothing. I long to see you in another life, Emily, but not until you have grown very old and very cross with all the world, do you hear me?'

'Louis ... I thought you had betrayed me ...' She wept silent tears at last as the fear and pain flooded outwards. 'Forgive me, I hated you.'

'There is nothing to forgive,' Louis told her. 'Do not weep, Emily. Just know, it wasn't me who gave the girl away. I think you know who it was now, and I beg you to forgive that person too. Fear can turn a soul against those they should love.'

'I will never forgive your death, Louis, not in a thousand years,' Emily swore. 'I will crush those who had a hand in it, depend on that.'

'No,' Louis barely shook his head. 'No, Emily, you will live and write and love and fight, but not for vengeance. Vengeance will only turn your soul to black. When I am gone, let me go and never think of me again: that is what you must do for me.'

'I will try,' Emily said. 'I will try for you.'

Emily bent her head over Louis', heard the name, and when he had spoken, she turned her face to his and kissed him briefly on his bloody lips.

'Emily,' he said, his voice no more than a whisper now. 'If life had been kinder to me, if there had been time enough, I would have wooed you until you fell in love with me, as I did with you from the first moment we spoke. And I *would* have been a good man for your sake.'

'You are a good man, Louis,' Emily said. 'You are for your own sake. When you come before God, he will see what you have done, he will know your heart and will take you into his arms and—'

'Could you have loved me, do you think?' Louis asked her. 'If we had had years and not days to know one another? Would you have loved me back?'

Emily felt his frozen fingers in her warm hand, and saw the shadows that crept around the edges of the fire, like scavengers waiting for their portion of the kill. The city that lived on above them was silent, and there was no one in the world to hear what she said next, except for her and a dying man. She would not lie to him.

'I could have, Louis,' she said. 'It is just as I lose you that I know that I do . . .'

He let out a long, rasping breath then and was still, his dark eyes becoming empty and dull in an instant. He was gone from this awful place.

Emily waited one moment more before letting go of his hand and, when she did, she realised he had given her a small square of tightly folded paper. Standing up, she slipped it into her pocket, straightened her shoulders, and left Louis in the cellar of a burning house, together with that corner of her soul where he would be kept secret for ever.

There was still work to do.

Anne

Anne came out of her hiding place and ran to Branwell as he struggled towards her, with the much taller Harry leaning heavily against him.

'Where's Emily?' she asked, as she inserted her shoulder under Harry, and together they limped back to the alleyway. They were unable to hide now, for more and more people were emerging from the buildings around them, attracted by the smoke that had begun to creep out of the ruin of the Dyott house.

'Fire!' someone shouted. 'Fetch your buckets, fetch water, we must not let it spread!'

'Emily!' Anne repeated frantically to Branwell. His face was as white as she had ever seen, and he seemed unable to speak. 'Dear God, is she killed?'

'No,' Branwell shook his head. 'At least, not when I left. Louis was there, he fought for us ... I don't know how it ended, but Emily wouldn't leave him.'

'Branwell, the building is on fire!' Anne shouted at him urgently. 'Emily is in there!'

Branwell could only stare at her. Leaving her brother and Harry, Anne raced towards the building, as groups of people began to form a chain, ferrying pails of water from a pump somewhere. The flames were just beginning to take hold of the ground floor, licking up the walls in delicate, deadly floral furls – a leaping, living entity.

'Don't go in there, miss!' a young man shouted, as Anne advanced to the door. Ignoring him, Anne clambered over the debris until she stood in the hallway.

'Emily!' she screamed. 'Emily, if you do not answer, I am coming down to find you.'

Anne drew one ragged, smoke-filled breath as Emily emerged into view, like a wraith who had clawed her way out of the earth to haunt the living. Her hair was tangled, her face marked with soot, her dress soaked in blood. Her expression, though, was blank with shock.

'I'm here,' she told Anne, emotionless, walking past her out into the street. Anne followed, half expecting her sister to faint dead away at any moment.

'Noose?' she asked.

'Dead,' Emily confirmed.

'Louis?' Anne knew the answer, but the look on Emily's face was unreadable, so she asked it anyway.

'Dead,' Emily said. She stopped walking and took in the scene as the people of The Rookery did their best to stop the fire from spreading and to save what little they had.

'Noose's men will be here all the sooner because of this. It doesn't matter that he is dead – there will be another all too willing to step into his shoes. You need to get Harry to safety now, as far away from here as you can.'

'We all do,' Anne said, troubled by Emily's failure to include herself in that plan. 'We all need to get away, though I'm not sure how we will move Harry. Look at him, Emily – it's likely that at least one of his ankles is broken. He cannot walk. I can't imagine where we will find sanctuary for him in time.'

'I know a place,' Moll spoke up. Anne had not registered her amongst the gathering crowd that circled round the Dyott house, which gave them some small shelter from scrutiny, at least for a few moments more.

'Moll, be careful,' Branwell said. 'We don't want to bring trouble to you.'

'You won't, not while he is saving all,' Moll assured them. 'He's never happier than when he can get them all to follow him – takes him back to his army days, I reckon. Besides, I know a place where you can take your friend – a house that we women use, and the men don't go near. For when we need assistance with . . .' She trailed off. 'There's a woman there, a midwife who knows something of doctoring too. She will be able to help with the pain, at least, and perhaps treat him some. And she will keep your secrets for a coin – she is very good at keeping secrets.'

Moll looked back at the line of people fighting the fire.

'You can hide there until I can get a cart to carry you off. I'll need money for that, though.'

'Moll, are you sure?' Anne asked her. 'I don't want you to pay a price for helping us.'

Moll glanced back at her husband, who was organising his neighbours very well in their endeavours, shouting and pointing and getting the blaze under control. It was clear he was well respected by the folk of The Rookery.

'I will pay a price no matter what I do,' Moll said. 'If I am silent and as still as a mouse, I pay a price. And you have saved my Clem. So, if I must pay, let it be for something worth my pain, at least. Come now, follow me. There's not much time.'

Just as they were about to depart, there was a clatter of hooves on the cobbles, and the imperious whinny of well-bred horses.

Anne stared, amazed, as a fine black carriage, its windows curtained by crêpe, and drawn by four black horses, stopped before the house. On the door of its carriage, the Monarch's insignia was painted.

'I don't understand,' Anne said, staring at the nightmarish spectacle.

'I do,' Emily said. 'Go with Moll and Branwell – get Harry out of here.'

'And what do you plan to do?' Anne asked Emily in alarm.

The door to the carriage opened, a set of steps swung down.

'I plan to take a ride in that carriage,' Emily said.

'Emily, you can't do this alone.' Anne grabbed her hand.

'I am not,' Emily said, with a smile. 'Once Harry is safe, you, Charlotte and Branwell will find me somehow, I have no doubt. And we will finish this together.'

Emily had vanished into the interior of the carriage before Anne could ask her how.

THIRTY-NINE

Charlotte

'Mr Murray,' Charlotte smiled, when the gentleman himself came to the front door. Her hands were on the shoulders of her small charge. 'I do beg your pardon, and I know we have asked so much of you already, but . . .'

It was only then that Charlotte took in the stricken expression on the face of Mr Murray, and saw how he could not meet her eye.

'What has happened, sir?' she asked.

'Soon after I arrived home with Lydia and Mary, men came,' he told her. 'They pushed their way into my home and took them both. They threatened to take my wife and kill me on the spot if I stood in their way. Miss Brontë, they wore the uniform of the police force. I . . . could not fight them. I'm sorry, I should never have become involved with this in the first place. I have my wife to take care of, my career . . . I'm sorry.'

He went to close his front door, but Charlotte prevented him from doing so with her foot, her face white and pinched with fear.

'Where did they take them?' she asked him steadily, careful to keep her contempt from her face, lest he decide to hide from her too. She knew she should not blame the gentleman – he loved his wife and treasured his life. And yet she did.

'I don't know, I didn't ask,' he said. 'Now if you will remove your foot from my door—'

'I will when you have given me some money, Mr Murray,' Charlotte said. 'Enough to acquire a hansom cab and keep it at my service, if you please. I anticipate that I will need to travel quickly if I am to attempt to save the lives of a pregnant woman and a child. Or will you refuse me even that help?'

Mr Murray swallowed hard as he turned his face from her, emptying a handful of coin he retrieved from his pocket into her palm.

'Good day, sir.' Charlotte removed her foot, the door slammed shut, and she heard it being bolted.

May God forgive me for my contempt, she prayed silently; not every soul can be made for battle. Putting the bitter thought behind her, her eyes raked the street as she searched for her next step. Then they alighted on the sign above the publishers, and she knew exactly what to do.

'Never fear,' Charlotte said to the child. 'I know just the person to help us. I met her on this very street. We shall go to Mrs Catherine Crowe.'

Fortunately the Chapter Coffee House where Mrs Crowe was lodging was only a ten-minute walk from their location, and in her urgent need Charlotte made the journey a little more quickly, the girl half flying, half trotting along at her side, her hand still fastened in Charlotte's as it had been since the moment they had left the Brontë siblings. As they walked, Charlotte fervently hoped that Mrs Crowe would be in residence at the coffee house, and not out and about in society.

Charlotte knew the establishment well – her father had stayed there as a youth, and they had passed through on their way to Brussels a few years earlier, their hearts alive with the thrill of widening their world. So, once she saw the attractive corner building, she could not help but break into a run, the little girl at her side.

Fortune was on their side, and Charlotte was able to locate Mrs Crowe at once, taking tea whilst attending to some correspondence. Without delay, Charlotte bypassed the young gentleman who was enquiring if she wished to be seated and went straight to Mrs Crowe's table.

'Mrs Crowe,' she said at once. 'There is no time to explain in detail, but I am in dire need of your help. The lives of my sisters and brother may depend on it.'

'Oh, my dear girl,' Mrs Crowe said, putting her pen down. 'Of course. I am at your service. Just tell me what you require.'

A moment later and the three of them were in the relative safety of Mrs Crowe's room, the child wrapped in a blanket and seated in the window with a drink of sweetened chocolate to sip from.

'I have a book here you may like,' Mrs Crowe told the girl, gently presenting her with a volume.

Tentatively, the child took the book, looking up at Mrs Crowe with her large, solemn eyes. What must be going through her mind? Charlotte worried. As a mother, Mrs Crowe was practised in soothing the child, and soon the little girl was absorbed in the pages of the book, and, Charlotte hoped, free from her troubles for a little while.

'Are you sure that all I can do to help you is to keep the child with me?' Mrs Crowe asked. It was the only question she had asked since Charlotte told her briefly that she had rescued the girl from abduction, but her sisters and brother were even now facing a deadly enemy and she was tasked with saving Lydia and Mary.

'I am putting you in danger as it is,' Charlotte whispered.

'My dear,' Mrs Crowe took her hand, tilting her head towards her. 'I don't generally make this known about myself, but I too am a detector of sorts . . .' She paused as if considering how to reveal what she meant. 'Let us just say that I am often privately engaged in the solving of more supernatural mysteries. I have faced death and danger and battled dark forces of evil more than once.'

'I would love nothing more than to have you at my side,' Charlotte said, without a moment's hesitation in accepting Mrs Crowe's revelation. 'But this dear child must be kept safe, and there is peril enough in asking you to do so. No, I need to find Lydia and Mary, and I'm afraid I must do it alone.' Charlotte shook at her desperate predicament. 'I have no idea where they would have been taken or where even to begin to look. What if I am too late?'

'Oh, well, I can help you with that at once,' Mrs Crowe said.

'How?' Charlotte asked her.

'Quite easily, if they are willing.' As she spoke, Mrs Crowe busied herself drawing the curtains around the child, who sat in the casement window, ensconcing her safely away from the business, and lighting a candle at her desk.

'I will ask the spirits,' Mrs Crowe went on, as if she were discussing dropping a postcard to a friend. 'We don't have enough time or enough people for a proper séance, I'm afraid, but I have a pencil and paper, so we will see if they will use my hand to write an answer. They see all, you know, and are often willing to help, if a cause is good and just and they are in a friendly mood.'

'Oh, but . . .' Charlotte simply didn't know how to respond to such an outlandish offer and so she said nothing. After all, few would ever believe her exploits and adventures, and as such she would never refute the possibility of anything without the evidence of her own eyes, particularly not when Mrs Crowe was being so trusting and kind. Besides, the whole thing would be over in a minute, and she could get back to searching for Lydia and Mary, and praying her siblings were having more success than her.

Catherine seated herself at the desk, her pencil poised over a fresh sheet of paper.

'Spirits, I beg your attention,' she called out, tilting her head back and closing her eyes. 'You have been with us as we talked of the matters that Miss Brontë has been battling against. Aid us, O spirits! Tell us where the lady Lydia Roxby and the child Mary are being held so that my friend Charlotte Brontë may free them from tyranny.'

The candle went out.

A moment later and Mrs Crowe had lit it again and pulled back the curtains to let in the summer evening, the girl still glued to her book, oblivious. She handed Charlotte the piece of paper which had several words scrawled across its creamy surface, in a steep, slanted hand that was nothing like the script that Charlotte had seen on Mrs Crowe's correspondence.

'Does it help?' Mrs Crowe asked.

Charlotte read the garbled messages.

'The devil's palace sits over Hades,' it read. 'Beware the heavenly, trust only in death.'

'Well?' Mrs Crowe asked, eagerly. 'They do often write very opaque messages, but I find given time, and a sort of loosening of thought, you can usually find meaning.'

Charlotte stared at the paper, willing its meaning to come into focus, or – at the very least – to spark some inspiration in her weary, terrified mind.

And then, she had it. Or part of it at least.

'Anne spoke of the arches underneath The Adelphi as a kind of hell,' Charlotte said, 'and she found the Monarch's mark there. But not painted or scratched on, carved into the fabric of the stone. That could be the devil's palace; yes, yes it could be!'

She grabbed Mrs Crowe's hands in her excitement.

'And the second part?' Mrs Crowe asked.

'I cannot fathom it,' Charlotte said, 'and for now I do not have time to try. I must go at once. Thank you, Mrs Crowe, thank you.'

'You will always have an ally in us,' Mrs Crowe said. 'Now, go and rescue your friend and the child. I'll be waiting for you here.'

FORTY

Emily

The moment she had stepped into the carriage, a soft black hood had been pulled over Emily's head – a blindfold that she accepted without a struggle. For it seemed to her that if the Monarch didn't want her to know where she was being taken, then there was some chance that he meant her to depart from the venue with breath in her body. In her hand she still held the square of folded paper that Louis had given her, with no idea what it contained, except that he must have thought it was the key to vanquishing the Monarch. Carefully she tucked it into her sleeve, certain to position it under the tight seams of her cuff, where it would not be lost.

Closing her eyes beneath the hood, she paid attention as best she could to every tilt, turn and rattle of the journey, pinching the back of her hand for every turn right, scratching her palm with a ragged nail for every turn left. Blindfolded or not she would find her way back from the Monarch the second she got the chance.

Thoughts of Louis, the look on his face, the touch of his cold hand in hers, the taste of blood on his lips, threatened to break her concentration every second. The simultaneous burning moment of knowing and losing love crowded around her heart so tightly that she thought it might stop beating, engulfed by anguish. Part of her would welcome the sudden escape from this pain, but not now. Emily could not die now, when there was still so much to be done. The astonishment and grief of her first and last love would have to wait for another time, another place – one that was very far away. One she might never come to find.

At length the carriage stopped, and Emily allowed herself to be handed out, stepping down into what she judged, by the echoing sound of the horses' hooves as the carriage drew away, to be a large, enclosed courtyard with tall buildings on all sides. Her elbow was taken and she was guided up first one set of steps, and then another sweeping staircase, which she could see, when she directed her gaze downwards, was made of white marble. Finally she was taken into an apartment – an excessively warm room, where she could hear the crackle of the fire despite the summer heat.

'Thank you, Skeet – continue with such efficiency and we shall do very well together,' a voice spoke; the same voice that had threatened Noose during their meeting in the Tall House.

This was it, then – she was to meet the Monarch. Emily was too exhausted, too angry and too hurt to be scared, but still she discovered that she was rather curious.

The hood was pulled from her head and, raising her hands to push her hair from her face, Emily saw she was in a richly appointed room, gold and velvet abounding. Then she met the gaze of the Red Monarch.

Not a half-man, half-beast then, as poor petrified Mary had remembered him. And not a monstrous fiend either, at least not in appearance. It was depressingly ever the case that when she came across evil, it was almost always utterly banal. This gentleman was no exception. He was a portly man of late middle age, complexion flushed by years of excess, hair greying and thinning. A man who might have been handsome once, but whose fleshy lids now hooded bloodshot eyes, filled with both cold contempt and a sense of superiority.

'I apologise for the blindfold,' the Monarch said. 'But I hope you will see the benefit of it in the long term.' He gestured at her bloody gown and hands. 'Miss Brontë, you have been in the wars. I must say you wear death very well.'

'Thank you, sir,' Emily said. 'Forgive me if I ask you why you have brought me here now. I did not know your identity. I still don't know it. You could be any one of a dozen overfed aristocrats, and I would not know which. What advantage can there be in your revealing yourself to me now?'

'All in good time, Miss Brontë,' he smiled. 'First, you might like to admire my stained-glass window,' and he gestured to a large glass panel set between two rooms. It contained, of course, a faithful rendition of a red monarch butterfly, executed with sublime artistry and craftsmanship, its large red wings more than six feet across, set in jewel-like glass flowers of blue and white. Here and there small panes of clear glass were set into the design, allowing an unimpeded view to the other side. At first Emily thought it must be an external window, but then she realised it could not be. The window had been set into a wall that divided them from another room.

'Feel free to examine it more closely,' the Monarch told her, gesturing towards the window. Doing her best not to look in the least bit interested, Emily went to the window, levelling her eyes to one of the clear pieces of glass. There she beheld a sight which made her blood run cold: Lydia, seated on a couch, her face rigid with fear, holding Mary in her arms. Both looked terrified beyond measure.

Emily resisted the urge to tap on the glass or to cry out, to let them know she was near. This was no time to show the Monarch anything beyond a placid countenance, for she sensed that he would derive enormous pleasure from witnessing distress or fear. No, she resolved, let his monstrous ego reveal what it would in his desperation to cow and terrorise her; she would hold her cards close until it came time to play them. Perhaps by then she might even know what they were.

'What do you propose to do?' she said calmly, turning back to the Monarch.

'Do you really not know who I am?' he asked her, the vain fool half enchanted, half infuriated by her ignorance.

'No, you are quite safe,' Emily said, as if she were rather bored.

'I am Sir John Conroy,' he told her with a half-bow. 'Delighted to make your acquaintance.' As he straightened, he searched her for some reaction to the name and found none.

'I wish I could say I felt the same,' Emily said. 'Sir, if you are to kill me, can we advance to that part? I find all this talk rather tiresome. My sisters would tell you I have never been one for small talk.'

'You are not familiar with the name?' he pressed. 'I was part of the Queen Mother's household for years. She was my . . . close confidante, and I hers. It was I, my judgement and decisions that all but raised Her Majesty, preparing her for the throne.'

'Oh yes,' Emily said. 'I do recall reading something about you now. Didn't Her Majesty exile you from court the moment she came of age, because she hated you and your devious manipulating and self-serving politicking so very much?'

'The little fool,' Conroy spat, throwing the glass he had been holding into the fire, so that the flames flared up as they met liquor.

'I had the throne in my grasp,' he went on, lost for a moment in his own bitter fury. 'I could have made this country great again, made it a force that would dominate the world – not let the complainers, the anti-slavers, the do-gooders and charitable fools corrupt us and drag us down to be a milksop nation of weaklings. But she, that foolish slip of a headstrong girl, would not let me lead her. Who was she to cast me out? The simpering little bitch!'

'Sir! You speak of our queen,' Emily said. 'Who was wise enough and clever enough to know that you would use your influence for your benefit only, and that this country would have been infected all the more quickly by your hate and greed.'

'The throne should have been mine,' Conroy roared, charging towards Emily, who did not flinch an inch as he blasted his foul breath into her face. 'It should have been mine, and she took it from me! Well, on that day I vowed to take my country back, one way or another, street by street, city by city, until at length I would have held all in my fist, one way or another.'

He held his clenched hand in front of Emily's face, spittle glistening in his beard.

'Marvellous,' Emily said. 'And how is that plan faring?'

'Very well, until you arrived,' Conroy told her, clearly deflated by her refusal to cry and beg for his mercy. 'Do you wish to know why I call myself the Red Monarch?'

'Not particularly,' Emily lied to annoy him. 'But I see that you are unlikely to refrain from telling me.'

'Here.' He picked up a wooden box from his desk, and delivered the small, glass-fronted case into her hands. Within, a red monarch butterfly had been preserved and pinned. Emily beheld the poor, tiny creature, the downy appearance of its body, the velvet splendour of its wings, the pin that secured it for eternity at the pleasure of man, and she felt the loss of its small soul, a life taken without thought, just as easily destroyed as the children sold to the highest bidder, or an actor who had burned to ashes in the cellar of a derelict house. She would have vengeance, for all of them.

'What a beautiful creature this would have been when it was living,' Emily said. 'Now I suppose it does make rather a pretty corpse. Does it symbolise your start as a murderer?'

'No, I had killed long before the title came to me.' Conroy waved the suggestion away. 'No, it marks the moment I knew that that brat at the palace would not be able to stop my rise.

I was at my desk one summer afternoon, just after that woman had banished me from court, when this butterfly flew into my apartment through the open window. At first I couldn't believe it. I have been a lepidopterist since boyhood, you see, so I knew that a red monarch is *never* seen in England – never! Of course I caught it and gassed it at once. And I discovered that the native people of America look upon this butterfly as a soul reborn – reborn to new purpose and destiny, again and again until it reaches perfection. And in that moment, I knew it was a message from God.'

'One might think it is not such a good idea to kill one's messages from God,' Emily said.

'He knew that I had been wronged,' Conroy told her. 'He knew that I had been wrenched from my true position behind the throne. And He sent me this butterfly, sent it a thousand miles away from its true migration to show me that whether the Queen says so or not, I was born to be a king. I was born to purify this foul world, purge it of the filth and deformity of the masses, who drag this country down under the weight of their *need*.'

'Oh, I see, so God instructed you to murder, and to steal children, only to sell them to . . .' Emily could not think of a word bad enough for the kind of men that would violate a child so. 'I beg your pardon, but it doesn't seem an awful lot like God. Perhaps more like the other one.'

'What can you know of God's plan?' Conroy told her. 'You whining radicals and reformers who want everyone to be sober and equal, you have no idea how the world works. Do you think God wants equality? Of course He doesn't. Where would He be in an equal world? Soon forgotten, and that's the truth.'

Emily yawned.

'I'm so sorry, but it's been a very long day. What do you want from me, Conroy?'

'Oh, it's quite simple, Miss Brontë,' he replied. 'I want you. Give yourself to me, and I will let Mrs Roxby and the brat go – neither of them is really equal to your value, it's true. But I will also let your siblings go free, and they will be able to live their lives without fear of my finding them one day. That seems like a fair bargain, does it not? Of course, I could just kill them all and take you, but I find I would prefer it if you gave yourself to me. Sacrifice tastes so very sweet to me.'

'What do you want me for?' Emily asked him. 'To kill me?'

Slowly Conroy's gaze travelled up from the hem of her skirts to meet her eyes.

'Eventually,' he said.

FORTY-ONE

Anne

Anne could only hope that they had made the right decisions when they left Harry in The Rookery with Moll. The moment the carriage had rolled off, with Emily in it, she had run after her brother and grabbed his arm.

'Moll, we have to go,' she told the woman. 'Keep safe – I'll send word to you as soon as I am able.'

There had not even been time to wait for Moll's consent, as she took Branwell's hand and raced him down a narrow, filth-sodden alleyway that ran parallel with the route taken by the carriage. Every few strides they would glimpse it passing at the end of a passageway, its speed slowed by the narrow streets, but as they began to leave the edges of The Rookery, it steadily began to pick up pace until they could no longer keep up with it.

'What now?' Anne asked her brother as the carriage rattled away.

'This way,' Branwell said, jerking Anne to her right, and taking her in completely the wrong direction.

'No, Branwell, we'll lose sight of it!' Anne protested, hardly able to catch her breath as her brother pulled her into another sprint.

'Not if it's heading where I think it is,' Branwell shouted back, letting go of her hand to increase his speed, so that Anne had to pick up her skirts to match his pace.

Gradually the streets became wider and cleaner, if no less busy. Anne had never apologised so much as she weaved and dodged in and out of the London crowds, and could only imagine how very unrespectable she looked, her long brown hair having come down entirely and now flying in the wind behind her. At last Branwell came to a skidding halt as the carriage hurtled by the corner on which they were standing.

'How did you know it would come this way?' Anne asked him, her cheeks pink with exertion, her hair damp with perspiration.

'Mary spoke of an opulent palace, and there were the marks of the butterfly carved into the stone in the columns,' Branwell said. 'It may not be his only home, but I'm certain that the Monarch is taking Emily to a house in the Adelphi. The road the carriage is taking bears out my theory. I am almost certain that I am correct, Anne. Will you chance it?'

Anne saw the light in her brother's eyes, and the colour in his face. And more than that, how very much he needed to be right about this, how he needed to prove his worth – not to them or to her or to any of them – but to himself. This was a matter of life and death – their sister's life and death. Branwell felt that just as keenly as she did, and he had, after all, pored over that map for hour after hour.

'There is no chance to take,' Anne said. 'I know you are right, Branwell. We must hurry.'

They arrived at the foot of the Adelphi, breathless and in disarray, but sure enough they saw the carriage leaving the grand arched entrance to the complex of grand town houses, empty of all occupants.

'How will we find a way in?' Anne whispered to Branwell. 'We can never gain entry for any legitimate reason – we both of us look quite mad. Perhaps we could force our way in. Did you retain Papa's pistol?'

Branwell patted his jacket and waistcoat.

'No, I must have lost it in the cellar,' he said. 'I fired it, in any case, and do not have any more shot or powder.'

'Fortunate that it was not Papa's favourite of the pair – I expect he will never notice,' Anne said, and found the thought oddly comforting, somehow, knowing that a few hundred miles away from here, life was carrying on as it always did. Papa would be working in his study, Tabby would be baking in the kitchen, tasking Martha with a hundred chores that the maid would undertake at a snail's pace. Anne could almost smell the bright Yorkshire air, and feel the cool west wind on her cheeks. Just knowing that home was still there gave her strength to carry on, though to what and where she was not exactly certain.

'Unarmed, and with not a friend in the world to help us, how are we to retrieve our sister, Branwell?' she demanded in despair.

'You may not have a friend to help you,' Charlotte said, climbing down from a hansom cab, 'but you have your older sister, Anne. And I am worth a hundred friends, am I not?'

There were a few moments of joy and relief as they embraced one another and hurriedly related what had happened during their separation.

'Louis is dead,' Charlotte shook her head. 'I can't quite believe it. He stood beside us, so full of life, only a few hours ago. I am sure now that it was not Louis who told Noose that we had Mary. He has shown us he was far too fine a man for that. Oh god, poor Emily. This will wound her very deep.'

Anne nodded in agreement.

'It was thanks to Branwell's cunning we followed the carriage here, but how on earth did you know to come here, Charlotte?'

'My friend Mrs Crowe,' Charlotte said, blinking rapidly. 'She is terribly well connected, it seems.'

'And now?' Anne asked. 'What are we to do now? We have lost all our weapons. How are we to storm this fortress?' She looked up at the formidable building.

'We have come this far without the aid of a weapon, have we not?' Charlotte said. 'Violence has never been our method; we fight with intellect and cunning. We shall make our plans as we advance, plot course while we travel, for sooner or later a resolution is bound to present itself. For now we have but one purpose: to stand beside our sister Emily and keep her safe. That is the first obstacle.'

Anne thought for a moment.

'Branwell, take us into the heart of the Adelphi. To a place where every house will be able to see us and hear us, if we make enough of a commotion.' Nodding, Branwell led them through an arched passageway into the central courtyard of the building. Anne went and stood in the middle of the rectangle.

'We are here for our sister Emily Brontë, held by the criminal the Red Monarch. Make yourself known!' she called out as loudly as she could. Charlotte and Branwell looked at one another, and when Anne went to repeat the demand, there were three voices ringing around the courtyard.

In less than a minute one of the doors opened, and a footman motioned them to be silent and then beckoned them to him.

Were they rescuers, or prey? Anne could not be certain, but she knew that to be either, they had to walk into the Monarch's lair, and face him, come what may.

CHAPTER

FORTY-TWO

Charlotte

When Charlotte saw Emily standing across the opulent room, it was all she could do not to run to her side, and she would have done so except that Emily subtly shook her head, warning her not to. From her look, Charlotte sensed that poise was all – they must not show the Monarch even a hint of fear. And yet, how she longed to go to Emily, who looked as if she had walked through the fires of hell to arrive at this moment. The sight of her, so bloody, ragged and pale, was more shocking than anything Charlotte had ever seen, and she could hardly bear it.

But her composure nearly failed her utterly when she realised she had met the Monarch before. For she was standing in the same room as 'Mr Smith', Kit's gentleman friend, though there was nothing gentlemanly about him. Kit had known of the Monarch, known his identity and plans all along.

Kit was their betrayer. God knows what threat was held over her if she did not comply, Charlotte told herself, for she could not believe that Kit would have wreaked so much havoc upon them for her own pleasure.

Emily stood erect, her chin held high, not a sign of the exhaustion and shock that must be coursing through her veins, and when she caught Charlotte's eyes, she smiled.

'How on earth did you find me?' the Monarch asked.

'Easily,' Charlotte told him, embellishing the truth a little. 'It seems your secret persona is unravelling as we speak. I

317

have heard your location mentioned in a coffee house as a matter of interest amongst respectable people. We have met before, sir, in the company of Kit Thornfield. Now, as your charade is nearly over, perhaps you'd like to avail me of your real name?'

The others exchanged dismayed glances at the revelation.

'Charlotte, Anne, Branwell,' Emily said, 'you won't recognise this gentleman, but he is the Red Monarch, otherwise known as Sir John Conroy.'

'Oh,' Charlotte said, taking her lead from Emily. 'I was rather hoping for a duke.'

'How dare you, madam!' Conroy said. 'Show me the respect that I am due – I'll thank you to remember that you are all my hostages now, and I will do with you as I please.'

'He is excessively fond of talking,' Emily told Charlotte, then turned to Conroy. 'Do you wish to tell them your secret plans at length once again, or can we advance to the crux of the matter?'

'I have already laid my offer on the table,' Conroy told Emily, 'just before these peculiar creatures arrived. It's just as well, too, as they are so unpleasant to look at, I might have them killed just to rid the world of their offensive appearances.'

'What is your offer?' Anne asked, who caught on to the need for a fearless demeanour at once. 'What will you give us to release you, Sir John?'

Conroy laughed out loud, a huge guffaw that made his belly tremble. Charlotte saw Emily directing her gaze to a huge glass butterfly set into a wall. Approaching it a little closer, she quickly made out Lydia and Mary in the next room. Now she knew where they were, it would ease their departure if it must come rapidly, which it certainly would, though the how of it still eluded her.

'Parensell's faked reports on your activities were all about Miss Emily Brontë, how fine she was, how strong and intelligent, how beautiful too. I thought at first what useless nonsense it was – nothing was ever vouchsafed to us that would help stop your meddling, so it was fortunate I had my pretty little plaything, the opera whore, to do my bidding too. Now I see why Parensell was quite smitten with you, Emily. He was filling his pages with love letters for you, and not one bit of useful intelligence. I honestly would never have guessed that the fop had it in him to actually feel anything. I do hope he didn't spoil you for me.'

'Sir, do not speak of my sister in that manner,' Branwell said. 'Your men might best me in a fight, but not before I have damaged you a deal.'

Conroy smirked at the threat as Charlotte moved away from the butterfly, searching every corner of the room for an escape route.

'I'm afraid there is no way out of this room save for the way you came in,' Conroy said, observing her, before continuing to taunt Emily. 'Yes, with Louis it was all "Emily this", and "Emily that", but I see now that you are all rather singular, are you not? If only I could keep you all pinned in place in a smart glass case. But I only keep one pet at a time and, once Kit is dispatched, knowing I have what Parensell could not will give me great pleasure, for he was a fool and a traitor.'

'I will not allow that to happen sir,' Charlotte said to him, surveying his magnificent desk of polished walnut, in the corner of which a small bronze of Aphrodite rising from the waves sat, next to a little porcelain doll dressed in white. A look out of the window behind the desk confirmed that they were on the second floor, with a sheer drop down to where the people of the Strand went about their usual business. Of course, Charlotte could not fathom how she would prevent it. All she did know was that none of her despair or fear must be seen by Conroy; for the moment he sensed any weakness, his game would be over and they would be finished.

Instead, turning back to the room, Charlotte assessed the position of her party. Branwell was nearest the door, Emily closest to Conroy, and Anne stood beside the great butterfly. How could she move these chess pieces to enable their escape? A dozen possibilities went through her mind in quick succession, each one ending in disaster.

'Anyway, I am a man of my word,' he went on. 'Emily will stay with me until I tire of her. You will take Lydia and the girl with you and go. If Harry Roxby is alive, you can take him too. And as long as no one ever speaks my name beyond this room, your sister will live.'

From her position at the window, Charlotte met Anne's eyes.

'Never,' Anne said at once, drawing the Monarch's attention. 'You will surrender to us. You will hand over Emily, Mrs Roxby, and Mary, and you will let us all go free without consequence.'

Conroy laughed again, this time finding his pocket handkerchief to wipe the tears of mirth from his eyes.

'And why exactly would I do that?' he asked.

They had come to the moment when they hoped that a solution would present itself, but Charlotte had no answer for the monarch.

However, it seemed that Emily did.

'Tell me, Conroy,' Emily said, retrieving a square of bloody paper from her cuff, and unfolding it. Charlotte watched as her sister scanned the piece of paper, and realised this was the first time she had seen its contents. She prayed to God there was something there to aid them. Whether there was or not, when Emily looked back up at her captor, it was as if she held all the cards in her hand. 'Were you a child when you injured your thumb so badly?'

'What are you talking about?' Conroy turned towards Emily, a quizzical expression on his face, and Charlotte had to admit she felt the same bewilderment.

'It must have been done a long time ago, and it must have hurt a great deal,' Emily said. 'How did you do it – peeling an apple, perhaps, or whittling wood? Maybe you were torturing a poor animal and your knife slipped.'

Charlotte shrugged slightly at Branwell, and glanced at Anne, unable to make out which direction Emily was leading them in, but trusting that Emily knew what she was doing.

'I have no idea what my thumb has to do with anything,' Conroy said, clasping his right hand around his left thumb as if it still hurt. 'But I was attempting to make a rabbit trap, if I recollect. I was sharpening spikes. Yes, it did hurt a great deal. Your concern is touching, but what has my thumb to do with this moment, Miss Brontë?'

'Because the cut left a deep scar in the thumb of your left hand,' Emily said. 'A unique, star-shaped scar. And here in my hand is a note that you sent to Noose commanding him to kill Harry and my brother, and to bring me to you. Signed here by the Red Monarch, and sealed with a stamp, do you see?'

'What does that matter?' Conroy said. 'Why should I be afraid of a childhood injury? It hardly matters to me if you have an order signed by a mysterious criminal. You will find nothing to tie that man to me.'

'Oh, but I will,' Emily said. 'In your eagerness to sanction murder, you used a little too much wax, and you left your thumbprint in it, sir, here, you see? A lovely clear thumbprint, and at its centre a star-shaped scar that will match yours exactly.'

Conroy narrowed his eyes. 'I can find you a dozen men with such a scar, and if I cannot, I will cut one into them myself.'

'Will all of them have a huge artwork of a butterfly installed in their homes that is a veritable signpost for the Red Monarch?' Emily asked. 'Or carvings of their secret sigil in the keystones of the arches directly beneath their homes? Really, sir, your ego will be your undoing.' Conroy began to speak but Emily spoke over him. 'Besides, there is more. In the theatre there is a safe full of receipts – false ones, I'm certain – that keep track of your dealings, money in, money out. Mr Roxby senior is your unwilling bookkeeper, is he not? Forced, under threat of ruin, to keep track of the corrupt fortune you are making on the back of other people's misery?'

Conroy said nothing, but his silence told Charlotte that Emily was right.

'Well, he may keep your books, but you seem to insist on writing every receipt yourself. The hand on those receipts matches the hand on this one exactly, Sir John. So really, the fact that you were in such a hurry to have my family killed that you used your family seal on this letter is almost incidental.'

Conroy lunged at Emily, who swiftly whipped the important piece of paper out of his reach, sidestepping him so that he tumbled into his own desk, and, winded, fell back on to the floor. Taking a paper knife from his desk, Emily stood over him, and the expression on her face showed Charlotte that her sister was as close to committing a mortal sin as she had ever been.

'So, you see,' Anne said, crossing to Emily's side and taking her sister's hand, and removing the paper knife from it, 'your offer doesn't meet our terms. As I said before, you will release Lydia, Mary and Kit to us at once. We will leave together tonight – and London, as soon as we are able – and in return you will never trouble us again.'

'I could call my men in here,' Conroy told her, as he clambered to his feet. 'There are ten just outside the door. I could have your evidence suppressed and all of you dead within the minute. So typical of modern women to think they are as clever as men, when in reality—'

He gave a strange sort of grunt, his eyes widened in surprise, and then Sir John Conroy crumpled softly to the floor.

Behind him, Kit Thornfield set the small bronze back down on the desk. At her back a secret servants' door, perfectly disguised as part of the wall, stood open.

'It was I,' Kit said, 'I who betrayed you to protect myself from death. But the moment it was done I knew I could not live with my weakness. I bribed the scullery maid, who hates him as much as any of us. Lydia and Mary are waiting in the corridor. Hurry, it won't be long before one of his men notices that he is no longer talking and comes in.'

'Well,' Charlotte said to Anne and Branwell. 'It appears that – on occasion – the use of a weapon is unavoidable after all.'

FORTY-THREE

Emily

Emily sat on the edge of Mrs Crowe's bed in her apartment at the Chapter Coffee House, dressed in one of the good lady's gowns. It was both too short and too broad for her, but at least it was clean of blood and soot, and in the hour that she had been left alone by their party to attend to her ablutions, she had crawled into the salve of solitude with weary gratitude. Warm water, fresh cotton and no other voices were all she allowed in those moments, for there was as yet no time or space to consider all that had happened. Emily thought perhaps there might never be.

Could it really have been but hours ago that she had held Louis' hand amid the fire that burnt around them, and said goodbye for ever? It seemed as if that had hardly happened in this life, let alone today. But she must not think of it now – she must push away all thoughts of him, bury them in the cold, hard ground under ten feet of never-melting snow. That was all she could do.

There was a gentle knock at the door and, after a while, Charlotte, Anne and Mrs Crowe entered.

'There you are,' Charlotte said gently, as if Emily might have been anywhere else. She sat next to her on the edge of the bed, while Anne sat at her feet. Mrs Crowe went to her desk, turning her chair to face the sisters. 'Are you well?'

'I am quite well,' Emily said, smiling at her. 'Thank you for your kindness, Mrs Crowe.'

'No need to thank me,' Mrs Crowe said, smiling at Charlotte. 'I knew the moment I met you, Miss Brontë, that our paths were meant to cross. I feel that this is just the beginning of our friendship.'

'I hope so,' Charlotte smiled.

'What about Harry?' Emily turned to her sister in a sudden surge of panic at remembering something lost. 'We left him in The Rookery.'

'Harry and Lydia have been lodged in the room next to Mrs Crowe's this last hour,' Anne told her. 'Branwell went to fetch him as soon as we were free from the Adelphi, found a cart to bring him down. He is in a poor way. But Mrs Crowe called in a doctor, who will see to them both. We owe you a great debt, Mrs Crowe, but we will send the funds on as soon as we have them.'

'You will not,' Mrs Crowe said. 'What kind of a woman would I be if I demanded payment for a little human decency? I saw the young man being brought in, his colour was good, and he was alert. My friends tell me that as long as no infection takes hold he will be well again.'

'The doctor has seen him already?' Anne asked.

'Oh no, sorry – my friends in spirit,' Mrs Crowe said.

'You talk to spirits?' Emily asked at once.

'Would you like me to pass on a message for you, my dear?' Mrs Crowe asked her gently. 'I'm sure they would oblige.'

Emily shook her head, dropping her gaze to her tight-knotted fingers.

'But will Harry be safe now?' she asked at length. 'Will any of us be safe again? Noose is dead, but Conroy still breathed when we left him, and he knows all of us, and Harry and Lydia. And the children – what about the children? How can they go home when he still has this hold over them?'

'I don't know,' Charlotte said, picking up the damaged and bloodstained receipt with which Emily had threatened Conroy at the Adelphi. 'But this is evidence that he is the Monarch. Louis gave it to you?'

'But what good is it, when we know that half the law is corrupt, and not which half? Conroy is untouchable, and now we and everything we love is in danger. He may be damaged today, but within a month all will be as it was, but worse.'

'Perhaps not,' Anne said, kneeling at Emily's feet as she looked at Mrs Crowe.

'How on earth not?' Emily asked.

'Mrs Crowe had rather a brilliant idea as to what to do about Sir John,' Charlotte said, sitting beside her and taking Emily's hand. Questioningly, Emily turned her gaze to Mrs Crowe.

'There is one person who can finish Conroy's evil empire once and for all,' Mrs Crowe told her. 'A lady who despises him as much as we do, and with just as good a cause – our true monarch, Her Majesty Queen Victoria.'

'Conroy does hate her,' Emily said. 'He spoke of her with such venom.'

'I'm not surprised. The moment she was crowned, she dismissed him from her household and kept him away from her mother, over whom he had a dangerous hold,' Mrs Crowe told them. 'Her Majesty saw him for the dangerous, power-hungry man he is. A man who wishes only to serve himself. He hates her for seeing it so clearly. That it was a young woman who stood in his way makes it all the worse for him, I'd wager. Now the truth is, though I'd never normally reveal such a private honour, Her Majesty read and enjoyed my *Susan Hopley*, and had the good grace to write me a most delightful note. Since then we have exchanged a letter or two – a humble correspondence on subjects we find interesting, and I can claim a very modest acquaintance with her.'

'Mrs Crowe knows the Queen,' Charlotte said proudly, as if the claim was her own, making Emily almost smile. 'Imagine knowing that our Queen has read your work. What a thrill that would be.'

'Well,' Mrs Crowe waved the compliment away, 'here is what I propose. You should each write down your account – anonymously, if you wish: everything he did, all his associates, how he structured his empire and kept his profits hidden. Write it all down, Miss Brontës, from the first moment to the last, and we shall parcel it up with the evidence you secured and send it to the palace. Be assured, our Queen will not let this stand, you may rely on that. Sir John Conroy is finished one way or another, and he'll be no threat to you or anyone else ever again, not once Her Majesty has finished with him, for I have an insight into her nature, her decency and deter-mination to protect her people. So you may be quite certain of that.'

'So there is hope?' Emily asked Charlotte. 'Could it really be over, Charlotte? Could we really be safe?'

'Yes, my dear,' Charlotte said. 'Yes, I believe everything that took place here in London is really at an end, or will be very soon. There will be shadows: deep hurts that linger on for months, perhaps even years, but eventually those painful memories will become like welcome ghosts, reminding us that we have lived, Emily. Though it has cost us, we have truly lived. One day you will welcome those ghosts.'

Emily nodded and rose from the bed.

'Mrs Crowe,' she said, 'might I borrow your writing slope and some materials? The sooner our dispatch is sent, the better.'

CHAPTER

FORTY-FOUR

Charlotte

'Can you ever forgive me?' were the first words Kit spoke to Charlotte as she crossed the street to stand at her side. Charlotte had been standing in the window when she had seen the young woman across the road, her hands clasped in uncertainty, as she paced to and fro outside.

'Kit, you saved our lives,' Charlotte said. 'We should never have found our way out of that room, at least without some kind of deadly battle, if it hadn't been for your ingenuity and . . . violence.'

Kit's mouth twisted into a little smile.

'I can't help but be rather proud of my daring plan,' she said. 'For a moment I was a detector too! Besides, it did not cost me much to hurt that man who took so much pleasure in hurting me. You showed me that I could be free, Charlotte. You showed me that I don't need any man's protection, let alone from someone so vile, to find my way in the world. I only wish I had learned it sooner.'

'Then I am glad,' Charlotte said.

'But I betrayed you,' Kit said unhappily. 'It was I who told Noose you had Mary, and I who told him you were to fetch the other child from St Patrick's. I told Conroy about the tunnels that ran from our theatre right to the church where she was hidden, so he might beat you to her sanctuary. My actions were all part of the chain that resulted in the death of my true friend Louis Parensell, and that almost killed you too, my dear Charlotte. I have Louis' blood on my hands and I cannot bear it. He did all he could to protect me, as a brother would; he gave me a portion of his earnings to add to my savings, so that I might be able to escape Conroy sooner, even though it made his life more difficult and dangerous. And for no more reason than that he wanted to do good. He never looked at me, or anyone, the way he looked at your sister. I believe he truly fell in love with Emily in those few short days he knew her.'

'I am certain Mr Parensell would gladly have risked all for my sister,' Charlotte said. 'I'm sure he always planned to be in that room when the critical moment came, knowing what was at stake. I only wish I could have had the opportunity to tell him that I mistook him at first – that in fact he was a man of fine character and honour.'

'Charlotte, if I could change what I did in a moment of fear and panicked desperation, I would go back, and I would change everything. For a single moment I thought I had no choice but, as soon as it was done, I saw I had been tricked into giving Mary away. I do so wish that we could go back.'

'But we never can.' Charlotte looked into Kit's face, her eyes hot with unhappiness and regret. 'I forgive you, Kit, but Emily never would. And my place is always at her side. We can never go back; such a thing is impossible. We can only ever say farewell to all we have lost and let it go.'

'You are telling me that now is the time for us to say fare-well?' Kit asked, though she knew the answer already.

'It is,' Charlotte nodded. 'It is time to put an end to this detection, and our acquaintance.' She paused. 'What will you do now? Noose might be dead, but there is a chance some other cad will attempt to impose himself on you.'

'My apprenticeship with Mr Blewitt begins in September, and I have given notice at the theatre. Celine Varens will disappear, perhaps to lead a scandalous life on the Continent, and Kit Thornfield will learn her trade and make another life for herself.'

'You will find a way to be happy, Kit,' Charlotte told her. 'I don't doubt it.'

'And you will finish your novel, and the world will come to know the name of Charlotte Brontë,' Kit said. 'I don't doubt that.'

'I wish I could be so sure,' Charlotte said.

'Charlotte, will you always remember me?' Kit asked her, suddenly taking her hands. 'For I know that I will never forget you, and I think it will give me strength to know that you think of me sometimes too.'

'I shall,' Charlotte said. 'Of course, I shall.'

'I will watch out for your novel,' Kit said. 'And I will look for my name amongst the pages to see if you have remembered me, and one day, far from now, I will write to you, and you will know it is me, for I will sign my name K.T. But we will correspond as if we had never met before, as if we are strangers, discovering for the first time that our tastes and minds are perfectly aligned, and that we are kindred spirits anew. Do you agree?'

'I agree,' Charlotte said. 'Goodbye, dearest Kit.'

'Goodbye, Miss Brontë,' Kit replied. 'Farewell, dear friend.'

FORTY-FIVE

Anne

The evening was as soft as gossamer. The intense, stifling heat of the last few days had ebbed away, and what remained of the lingering warmth was threaded through with a light breeze. In the coppery light of the last hour of the day, the home-filled streets that the cab had brought them to seemed almost beautiful to Anne. Countless invisible lives were lived here on these tree-lined avenues. These houses weren't grand, but they were as precious as any palace, for each one contained a family who loved one another unconditionally.

That afternoon, funded by Mrs Crowe's generosity, the cab had taken them to the opposite end of the city, almost as far south as it reached, to dockland streets filled with warehouses, and ships from all around the world, which flowed in and out of the city, circulating through the pumping heart of London. They had stopped on the corner of short Neptune Street, where three narrow houses stood between two great warehouses, the industry of the river running just behind them.

'Now, Cora,' Charlotte turned to the girl, who had been at her side since they had taken her from Mornington Crescent. 'We can't come to the door with you, but should your mama and papa want to know who brought you home, tell them the Misses Bell found you lost, and you cleverly told them your name and address. Will you remember?'

The fact that Cora Blake hadn't been able to speak until that very morning, when she had lain with her head in Charlotte's lap as Charlotte read to her, was neither here nor there.

'Yes, miss,' Cora said, her voice light and sweet. She had continued to hold Charlotte's hand, her large brown eyes fixed on Charlotte's face. 'Miss, I don't really know what danger you took me from. Thank you for your kindness. You are my friends, and I shall never forget you.'

'You are our friend too,' Charlotte had said, with a tender expression. 'My dear child, I shall never forget you either.'

They had embraced one last time, and the driver had lifted Cora out of the cab. Anne and Charlotte had watched as she ran down the street, turning into the middle house. Their view on the corner was obscured, but they heard a shriek of joy, a father called and sobs of relief. They waited for a while until all fell quiet, and then, when they were sure Cora was safe in the arms of her family again, the cab drove on.

Now here they were outside Mary's home, or rather across the street and a little further on. It was after Cora spoke to Charlotte that Mary had found the courage to tell them she had remembered her name, and her house, for some time, though she was so afraid to go back there.

'What if they don't want me, miss?' Mary had asked her. 'What if they've moved away? Or what if they cannot bear the shame of what I have done? I shall be lost again, only it will hurt all the worse.'

'If they've moved away, then we will only have to look a little further for a little longer,' Anne had said. 'And if they don't want you, Mary . . . Well, I feel certain that they will, but if they don't, then we want you. We would take you home with us, and take care of you for the rest of your life.'

'Would you, miss?' Mary's eyes had grown large.

'Yes, but you must try, Mary. Remember how you spoke of your kind parents and your siblings? And how much love you felt in those memories? You must give them a chance to have back the beloved girl who was stolen from them.'

They had found a decent dress for her on the market, which Emily had swiftly altered, and though her hair was all but gone, Anne gave her the straw bonnet that once belonged to Kit, and tied the sage-green ribbon under her chin, and what a pretty, delicate girl she was. What – given the chance – a fine young woman she would become.

'Now . . .' Anne began to remind her of their planned discretion concerning their identity.

'I know – you are the benevolent Misses Bell,' Mary said, clutching Anne's hand as the moment came near. 'What if they hate me, Anne? What if I disgust them? When I think of everything I've done, how could they ever love me . . .?'

Anne didn't know how to answer in the moment, but Charlotte did.

'Mary, I have yet to know the delight of motherhood for myself, but I have watched over my brother and sisters since they were but babes. I know there is nothing they could do that would make me hate them. I feel anger, pity, sorrow and regret from time to time, but underneath it all, *always*, is love. My love for them and God's love for us all. You are born anew, everything past is gone, washed away. Go home to your family, and trust in the strength of love.'

Mary nodded, and, embracing Anne and Charlotte once more, was let out of the cab.

Taking a deep breath, she went towards the house where a lamp glowed in the front window, calling her home. This time Anne and Charlotte had a perfect view as the door opened, and a small boy looked up at Mary.

'Ma, there's a girl here says she knows us?' they heard the thin, high voice call out.

A woman came to the door, wiping her hands on her apron. She stared at Mary for a long moment as the girl murmured something.

'Oh, dear Lord, oh my Lord, can you be real?' they heard Mary's mother cry out as she embraced her daughter, held her away from her so she could look her all over, and then held her tight once again.

'Frank!' she called out. 'Frank, come quick – it's a miracle!'

Mary was gone in and the door was shut. Anne looked at Charlotte.

'What would it be like to open our door and see Maria and Elizabeth there once again?' Anne said. 'And Mama?'

'Would we could return all of the lost so easily,' Charlotte smiled forlornly.

'It was hardly effortless,' Anne said, motioning for the cab to take them back to Paternoster Row. 'Indeed, I fear for Emily, Charlotte. The burden of reality has invaded her heart and mind and, I fear, almost defeated our fearless warrior.'

'Emily will make her peace with it somehow, Anne,' Charlotte said. 'Though she will never speak of it to us, or anyone, she will find her way to reconcile everything she has found with everything she has lost, and she will spin it into silver and gold with her poetry, believe me. Our sister will return to us, not as she was before, but whole and made something more by what she has lost. For it was ever thus.'

FORTY-SIX

Emily

How glad Emily was to be home, safe in the arms of her homeland once again. The moment she had set foot through the door of the parsonage, she swore never to leave Yorkshire again, and certainly never to return to London, no matter the circumstances.

Emily had suffered through dinner while Charlotte and Branwell chattered to Papa about everything they could think of, to prevent him from asking how their trip had been.

She had watched as Mr Nicholls gazed lovingly at Charlotte, so openly beguiled by her that she wondered how her sister was able to keep any of her supper down, never mind remain completely ignorant of his feelings towards her. And then, as soon as she had this uncharitable thought, she retracted it, perhaps a little softened towards the vagaries of love and how they could alter a person, after all. Though she was fairly certain such warmth could not last when it came to Arthur Bell Nicholls, the world's most tedious man.

'Ah,' Papa had said, as Tabby and Anne began to clear away the dishes, 'this magazine came for you, Charlotte, I quite forgot to mention it. I didn't know you took *The Critic*.'

'Oh, I don't, usually,' Charlotte said, taking the publication at once. 'I was just interested in a particular review, for no reason really – just a passing interest. I think I shall read it now.'

Glancing at her sisters, Charlotte excused herself and took the paper into the hallway.

'One moment, Papa,' Anne said, following her, and, supposing she too ought to be present at her own judging, Emily sighed and rose from the table, just as her papa caught her hand.

'Where do all my daughters go?' Patrick asked, perplexed, turning his cataract-dimmed eyes towards her. 'When you are only just returned.'

'You know Charlotte, Papa,' Emily said, kissing her father's hand. 'She's always got something urgent to be passionate about. It's my duty as her sister to go and soothe her nerves with reason and good sense.'

'You are a good girl, Emily Jane,' Papa told her as she left.

Charlotte and Anne were seated on the stairs, Anne just above Charlotte, reading over her shoulder. As Charlotte looked up, Emily saw her eyes shining with tears.

'Is it so very bad?' Emily asked.

'Bad? Not bad at all,' Charlotte replied, reading aloud. '"It is long since we have enjoyed a volume of such genuine poetry as this, this book has come like a ray of sunshine, gladdening the eye with present glory and the head with promise of bright hours in store." Emily, it is an excellent review, a favourable review.' She reached over her shoulder for Anne's hand, her smile radiant.

'This is the beginning, sisters, I am sure of it. From this moment on, we are authors of note.'

Emily wanted to be as thrilled as her sisters, but she couldn't find pleasure in the review – not yet. It seemed to her as if it had been written for someone else, a poet who no longer walked these hallways. And so she had kissed them both on the tops of their heads and left them to their delighted, whispered plans for their brilliant careers, and went to help with the washing up.

Tabby had caught her and Keeper in the back kitchen, about to slip out.

'Where do you think you're going to at this hour, my lady?' Tabby said, grabbing her shoulders, and holding her still so she could search Emily's face. 'Lord, what's befallen you, my girl? You look sickly and hollow. I shall not be letting ye out at this hour. Your own bed, and some onions in your stockings to ward off a cough, that's what you need.'

'I am not ill, Tabby,' Emily assured her. 'Only . . .' She looked out of the open door. 'Only heartsick for my moors, for I've been away too long. I beg you – let Keeper and me out for a little while. We shall not tarry long, but there are rabbits to chase and owls to see swooping.'

Tabby pressed her calloused palm to Emily's face.

'Go on, then, as it's a warm evening,' she said. 'But if you are more than an hour . . .'

'Two hours,' Emily bargained.

'If you are more than that, I shall come and find you myself, and bend you over me knee, you hear me?'

'Thank you, Tabby dear, I love you so.' Emily engulfed the old woman in a hug so fierce that when she withdrew Tabby's expression was one of wonder and joy, her eyes filled with tears.

'Will you be well, lass?' Tabby said, turning away to hide her emotion. 'Whatever it was that has touched you so, will you recover from it?'

'I will,' Emily said, to herself as much as Tabby. 'I shall be quite myself by morning.'

Now she sat on the rocky crag of Ponden Kirk, which jutted out over the valley below. Keeper leaned solidly into her shoulder, his heavy paw on her knee, as if he were determined to prevent her from leaving him again, and at last she could breathe. Up here in the heights of the moor it was easy to believe that she had been unleashed from gravity and floated free amongst the stars. Heavenly fire burned bright above her, and hearth-light pinpointed moorland abodes below. The whispering wind welcomed her home, and the cool, dark night embraced her and told her she was safe from harm.

Something in Emily had altered for ever – Tabby had seen that right away. There was something sharp embedded in her heart now – a precious cargo that she would carry in her soul and mind for ever more. And when it sang to her, as she knew it often would, she would write its song into the starry sky, where it would burn for ever.

Epilogue

'Goodness,' Anne said, as she read the London paper that afternoon.

'What on earth has happened now?' Charlotte asked her.

'The tigress that we saw at the theatre? It seems that on the day we left London, she somehow escaped her cage and mauled her trainer to death! She is now in the care of the Regent's Park Zoo, where she is to be given a large enclosure and displayed as a man-killer. Can you believe it?'

'I can,' Emily said with a small, secret smile. 'I can believe it very well.'

Acknowledgements

This is the second book in this series to be written in the grip of a pandemic, and everything was different for everyone except me, since I work mostly from home and tend towards the more hermitish side of the social spectrum. But I couldn't have written this book without the support of many brilliant people who had to adapt to sudden change and a whole new world.

So thank you to my amazing team at Hodder; my brilliant, insightful editor Melissa Cox and Steven Cooper, publicity genius. To Morgan Springett for keeping it all together, and to Maddy Marshall, who, though now gone to pastures new, was a joy to work with. Also huge thanks to William Speed who designs these utterly beautiful books.

Huge thanks are also due to my fantastic agent Hellie Ogden, and to the whole team at Janklow & Nesbitt, especially Ma'sumi Amiri, Emma Winter, Maimy Suleiman and Kirsty Gordon.

I can't write these books without my darling friend Julie Akhurst who is my touchstone and muse and to whom I wish all the love in the world.

Also the whole of the Brontë community who inspire and support me: my hero Ann Dinsdale; my friend and bookseller extraordinaire Diane Park of Wave of Nostalgia, Haworth; the wonderful team at the Brontë Parsonage who have kept this most precious museum going through difficult times, especially Rebecca Yorke; genius Brontë biographer, historian and friend Sharon Wright; Kay Fairhurst Adams, Nina Oaken, Sarah Mason Walden, Sarah Goodenough, Emily Ross, Rachel Maria Bell, Emmeline Burdett, Leza Blacklock, Mary Jayne Baker, Maggie Gardiner, Christina Rauh Fishburne, Charlie Rauh, Catherine Redpath Maud Servignat, Deborah Jones, Tim Rideout, Deborah Jones and ALL the members of my favourite place on the internet 'A Walk Around the Brontë Table' on Facebook.

Thank you to Anne Booth, who is always so generous with her knowledge and enthusiasm, Simon Trewin, theatrical fan and finder of brilliant playbills! To my writer friends without whom I just couldn't do this job: Julie Cohen, Kate Harrison, Miranda Dickinson, Angela Clarke, to name a few.

Love to my number one reader Eunice Brown, and to Steve, Kizzy and Noah Brown, my adopted family and friends for life.

Finally thank you to my husband Adam Evans, who has been endlessly supportive even with a broken leg, and to my amazing daughter Lily for stepping up to help me while kept away from university because of the pandemic. To my adorable, hilarious sons who keep me going, and my brilliant dogs: Blossom, my spirit animal and Head of Security, and Bluebell Chief Procurer of Snacks.